The
HOSTAGE
BRIDE

Also by Jane Feather

JANE FEATHER

The HOSTAGE BRIDE

BANTAM BOOKS

New York   Toronto   London   Sydney   Auckland

THE HOSTAGE BRIDE
A Bantam Book / June 1998

ISBN 1-56865-817-6

PRINTED IN THE UNITED STATES OF AMERICA

After eleven books for Bantam, it's way past time that I expressed my gratitude to Wendy McCurdy, my editor. Her support, painstakingly hard work, and unerring sense of what will and will not work have piloted back on course more drifting manuscripts than I care to admit. It's a lucky writer indeed to have such an editor in her corner. Thank you, Wendy, for a great partnership.

Preface to
The Brides Trilogy

LONDON, MAY 11, 1641

Phoebe swiped one hand across her eyes as she felt for her handkerchief with the other. The handkerchief was nowhere to be found, but that didn't surprise her. She'd lost more handkerchiefs in her thirteen years than she'd had hot dinners. With a vigorous and efficacious sniff, she crept around the hedge of clipped laurel out of sight of the clacking, laughing crowd of wedding guests. The high-pitched cacophony of their merrymaking mingled oddly with the persistent, raucous screams of a mob in full cry gusting across the river from Tower Hill.

She glanced over her shoulder at the graceful half-timbered house that was her home. It stood on a slight rise on the south bank of the river Thames, commanding a view over London and the surrounding countryside. Windows winked in the afternoon sunlight and she could hear the plaintive plucking of a harp persistent beneath the surge and ebb of the party.

No one was looking for her. Why should they? She was of no interest to anyone. Diana had banished her from her presence after the accident. Phoebe cringed at the memory. She could never understand how it happened that her body seemed to get away from her, to have a life of its own, creating a wake of chaos and destruction that followed her wherever she went.

But she was safe for a while. Her step quickened as she made for the old boathouse, her own private sanctuary. When her father had moved the mansion's

water gate so that it faced the water steps at Wapping, the old boathouse had fallen into disrepair. Now it nestled in a tangle of tall reeds at the water's edge, its roof sagging, its timbers bared to the bone by the damp salt air and the wind.

But it was the one place where Phoebe could lick her wounds in private. She wasn't sure whether anyone else in the household knew it still existed, but as she approached she saw that the door was not firmly closed.

Her first reaction was anger. Someone had been trespassing in the one place she could call her own. Her second was a swift pattering of fear. The world was full of beasts, both human and animal, and anyone could have penetrated this clearly deserted structure. Anyone or anything could be lying in wait within. She hesitated, staring at the dark crack between door and frame, almost as if the tiny crack could open to reveal the dim, dusty interior for her from a safe distance. Then her anger reasserted itself. The boathouse belonged to *her*. And if anyone was in there, she would send them off.

She turned into the rushes, looking for a thick piece of driftwood, and found an old spar, rusty nails sticking out in a most satisfactory fashion. Thus armed, she approached the boathouse, her heart still pattering, but her face set. She kicked the door open, flooding the dark mildewed corners with light.

"Who are you?" she demanded of the occupant, who, startled, blinked but didn't move from her perch on a rickety three-legged stool by the unglazed window where the light fell on the page of her book.

Phoebe entered the shed, dropping her weapon. "Oh," she said. "I know who you are. You're Lord Granville's daughter. What are you doing here? Why aren't you at the wedding? I thought you were supposed to carry my sister's train."

The dark-haired girl carefully closed her book over

her finger. "Yes, I'm Olivia," she said after a minute. "And I d-d-didn't want to b-be in the wedding. My father said I d-didn't have to b-be if I d-didn't want to." She let out a slow breath at the end of this little speech, which had clearly cost her some effort.

Phoebe looked at the girl curiously. She was younger than Phoebe, although she was as tall, and enviably slim to the eyes of one who constantly lamented her own intractable roundness. "This is my special place," Phoebe said, but without rancor, sitting on a fallen beam and drawing a wrapped packet from her pocket. "And I don't blame you for not wanting to be in the wedding. I was supposed to attend my sister, but I knocked over the perfume bottle and then trod on Diana's flounce."

She unwrapped the packet, taking a bite of the gingerbread it contained before holding out the offering to Olivia, who shook her head.

"Diana cursed me up hill and down dale and said she never wanted to lay eyes on me again," Phoebe continued. "Which she probably won't, since she's going to be in Yorkshire, miles and miles away from here. And I have to say, if I never lay eyes on her again, I won't be sorry." She looked defiantly upward as if braving heavenly wrath with such an undutiful statement.

"I d-don't like her," Olivia confided.

"I wouldn't like her for a stepmother either. . . . She'll be absolutely horrible! Oh, I'm sorry. I always say the wrong thing," Phoebe exclaimed crossly. "I always say whatever comes into my head."

"It's the t-truth, anyway," the other girl muttered. She opened up her book again and began to read.

Phoebe frowned. Her stepniece, as she supposed she now was, was not the friendliest of creatures. "Do you always stammer?"

Olivia blushed crimson. "I c-c-can't help it."

"No, of course you can't," Phoebe said hastily. "I was just curious." In the absence of a response from

her companion, she moved on to the second piece of gingerbread, idly brushing at a collection of tiny grease spots that seemed to have gathered upon her pink silk gown. A gown specially made for her sister's wedding. It was supposed to complement Diana's pearl-encrusted ivory damask, but somehow on Phoebe the effect didn't quite work, as Diana had pointed out with her usual asperity.

There was a sudden whirlwind rush from the door that banged shut, enclosing the girls in semidarkness again. "God's bones, but if this isn't the peskiest wedding!" a voice declared vigorously. The newcomer leaned against the closed door. She was breathing fast and dashed a hand across her brow to wipe away the dew of perspiration. Her bright green eyes fell upon the boathouse's other occupants.

"I didn't think anyone knew this place was here. I slept here last night. It was the only way I could get away from those pawing beasts. And now they're at it again. I came here for some peace and quiet."

"It's my special place," Phoebe said, standing up. "And you're trespassing." The newcomer didn't look in the least like a wedding guest. Her hair was a tangled mass of bright red curls that didn't look as if it had seen a brush in a month. Her face looked dirty in the gloom, although it was hard to tell among the freckles what was dirt and what wasn't. Her dress was made of dull coarse holland, the hem dipping in the middle, the perfunctory ruffles on the sleeves torn and grubby.

"Oho, no I'm not," the girl crowed, perching on the upturned holey hull of an abandoned rowboat. "I'm invited to the wedding. Or at least," she added with scrupulous honesty, "my father is. And where Jack goes, I go. No choice."

"I know who you are." Olivia looked up from her book for the first time since the girl had burst in upon them. "You're my father's half b-brother's natural child."

"Portia," the girl said cheerfully. "Jack Worth's bastard. And so you must be Olivia. Jack was talking about you. And I suppose, if you live here, you're the bride's sister. Phoebe, isn't it?"

Phoebe sat down again. "You seem to know a great deal about us."

Portia shrugged. "I keep my ears open . . . and my eyes. Close either one of 'em for half a second and the devils'll get you."

"What devils?"

"Men," Portia declared. "You wouldn't think it to look at me, would you?" She chuckled. "Scrawny as a scarecrow. But they'll take anything they can get so long as it's free."

"I loathe men!" The fierce and perfectly clear statement came from Olivia.

"Me too," Portia agreed, then added with all the loftiness of her fourteen years, "But you're a little young, duckie, to have made such a decision. How old are you?"

"Eleven."

"Oh, you'll change your mind," Portia said knowledgeably.

"I won't. I'm never going to marry." Olivia's brown eyes threw daggers beneath their thick black eyebrows.

"Neither am I," Phoebe said. "Now that my father has managed to make such a splendid match for Diana, he'll leave me alone, I'm sure."

"Why don't you want to marry?" Portia asked with interest. "It's your destiny to marry. There's nothing else for someone as wellborn as you to do."

Phoebe shook her head. "No one would want to marry me. Nothing ever fits me, and I'm always dropping things and saying just what comes into my head. Diana and my father say I'm a liability. I can't do anything right. So I'm going to be a poet and do good works instead."

"Of course someone will want to marry you,"

Portia stated. "You're lovely and curvy and womanly. I'm the one no one's going to marry. Look at me." She stood up and gestured to herself with a flourish. "I'm straight up and down like a ruler. I'm a bastard. I have no money, no property. I'm a hopeless prospect." She sat down again, smiling cheerfully as if the prophecy were not in the least disheartening.

Phoebe considered. "I see what you mean," she said. "It would be difficult for you to find a husband. So what will you do?"

"I'd like to be a soldier. I wish I'd been born a boy. I'm sure I was supposed to be, but something went wrong."

"I'm going to b-be a scholar," Olivia declared. "I'm going to ask my father to get me a t-tutor when I'm older, and I want to live in Oxford and study there."

"Women don't study at the university," Phoebe pointed out.

"I shall," Olivia stated stubbornly.

"Lord, a soldier, a poet, and a scholar! What a trio of female misfits!" Portia went into a peal of laughter.

Phoebe laughed with her, feeling a delicious and hitherto unknown warmth in her belly. She wanted to sing, get to her feet and dance with her companions. Even Olivia was smiling, the defensive fierceness momentarily gone from her eyes.

"We must have a pact to support each other if we're ever tempted to fall by the wayside and become ordinary." Portia jumped to her feet. "Olivia, have you some scissors in that little bag?"

Olivia opened the drawstrings of the little lace-trimmed bag she wore at her waist. She took out a tiny pair of scissors, handing them to Portia, who very carefully cut three red curls from the unruly halo surrounding her freckled face.

"Now, Phoebe, let me have three of those pretty

fair locks, and then three of Olivia's black ones." She suited action to words, the little scissors snipping away. "Now watch."

As the other two gazed, wide-eyed with curiosity, Portia's long, thin fingers with their grubby broken nails nimbly braided the different strands into three tricolored rings. "There, we have one each. Mine is the one with the red on the outside, Phoebe's has the fair, and Olivia's the black." She handed them over. "Now, whenever you feel like forgetting your ambition, just look at your ring. . . . Oh, and we must mingle blood." Her green eyes, slanted slightly like a cat's, glinted with enthusiasm and fun.

She turned her wrist up and nicked the skin, squeezing out a drop of blood. "Now you, Phoebe." She held out the scissors.

Phoebe shook her fair head. "I can't. But you do it." Closing her eyes tightly, she extended her arm, wrist uppermost. Portia nicked the skin, then turned to Olivia, who was already extending her wrist.

"There. Now we rub our wrists together to mingle the blood. That way we cement our vow to support each other through thick and thin."

It was clear to Olivia that Portia was playing a game, and yet Olivia, as her skin touched the others, felt a strange tremor of connection that seemed much more serious than mere play. But she was not a fanciful child and sternly dismissed such whimsy.

"If one of us is ever in trouble, then we can send our ring to one of the others and be sure of getting help," Phoebe said enthusiastically.

"That's very silly and romantical," Olivia declared with a scorn that she knew sprang from her own fancy.

"What's wrong with being romantic?" Portia said with a shrug, and Phoebe gave her a quick, grateful smile.

"Scholars aren't romantic," Olivia said. She frowned fiercely, her black eyebrows almost meeting

over her deep-set dark eyes. Then she sighed. "I'd b-better go back to the wedding." She slipped her braided ring into the little bag at her waist. With a little reflective gesture, as if to give herself courage, she touched her wrist, thinly smeared with their shared blood, then went to the door.

As she opened it, the clamor from the city across the river swelled into the dim seclusion of the boathouse. Olivia shivered at the wild savagery of the sound. "C-Can you hear what they're saying?"

"They're yelling, 'His head is off, his head is off!' " Portia said knowledgeably. "They've just executed the earl of Strafford."

"But why?" Phoebe asked.

"Lord, don't you know anything?" Portia was genuinely shocked at this ignorance. "Strafford was the king's closest advisor and Parliament defied the king and impeached the earl and now they've just beheaded him."

Olivia felt her scalp contract as the bloody, brutal screech of mob triumph tore into the soft May air and the smoke of bonfires lit in jubilation for a man's violent death rose thick and choking from the city and its surroundings.

"Jack says there's going to be civil war," Portia continued, referring to her father with her customary informality. "He's usually right about such things . . . not about much else, though," she added.

"There couldn't be civil war!" Olivia was horrified.

"We'll see." Portia shrugged.

"Well, I wish it would come now and save me having to go back to the wedding," Phoebe said glumly. "Are you going to come, Portia?"

Portia shook her head, gesturing brusquely to the door. "Go back to the party. There's no place for me there."

Phoebe hesitated, then followed Olivia, the ring clutched tightly in her palm.

Portia remained in the dimness with the cobwebs for company. She leaned over and picked up the piece of gingerbread that Phoebe had forgotten about in the events of the last half hour. Slowly and with great pleasure, she began to nibble at it, making it last as long as possible, while the shadows lengthened and the shouts from the city and the merrymaking from the house gradually faded with the sunset.

The HOSTAGE BRIDE

Prologue

"*M'lord, they're coming!*"

William Decatur, Earl of Rothbury, lifted his gaze from the parchment he was penning and carefully laid his quill across the top of the silver inkwell. His eyes, as vivid blue as summer lightning, seemed to look right through the messenger.

"How far are they?"

"A mile behind me, m'lord . . . riding hard." The messenger wiped his brow with a grubby linen kerchief. The reek of sweat and horseflesh hung like low clouds around him.

The earl sanded the parchment, dropped wax from a lit taper alongside his signature, and pressed his signet ring into the wax. Without urgency, he pushed back his carved oak chair and rose to his feet. His countenance revealed nothing. "How many of them?"

"At least a full battalion, sir. Cavalry and infantry."

"Under whose charge?"

The messenger hesitated.

"*Under whose charge?*" The question crackled like musket shot.

"They're flying the Granville standard, sir."

William Decatur exhaled softly.

The door opened behind the messenger. It opened quietly, hesitantly, but the woman who entered was neither quiet nor hesitant. "They are coming?" Her eyes fixed upon the earl with painful intensity. "They are coming to put us out of our house. Is it so, my lord?"

"Aye, Clarissa, it is so." Her husband's blue gaze was unreadable as it rested on the brown-haired woman and the young boy standing wide-eyed beside her. The child that Clarissa carried beneath her belt, with its great ring of household keys, was visible only in the slight thickening of her waist, but one hand rested on her belly, the other on her son's already sturdy shoulder, in unconscious protection of the life both born and unborn.

"They will take you away," she said, and the struggle to control the tremor in her voice was harsh on her countenance. "And what will become of us, my lord?"

William flinched from the hard bitterness of her resentment, of her refusal to understand the driving power of conscience that forced him to make this sacrifice, to drive his family into penniless exile, to besmirch a proud family name with the vile tag of traitor.

Before he could answer, however, the thundering roll of hooves surged through the open window. Clarissa gasped and the boy, Rufus, Viscount Rothbury, son and heir to the now disgraced earl of Rothbury, stepped away from his mother, moving closer to his father as if to separate himself from a woman's weakness.

The earl glanced down at the red-haired boy and met the child's clear blue gaze, as vivid and as steadfast as his father's. William smiled, a half smile that yet carried deep sorrow for this child whose birthright was to be snatched from him, who was to be condemned to an outlaw's life. Then he placed his hand on his son's shoulder and drew him beside him as he faced the open window.

In the gathering dusk, the invading force swept inexorably, rank after rank, onto the gravel sweep before the soft weathered facade of the Elizabethan manor house. They carried pikes and muskets, infantry filing behind the three ranks of cavalry. The royal standard of James Stuart, King of England, snapped in the evening breeze.

But it was not his king's standard that set the lightning forks blazing in the earl's eyes. It was the banner that flew beside it. The banner of the house of Granville. And beneath it, George, Marquis of Granville, sat on his great black steed, his head bare, his gloved hands resting lightly on his saddle.

A herald's trumpet blew a long note, and a voice bellowed from below, "William Decatur, Earl of Rothbury, you are hereby commanded in the king's name to surrender yourself to His Majesty's justice."

It was as if a spell had been broken in the room. The earl swung from the window. He strode to the fireplace. His fingers moved across the stones and slowly, silently, the great fieldstone swung back, revealing the black cavernous space of a priest's hole. "You know what to do, Clarissa. Take Rufus and go. My brothers are waiting for you beyond the coppice. I'll hold this scum here until you're safe away."

"But, William . . ." Clarissa's voice died, and the hand she extended toward her husband hung as if forgotten in midair.

"I will follow you," he said shortly. "Now do as I bid, and go."

A wife did not disobey her husband, not even in this extremity. Clarissa reached for her son's hand, but he snatched it away.

"I will stay with Father." He didn't look at his mother; his gaze was fixed intently upon his father. And William understood that his son knew the truth. The earl of Rothbury would not be following his wife and son into exile. He would not run from the king's justice and earn the name of coward as well as traitor.

He took the boy by the shoulders and said softly, "You are your mother's keeper, Rufus. You are her shield and buckler now. And it is for you now to avenge our honor."

He turned aside to the table and took up the parchment, rolling it carefully. He held it out to the boy. "Rufus, my son, I lay upon you now the most solemn trust: that you will be avenged upon the house of Granville, and you will bear our name with pride even in the face of those who call it dishonored. You will by your deeds make the house of Rothbury a watchword for truth, justice, and honor even though you are condemned to live outside the law, to create your own world, your own truth, your own honor."

Rufus swallowed as he took the rolled parchment. His throat seemed to have closed under the dreadful weight of his father's words. He was eight years old, but his shoulders stiffened as if all the better to bear the great burden of this responsibility his father had laid upon him.

"Do you swear so to do?"

"I swear." Rufus found the words, though they sounded strange, as if coming from a great distance.

"Then go." His father laid a hand on the boy's head in a moment's benediction, then he kissed his wife and urged her toward the priest's hole. Rufus looked back for an instant, his hair ablaze in the light of the oil lamp the messenger held high; his eyes, no longer the innocent, candid eyes of an eight-year-old boy, were filled with the foreboding of loss and the dreadful knowledge of duty. Then he turned and followed his mother into the darkness.

The messenger followed them, and the stone on well-oiled hinges closed silently behind them.

William strode from the chamber. He walked down the wide sweep of stairs to the stone-flagged hallway and out into the dusk, to stand on the top step and survey his accusers. To look in the eye of the man he had once called friend . . . the man who had now come to dispossess him of his house, his lands, his family honor.

For a moment the two men looked at each other, and the silence stretched taut as a bowstring between them. Then William Decatur spoke, his voice low, yet each bitter word thrown with the power of lead shot. "So, this is how you honor the vows of friendship, Granville."

George, Marquis of Granville, urged his horse forward, away from the line of cavalry. He raised one gloved hand as if in protest, "William, I come not in enmity, but in—"

"Don't insult me, Granville!" The furious words cut through the other man's speech. "I know you for what you are, and you will pay, you and your heirs. I swear it on the blood of Christ." His hand moved from his side, lifted, revealing the dull silver barrel of a flintlock pistol.

Rooks wheeled and shrieked over the gables as the hideous shock of the explosion faded into the stunned silence. William Decatur, Earl of Rothbury, lay at the foot of the steps to his house; blood, a thick, dark puddle, spread beneath his head. His eyes, sightless now, stared upward at the circling rooks, the scudding clouds, the first faint prick of the evening star.

A soldier stepped forward, carrying a pitch torch. The flame flared, blue and orange under a gust of wind. He stepped over the fallen man and hurled his torch into the open doorway.

George Granville sat his horse, immobile. He had come

here to oversee the king's justice. He had come to mitigate that justice, to work with his old friend to avoid the worst. But his intentions were so much chaff in the wind now.

The earl of Rothbury lay dead at the foot of his burning house, and his heir, a lad of eight summers, was cast out into the world beyond the laws of man with a burden of vengeance that sat ill on the shoulders of a child, but that, George Granville knew, the lad would grow into. Rufus Decatur was his father's son.

1

EDINBURGH, SCOTLAND, DECEMBER, 1643

Acrid smoke billowed around the windowless room from the peat fire smoldering sullenly in the hearth. The old crone stirring a pot over the fire coughed intermittently, the harsh racking the only sound. Outside, the snow lay thick on a dead white world, heavy flakes drifting steadily from the iron gray sky.

A bundle of rags, huddled beneath a moth-eaten blanket, groaned, shifted with a rustle of the straw beneath the stick-like frame. "Brandy, woman!"

The crone glanced over her shoulder at the hump in the corner, then she spat into the fire. The spittle sizzled on the peat. "Girl's gone fer it. Altho' what she's usin' to pay fer it, the good Lord knows."

The bundle groaned again. A wasted arm pushed feebly at the blanket, and Jack Worth struggled onto his elbow. He peered through slitted eyes into the smoke-shrouded room. Nothing had improved since he'd last looked, and he sank back into the straw again. The earth floor was hard and cold beneath the thin and foul-smelling straw, pressing painfully into his emaciated body.

Jack wanted to die, but the flicker of life was persistent. And if he couldn't die, he wanted brandy. Portia had gone for brandy. His enfeebled brain could hold that thought. But where in the name of Lucifer was she? He couldn't remember what time she'd gone out into the storm. The blizzard obliterated all signs of time passing, and it could as well be midnight as dawn.

His pain-racked limbs were on fire, his eyes burned in their sockets, every inch of his skin ached, and the dreadful craving consumed him so that he cried out, a sound so feeble that the crone didn't even turn from the fire.

The door opened. Frigid air blasted the fug, and the smoke

swirled like dervishes. The girl who kicked the door shut behind her was wire thin yet exuded a nervous energy that somehow enlivened the reeking squalor of the hovel.

"Brandy, Jack." She came to the mattress and knelt, drawing a small leather flask from inside her threadbare cloak. Her nose wrinkled at the sour stench of old brandy and decaying flesh exuding from the man and his sickbed, but she pushed an arm beneath his scrawny neck and lifted him, pulling off the stopper of the flagon with her teeth. Her father was shaking so hard she could barely manage to hold the flask to his lips. His teeth rattled, his lifeless eyes stared up at her from his gaunt face, where the bones of his skull were clearly defined.

He managed to swallow a mouthful of the fiery spirit, and as it slid down his gullet his aches diminished a little, the shivers died, and he was able to hold the flask in one clawlike hand and keep it to his lips himself until the last drop was gone.

"Goddamn it, but it's never enough!" he cursed. "Why d'ye not bring enough, girl!"

Portia sat back on her heels, regarding her father with a mixture of distaste and pity. "It's all I could afford. It's been a long time, in case you've forgotten, since you contributed to the family coffers."

"Insolence!" he growled, but his eyes closed and he became so still that for a moment Portia thought that finally death would bring him peace, but after a minute his eyes flickered open. Saliva flecked his lips amid his thick uncombed gray beard; sweat stood out against the greenish waxen pallor of his forehead and trickled down his sunken cheeks.

Portia wiped his face with the corner of her cloak. Her stomach was so empty it was cleaving to her backbone, and the familiar nausea of hunger made her dizzy. She stood up and went over to the noisome fire. "Is that porridge?"

"Aye. What else'd it be?"

"What else indeed," she said, squatting on the floor beside the cauldron. She had learned early the lesson that beggars could not be choosers, and ladled the watery gruel into a wooden bowl with as much enthusiasm as if it was the finest delicacy from the king's table.

But it was a thin ungrateful pap and left her hunger barely

appeased. Images of bread and cheese danced tantalizingly before her internal vision, making her juices run, but what little she could earn in the taproom of the Rising Sun, drawing ale, answering ribaldry with its kind, and turning a blind eye to the groping hands on her body so long as they pushed a coin into her meager bosom, went for brandy to still her father's all-consuming addiction. The addiction that was killing him by inches.

"Port . . . *Portia!*" He gasped out her name and she came quickly over to him. "In my box . . . a letter . . . find it . . . quickly." Every word was wrenched from him as if with red-hot pincers.

She went to the small leather box, the only possession they had apart from the rags on their backs. She brought it over, opening it without much curiosity. She knew the contents by heart. Anything of worth had been sold off long ago to pay for brandy.

"At the back . . . behind the silk."

She slipped her fingers behind the shabby lining, encountering the crackling crispness of parchment. She pulled it out, handing it to her father.

"When I'm gone, you're to s . . . se . . ." A violent coughing fit interrupted him, and when it subsided he lay back too exhausted to continue. But after a minute, as Portia watched his agonizing efforts, he began again. "Send it to Lammermuir, to Castle Granville. Read the direction."

Portia turned the sealed parchment over in her hand. "What is it? What does it say?"

"Read the direction!"

"Castle Granville, Lammermuir, Yorkshire."

"Send it by the mail. When I'm gone." His voice faded, but his hand reached for her and she gave him her own. "It's all I can do for you now, Portia," he said, his fingers squeezing hers with a strength she hadn't known he still possessed; then, as if defeated by the effort, his hand opened and fell from hers.

An hour later, Jack Worth, half brother to Cato, Marquis of Granville, died much as he had lived, in a brandy stupor and without a penny to his name.

Portia closed her father's eyes. "I must bury him."

"Ground's iron hard," the crone declared unhelpfully.

Portia's lips thinned. "I'll manage."

"Ye've no money for a burial."

"I'll dig the grave and bury him myself."

The old woman shrugged. The man and his daughter had been lodging in her cottage for close on a month, and she'd formed a pretty good idea of the girl's character. Not one to be easily defeated.

Portia turned the sealed parchment over in her hand. She had no money for postage, knew no one who could frank it for her. She didn't even know if the mail services still operated between Edinburgh and York now that civil war raged across the northern lands beyond the Scottish border. But she could not ignore her father's dying instructions. He wanted the letter delivered to his half brother, and she must find a way to do so.

And then what was she to do? She looked around the bleak hovel. She could stay here throughout the winter. There was a living of sorts to be made in the tavern, and the old woman wouldn't throw her out so long as she could pay for the straw palliasse and a daily bowl of gruel. And without Jack's addiction to supply, she might be able to save a little. In the spring, she would move on . . . somewhere.

But first she had to bury her father.

"*My* lord . . . *my lord* . . . *Beggin' yer pardon, my lord . . .*"

Cato, Marquis of Granville, looked up at the voice, ragged for lack of breath, gasping behind him in the stable courtyard of Castle Granville. He turned, his hand still on the smooth black neck of the charger he was examining.

"Well?" He raised an eyebrow at the lad, who, unable to catch his breath for further speech, wordlessly held out a sealed parchment, then hugged his frozen hands under his armpits against the vicious January wind blowing off the Lammermuir hills.

Cato took it. The untidy scrawl was unknown to him. The letters wandered all over the paper as if the hand that had penned them had had little strength to hold the quill.

He turned the parchment over and inhaled sharply. The

seal was his half brother's. "I'll not ride out this morning, after all, Jebediah."

"Aye, m'lord." The groom took the charger's halter and led him back in the direction of his stall.

"Oh, you, lad." The marquis paused, glancing over his shoulder at the abandoned messenger, who stood, his recaptured breath steaming in the bitter air, his nose scarlet with cold. "You're from the mail office in York?"

The lad nodded vigorously.

"I didn't realize the mails were still running."

"They don't always gets through, m'lord. But the carrier what brought the bag that this come in took safe passage from Lord Leven when 'is lordship crossed the border."

Cato's nod of understanding was somber. "Go to the kitchen. They'll look after you there before you return to the city."

The marquis continued on his way, crossing the inner bailey to the great donjon, where the family resided. The blast of a trumpet came over the frosty air from the fields beyond the castle moat. It was followed by the carrying voice of a drill sergeant, the roll of a drum. But the marching footsteps of the drilling militia were muffled in the snow of the parade ground that had once been a peaceful wheat field.

The marquis entered the building through the narrow door. Pitch torches in sconces flickered over the ancient stone walls, lit the heavy slabs beneath his feet. Despite the tapestries hung upon the walls in the great hall, it was hard to soften the military, defensive nature of this inner keep that for centuries had protected the families of the house of Granville from the marauders and moss-troopers who menaced the border between Scotland and England, and from the lawless armies who had periodically ravaged the land since the Conqueror.

He ascended the stone stairs running off the hall, and the atmosphere changed, became more domestic. Windows had been widened and glassed, to let in both light and air, carpets softened the flagstones, and the tapestries were thick and plentiful. He turned down a corridor and entered his own sanctum in the bastion.

He threw off his thick cloak and drew off his leather

gauntlets. A log fire blazed in the hearth and he bent to warm his hands, before straightening, turning slowly before the fire's heat like a lamb on a spit, and breaking the seal on the parchment as he opened his half brother's missive.

St. Stephen's Street, Edinburgh, December, 1643

My dear brother,

When you read this, you may be certain that I have gone to my just reward. The pits of hell, I have no doubt! But I willingly pay the price for such a life as I have had. (Ah, I can see your pained frown, Cato. Such an upright soul as you could never understand the pleasures of excess.) But know that I am now paying for my sins, such as they are, and grant me one boon out of the goodness of your heart and the charity that I know flows so sweetly in your veins! My daughter, Portia. She has suffered with me but should not suffer without me. Will you take her in and treat her kindly? She has no family claims upon you—poor little bastard—and yet I ask this favor of the only person who could grant it.

Ever your degenerate brother,

Jack

Cato scrunched up the parchment. He could hear Jack's ironical, mocking tone in every word. No doubt the man was now stoking the fires of hell, as unrepentant as ever.

He bent to throw the missive into the flames, then paused. With a sigh, he smoothed out the sheet, laying it upon the oak table, flattening the creases with his palm. When had Jack died? The letter was dated the previous month. It would have taken anything up to three weeks to reach Granville. Was the girl still in Edinburgh? Still to be found on St. Stephen's Street? And how in the name of grace was he to find her with the border in an uproar?

He had known that sunny afternoon of his wedding two

and a half years ago that civil war had become inevitable. King Charles had pushed his country too far in his pursuit of absolute rule. The worm, as embodied in Parliament, had turned. For two years now the country had been torn apart, with families divided brother against brother, father against son. There had been battles, many of them, and yet out of the hideous slaughter had come no decisive victory for either side. Winter had brought an end to pitched battle, and in the cold new year of 1643, the king's supporters held the north of England. But they faced a new challenge now. The Scots army had raised its standard for Parliament and with Lord Leven at its head had just crossed the border into Yorkshire, bringing reinforcement against the king's military strength in the north.

Cato walked to the narrow window in the turret. From here he could see his own militia drilling. A militia he had originally raised in the king's name. The soldiers believed they were armed and ready to fight for King Charles at their lord's command, little knowing that their lord's loyalties were no longer a simple matter.

At the very beginning of this civil strife, Cato had seen no alternative to supporting his king and the royalist cause. It had seemed then morally unthinkable for a Granville to do otherwise than support his king in the face of civil insurrection.

He had raised men and money in the king's name and continued to hold his border castle for his sovereign. But slowly, inexorably, the conviction had grown that the king's cause was wrong . . . that the king was destroying the lives and liberties of his subjects. He was led astray by advisors who were mistaken if not downright evil, and no man who truly loved his country could support a sovereign so wrongheaded. So blind to the needs and rights of his people. Now, in the second year of war, Cato Granville was ready to turn his back on his king and raise his standard for Parliament and the cause of liberty.

And yet to oppose his sovereign went against every tenet of his heritage, and he had not yet spoken of his change of allegiance within his own walls, let alone declared himself publicly for Parliament.

But the time when he would have no choice was imminent, and each day he prepared himself anew.

Cato turned back from the window with a brusque impatient shake of his head and once more picked up Jack's letter.

He'd seen the child but once, at his own wedding, the day they had beheaded Strafford on Tower Hill. He had only a vague memory of her. Thin, dirty, freckles, startling red hair, and Jack's eyes, green and slanted like a cat's, with the same sharp, mocking glitter as her father's. She'd had the same insolent tone too, he recalled, his lip curling with remembered distaste.

He had enough to deal with at the moment without taking in an abandoned waif with neither family nor fortune to recommend her. He scrunched the letter again in his hand, prepared to toss it into the fire. And then again he paused. He could not refuse his brother's dying request. A dying request had all the force of moral imperative, and however disinclined he was, he had to do something for the girl.

He left the bastion room and made his way down the corridor to the square dining parlor, where he found his wife and daughter at breakfast. He had the unmistakable sense that he'd interrupted something unpleasant.

Diana looked up at his entrance. Her mouth was a little tighter than usual, her fine hazel eyes snapping, her well-plucked eyebrows lifted in an irritable frown. But at the sight of her husband, the irritability was smoothed from her features as easily as a damp cloth would expunge chalk from a blackboard.

Olivia, her large black eyes slightly averted, pushed back her chair and curtsied before resuming her seat.

"G-good morning, sir."

"Good morning, Olivia." Cato frowned, wondering what had caused the present tension between his wife and her stepdaughter. Olivia never seemed to treat her stepmother with anything but stiff and almost mute courtesy, although Diana, as far as he could tell, only had the child's best interests at heart.

Diana said, "My lord, you are not accustomed to taking breakfast with us." Her voice was light, but there was an underlying edge to it that defied concealment.

Even so, Olivia often wondered if her father was aware of Diana's dissatisfaction with her life in the frozen north, ensconced in a fortified castle, far from the gaiety and pleasures of the court. He seemed oblivious of his wife's daily sighing reminiscence of past glories of court life, of her wistful murmurs about how guilty she felt at not being at the queen's side during these trying times. He seemed not to notice, either, her occasional pointed remarks about how valuable the marquis of Granville would be to the king and his advisors, if only he could see his duty clear and join the king at Oxford, where the court had been sequestered since the beginning of the war.

But then, there was much that he didn't notice, Olivia reflected glumly, although what he could or would do if he understood what went on between his daughter and her stepmother, she didn't know.

"I was intending to ride out, madam, but a messenger arrived from Edinburgh with news of my half brother's death." Cato sat in the carved elbow chair at the head of the table and took up the tankard of ale that had appeared as if by magic at his elbow. He drank, forked sirloin onto his plate, and spread golden butter thickly onto a slice of barley bread.

Olivia felt a shiver of anticipation and she broke her customary defensive silence in a little rush of words. "Is that P-Portia's father, sir?"

"If you would breathe deeply, my dear Olivia, as I have told you so many times, I am sure you could control that unfortunate defect," Diana said with one of her sweet smiles. "You will find it hard to catch a husband if you cannot converse clearly." She patted Olivia's hand.

Olivia removed her hand abruptly and tucked it in her lap. She compressed her lips and lowered her eyes to her plate, the urge to speak demolished.

"It was of Portia that my brother wrote," Cato said.

Olivia's eyes lifted from her plate; it was impossible to pretend indifference. Cato continued calmly, "His deathbed wish is that I take the child into my household."

"You have no family responsibility to provide for a bastard, my lord," Diana pointed out with a gentle smile.

"My brother acknowledged that. But in all conscience, I cannot abandon the girl. She is my niece in blood."

Diana would ruin this wondrous possibility, given half a chance. Desperation and excitement catapulted Olivia into speech. "I would like her to c-come," she gasped, her usually pale cheeks flushed.

Diana's eyebrows disappeared beneath the artful froth of curls clustered on her white forehead. "My dear Olivia, she can be no fit companion for you . . . that dreadful man for a father." She shuddered with delicate distaste. "Forgive me, my lord, for speaking so frankly of your half brother, but . . . well, you know what I mean."

Cato nodded grimly. "I do indeed."

"I would very *much* like P–Portia to c–come!" Olivia repeated, her stammer more pronounced than usual under the pressure of emotion.

Diana snapped open her fan. "It's not for you to say, my dear," she chided, her eyes shooting darts of fire at Olivia from behind the fan.

Cato didn't appear to hear his wife's comment. "I was forgetting that you met her the once, at the wedding, Olivia. Did you take to her so strongly then?"

Olivia nodded, but didn't risk further speech.

"You could perhaps teach her our ways," Cato mused. The idea of a companion for his daughter had been much on his mind. He had once or twice proposed that Diana's younger sister Phoebe should pay them an extended visit, but whenever he had brought up the subject, Diana had always produced some reason against it. Cato knew that she didn't really care for her sister, whom she found clumsy and exasperating, so he hadn't pressed the subject.

"How old is the child?" Diana realized she was frowning again and hastily altered her expression, smoothing out any residue of lines with her forefinger.

Cato shook his head. "I don't really know. Older than Olivia, certainly."

"Yes, she is," Olivia ventured with a spark of defiance in her eyes. She knew that if she backed out of the conversation completely as Diana intended, Portia would not come. Diana's husband would give in to his wife with his usual dismissive shrug because he had too many more important things to concern him. Everything, it seemed to Olivia, was more important to her father than herself.

Olivia surreptitiously clasped the little silver locket at her neck. Inside was the braided ring of hair. The memory of those wonderful moments of friendship that had filled the decaying boathouse on that May afternoon gave her courage.

"Too old surely to learn new ways?" Diana suggested with another of her insidious smiles.

It was Cato's turn to frown. "Are you really against this, madam? I feel most strongly that I must honor my brother's dying request."

"Of course you must," Diana said hastily. "I wouldn't suggest otherwise, but I wonder if, perhaps, the girl wouldn't be happier lodging with some suitable family . . . a good bourgeois family where she could learn a trade, or find a husband of the right class. If you dowered her, perhaps . . ." She opened her palms in an indulgent gesture.

Olivia saw that her father had taken Diana's point. He was about to give in. She said in a voice so soft and pleading it surprised her, "P-*please*, sir."

The tone surprised Cato as much as it did Olivia. He looked at her with an arrested expression, suddenly remembering the warm, outgoing, bright little girl she had once been. Then had come the winter when the stammer had appeared and she had become so withdrawn. He couldn't remember when she had last asked him for something.

"Very well," he said.

Diana's fan snapped shut, the delicate ivory sticks clicking in the moment of silence.

Olivia's face glowed, the shadows in her eyes vanished, and her smile transformed the gravity of her expression.

Cato turned to his wife. "I'm sure Portia will learn to adapt to our ways, Diana. With your help."

"As you command, sir." Diana inclined her head dutifully. "And perhaps she can be of some use. In the nursery, maybe, with some of the lighter tasks. She'll wish to show her gratitude for your generosity, I'm sure."

Cato pushed back his chair and got to his feet. "Playing with the babies, acting as companion to Olivia, of course.

That would be very suitable, and I leave the details in your more than capable hands, my dear." He bowed and left the dining room.

Diana's sweet expression vanished. "If you have finished your breakfast, Olivia, you may go and practice your deportment. You're developing a veritable hunchback with all the reading you do. Come." She rose from the table, graceful and stately, not the slightest curve to her back or shoulders.

But then, no one could accuse Lady Granville of ever having her head in a book, Olivia thought, as she reluctantly pushed back her chair and followed her stepmother to her bedchamber, where Diana would strap the dreaded backboard to her stepdaughter's frail shoulders.

Cato, ignorant of his daughter's daily torture, strode out of the castle and onto the parade ground, where the militia continued to drill. He stood to one side, watching the maneuvers. Giles Crampton, the sergeant at arms, was a past master at turning a bunch of red-handed, big-footed farmhands and laborers into a disciplined unit.

Disciplined enough for Parliament's army. In fact, they would be a credit to it. And Giles Crampton had just that end in view. He alone was party to Lord Granville's change of allegiance, and Giles Crampton was absolutely behind his lord.

The sergeant, aware of his lordship's presence on the field, gestured to his second to take over the drill and marched smartly across to Lord Granville, his booted feet cracking the frozen ground with each long stride.

"Mornin', m'lord."

Cato gestured that he should walk with him. "I have a task for you, Giles. I don't know anyone else I can send."

"I'm your man, m'lord. You know that."

"Aye, but this is a task you may not take to." Cato frowned. "A nursemaid's task, you might call it. And it comes at the devil's own time. I can't easily spare you."

Giles's firm stride didn't falter. "Go on, sir."

"I need you to go to Edinburgh and bring back my niece." Cato explained the situation, and Giles said nothing until the explanation was finished.

"You want me to go today?"

"The sooner the better. There's no fighting close to the border yet. Leven is still bringing his troops down."

"And we'll be joinin' him, will we, m'lord?"

"Aye. When you get back from Scotland with the girl, we'll raise the standard for Parliament."

A beam spread slowly over Giles's rough-hewn countenance. "Now, that'll be a rare sight, m'lord."

"Will the men take up the standard?"

"Aye. They'll follow orders. Those who think at all already have leanings toward Parliament."

"Good." Cato drew out a heavy leather purse from his pocket. "This should see you through."

"And if the girl is unwilling . . . ?"

"Then don't force her. If she has plans of her own, so much the better." His brother couldn't expect him to do more than offer the girl a home.

Giles nodded again. " 'Appen I'll go over the moors. Less chance of meetin' an army." He grinned slyly.

"More chance of meeting moss-troopers," Cato said with a grim smile. "Rufus Decatur will have his spies out, and there's nothing he'd like better than to ambush a party of Granville men."

"I've heard tell he's raisin' his own militia for the king," Giles said.

"I suppose it was only to be expected that he'd become embroiled in the war," Cato said dourly. "He's bound to see fat pickings somewhere in the chaos of conflict. Just the kind of anarchy Decatur thrives upon."

He returned to the castle, his brow knotted as always by a train of thought that brought only frustration and anger. For twenty-six years the outlawed Decatur clan had lived in the wild, barren lands of the Cheviot Hills, from where they carried on a war of nerves and depredation against the lands, properties, and livelihoods of all bearing allegiance to the Granville standard.

The bands of moss-troopers who throughout the reigns of Elizabeth and James had turned the northern border into their own lawless territory had finally been subdued, but the Decaturs remained, protected in their isolated stronghold, moving easily back and forth across the Scottish border, raiding Granville property, remaining always outside the law, and always evading pursuit and capture.

Rufus Decatur led this band of outlaws. He was a man of huge reputation in the countryside, and the legends accompanying his name were larger than life. It didn't matter that he was master of a band of brigands and thieves, the people loved him for it, and he repaid their affection in kind. From them, he took nothing that was not freely given, and gave generously where help was needed. Even from his own jaundiced viewpoint, Cato was forced to acknowledge that the outcast house of Rothbury was as much a force for good throughout the countryside as it had been when the family had been in possession of their estates and fortune.

Except when it came to Granville matters. There Decatur's loathing and malice were unbounded. He hounded and persecuted, raided, destroyed, never missing an opportunity for mischief wherever it would hurt the marquis of Granville the most.

Every day of his adult life, Cato had felt himself pitted against Rufus Decatur. They were of an age. And each had succeeded to his father's title. But whereas Cato on the death of his father had assumed the mantle and trappings of a powerful noble of the borderlands, Rufus had only an empty title and forfeit estates, and the memory of a father who had died by his own hand rather than face trial for treason, and the execution or slow, lingering death in prison that would have followed.

Cato understood that he had inherited his father's guilt in the eyes of Rufus Decatur. His father had been a man of rigid temperament, acknowledging no gray areas in matters of honor and conscience. When William Decatur had dared to speak out openly against King James's actions, had dared to conspire against the king's destructive advisors, George Granville had had no hesitation in condemning his old friend. As Lord Marshal of the borderlands, it had been his task to arrest the traitor, to oversee the king's justice, and he had not hesitated to perform that task.

Cato didn't know whether he himself would have been able to do as his father had done in such circumstances. He shared none of his father's rigidity and was plagued too much by the ability to see both sides of an issue. But he knew that as far as Rufus Decatur was concerned, it didn't matter a tinker's damn how the son would have reacted. William Decatur had died and his family was disinherited because of the actions of George Granville, and Rufus wanted his vengeance. The battle he fought with George's son was a personal one, and Cato was forced to fight whether he wished to or not.

And if Rufus Decatur was about to enter the civil war on the side opposite to Cato Granville, their personal enmity would assume a greater dimension.

Part of Cato relished the prospect of meeting his enemy face-to-face on the battlefield, where there would be something cold and clear and comprehensible about the encounter.

2

"*Where are you goin', Rufus?*" *The sleepy voice, sound-*ing somewhat aggrieved, emerged from the tangle of bed-clothes. There was a heave beneath the fur coverlet, and a woman struggled onto an elbow. A work-roughened hand pushed aside the veil of dark hair to reveal a pair of brown eyes.

"I've work to do, Maggie. And well you know it." Rufus Decatur broke the ice in the pitcher with a balled fist and poured the freezing water over his head with a groan of min-gled pain and exhilaration. He shook his head and drops of ice water flew around the small loft. The woman retreated be-neath the fur with a muttered curse.

Rufus toweled his head vigorously, ignoring the curses and complaints, and after a minute Maggie sat up in the wide bed, drawing the fur to her chin, and surveyed the master of De-catur village with a disgruntled frown.

"It's not even dawn."

"And you're a lazy wench, Maggie, my love," Rufus declared, reaching for his shirt where it lay over the rail of the bed.

The woman's eyes narrowed at the tone and she leaned back against the carved headboard. "Come back to bed." He was a fine, strong man, this Rufus Decatur, and she was never averse to a summons to his bed. The nights she spent there brought her a deal more pleasure than she was accustomed to from her usual customers.

Her eyes ran lasciviously down his body. The same red-gold hair that fell to his shoulders and bearded his square chin clustered on his chest and sprang in a curly bush at his groin. It glistened in the candlelight on his forearms and on his legs, red against the weather-browned limbs. He carried no spare flesh, but there was something about the sheer size of the man that made him seem larger than life, as if the loft was too small to contain him.

"Get up," was all she received for her pains. He swooped over her and pulled back the covers. "Up! I've a busy day ahead of me!" There was something in the vivid blue eyes that brought his bedmate to her feet, shivering and grumbling. Rufus Decatur had a temper to match his red hair, and in certain moods he was not to be denied.

"Y'are raidin' again?" She sat on the bed to draw on her woolen stockings, then stepped into her flannel petticoat, before thrusting her head into the opening of her woolen chemise.

"Maybe." He pulled on a buff leather jerkin and bent to stir the embers in the hearth. A flame shot up and he threw on kindling until the blaze roared up the chimney.

Maggie moved closer to the heat to finish dressing. "Talk is that y'are goin' to declare fer the king," she observed, casting him a sly look. "Take yer men to join up wi' the king's men."

"Talk's cheap." Rufus swatted her ample rear as he passed her. "You'll find your purse in the usual place." He gave her a quick smile before he disappeared from view down the rickety staircase to the square cottage room below.

Maggie was satisfied with the smile. Rufus was not one to share his business, and he could well have snubbed her with uncomfortable asperity. Matters in Decatur village took place out of the public eye. There were no women. Maggie and her friends visited when summoned, and for all other domestic needs the men took care of themselves.

Everyone knew that the village was more of a military encampment than a civilian community, and it was only reasonable to assume that Rufus was preparing to throw his well-trained band of brigands into a war that was bidding fair to leave no man and his conscience untouched. But so far no one beyond the borders of Rufus's stronghold had any true inkling which side of the conflict appealed to the master of Decatur village, and it was a matter of some considerable interest and importance.

Rufus was well aware of the local speculation and guessed that Maggie had been put up to her probing by the inquisitive

Mistress Beldam, who managed the affairs of the women who took care of the men of Decatur village. But their curiosity would soon be satisfied. His decision was made and would be common knowledge within a day or two.

The banked fire threw off an ashy glow that provided dim light in the simply furnished room. Rufus trod softly over to a curtained alcove in the far corner of the room. He peered behind the curtain and was surprised to see that the two small heaps beneath the covers on the cot were not yet ready to resume the tempestuous course of their daily life. They were usually awake before the first cock crow, even in the dead of winter, but he knew they'd be up as soon as they heard Maggie leave. In the meantime, their father could enjoy this small and rare extension of dawn peace.

He caught up his cloak hanging from a nail in the wall by the door, threw up the heavy wooden bar, and pushed open the door. It had snowed heavily in the night, and it required a heave from his shoulder to push through the drift piling up against the base of the door.

The last stars were fading in the sky and the moon hung low over the Cheviot Hills as he emerged into the frigid dawn. The cluster of stone cottages was nestled in a deep fold of the rolling hills, inaccessible by road. On the hilltops around, watchmen's fires burned as guards kept sentinel over the barren, inhospitable countryside that stretched to the Scottish border.

Rufus made his way through the village to the river that flowed so conveniently past his stronghold. The water ran sluggishly now beneath its frozen surface, but it still provided water for the village and a thoroughfare into the world beyond—by sled in the frozen depths of winter, by boat in other seasons.

A group of youths was gathered at the river's edge, their cloaks discarded beside the line of buckets that stood waiting on the bank, as they swung pickaxes at the ice to free the water hole that had frozen over in the night. They straightened as Rufus approached, and stood waiting, their cheeks pink from cold and exertion.

"Mornin', m'lord."

"Morning, lads." Rufus exchanged greetings and small

talk, acknowledging each one by name. If he was aware of the naked adoration in their eyes as they gathered around him, he gave no indication.

These were his novitiates, the most recent recruits to the Decatur band. Many had followed fathers, brothers, uncles into the world beyond the law. Some were fugitives from the law themselves, some merely imbued with the spirit of adventure. They all, however, had one distinguishing feature. They were utterly and unswervingly devoted to the house of Rothbury and held no loyalty above loyalty to their cadre.

"Is it true, master, that we're to declare for the king?" A tall young man, whose bearing made him the clear leader of the group, spoke for them all. Ten pairs of eager eyes rested on Rufus's countenance.

"You think His Majesty will accept the aid of a band of moss-troopers, Paul?" Rufus inquired, and his bland tone deceived none of them. His eyes had a glitter that seemed to reflect the icy surface of the river under the fading stars. "The aid of a family dispossessed for treason? The hand of an outlaw, stained with years of cattle stealing, highway robbery, and God knows what other crimes against the law-abiding countryside?"

Paul met his eye. "I think His Majesty'll accept any hand that's offered, sir," he declared. "With Lord Leven marching in from Scotland, seems to me the king hasn't much choice."

The master's mouth quirked, but with more derision than amusement. "Aye, I believe you're right, lad. A whole mountain of grievance will be buried under the banner of loyalty, you mark my words. And with a king's gratitude, what could a man not achieve?" He raised a hand in farewell and strode off, his cloak swirling around his ankles with the sudden energy of his stride.

With a king's gratitude, a man could achieve reinstatement . . . a full pardon. . . . The house of Rothbury could once more take its rightful place in the world inside the law. Oh yes, there was little that a grateful king could not do for a loyal subject.

Rufus laughed shortly to himself. He would play this conflict for his own ends. He had no time for the king's cause. Charles was as much a fool as his father, James, had been. But

Rufus would not make the mistake of his own father. He would support this king in his folly, and he would reap the rewards of that support. He would exact the goodly price of restitution.

He made his way up the narrow path that snaked up the hillside to the first of the watchmen's fires. The stars had disappeared when he reached the hilltop, but the ring of fires surrounding the valley still burned brightly, as they would throughout the day, providing warmth for the watchmen who guarded the Decatur sanctuary twenty-four hours a day.

"Morning, Rufus." A tall, lean man in his early twenties turned from the fire where he was warming his hands. "Coffee?"

"Thanks, Will." Rufus nodded at his cousin. He was particularly fond of the younger man, whose father had guided the fatherless Rufus through all the pitfalls of youth. Will was Rufus's uncle's son, sired when the old man should have been sitting by the fire nodding in peaceful senility instead of rampaging through the countryside by day and lying each night with his bedmate with all the vigor and virility of a man in his prime. "Peaceful night?"

"Aye. But Connor's men reported troop movements to the north. Leven's men, we reckon."

Rufus took a beaker of hot spiced mead from a man armed with pike and musket. "We'll send out scouts later this morning. If Fairfax and Leven join up with Parliament's forces, the king'll be in a pretty pickle. He can wave goodbye to a superior force in the north." He sounded as if the issue didn't concern him unduly, but Will was not deceived by the calm, matter-of-fact tone. He knew what Rufus had invested in this choice he'd made.

"You think we might be able to delay Leven?" Will blew on the surface of his own mead to cool it. "A little judicial harassment perhaps?"

"Aye, that's precisely what I thought." Rufus chuckled suddenly, and his expression lightened, his eyes losing their earlier glitter. "We'll give the king's command a little unofficial aid. My lords Bellasis and Newcastle should prove grateful."

Will grinned, recognizing that Rufus had lost his seriousness and was now contemplating this little jaunt in the same light as he planned their more mischievous raids.

"Granville's for the king, too," he observed after a minute.

Rufus did not immediately respond, but stared out over the hills as the night clouds rolled away from the eastern hills. "We'll see. I've a feeling that he's not committed as yet. If he goes for Parliament, all the better. We'll really tweak his tail then."

"But it's said he's raising a militia for the king." Will couldn't hide his puzzlement.

"We'll see," Rufus repeated. He didn't know why he was so sure of Cato Granville's ambivalence, but he felt it as if it were his own. He'd spent all his life ranged against this man, watching his movements, trying to second-guess him, until sometimes he felt he lived inside the man's head.

He handed his beaker back to the pikeman. "I'll take a few men and ride out toward Selkirk. See what tidbits we can pick up on the Edinburgh road."

"Have a care."

"Aye." Rufus strode away down the narrow track to the village below.

The sounds of shrill altercation coming from a garden at the edge of the village gave him pause. His expression lost its air of somber distraction. He turned aside through a wooden gate into a small kitchen garden. The ground was iron hard and barren of produce, but a clutch of hens was squabbling over grain scattered before the kitchen door. Two very small bundled figures rolling in the snow were the source of the altercation.

Two strides took him beside them. Fortunately they'd gone to bed in their clothes the previous night. In the absence of supervision they would probably have rolled out of bed and into the snow in their nightshirts. As it was, little Luke seemed to have his boots on the wrong feet and his fingers were all tangled in his gloves.

Rufus seized a collar in each hand and hauled the pair apart. Towheaded, blue eyed, they faced each other, glaring, red faced, furious.

"It's *my* turn to collect the eggs!"

"No it's not, it's *mine!*"

Rufus surveyed the two boys with a degree of indulgent amusement. They were such a tempestuous pair, born a year apart, and they both had inherited the Rothbury temper. It made for an unquiet life, but he recognized so much of himself in his sons that he rarely took forceful objection to their whirlwind passions. "What a pair of scrappy brats you are. It's too cold to be rolling in the snow."

"It's *my* turn for the eggs because I'm older," young Tobias declared, lunging against the hand that merely tightened on his collar.

"You did it yesterday. You *always* say you're older." Tears clogged his little brother's voice as he stated this unassailable truth.

"Because I am," Toby said smugly.

"It's *not* fair!" Luke wailed. " 'Tisn't!"

"No, such things rarely are," Rufus agreed. "But sadly, they can't be changed. Who collected the eggs yesterday?"

"Toby did!" Luke swiped his forearm across his button nose. "He *always* does it 'cause he's older."

"I'm *better* at it than you, 'cause I'm older." Toby sounded very sure of his ground.

"But how's Luke to get better at it if he never gets any practice?" Rufus pointed out, aware of the sudden frigid gust of wind whistling around the corner of the house from the hilltop. "The eggs will have to wait now. It's breakfast time."

Ignoring the barrage of protests, he tightened his hold on their collars and propelled them ahead of him toward the low stone building that contained the mess.

The children's mother had died soon after Luke's birth. Elinor had been Rufus's regular bedmate for five years. She hadn't lived in the village, but their relationship had transcended the simple financial exchange that characterized his dealings with Maggie and the other women of Mistress Beldam's establishment. Her death had affected him deeply, and in the face of all practicality, once Luke was out of swaddling clothes, Rufus had taken the boys himself. A martial encampment was hardly the perfect place to bring up two small children, but he had sworn to their mother that they would bear his name and he would take care of them himself.

Mind you, their futures would be a lot rosier if their father's gamble paid off and his lands were restored to him by a grateful monarch, Rufus reflected with cold cynicism, ushering the children into the crowded aromatic warmth of the mess.

Portia pulled the hood of her cloak tighter around her face, against the sleet-laden wind whipping down through the Lammermuir Hills. Her horse blew through his nostrils in disgust and dropped his head against the freezing blasts. It was late morning and she hoped they would stop for dinner soon, but there were no signs of comforting habitation on this stretch of the Edinburgh road, and Portia's companions, the dour but not ill-disposed Giles Crampton and his four men, continued to ride into the teeth of the wind with the steadfast endurance she'd come to expect of these Yorkshiremen.

It had been a week since Sergeant Crampton, as he called himself, had come to the Rising Sun. She'd been drawing ale and dodging the wandering hands of the taproom's patrons when this burly Yorkshireman had pushed open the door, letting in a flurry of snow and earning the grumbling curses of those huddled around the sullen smolder of the peat fire. . . .

"Mistress Worth?"

"Who wants her?" Portia pushed the filled tankard across to the waiting customer and leaned her elbows on the bar counter. Her green eyes assessed the newcomer, taking in his thick, comfortable garments, his heavy boots, the rugged countenance of a man accustomed to the outdoors. A well-to-do farmer or craftsman, she guessed. But not a man to tangle with, judging by the large, square hands with their corded veins, the massive shoulders, thick-muscled thighs, and the uncompromising stare of his sharp brown eyes.

"Crampton, Sergeant Crampton." Giles thrust his hands into his britches' pockets, pushing aside his cloak to reveal the bone-handled pistols at his belt, the plain sheathed sword.

Of course, Portia thought. A soldier. Talk of England's civil war was on every Scot's tongue, but the fighting was across the border.

"What d'ye want with me, Sergeant?" She rested her chin

in her elbow-propped hand and regarded him curiously. "Ale, perhaps?"

"Drawing ale is no work for Lord Granville's niece," Giles stated gruffly. "I'd count it a favor if ye'd leave this place and accompany me, Mistress Worth. I've a letter from your uncle." He drew a rolled parchment from his breast and laid it on the counter.

Portia was conscious of a quickening of her blood, a lifting of her skin. She had had no idea what Jack had written to his half brother, but it had clearly concerned her. She unrolled the parchment and scanned the bold black script.

Giles watched her. A lettered tavern wench was unusual indeed, but this one, for all that she looked the part to perfection with her chapped hands, ragged and none too clean shift beneath her holland gown, and untidy crop of orange curls springing around a thin pale face liberally sprinkled with freckles, seemed to have no trouble ciphering.

Portia remembered Cato Granville from that hot afternoon in London when they'd beheaded the earl of Strafford. She remembered the boathouse, the two girls: Phoebe, the bride's sister; and Portia's own half cousin, Olivia. The pale, solemn child with the pronounced stammer. They'd played some silly game of mixing blood and promising eternal friendship. She'd even made braided rings of their hair. She seemed to remember how they'd all had the most absurd ambitions, ways by which they'd ensure their freedom from men and marriage. She herself was going to go for a soldier and maintain her independence by following the drum.

Portia almost laughed aloud at the absurdity of that childish game. She'd still had the ability to play the child three years ago. But no longer.

Her uncle was offering her a home. There didn't seem to be any conditions attached to the offer, but Portia knew kindness never came without strings. But what could the illegitimate daughter of the marquis's wastrel half brother do for Lord Granville? She couldn't marry for him, bringing the family powerful alliances and grand estates in her marriage contracts. No one would wed a penniless bastard. He couldn't need another servant, he must have plenty.

So why?

"Lady Olivia asked me to give you this." Sergeant Crampton interrupted her puzzled thoughts. He laid a wafer-sealed paper on the counter.

Portia opened it. A tricolored ring of braided hair fell out. A black lock entwined with a fair and a red.

Please come. They were the only two words on the paper that had contained the ring.

This time Portia did laugh aloud at the childish whimsy of it all. What did games in a boathouse have to do with her own grim struggle for survival?

"If I thank Lord Granville for his offer but would prefer to remain as I am . . . ?" She raised an eyebrow.

"Then, 'tis your choice, mistress." He glanced pointedly around the taproom. "But seems to me there's no choice for a body with half a wit."

Portia scooped the ring back into the paper and screwed it tight, dropping it into her bosom. "No, you're right, Sergeant. Better the devil I don't know to the one I do. . . ."

So here she was three days' ride out of Edinburgh, serviceably if not elegantly clad in good boots and a thick riding cloak over a gown of dark wool and several very clean woolen petticoats discreetly covering a pair of soft leather britches so she could ride comfortably astride. Midwinter journeys on the rough tracks of the Scottish border were not for sidesaddle riders.

Sergeant Crampton had given her money without explanation or instruction, for which Portia had been grateful. She didn't like taking charity, but the sergeant's matter-of-fact attitude had saved her embarrassment. And common sense had dictated that she accept the offering. She certainly couldn't have journeyed any distance in the clothes she had on her back.

Despite the bitter cold and the constant freezing damp that trickled down her neck whenever she shook off her hood, Portia was pleasantly exhilarated. It had been several years since she'd had a decent horse to ride. Jack had been very particular about horseflesh, refusing to provide either himself or his daughter with anything but prime cattle, until the drink had ended both his physical ability to ride and his ability to keep them from total penury with his skill at the gaming tables.

"Y'are doin' all right, mistress?" The sergeant brought his mount alongside Portia's. His eyes roamed the bleak landscape even as he spoke to her, and she sensed an unusual tension in the man, who was generally phlegmatic to the point of apparent sleepiness.

"I'm fine, Sergeant," Portia replied. "This is a miserable part of the world, though."

"Aye," he agreed. "But another four hours should see us home. I'd not wish to stop before, if ye can manage it."

"Without difficulty," Portia said easily. She was accustomed to hunger. "Is there danger here?"

"It's Decatur land. Goddamned moss-troopers." Giles spat in disgust.

"Moss-troopers! But I thought they'd been run out of the hills years ago."

"Aye, all but the Decaturs. They're holed up in the Cheviots, where they prey on Granville land and cattle. Murdering, thieving bastards!"

Portia remembered what Jack had told her of the feud between the house of Rothbury and the house of Granville. Jack had had grim memories of the father he and Cato had shared. A man of unbending temperament, a harsh disciplinarian, a father who had no interest in gaining the affection of his sons. But Jack had had even less regard for Rufus Decatur, Earl of Rothbury, and his outlaw band. It was one area of agreement between Jack and his half brother. Nothing that had happened in the past justified the lawless actions and private malice of Decatur and his men. They were a scourge on the face of the borderlands, no better than the criminal bands of moss-troopers who had been hunted down and exterminated like so many rats in a stubble field.

"They're still as active, then?"

"Aye, and worse than usual these last months." Giles spat again. "Cattle-thieving murderers. Decatur, that devil's spawn, will be usin' the war for 'is own ends, you mark my words."

Portia shivered. She could see how a world at war could lend itself to the pursuit of a powerful personal vendetta. "Is Lord Granville for the king?"

Giles cast her a sharp look. "What's it to you?"

"A matter of interest." She looked sideways at him. "Is he?"

"Happen so," was the short response, and the sergeant urged his mount forward to join the two men who rode a little ahead of Portia. The other two brought up the rear, giving her the feeling of being hemmed in. It seemed her father's half brother wanted her protected—a novel thought.

She slipped her gloved hand into the pocket of her jacket beneath her cloak. Olivia's braided ring was still wrapped in the screw of paper, and Portia had found her own in the small box where she kept the very few personal possessions that had some sentimental value—her father's signet ring; a silver coin with a hole in it that had been given her as a child and that she believed had magic powers; a pressed violet that she vaguely thought her mother had given to her, except that she had no image of the woman who had died before Portia's second birthday; an ivory comb with several teeth missing; and a small porcelain brooch in the shape of a daisy that Jack had told her had belonged to her mother. The box and its contents were all she had brought with her from Edinburgh.

What was Olivia like now? She had been such a serious creature . . . unhappy, Portia had thought at the time, although it was hard to understand how someone who had never known want could be unhappy. Olivia had been worried about her new stepmother, of course. Phoebe, the bride's sister, had certainly had a very poor opinion of her elder sister. Portia wondered if Olivia was in some sort of trouble. And if so, did she really think Portia could be of any help? Portia, who had enough trouble keeping her own body and soul together and her spirits relatively buoyant.

Portia's stomach rumbled loudly and she huddled closer into her cloak. A week of regular and substantial meals had lessened her tolerance for an empty belly, she reflected.

A shout, the thudding of hooves, the crack of a musket, drove all thoughts of hunger from her mind. Her horse reared in panic and she fought to keep him from bolting, while around her men seemed to swarm, horses whinnying, muskets cracking. She heard Sergeant Crampton yelling at his men to close up, but there were only four of them against eight armed riders, who quickly surrounded the party, separating the Granville men from each other, crowding them toward a stand of bare trees.

"Now, just who do we have here?"

Portia drew the reins tight. The quivering horse raised its head and neighed in protest, pawing the ground. Portia looked up and into a pair of vivid blue eyes glinting with an amusement to match the voice.

"And who are you?" she demanded. "And why have you taken those men prisoner?"

Her hood had fallen back in her struggles with the horse, and Rufus found himself the object of a fierce green-eyed scrutiny from beneath an unruly tangle of hair as orange-red as a burning brazier. Her complexion was white as milk, but not from fear, he decided; she looked far too annoyed for alarm.

"Rufus Decatur, Lord Rothbury, at your service," he said solemnly, removing his plumed hat with a flourish as he offered a mock bow from atop his great chestnut stallion. "And who is it who travels under the Granville standard? If you please . . ." He raised a red eyebrow.

Portia didn't answer the question. "Are you abducting us? Or is it murder you have in mind?"

"Tell you what," Rufus said amiably, catching her mount's bridle just below the bit. "We'll trade questions. But let's continue this fascinating but so far uninformative exchange somewhere a little less exposed to this ball-breaking cold."

3

$\mathcal{P}$ortia reacted without thought. Her whip hand rose and she slashed at Decatur's wrist, using all her force so that the blow cut through the leather gauntlet. He gave a shout of surprise, his hand falling from the bridle, and Portia had gathered the reins, kicked at the animal's flanks, and was racing down the track, neither knowing nor caring in which direction, before Rufus fully realized what had happened.

Portia heard him behind her, the chestnut's pounding hooves cracking the thin ice that had formed over the wet mud between the ridges on the track. She urged her horse to greater speed, and the animal, still panicked from the earlier melee, threw up his head and plunged forward. If she had given him his head, he would have bolted, but she hung on, maintaining some semblance of control, crouched low over his neck, half expecting a musket shot from behind.

But she knew this was a race she wasn't going to win. Her horse was a neat, sprightly young gelding, but he hadn't the stride or the deep chest of the pursuing animal. Unless Rufus Decatur decided for some reason to give up the chase, she was going to be overtaken within minutes. And then she realized that her pursuer was not overtaking her, he was keeping an even distance between them, and for some reason this infuriated Portia. It was as if he were playing with her, cat with mouse, allowing her to think she was escaping even as he waited to pounce in his own good time.

She slipped her hand into her boot, her fingers closing over the hilt of the wickedly sharp dagger Jack had insisted she carry from the moment he had judged her mature enough to attract unwelcome attention. Maturity rather than physical appeal had clearly been the issue. She'd learned rapidly that men didn't seem to care if their female prey was ragged, poxed, and looked like the back end of a beer keg when they had sex on their minds.

By degrees, Portia drew back on the reins, slowing the horse's mad progress even as she straightened in the saddle. The hooves behind her were closer now. She waited, wanting him to be too close to stop easily. Her mind was cold and clear, her heart steady, her breathing easy. But she was ready to do murder.

With a swift jerk, she pulled up her horse, swinging round in the saddle in the same moment, the dagger in her hand, the weight of the hilt balanced between her index and forefingers, steadied by her thumb.

Rufus Decatur was good and close, and as she'd hoped his horse was going fast enough to carry him right past her before he could pull it up. She saw his startled expression as for a minute he was facing her head-on. She threw the dagger, straight for his heart.

It lodged in his chest, piercing his thick cloak. The hilt quivered. Portia, mesmerized, stared at it, for the moment unable to kick her horse into motion again. She had never killed a man before.

"Jesus, Mary, and sainted Joseph!" Rufus Decatur exclaimed in a voice far too vigorous for that of a dead man. He pulled the dagger free and looked down at it in astonishment. "Mother of God!" He regarded the girl on her horse in astonishment. "You were trying to stab me!"

Portia was as astonished as he was, but for different reasons. She could see no blood on the blade. And then the mystery was explained. Her intended victim moved aside his cloak to reveal a thickly padded buff coat of the kind soldiers wore. It was fair protection against knives and arrows, if not musket balls.

"You were chasing me," she said, feeling no need to apologize for her murderous intent. Indeed, she sounded as cross as she felt. "You abducted my escort and you were chasing me. Of course I wanted to stop you."

Rufus thought that most young women finding themselves in such a situation, if they hadn't swooned away in fright or thrown a fit of strong hysterics first, would have chosen a less violent course of action. But this tousled and indignant member of the female sex obviously had a more down-to-earth attitude, one with which he couldn't help but find himself in sympathy.

"Well, I suppose you have a point," he agreed, turning the knife over in his hand. His eyes were speculative as he examined the weapon. It was no toy. He looked up, subjecting her to a sharp scrutiny. "I should have guessed that a lass with that hair would have a temper to match."

"As it happens, I don't," Portia said, returning his scrutiny with her own, every bit as sharp and a lot less benign. "I'm a very calm and easygoing person in general. Except when someone's chasing me with obviously malicious intent."

"Well, I have to confess I do have the temper to match," Rufus declared with a sudden laugh as he swept off his hat to reveal his own brightly burnished locks. "But it's utterly dormant at present. All I need from you are the answers to a couple of questions, and then you may be on your way again. I simply want to know who you are and why you're riding under Granville protection."

"And what business is it of yours?" Portia demanded.

"Well . . . you see, anything to do with the Granvilles is my business," Rufus explained almost apologetically. "So, I really do need to have the answer to my questions."

"What are you doing with Sergeant Crampton and his men?"

"Oh, just a little sport," he said with a careless flourish of his hat. "They'll come to no real harm, although they might get a little chilly."

Portia looked over her shoulder down the narrow lane. She could see no sign of either the sergeant and his men or Rufus Decatur's men. "Why didn't you overtake me?" She turned back to him, her eyes narrowed. "You could have done so any time you chose."

"You were going in the right direction, so I saw no need," he explained reasonably. "Shall we continue on our way?"

The right direction for what? Portia was beginning to feel very confused. "You're abducting me?"

"No, I'm offering you shelter from the cold," he corrected

in the same reasonable tone. "Since you can't continue on your way for a while longer . . . until my men have finished their business . . . it seems only chivalrous to offer you shelter."

"Chivalrous?" Portia stared at him and quite unconsciously her voice mimicked the mockery she had so often heard from her father on the subject of Decatur honor. "A Decatur, *chivalrous!* Don't make me laugh!"

"Oh, believe me, nothing is further from my intention," Rufus said softly, and Portia's confusion gave way to downright fear. Some demon had sprung into the bright blue gaze, and Decatur's dormant temper was clearly wide-awake now. She could almost feel as a palpable force the power he was using to control it.

She realized with a sick feeling that he was waiting for an apology, but Jack would turn in his grave if his daughter apologized to a Decatur. And then, embarrassingly, her stomach growled loudly in the tense silence.

Quite suddenly, the demon vanished from Decatur's eyes, and when he spoke his voice was once more coolly reasonable. "We both seem to be in need of our dinner," he observed. "Let's put that unfortunate exchange down to an empty belly and the fact that you don't know me very well as yet. . . . When you do," he added almost reflectively, "you'll know to be a little more careful where you tread." He turned his horse on the narrow path. "Come, let us go in search of dinner."

Portia wanted to respond that she had neither the interest in nor intention of furthering their acquaintance, but she opted for an indifferent shrug instead. "At least let me have my dagger back."

"Oh, certainly." He presented it to her politely, hilt first, watching with interest as she tucked it back into her boot. "You threw it like an expert assassin."

"As it happens, I've never tried to kill anyone before, but I know how to, should the need arise." She turned her horse beside his. "Where are you taking me?"

"A farmhouse up the road."

"And you'll force them to give succor to an outlaw," she said acidly, and then immediately cursed her unruly tongue.

However, to her relief, Rufus merely chuckled. "No, no,

on the contrary. The Boltons will be delighted to see me. I hope you have a good appetite, because Annie's likely to get offended if her plates aren't cleaned."

Portia glanced back again over her shoulder. She couldn't see what she could do to aid the sergeant and his men, even if she knew where they were.

"Shall we canter?" Rufus suggested. "You're looking very pinched and cold."

"I always look cold. It's because I'm thin," she returned with a snap. "Like a scarecrow, really." She nudged her mount into a canter, keeping pace with the chestnut's easy lope until they drew rein outside a stone cottage set back from the road behind a low fieldstone wall. Smoke curled from the twin chimneys, and the windows were shuttered against the cold.

Rufus leaned down to open the gate and moved his horse to one side so she could precede him into the small front garden, where cabbage stalks poked up from the snow-covered ground. The door flew open and a small boy exploded into the garden.

"It's Lord Rufus," he yelled excitedly. "Grandmama, it's Lord Rufus."

"Lord bless ye, lad." A plump woman appeared behind him in the doorway. "There's no need to shout it from the rooftops." She came out of the cottage, drawing a shawl over her head. "It's been overlong, m'lord, since ye've paid us a visit."

"Aye, I know it, Annie." Rufus swung down from his horse and embraced the woman, who seemed to disappear into his cloak for a minute. "And if you'll not forgive me, I'll not sleep easy for a se'enight."

"Oh, get on wi' ye!" She laughed and slapped playfully at his arm. "Who's the lass?"

"That I don't know as yet." Rufus turned back to Portia, still sitting her horse. "But I expect to discover very shortly." Before she realized what he was about, he had reached up and lifted her out of the saddle, his hands firm at her waist. "You'll not be holding secrets, will you, lass?"

He held her off the ground and there was an unmistakable challenge behind the laughter in his voice. Portia's hackles rose in instant response as she glared down into the bright blue gaze.

He chuckled softly and lifted her a little higher. His large hands easily spanned her waist, and Portia suddenly felt acutely vulnerable, like a doll made of twigs. "Put me down," she demanded, resisting the almost uncontrollable urge to kick and struggle.

To her relief he did so immediately, saying over his shoulder, "We're both right famished, Annie. Freddy, bait the horses and rub 'em down, lad."

"Aye, m'lord." The boy's gaze was adoring as Rufus ruffled his shock of spiky dark hair.

" 'Ow's those lads of your'n, m'lord?" Annie inquired, hustling them into the cottage.

"Squabbling," Rufus said with one of his deep laughs, unclasping his cloak and hanging it on a nail beside the door. He held out a hand for Portia's in a gesture as matter-of-fact as it was commanding.

Rufus took the cloak from her, then held it for a minute before hanging it up, running his eyes over her in an unabashed appraisal that made her feel uncomfortably exposed.

"Mmm. See what you mean about the scarecrow," he said. "You've no meat on your bones at all. What's a Granville protégée doing half-starved?" He gestured to the fire as he hung up her cloak. "Sit close to the warmth. You're frozen."

"Lord, but the lass is white as a ghost!" Annie exclaimed, encouraging her to take a stool almost inside the inglenook. "But it's a coloring that goes with the carrot top, I daresay." She fetched a leather flagon from a shelf above the hearth. " 'Ere, a drop of rhubarb wine'll put the blood in yer veins, duckie."

Portia accepted the pitch tankard she was offered. She was not particularly offended by Annie's personal comments on her appearance; she'd been hearing their like all her life and had few illusions of her own. But for some reason Rufus Decatur's unflattering appraisal seemed to be a different matter, even if he was only echoing her own comments.

"I've potato and cabbage soup and a pig's cheek," Annie said. "It'll take me but a few minutes to get it to table. Would ye slice the loaf, m'lord?"

Rufus took up a knife and a loaf of barley bread from the table and, holding the loaf against his chest, began to slice it with all the rapid expertise of a man accustomed to such household tasks.

Portia watched with unwilling fascination. Such a homely skill seemed quite incongruous in the large hands of this red-bearded giant. Remarkably well-shaped hands they were, too. The fingers were long and slender, the knuckles smooth, the nails broad and neatly filed. But his wrists, visible below the turned-back cuffs of his shirt, were all sinew, dusted with red-gold hairs.

"So," Rufus said, putting the sliced bread back on the table. "An answer to my question before we eat. Who are you?"

The diversion was a relief. "Portia Worth." She had no reason to hide her identity.

"Ah." He nodded and took up his tankard again. "Jack Worth's spawn." He regarded her with a hint of sympathy. "Don't answer this if you don't wish to, but is it by-blow?"

Portia shrugged. "Jack wasn't the marrying kind."

"No, that he wasn't."

"You knew him?" She was startled into a show of interest.

"I knew of him. I knew he took his mother's name." Rufus gave a short laugh. "Some misguided sensibility about sullying the Granville name with his misdeeds! As if such a name weren't sufficiently tainted. . . . Come, sit at the table." He gestured to a stool at the table as Annie placed wooden bowls of steaming soup before them.

Portia was not in the habit of defending her father's family, because she was not accustomed to hearing them attacked. Even Jack through his drunken cynicism had accorded Cato, his half brother, a degree of careless respect bordering on what could almost pass for a measure of sibling affection. But base-born though she was, she was still half a Granville and she'd been taught to view the lawless viciousness of the outcast Decaturs with her father's eye. Her blood rose hot and she forgot caution.

"When it comes to misdeeds, you should maybe look to your own," she said tautly. "Murder, robbery, brigandage—"

"Now, now, missie, there's no cause to be throwing such words around my table." Annie, her cheeks pink with indignation, spun around from her pots on the fire. "Lord Rufus is an honored guest in my 'ouse, an' if ye wish to—"

Rufus's response was utterly surprising in the light of their previous contretemps. He interrupted the woman's diatribe with a lifted hand. "Hush, Annie, the lass is only standing up for her own. I'd think less of her if she did otherwise."

"Is that supposed to make me feel complimented?" Portia demanded. "I couldn't give a hoot in hell what you think of me, Lord Rothbury."

"So far, I haven't made up my mind on the subject," he said. "Your Granville blood is definitely against you, but I'll not hold your loyalty against you, even if I consider it misplaced." He took up his spoon. "Just beware of making groundless accusations. Now, sit down and use your breath to cool your soup." He turned his attention to his own soup as if signaling a definitive end to the subject.

She would make no points by starving herself. Portia hitched out the stool with her foot and sat down. Nothing further was said until she was halfway through her bowl and Rufus had finished his.

Then he said, "And why are you journeying to Cato's domain?"

"Jack died."

He caught the quick shadow that crossed her eyes and said quietly, "I'm sorry."

"He was all I had," she responded, the matter-of-fact tone belying her emotions. She still wept for her father in the dark and dead of night.

"So, you're throwing yourself upon Granville mercy?"

It was the same bitter, sardonic tone, the flash of sympathy vanished, and it brought Portia back to the reality of her situation. Half-kidnapped, while the devil only knew what Decatur's men were doing to her Granville escort. She put down her spoon with a gesture of finality.

"Finish your soup," Rufus said. "Annie will be upset if you leave any."

She pushed the bowl from her.

Rufus raised an eyebrow. "Where have you come from?" he asked, his tone neutral.

"Edinburgh," she said dully.

"Cato sent men to fetch you?"

"What business is it of yours?" she flashed, pushing back her stool. "What possible interest can that be to you?"

"Everything Cato does is of interest to me," he responded calmly. "Sit down and finish your soup. What good will it do to starve yourself?"

"Oh, I'm perfectly accustomed to starvation," she said bitterly, stalking to the door. "I'll not sit here and meekly betray my uncle for a bowl of soup." Icy air gusted into the cottage as she opened the door and then slammed it behind her.

Rufus wondered how long it would take before she realized she'd forgotten her cloak in her anger.

"What's with the lass?" Annie set the pig's cheek and a dish of turnips on the table. "She eatin' or not?"

Rufus, to his surprise, found he was not inclined to leave the uncooperative Mistress Worth to the consequences of her stubbornness.

"Yes, she's eating." He got up and went to the door. Portia was standing at the garden gate. Freddy wouldn't produce her horse without Rufus's orders, and she was clearly contemplating her situation. He caught himself reflecting that Jack Worth's daughter for all her youth had an old head on her shoulders.

There was something about her that disturbed him. Something he found moving in the way she held her frail body rigid against the renewed flurries of snow. Her bright hair was veiled in white, and when she turned her head at the sound of his step, the sharp angularity of her profile looked pinched and drawn.

"Portia." He came down the path toward her, clapping his hands across his chest against the cold. "No more questions. Come inside now."

"You've discovered all you need to know, I suppose."

"No," he said frankly. "I'll never discover all I need to know about Cato Granville's affairs. However, I want you to come inside and finish your dinner."

"I'll not come in while my uncle's men are being used as sport."

Rufus abruptly lost patience. He'd done what he could,

coaxed and cajoled enough to save a damned Granville from an empty belly and an ague.

"Please yourself then." He turned and went back inside. He took her cloak from beside the door and tossed it along the path toward her. Then he stepped back into the warmth and closed the door.

Portia ran to pick up her cloak before it became soaked on the snow-covered ground. The flakes were now thick and growing heavier. She wrapped herself in the garment and walked purposefully around the side of the cottage, following the horses' hoofprints. There would be a stable, and stables were a damn sight warmer than the open air.

She found a substantial wooden structure at the rear of the cottage. Four horses, two of them shires, filled the small space with steaming breath and the rich smell of horseflesh. Tack hung on the wall, and she found her own saddle slung over a crossbeam.

There was no sign of the boy. Nothing to stop her saddling up and riding out. She stood frowning. Would escape be this easy? She had nothing to lose by finding out.

"Come on then, Patches." She backed the originally named piebald out of the stall. He turned his head and whickered at the smell of snow from the open door behind her. "Yes, I'm sorry, but we have to go out there." She hoisted the saddle off the beam and flung it over his back. "Even if we can't find the sergeant and his men, there's got to be a town or hamlet friendly to the Granvilles somewhere close by in this godforsaken land."

Her fingers were numb even within her gloves, and buckling bridle and girth took longer than it should have done. However, finally she was ready. She vaulted onto the piebald's back and rode him out of the stable.

The small backyard was fenced and contained a well, a henhouse, and a group of rabbit hutches. She rode toward a gate opening onto a field, reasoning that she could then ride parallel to the lane. Her heart was hammering. It all seemed too easy. Why would Rufus Decatur go to all that trouble to abduct her and then stand aside as she escaped?

It *was* too easy. As she leaned down to open the gate, the

back door of the cottage opened. The earl of Rothbury stood in the doorway, his tankard in one hand, a hunk of bread and cheese in the other. He had an air of careless relaxation, his gaze disconcertingly mild as if he had no particular interest in her present movements.

"Leaving so soon?" He raised the tankard to his lips.

Portia's numb fingers slipped on the latch of the gate and she swore.

"My apologies if the hospitality was not up to Granville standards," he said. "A lack for which your father's brother must bear responsibility."

He hadn't taken a step toward her. Perhaps he wasn't going to stop her. Portia didn't say anything. She finally had a grip on the latch and nudged open the gate with one knee.

"When you reach Castle Granville, inform Cato that Rufus Decatur sends his regards," the earl of Rothbury said pleasantly. "And you may tell him too that I'll see him in hell." The door closed behind him, and Portia was left alone in the yard.

She urged Patches through the narrow gate and closed it behind her, too well trained in country law to leave it open even in emergency.

She reached the road but it was hard to see the lane in front of her in the now driving snowstorm. Patches was not happy as he picked his way through the thick white stuff and was very reluctant to increase his speed. With a tremor of fear, Portia realized that she'd made a mistake leaving the sanctuary of the cottage. She should have swallowed her damned pride and ignored Decatur's prating. It would have done her less harm than finding herself lost in a blizzard.

There was no sign of life around her, and she seemed enclosed in a white swirling cloud. And then she heard the hooves behind her and the great chestnut stallion loomed up, a grayish shadow amid the white, his rider cloaked in snow. Only the vivid blue eyes pierced the uniform dullness with life and color.

"God's grace! You don't have the sense to know when you're well off!" Rufus declared, leaning forward to grab her bridle. "And neither, it seems, do I." He swore vigorously, as much at his own misguided urge to rescue her from her obstinacy as at

Portia herself. He hauled her mount up alongside the chestnut. "I'll lead your horse; he'll follow Ajax more easily than make tracks on his own."

"But what of Sergeant Crampton?" Portia demanded, her fear forgotten, her original grievance taking its place. She swallowed snow as it drove into her momentarily opened mouth. "You can't leave them—"

"They're not out in this," he said curtly. "Don't talk, and keep your head down."

Portia did as she was told, since it was the only thing that made any sense. She'd expected him to turn their horses back to the cottage, but instead they kept going toward the place where the ambush had occurred. In the featureless gray-whiteness, she could recognize nothing, and the blanketing silence was eerie, even their own hoofprints muffled.

The stand of bare trees rose up suddenly, taking her by surprise. Rufus swung his horse off the track, and Patches followed perforce. They rode into the trees, and after a few yards, Rufus drew rein.

He pointed with his whip. "Go straight ahead until you reach a rock face. There's a cave inside. You'll find the Granville men in there." Before Portia could speak, he brought his whip down on the flanks of her horse and the animal started forward.

"Don't forget my message to Cato!" The words came clearly for an instant and then were lost. Portia wrenched her head around against the wind. For a second she could make out a gray shape in the trees, and then it was gone too, and she was alone, and now very frightened.

Her horse plunged through the trees and she gave him his head. There was a chance he knew where he was going. Portia certainly didn't. The rock face sprang up out of the white-shaded gloom, but she couldn't discern an opening. "Whoa!" She pulled back on the reins, forcing the trembling horse to a standstill as she stared fixedly at the blank wall in front of her. Then she heard it. The faint whicker of a horse. It was coming from inside the rock.

She urged Patches forward and gradually through the blinding snow a dark shadow in the rock face appeared. She rode straight for it, kicking Patches urgently when he shied. It was like riding through porridge, but the shadow gave way before them and they found themselves out of the snow, in a small, dark space.

Portia wiped snow from her eyes and face. Her eyes took a minute to accustom themselves to the change in light. But while she was still blinking, a voice she recognized declared from the gloom, "Why, it's the maid."

"Aye, so 'tis." Giles Crampton appeared out of the dimness. "Lord be thanked! The filthy bastard let you go." He reached up to help her from her horse. "Are ye all right, lass? Did he 'urt ye?" The anxiety rasped in his voice. "If he put his filthy 'ands—"

"No, no, nothing happened!" Portia interrupted. "And he brought me back to you. But what happened?" She could make out all five men now and wondered stupidly what it was that was so different about them. Their coats were undone . . . had no buttons, she saw. It looked as if the buttons had been sliced off. And then she realized what was different. They had all sported some form of facial hair—beards, sideburns, mustaches. But they were now all clean shaven, faces shining pink and bare as a baby's bottom.

She was about to exclaim and then some deep female instinct kept her silent. Such humiliation left them naked, exposed, a prey to their own self-disgust.

"I suppose the Decatur men robbed you?" she asked, clapping her hands together, shivering in the icy cave.

"Aye, thieving, murderin' swine! Took every last coin we had. Everything worth more than a groat . . . includin' our weapons." Giles turned away from her, unable to hide his mortification. "We're lucky they left us the horses."

"Aye, they left 'em, but wi'out saddles or bridles," one of the others said bitterly. "Come into the back, mistress. We've lit a bit o' fire. Not much like, but better'n nothing."

Portia went eagerly toward the small red glow at the far back of the cave. They'd found a few sticks of kindling, and the fire, though small, was as welcome as a yule log in a Christmas inglenook.

"How long will the storm last, do you think?" She bent to warm her frozen hands.

Giles came back from the cave entrance. " 'Tis a nor'easter. They usually blow 'emselves out in a couple of hours."

"And it's four hours' ride to Granville Castle?"

"Four hours *fast* riding. But we'll be lucky to do more 'an two miles an hour through the drifts."

It was a bleak prospect. Portia shivered, hugging herself convulsively.

"What did the bastard Decatur want wi' you, mistress?"

"He wanted to know who I was," she replied to Giles's question.

Giles frowned. "And ye told 'im and 'e brought ye back 'ere?"

"Basically," she said, realizing that she didn't wish to talk of Annie's cottage and soup and pig's cheek and fire in front of these men, who, on Rufus Decatur's orders, had been tormented and humiliated and robbed.

Giles grunted, but he seemed to know she'd left much unsaid. He left her and returned to the mouth of the cave.

Portia felt the eyes of the men on her. They were clearly speculating, and they were now rather less friendly than before. Obviously, to receive anything other than ill treatment from a Decatur gave rise to suspicion, although she couldn't imagine what they were suspecting. Consorting with the enemy . . . fraternizing with an outlaw brigand?

It was all very uncomfortable and she was overwhelmingly glad when Giles announced that the blizzard had let up enough to enable them to leave. The men rode their horses bareback, drawing their cloaks tightly across their opened jackets in a vain effort to keep out the piercing stabs of cold.

They rode in the same formation as before, Portia with Giles sandwiched between the other four. It provided Portia with a windbreak, but the morose silence of her companions was little comfort. They rode through silent shuttered hamlets like ghosts in the night. Not even the taverns showed a welcoming light.

"Is this still Decatur land?" Portia ventured after they'd been riding for an hour.

"Half an' 'alf," Giles replied. "But we'll not risk askin' fer succor until we're well into Granville territory."

"It's wretched weather for armies on the move," she said,

trying to make conversation, to turn their minds to broader issues.

"Like as not, they'll be 'oled up someplace."

"I hope so for their sakes. King or Parliament, you wouldn't want to be fighting more than the weather," Portia observed, steadying Patches as he stumbled into a drift up to his hocks. Giles merely grunted in response, reaching over to grab her bit to haul her horse forward through the snowbank.

Portia abandoned conversation and let her mind wander into a world where fires burned bright and hot, tables groaned under laden platters of meat and pitchers of wine and ale, beds were deeply feathered with thick quilted comforters atop. It was a fantasy she'd often employed in the past to deal with the grimmer reality and was so adept at it she could actually taste the food on her tongue and feel the warmth licking her limbs.

The snow had stopped, bright starlight now filling an achingly clear sky when they reached Castle Granville. Portia stared upward at the forbidding gray structure, with its donjon and keeps, its parapets and battlements. It bore no relation to a family home, and she remembered the gracious half-timbered manor house on the banks of the Thames where Cato had married his second wife, the impossibly beautiful and elegant Lady Diana Carlton.

It was hard to imagine that lady making a home for herself here.

As they clattered over the drawbridge that lay across a wide frozen moat, the iron portcullis was raised to admit them into the outer bailey. The opposing armies might be holed up by the warmth of their separate fires, but the country was still at war and Lord Granville's castle was closed to the outside world.

Men ran forward to take their horses, shouting questions, exclaiming at the lateness of the hour. The snow had been swept from the cobbles and lay in huge piles against the walls, rosy and glittering in the light of the pitch torches flaring from poles. Patches shuffled in the straw scattered over the cobbles to prevent slipping on the ice-slick surface. Portia wondered what to do.

Her escorts had all dismounted and were surrounded by

their own comrades. Giles was striding toward the archway leading to the inner bailey. Before he reached it, a slender cloaked figure emerged into the bailey. The girl began to run toward Portia and Patches.

"P–Portia . . . I am *so* glad you're here!" Olivia exclaimed as she took hold of Patches' bridle, her black eyes shining in the torchlight. "I c–*can't* tell you how *glad* I am."

"I'm rather glad to be here myself," Portia said a little awkwardly. She remembered that Olivia had seemed tall for her age when they'd met at the wedding, and that had not changed. Indeed, she was now almost as tall as Portia, her small head crowned with dark braids, and despite the glow of pleasure in her eyes, there was still an underlying somberness to her expression.

Portia swung down to the cobbles. She didn't know what to do next, but something seemed required. She stuck out her hand. "How are you? Three years is a long time."

Olivia took the proffered hand and shook it, smiling shyly. "I'm quite well, thank you."

"Welcome to Castle Granville, Portia."

Portia turned at the quiet voice. Her father's half brother was a tall, lean man with brown eyes, an aquiline nose, and a well-sculptured mouth. His brown hair receded from his forehead in a pronounced widow's peak. He drew off his glove and extended his hand.

Hastily Portia followed suit.

"You're cold," he said, chafing her fingers. "You've had a dreadful journey in that blizzard." He nodded toward Giles, who had retraced his steps to come up beside his lord.

"We ran into an ambush, sir."

Cato's expression lost its benevolence. "Decatur?"

"Aye, sir." Giles nodded.

Cato released Portia's hands. "Take your cousin into the warmth, Olivia, and see to her needs. She's half frozen." He turned to Giles. "Come, man, let's hear it."

They walked off toward the keep, where the men were housed. Portia pulled on her glove again.

"This way." Olivia led the way to the arch leading to the inner bailey and the donjon.

Portia squared her shoulders and followed her.

4

"*This is to be your chamber.*" *Olivia opened the door on* a small bastion room. "It's n—not a very nice room," she said apologetically. "But D—Diana says you're to have it."

Portia stepped into the chamber. The stone walls were softened by a few threadbare tapestries, and there was rush matting on the floor. A sullen fire burned in the hearth, and tallow candles flickered from a double pewter candlestick. The high window recessed into the thick stone was sealed with oiled parchment that rattled under the gusts of icy wind. Apart from the low, narrow bed, there was a stool, a small table and washstand, and a linen press.

Portia absorbed all this in a sweeping glance. The bare furnishings told her much about her position in this household. "Am I to share it?"

"Oh, no!" Olivia was shocked. "No, of c—course not."

"Then it's a palace," Portia declared cheerfully, pulling off her gloves. "A deal more comfortable than I've been accustomed to, I can tell you."

Olivia looked doubtful. "I expect they'll be bringing up your b—baggage in a minute. It'll be c—cozier when you have your own things around you."

Portia laughed. "What baggage? All I have is what I stand up in. Oh, except for my little box that was strapped to Patches' saddle. I wouldn't want to be without that." Her smile faded for a minute. "It's little enough to show for seventeen years in the world, but it's all I have." All she had to prove who she was, she thought. Those little keepsakes, pathetic though they would seem to some eyes, were her only anchors to the life she'd known and the only parent she'd known.

"You don't have any other clothes?" Olivia stared.

Portia shook her head, saying with a return to her previous

cheerfulness, "Only what I'm wearing. And they're a vast improvement on what I was wearing before Sergeant Crampton found me." She unclasped her cloak and tossed it on the bed before bending to poke at the sullen smolder in the grate. "The wood is green," she observed. "Maybe I can find some seasoned logs when I've learned my way around."

Olivia frowned. She suspected that the servants who'd prepared the chamber had been given the impression by Lady Granville that they need not put themselves out to make the new arrival particularly comfortable.

"I should t–take you t–to D–Diana."

Portia straightened. Olivia's stammer seemed to become worse at the prospect of her stepmother.

"Is she a gorgon?"

Olivia nodded. "She's quite *horrid*."

"Oh." Portia nodded. "I suppose she doesn't want me here."

Olivia nodded again.

"Does Lord Granville know?"

Olivia shook her head. "No! D–Diana never shows him her b–bad side. He thinks she's wonderful and k–kind."

"Men are always so blind," Portia observed with weary knowledge. "Even the nicest ones don't see what's under their noses. Well, let's go and brave the gorgon, then."

Olivia's smile chased away the shadows on her pale, composed face, and her black eyes lit up, transforming her countenance. "I'm so glad you're here."

Portia was reserving judgment in the light of what she'd learned in the last few minutes, but she said only, "Castle Granville is a vast improvement on St. Stephen's Street."

Diana was waiting for them in her parlor. She set down her tambour frame and regarded Portia with sharp, unfriendly eyes. "Olivia has shown you your chamber."

"Yes, madam." Portia curtsied politely. "I am most grateful for your hospitality."

"Yes, I believe it's rather above the call of family duty," Diana said coldly. "I expect you to repay my husband's generosity in kind."

Ah, thought Portia. *Now we're coming to it.* "I don't believe you'll find me lacking in gratitude, madam."

"Your chamber is very close to the nursery. You will be able to hear the babies if they cry in the night and be on hand to give the nursemaid any help she needs. Do you sew?"

"I'm not unskilled in the domestic arts, madam."

"Good, then you'll be able to take care of Olivia's wardrobe. My own seamstress is really too busy to give it adequate attention. Also, there will be household mending. I'm sure you'll be glad to make yourself useful wherever you can."

Portia merely curtsied again. She could feel Olivia beside her thrumming with the desperate need to speak out and the dreadful frustration of knowing that she would not be coherent. Portia gave her a quick sidelong look and allowed one eyelid to drop in an almost imperceptible wink.

The door opened behind her with a vigor that set the logs blazing in the deep fireplace, and Cato Granville entered, stamping the snow off his boots and pulling off his gloves. "Christ, but it's cold out there! I'm sorry you had such an eventful journey, Portia." His smile was pleasant enough, but there was a question in his eyes.

"Eventful?" Diana inquired, smiling, her gray eyes shuttered.

"Decatur," her husband said shortly. He turned to the oak sideboard and picked up a decanter of sherry. "A glass of wine to welcome you, Portia?"

"Thank you, sir." Portia accepted the offer with another polite curtsy.

"My dear?" Cato handed his wife a glass, poured a small measure for Olivia, then hesitated for a second over the amount to pour in the third glass. But the girl was full grown, three years older than Olivia. He filled the glass to the brim and offered it to Portia.

"So, welcome to Castle Granville, Portia." He inclined his head as he drank to her, but his eyes were still sharply questioning. "You must be exhausted after the journey. From Giles's description, it was a nightmare."

"The blizzard didn't help matters," she agreed. "But your men had the worst of it, sir."

"Yes, so I gather." He refilled his glass, examining her carefully, eyes slightly narrowed. "Giles assures me you were unharmed."

"Yes, sir." The simple response seemed best. The sherry on her empty belly was going to her knees, and she set down her glass.

"Goodness me, whatever happened?" Diana sipped delicately from her own glass, regarding her husband in wide-eyed alarm.

"Decatur ambushed my men and robbed them," Cato said. "He abducted Portia for a short while." He turned back to Portia, eyes still narrowed. "What happened, exactly?"

"Nothing of any particular interest, sir," Portia said judiciously. "He obliged me to go with him, although I tried to kill him with my dagger, and—"

"You did *what?*" Cato stared in disbelief.

Diana's glass slipped from her suddenly inert fingers. Tawny liquid splashed onto the carpet at her feet. She gave a gasp of annoyance.

"Oh, forgive me, madam. I didn't mean to shock you." Portia was all apologetic concern. She dropped to her knees, pulling out her handkerchief to mop up the spill. "I don't believe it's stained your gown."

"For mercy's sake, girl, leave it alone!" Diana pushed her away. "Rubbing it like that will only make it worse. Olivia, ring the bell for Clayton." She fanned herself vigorously. "I cannot have heard you aright."

"I threw my dagger at Lord Rothbury, madam, but he was wearing a buff coat and it didn't penetrate far enough to kill him," Portia explained with an air of frank innocence.

Olivia choked back her laughter. She was as astounded as Diana, but she also guessed that Portia was having great fun at the expense of Lady Granville.

"Where did you get this knife?" Cato demanded, waving a hushing hand at his wife in a most uncharacteristically impatient gesture.

"Jack gave it to me. To protect myself against unwanted advances," Portia said with yet more devastating effect. "Although you wouldn't think to look at me that I'd be on the receiving end of too many of them, would you?" She smiled serenely at the marquis and his wife. "But I've had a few unpleasant encounters, I can tell you."

Cato struggled to take control of the situation. He said

repressively, "I don't think that's a topic for my wife's parlor. To return to Rothbury. Did he question you?"

"He wished to know who I was, sir, and why I was traveling under Granville protection. He took me to a crofter's cottage where the mistress of the house offered us both dinner."

"How considerate of him," Cato observed sardonically. "He must have had some ulterior motive."

Diana had recovered herself and now said, regarding Portia with the deepest distaste, "Olivia, why don't you take the girl back to her chamber? She can sup there alone. From the tone of her conversation it's clear she's not accustomed to polite company, and we don't wish for her to feel out of place. I imagine her baggage has been brought up by now, and she'll be able to unpack."

"As to that, ma'am, I've no baggage to speak of," Portia said swiftly, unable to help herself. "But I'll own I'm fair clemmed and me belly's cleavin' to me backbone."

Olivia shot her a startled look. Portia's voice had taken on the broad cadences of a Yorkshire alley. Diana's nose wrinkled with disgust but Cato's eyebrows climbed into his scalp. Their visitor had been speaking in perfectly accentless tones a minute before. He wondered if perhaps she'd been trying very hard to impress them before and had accidentally slipped back into her more customary mode of speech.

And then, as he looked more closely at her, he was suddenly forcibly reminded of his half brother. The girl's slanted green cat's eyes were narrowed, but they were sharp and bright and shrewd, and he realized that for all her impecunious youth, Jack's daughter was no one's fool. The girl was answering Diana's unpleasant condescension in her own fashion.

He glanced at Olivia. His somber, withdrawn child was unmistakably grinning.

While he was still trying to decide how he should react to this, Olivia plunged into speech. "Come, Portia. I'll sup with you and tell you about everything. That will be best, sir, d–don't you think?"

Portia took up her cue, her speech once more impeccably moderated. "Thank you, sir," she said, as if he had agreed to Olivia's suggestion. "I own I'm fatigued. Unless there's anything else you wish to know about my meeting with Lord Rothbury?"

"In the morning," he said, waving her away even as he was wrestling with this strange feeling that the ground had just been swept from beneath his feet.

She curtsied again and turned with Olivia to the door. Then she paused and looked over her shoulder. "He did give me a message for you. It was not very polite but he was most insistent that I remember to deliver it."

Cato was very still, one hand resting on the carved mantelpiece, the other holding his glass. His eyes fixed on Portia's pale freckled face. "Then deliver it."

"He sends his regards . . . and that he'll see you in hell."

There was a gasp of anger from Diana and a quick dart of fury flashed across Lord Granville's steady brown gaze.

With a little nod of farewell, Portia departed the room, Olivia on her heels.

ater, Portia lay awake in her narrow bed watching the firelight on the arched ceiling. The wind rattled the oiled parchment at the window and she huddled closer under the thick quilts, relishing the warmth and security of this private chamber behind a securely locked door. She didn't know why she'd locked the door, except that it was a habit acquired over the years of traveling with Jack in frequently insalubrious places, where one was as likely to get one's throat cut for a farthing as spend a peaceful night.

She was unlikely to get her throat cut in Castle Granville, but if Diana, Lady Granville, had anything to do with it, she'd be swiftly cut down to size.

Olivia had taken her to see the two baby girls asleep in their cradles. Hitherto, Portia had had little to do with infants and even less interest in them. But she could tell immediately from the nursemaid's somewhat patronizing attitude that she was expected to perform as a maid-of-all-work in the nursery, at the disposal of Miss Janet Beckton.

Portia curled on her side, drew her knees up to her narrow chest and hugged them vigorously. She was warm and dry and well fed, a reasonable exchange surely for loss of independence. This castle in the desolate Lammermuir Hills was too far from urban civilization to afford the opportunity for work elsewhere. And while in the depths of winter the fighting was in abeyance, the uneasy truce wouldn't last long. Once Lord Leven and his Scots reinforcements joined up with Parliament's army under Lord Fairfax, then the royalist cause would be greatly threatened by an outnumbering enemy. A kinless woman roaming the battlefields would have but one way of supporting herself.

And that way was one Portia had long ago rejected, even when it had offered the only possibility of bread and a roof over her head.

Of course, if she were a man, she could go for a soldier and follow the drum. Food and pay would then be forthcoming. A reluctant smile touched her lips as she remembered that once upon a time such a plan hadn't seemed unreasonable. But then she'd been a mere child who hadn't quite lost a child's belief in magic.

Portia yawned as a wave of overpowering weariness broke over her. Her body ached in every limb. Things would look better in the morning. They always did.

Portia yielded to sleep, unaware that she was still smiling. Her last waking thought was of the big redheaded Rufus Decatur, slicing bread with all the neat expertise of a housewife. . . .

She awoke to a banging on her door and sat up, instantly awake but disoriented. She blinked around the unfamiliar chamber, lit palely from the recessed window.

"Portia!" The banging was repeated and memory returned in full.

"Just a minute." She slid out of bed, shivering in the freezing air, drawing a quilt around her as she padded barefoot to the door and turned the key. "Lord, what time is it?" She yawned.

"Gone eight o'clock." Olivia pushed past her. "The most amazing th– . . ." She struggled desperately for what seemed to Portia to be an agonizing eternity as she tried to get out the word. "Thing," she managed at last. "Amazing *thing* has happened!"

Portia jumped back into bed, pushing her freezing feet deep down into the night's warmth of the blankets. "What?"

"My father!" It was hard to tell from her wide-eyed excitement whether Olivia believed her news to be good or dreadful. Portia waited patiently as the other girl mastered her thoughts.

"He . . . he has d–declared for P-Parliament!" Olivia finally got out. "He's raising the standard this morning."

"Now, that *is* interesting," Portia said thoughtfully. The Granvilles were the most influential noble family in the north. Their allegiance to Parliament's cause would be a big blow to the royalists.

"My stepmother has taken to her bed." Olivia took a deep breath, then said all in a rush, "She does that when something's happening that she doesn't like." She exhaled noisily at the end of that effort and regarded Portia with the air of one who had done all that could be expected of her.

"Well, that should give everyone a little relief," Portia observed and was rewarded by a chuckle from Olivia. Portia pushed aside the covers again with an air of resolution. "I should get up."

"J–Janet was wondering where you were."

"The nursemaid?" Portia pulled a face as she unraveled herself from the quilts and stood shivering for a minute in her shift. "I think that lady and I are going to find it difficult to get along." She dressed rapidly, her fingers turning blue in the cold. "But first I need wood for the fire, and washing water. Where can I find it?"

"Summon a maid."

Portia shook her head. "I don't think anyone in Castle Granville is going to take kindly to waiting upon me. And I'm quite capable of looking after myself." She slung her cloak around her shoulders, muttering, "I wish I didn't feel the cold so dreadfully." She hurried to the door, Olivia trailing behind her.

"Let's go to the kitchen first."

Olivia shrugged agreeably and followed the whirlwind who had entered her life, as Portia half ran down the corridor, her cloak swirling around her. In the kitchen, Olivia watched as Portia in a relaxed and easy fashion made herself known to the servants and the cook toiling amidst bubbling kettles and turning spits. In a matter of minutes she was provided with a jug of steaming hot water to wash with in the scullery, and on her return to the kitchen sat down to a dish of veal collops and eggs.

"Have you broken your fast, Olivia?" she inquired, hungrily spreading golden butter on a hunk of barley bread. "These eggs are very good." She gestured with her knife to the bench beside her.

"Goodness me, Lady Olivia can't be eatin' in the kitchen!" the cook exclaimed. "Off you go, m'lady. This is no place for you."

"But I don't *wish* to go," Olivia declared with a stubborn air that Portia noted with interest. Olivia sat down beside Portia and looked defiantly around the room.

"Lord love a duck!" muttered a servitor from the pantry. " 'Er ladyship'll 'ave a apoplexy!"

"Not bleedin' likely!" laughed a rotund, red-cheeked pastry maker. "Not that one. She's all ice. She'll freeze us all like Lot's wife. That's what 'er ladyship'll do." She slapped the rolling pin onto the sheet of pastry, sending flour rising into the air in a fine mist.

"Now, you 'old yer tongue!" the cook chided, gesturing significantly to Olivia, who didn't appear to be listening anyway. However, a somewhat uneasy silence fell, disturbed only by the sounds of pots and pans, until the kitchen door burst open, letting in a blast of icy air, and Lord Granville came in with Giles Crampton.

"How many kegs of ale have we in the scullery, Garsing?" Cato inquired cheerfully of the castle butler, a man distinguished from the other servants by the heavy cellar keys attached to his belt. "I want at least half a dozen in the outer ward tomorrow morning.

"And we'll have barons of beef, suckling pig, and a couple of sheep on spits over the bonfires. Can you take care of that, Mistress Quick? There's some celebrating to be done." He stamped his feet and blew on his hands, his cheeks reddened with cold. But his eyes were bright, his whole body radiating energy and purpose.

And then his eye fell on the two girls at the table. He frowned. "What are you doing in here, Olivia?"

Portia jumped up and answered for her. "She was keeping me company, my lord, while I broke my fast."

"And why are you breaking your fast in the kitchen?" His frown deepened.

"I didn't consider it seemly that your servants should wait upon me, sir."

Cato glanced around the kitchen, and his servants avoided his eye. He returned his gaze to his daughter, his frown deepening. "Where is your stepmother? Surely she would not have approved your presence here."

Olivia pinkened with the effort of gathering the sounds together. Cato waited, slapping his gloves into the palm of one hand. Portia, without resuming her seat, surreptitiously chased the last mouthful of veal collop onto her fork.

"Madam my m—mother is abed, sir."

Cato frowned. As he'd feared, Diana was seriously upset by his decision to change allegiance. But she was his wife. She'd support him once she'd become accustomed to the idea.

He lost interest in his daughter's presence in the kitchen and turned back to Giles, who was waiting patiently by the door. "Giles, declare tomorrow a holiday for the men and tell them to bring their families to the feast. Open the gates and bid the villagers welcome, too. All those, at least, who'll stand up for Parliament with their lord," he added, but in a tone that indicated any dissenters would surprise him. "If it doesn't snow again, we'll find some music, have dancing. A holiday feast for all who choose to join us." He gestured expansively.

"The men'll be right glad of it, sir." Giles beamed. "They're in 'oliday spirits already. Ye'll not find any turnin' their back on the standard."

"Good." Cato nodded his satisfaction and headed for the door again. Then he paused and glanced across at Portia, who, no longer the focus of attention, had resumed her place at the table and was finishing her breakfast.

Cato examined her pale freckled face as intently as if he could read the thoughts behind the clear green eyes. Why did he have the impression that this newcomer to his household was as unreadable as a cipher? With a sudden decision to catch her off balance, he asked abruptly, "What personal impression did you gain of Lord Rothbury, niece?"

The question took Portia completely by surprise, but she answered calmly enough, "I don't think I gained one at all, my lord. At least, I didn't find him very interesting."

Cato raised an eyebrow. If his niece had not found Rufus Decatur interesting, she was a most unusual member of her sex, if rumor was to be believed. It was said the man rampaged around the countryside like a rutting stallion, leaving a trail of broken hearts and bastard children in his wake. But then, judging by the dagger-throwing episode, Jack's daughter was a most unusual creature.

He turned again to the door. "Olivia, you should visit your stepmother without further delay. She may have need of you." He drew on his gloves again and banged out of the kitchen in another icy blast.

Outside, he strode to the parade ground, where the men were falling out after the morning's drill. Cato paused to look back up at the castle battlements where the pennants snapped, flying the colors of Parliament. They made a brave show against the ice blue sky. The air was so cold it hurt to breathe deeply, and the sun was a pale yellow round hanging low over the hulking Lammermuir Hills without a thread of warmth to it.

Where was Rufus Decatur at this moment? Holed up in his private fold of the Cheviot wasteland? The earl of Rothbury had known since the previous afternoon that Cato Granville was declaring for Parliament. The information had been pricked out of one of Giles's less stoic companions during their ordeal at the hands of Decatur moss-troopers while the robber baron himself had entertained Granville's niece by a cottager's fireside. Cato was in little doubt that the attack on his men had been primarily designed to produce the information.

Not that it made any difference, since the information was now as public as it could be, flying for all to see for miles around from the battlements of Castle Granville. But Cato would have dearly liked to know which way his enemy was going to jump. Was Rufus still sitting on the fence, watching the turmoil unfolding across the land with an ironical observer's eye, planning his own entrance into the anarchy where it would bring him and his band the most benefit?

Cato could not believe that Rufus would make his decision based on anything other than self-interest. If Decatur allied himself with the winning side, then he could expect rewards. He could expect that the house of Rothbury would be returned to its former position of wealth, influence, and prestige.

If indeed that was what he wanted. Rufus Decatur was a born outlaw, and a born leader. He attracted men like bees to pollen. Good men and bad. Men in search of excitement. Men unwilling or unable to live within the ordinary laws of society. Would such a man ever be able to return to the civilized world?

But there was a war to be fought before such questions could be answered. And for all the excitement among the men leaving the parade ground, for all Cato's own jubilation, the marquis of Granville saw the shadow of a bloody death across all their futures.

5

"*Well, well, will you look at that, now.*" Rufus smiled within his red beard, but his bright blue eyes were hard as diamonds. He sat his horse and looked across the roll of low hills spread out before him to where Castle Granville stood on its own hill, higher than the rest, Parliament's flags flying from keep and buttress.

"Cock of the dunghill," he said scornfully. "Crowing defiance and boastful pride."

"Seems like they're having some kind of feast," Will observed, shading his eyes with his hand. "You can smell the roasting meat from here." There was a wistful note in his voice; they'd left Decatur village just after sunup and it was now nearly noon.

"Aye, an' there's 'alf the countryside goin' in to join 'em, looks like," their companion muttered.

In silence the three men watched the scene below them. Folk in holiday dress were pouring across the drawbridge into the castle, children pranced and darted, and the sound of drums and pipes drifted upward, the music both martial and merry.

"I reckon they're celebratin' Granville comin' out for Parliament."

"So it would seem, George," Rufus agreed absently. He tapped his whip against his boot in the stirrup, his gaze fixed on the activity below, the snapping banners, a pair of skaters on the frozen moat, a beer keg being rolled across the drawbridge by a group of exuberant youths. "So it would seem," he murmured again.

Will glanced sideways, his expression immediately alert. He knew that tone. And when Rufus turned his vivid blue gaze toward him, Will's heart sank. Pure mischief raced across those serenely smiling orbs, and the full-lipped mouth within the red-gold beard had a curve to it that filled Will with familiar foreboding.

"What are you thinking, Rufus?" he inquired uneasily.

Rufus's smile broadened. "Oh, I thought maybe we should beg a little hospitality from our friend Granville. It's been a long time since breakfast, and that meat certainly sets a man's juices running."

"You're goin' along there, m'lord?" George sounded more resigned than horrified. "Reckon you can get lost in the crowd?"

"Why not?" Rufus shrugged carelessly, kicking his chestnut into motion. The others followed as he rode down into the valley and halfway up the hill topped by Castle Granville.

Rufus drew rein behind a screen of holly bushes, observing, "This is about as close as we can get."

"You're mad!" Will exclaimed. "Granville will hang you from the highest battlement."

"He might if he knew I was there," Rufus agreed amiably. He swung from his horse and unstrapped a blanket roll from his saddle. "Give me a hand with this, George."

George dismounted. He knew exactly what was required of him. Rufus Decatur, among other talents, was a master of disguise.

Rufus shrugged off his cloak and fashioned a pad out of the blanket. With George's help, he fastened the pad to his shoulder as Will watched with resignation.

"Now, how does it look?" Rufus slung his cloak of dark homespun over his shoulder, drawing the hood up, clasping it tightly at his throat. He was transformed. His tall, powerful frame was suddenly frail, bent, one shoulder higher than the other, a hump disfiguring the straight lines of his back.

"You'll pass," Will said with a reluctant grin. He'd seen the disguise many times, but it still astonished him. It was so simple—a transformation of the very features, his height and commanding presence, that made Rufus Decatur so distinctive. Without those features, the name of Decatur would never spring to mind.

George cut a stout stick from a sapling and handed it to the master of Decatur, and the transformation was complete. Bent and supported by his stick, in his homespun country garments of cloak, jerkin, and britches, the hood pulled low over his eyes, Rufus had become a local villager.

"I'm going in alone," he said, waving away Will's immediate protests. "One interloper is less risky than three."

"*Why?*" Will demanded. "What can you possibly hope to gain from taking such a risk?"

"I thought you were hungry," Rufus said in mock surprise. "I certainly am. I'm going to forage at Cato Granville's feast — what else?"

"What else indeed?" Will muttered, watching as Rufus moved discreetly from the concealment of the bushes. "He's up to something else, isn't he, George?"

"Reckon so," George agreed phlegmatically. "But I could still use some o' that meat. Smells powerful good from 'ere." He gave an appreciative sniff as the wind brought the rich aromas of roasting meat mingled with wood smoke to tantalize his taste buds.

Rufus moved alone for no more than five minutes, then blended in with the stream of people climbing the hill from the village at its base, and Will had difficulty keeping him in sight as he shambled upward, leaning heavily on his stick. When the crowd reached the drawbridge, Rufus disappeared from view and Will was left to chew his nails in anxiety.

Rufus glanced sideways down into the moat as he crossed the drawbridge. The two figures he had seen earlier were still skating. He was not prepared for the strange jolt of recognition in the pit of his belly when Portia Worth swirled beneath him, the hood of her drab cloak thrown back, her orange hair fizzing in a shaft of weak sunlight.

It wasn't that he was surprised to see her. He'd known she'd be somewhere in the castle. And yet he was aware of a most peculiar sense of disturbance . . . the disquieting thought that he'd come to Granville's castle to look for her. Which was, of course, quite ridiculous.

Then she was gone, disappearing beneath the drawbridge below, and he had entered under the raised portcullis and was in enemy territory with the need to keep all his wits about him.

Great fires burned in the center of the outer ward, and barons of beef, whole sheep, and suckling pigs were roasting over the fires, pairs of young lads turning the spits, their cheeks scarlet from the heat and the contents of the ale pitchers from which they refreshed themselves, their eyes watering from the smoke.

A fiddler was playing in the corner of the ward, and a troupe of Morris dancers was entertaining the crowd, their bells melodious amid the exuberant shouts and cheers of their audience. Trestle tables laden with mounds of potatoes, breads, cakes, cheeses, and rounds of golden butter stood against the walls, but the greatest activity was centered around the kegs of ale.

Rufus blended seamlessly into the throng. Will had guessed aright that the master of Decatur had more than pure deviltry in mind in this escapade. He was in search of information. Any little tidbit, any piece of gossip, anything that would give him a sense of the size of Cato Granville's militia and an insight into the man's intentions, into how he was going to proceed in his support for Parliament.

Rufus approached the kegs of ale and took a tankard cheerily passed to him by a red-faced farmer who held a roasted potato between his gloved finger and thumb, taking hearty bites while he regaled a group of merrymakers with a particularly ribald tale.

Rufus could see no sign of Cato and he thought sardonically that mingling with his peasantry was probably beneath Granville. He'd provide them with the wherewithal to celebrate a decision that would leave widows and orphans across Granville land, while holding himself aloof.

Then he saw him, at the far side of the court. Rufus's blood flowed swift. Cato was talking with three of the most prominent landowners between Lammermuir and York. It could mean only one thing. Viscount Charter, the earl of Fairoaks, and Sir Graham Preston were following Granville's lead and throwing in their lot with Parliament. Theirs was a conversation Rufus Decatur thought might prove interesting for an eavesdropper.

He shuffled casually through the throng, drinking his ale, shielding his body among the knots of people, moving almost shadowlike, so inconspicuous that people barely noticed his passing.

On the moat, Portia skidded to a stop against the castle's curtain wall. She was laughing as she steadied herself, enjoying the heady sense of freedom that skating gave her, the icy freshness of the air after the fetid urban stews she'd been inhabiting for the last several years. Leisure for skating had not often come her way, and these bone skates strapped to her boots were wonderfully sharp edged, adding to the exhilaration even as they showed up her lack of skill.

"One of these days, I need to learn to stop without having to run into something," she called to Olivia, who, a much more accomplished skater, came to an elegant halt beside her.

Portia glanced up at the crowds still pouring across the drawbridge and her eyes narrowed. "What do you think about joining the festivities, Olivia?"

Olivia looked startled. "But we haven't b–been invited."

"No, but as your father's daughter, don't you think you should play hostess a little?" Portia casually smoothed her gloves over her fingers, waiting to see how Olivia would respond to this novel suggestion.

"I never have done," Olivia said doubtfully. "It's D–Diana's place."

"But Diana's not coming out of her bedchamber today," Portia pointed out. She was leaning against the wall, arms folded, her green gaze bright and questioning and more than a little shrewd.

Olivia absorbed this in thoughtful silence. She glanced up at the gray castle walls, towering above her. The sounds of music, of voices raised in merriment, billowed forth from the outer ward.

"It would make Diana look remiss," she said slowly.

"Precisely." Portia chuckled. "Come." She skated to the bank, Olivia following, and sat down to remove her skates. "And it'll keep me out of Janet Beckton's clutches for a while longer this morning, too."

Olivia's laugh was both nervous and excited as they made their way across the drawbridge back into the castle.

Cato was surprised to see the girls mingling with the merrymakers in the outer ward, but he was pleased to see the confident manner in which Olivia was supervising the filling of the tables. She seemed to know what she was doing.

Portia, deciding that Olivia didn't need her assistance in her domestic overseeing, veered toward the fires, attracted by the aromas of roasting meat. Hunger was still such a lively memory that Portia never passed up the opportunity to eat when it presented itself.

She wriggled through the crowds around the spit where a suckling pig was turning over the flames. An elderly man, his back misshapen beneath a homespun cloak, stood beside the spit, slicing through the crisp pork with his dagger, spearing succulent meat on the point of his knife and offering it to his neighbors.

"I'll have a slice, goodman," Portia said cheerfully, stripping off her gloves, holding her bare hands to the fire's warmth as she waited for meat. She was standing very close to the man, and the strangest sensation rippled over her skin, the fine hairs lifting as if a ghost had crossed her path. She froze, her extended hands motionless, her breath stopped in her chest. Impossible recognition crackled in her veins.

"D'ye care for the crisped skin, mistress?" The man spoke in an old and creaky voice, his Yorkshire burr very pronounced as he sliced deep into the carcass, cutting off a thick chunk of meat with its crisp golden skin. He turned toward her, his eyes blue sparks beneath the concealing hood, drawn low over his forehead.

Portia stared at Rufus Decatur, incredulous. What was he doing here? Lord Granville's mortal enemy standing casual as you please within the castle walls, cheerfully helping himself to Granville meat. She took a step backward out of the circle around the fire, whether for her own protection or Decatur's she wasn't sure. But Rufus Decatur stepped back with her, his offering still poised on the tip of his dagger.

"Are you run quite mad?" she whispered, unknowingly echoing Will.

Rufus seemed to consider this, but his bright eyes were far from serious as they rested on her upturned face. He was laughing at her, and she had the unmistakable impression he was inviting her to share in the jest.

"Are you mad?" she repeated in a bare whisper, trying to tear her own eyes away from the lodestone of that gaze.

"I don't believe so, Mistress Worth," he said thoughtfully.

"But it might be safer if you could manage to look a little less like a mesmerized rabbit. I'm afraid you might draw unwelcome attention, when I've gone to such great lengths to make myself inconspicuous." He offered an apologetic smile but his eyes were still laughing at her.

Portia couldn't help a guilty glance at the people around them, and Rufus tutted reproachfully. "That's a sure way to draw attention to oneself," he murmured.

He moved an arm and his cloak swirled out like a bat's wing, and without Portia's knowing quite how it happened, she was moving within the shield of this wing. Being moved rather than moving of her own volition, she decided numbly. And when she came to a halt, again without her own volition, she found herself in a secluded corner of the court, sheltered from the crowd by the massive outcrop of a buttress.

"What do you want?" she demanded in a hiss. She was still contained within the swirling wing of his cloak, standing so close to him she could feel the heat of his body, smell the leather of his buff jerkin, the rough wool of his homespun shirt and britches. The world seemed to have shrunk to this small, dim, aromatic spot, and the boisterous sounds of a merry-making crowd came from a great distance.

Rufus didn't answer. He merely offered her the meat that he still carried on the tip of his knife. Without thinking, she reached to take it and then gave a little cry as it seared her bare fingers.

"Careful!" he warned, sounding genuinely concerned. He took the meat with his own bare hand and blew on it. "Try it now." He held the succulent morsel to her lips, and in a kind of daze Portia opened her mouth to take it. It was delicious, the skin crisp and slightly scorched, the meat beneath juicy and tender. She savored it with all the delicacy of one who really relished her food, forgetting their surroundings in the moment of pleasure and failing to see the appreciative glimmer in her companion's eyes as he watched her.

"Good?" he inquired, his voice so low it increased the sense of their complete intimacy in the thronged and noisy yard. He licked his fingers and then, with a little frown of concentration, rubbed the pad of his thumb over Portia's lips and chin, where there was a smear of meat juice. The skin of his thumb was roughened, and her mouth tingled beneath the firm pliancy of his touch. For a fleeting instant his palm cupped her cheek and she could feel the swordsman's calluses against her own delicate skin. The fine hairs on her nape lifted, a current of tension jolted her belly, then his hand dropped from her face. She watched, mesmerized, as he deliberately licked his thumb again, before sheathing his dagger and replacing his glove.

Slowly the world stopped spinning and she struggled to renew her grasp on reality. "What do you want here?" she demanded yet again.

"Oh, I am, how does the bard put it . . . ? 'A snapper up of unconsidered trifles,' " he replied with a nonchalant gesture that seemed to encompass the entire scene.

"You're spying?"

"If you choose to put it that way," he agreed.

"But Lord Granville will have you hanged!" She had a sudden vivid image of Granville's soldiers descending upon them in this quiet corner. One man, even one as powerful as this one, would be helpless. They'd beat him to a bloody pulp before . . . She'd seen hangings. She knew what a body looked like swinging from a gibbet, the head at an unnatural angle, tongue protruding, face blue, eyes popping. . . . She felt queasy and the meat she'd just eaten with such relish felt like greasy lead in her belly.

"Granville will have to discover me first." Rufus's eyes traced her face, where the freckles stood out against her pallor with the intensity of her expression. "What is it?" he asked involuntarily, seeing the horror in her slanted green eyes. "You look as if you've seen the devil."

"Perhaps I have," she said, snapping back to herself. "The devil as Rufus Decatur. Don't you realize that all I have to do is raise my little finger and Lord Granville's men will fall on you like flies on a carcass?"

"But you're not about to betray me, are you, Mistress Worth?" He moved his arm and the folds of his cloak caught around her again, so that she was somehow drawn closer to his body.

This strange and disturbing proximity made her feel implicated in his presence in the heart of enemy territory. She struggled to banish the feeling, demanding, "Why would I not?"

"Oh, several reasons," he said with a tiny smile. "For one, I don't believe you have it in you to condemn a man to death."

"I could condemn a Decatur," she snapped, wishing she could move away, but the wall was at her back, his body like a shield in front of her, the cloak and the buttress separating her from the rest of the world, isolating her in this intimate seclusion. "You forget, I'm a Granville, Lord Rothbury."

He shook his head. "No, I don't forget that. Nevertheless . . ." His smile deepened and she saw the little creases around his eyes, white against the weather-bronzed complexion. "Nevertheless, we have something in common, you and I," he said softly. "I don't belong here, but neither, my sweet, do you."

It was such a startling truth, Portia simply stared at him.

Rufus chuckled. "Cat got your tongue?" He caught her chin on one finger and with a swift movement bent and kissed her mouth. "To seal a bargain between outcasts," he said, straightening. As he did so, he allowed the cloak to fall away from her and stepped back from the buttress, opening a door onto the world again.

The loss of isolation, the returning sense of space, was so sudden, Portia felt momentarily dizzy. Her head was whirling. She could no more make sense of what had just happened than she could have read Chinese.

Rufus glanced around and said casually, "Is that Granville's daughter? The girl in the blue cloak?"

The question broke whatever charm had kept Portia in thrall. With a flash of panic she remembered who this man was. A deadly enemy, a lethal menace to the welfare of any Granville. "Why do you wish to know?" Her voice sounded croaky and she cleared her throat.

"A matter of interest."

"What possible interest could Olivia be to you?" Portia moved as if she could somehow block Decatur's view of Olivia, although she knew it was futile.

"Not much," he returned with a careless shrug. "Granville's girl children don't hold much interest. If and when he sires a son, that would be different." He shrugged again. "Farewell, Mistress Worth."

Abruptly he turned from her and shuffled off through the throng, his homespun cloak hunched over his bent and deformed back . . . the veritable incarnation of a frail old peasant.

Portia stood still amid the raucous merrymaking, trying to find herself again. She was adrift in a maelstrom of confusion from which she understood only one thing. She'd been manipulated. Rufus Decatur had twisted her emotions, piqued her senses, and laughed at her as he'd done so. He'd treated her with the careless familiarity of a man who knew he could twist any woman around his little finger. And she'd allowed him to do it. She had enough experience of the way men trifled with women to have known what was happening, and yet she'd allowed Rufus Decatur to make mock of her.

Furious with herself and with Decatur, she made her way to Olivia, her eyes ablaze. At this moment she would happily have betrayed Rufus Decatur, but the old man in the homespun cloak was nowhere to be seen.

The square room on the ground floor of Rufus's cottage was brightly lit and warm from the great logs blazing in the hearth. It was a welcome haven after the three-hour ride back from Castle Granville, the last hour under a steady snowfall that had left men and horses white-coated, ghostly figures in the white-shot darkness.

"Who's looking after the boys?" Will inquired, shaking snow off his cloak inside the cottage doorway.

"They're with Silas tonight . . . at least I hope they are," Rufus added, closing the door behind him. "It's where they're supposed to be." He went through into the scullery at the rear of the room to fetch a pitcher of mead.

Will chuckled, divesting himself of his dripping outer garments. "Someone'll have an eye out for them."

"Aye." Rufus filled two tankards with mead and handed one to his cousin. He was not concerned about his sons' whereabouts. They'd be somewhere in the encampment under someone's eye. They ate at whatever table happened to be closest when they were hungry, and rolled themselves into balls of sleep wherever they happened to fall. It was a somewhat haphazard method of growing up, but Rufus couldn't see that it was doing them any harm.

"Drink, and we'll sup in the mess in a while." Rufus raised his tankard in a toast. Will saw that his cousin's expression was now reflective, somber even, and he prepared himself to hear what Rufus had gleaned during his sojourn to Castle Granville.

Rufus stood before the fire, one booted foot on the fender. Melted snow puddled on the clean-swept floor, but he didn't seem to notice it. "Granville and his cronies are setting up a collection for Parliament," he said tersely, carrying his tankard to his mouth.

"Where from?"

"Across the county. Charter, Fairoaks, and Preston have a long reach."

"They've joined with Granville?" Will's eyes widened as he absorbed the implications of this.

"Aye. They'll be plundering York, Nottingham, Bradford, and Leeds in the name of Parliament. They'll know exactly whom to call upon, exactly who can be turned in their favor."

Rufus refilled his tankard and gestured to the pitcher, inviting Will to help himself. His mouth was a thin line, almost invisible within his beard, and his voice was without expression. "Fairoaks was talking of gathering church plate . . . chalices and suchlike. They'll get quite a pretty haul, I shouldn't wonder."

Will felt his shoulders stiffen in apprehension. He didn't like the way Rufus was talking; all the humor, the daredevil amusement had left him, and both voice and countenance were as hard as agate. Rufus was going somewhere with this account of his discoveries, and Will couldn't guess where. But it was not a happy destination, that much he knew.

"Burghers' wives will give up their jewels; merchants will yield silver plate, pewter, gold, anything that can be melted down or sold. And Granville's going to be collecting lead and iron for bullets and cannon."

The blue eyes were ciphers as they rested on Will's face. "And where else do you think Granville's going to be looking for revenue, Will?"

Will swallowed uneasily under the pitiless gaze. He was expected to come up with an answer, but he couldn't think what would be the correct response.

Rufus drummed his fingers on the mantelpiece, his short, well-shaped nails clicking against the wood, waiting for Will to catch up. After a moment's silence, he prompted softly, "Presumably, Granville will contribute from his own resources too."

"Well, yes, I suppose so," Will said, frowning as he wrestled to find the answer that would satisfy his cousin. "He's raised his own militia, and that'll cost a pretty penny. And if he's establishing his own armory . . ."

"Yes, I would imagine Cato is intending to make free with any source of revenue he can lay hands on," Rufus said, and his voice now would have corroded alchemist's gold.

Will stared at him as the implication slowly became clear. "You . . . you think he'll use Rothbury?"

Rufus's eyes were fixed on a point above Will's head, but even so the younger man shivered at the deadly venomous spark flickering across the cold blue surface.

"Why wouldn't he?" Rufus said in the same corrosive tone. "Why wouldn't he?" He moved abruptly toward the table, swinging one booted foot, and a stool skittered across the flagged floor to fall on its side against the wall. "Cato Granville holds the stewardship of the Rothbury estates. Why wouldn't he use their revenues to support his own cause?"

Will rarely saw his cousin's almost legendary temper, because Rufus had learned many years ago to keep it well under control. But he sensed now that Rufus was very close to the brink, and Will understood why.

"He holds the stewardship for the crown," he suggested tentatively. "Surely he couldn't divert such revenues to use against the crown."

"Why not?" Rufus demanded. "The man's a cheat, a liar, a traitor. He's broken his oath of fealty to his sovereign. What possible moral code do you think he has? Don't be naive!" He paced the room, and the walls seemed to close in on Will as his cousin's powerful presence and enraged spirit filled the space until it seemed it couldn't possibly contain him.

Suddenly Rufus slammed his clenched fist against the wall

and a shelf of crockery above shivered, setting pewter and stoneware rattling against each other. Will, for all that he knew that he personally was safe from any explosion, began to wish he could slip from the room unnoticed.

"I will not permit it," Rufus said, and his voice was now as quiet and as venomous as an adder's sting. "That cur will not divert Rothbury revenues for his own purposes. I will have those for the king. And when he's gathered his treasure, then I will have that too. I will have every piece of silver, every golden guinea, every jewel, every lead bullet and steel pike that he collects. I will have them for the king."

Will didn't know whether he should respond. His cousin didn't seem to be speaking directly to him; this soft, vicious promise was a personal one. But Will couldn't help himself. Into the ensuing silence, he said hesitantly, "How?"

Rufus came back to the table, and his eyes now were alight, the terrifying tension of his contained rage gone from his powerful frame. "I've a plan as nasty and as devious as Cato Granville himself, Will." He picked up his tankard and drained it, before hooking a finger into the handle of a stone jar and hefting it from the shelf, holding it against his shoulder as he drew the cork with strong white teeth.

"Are you man enough for this, Will?" He gestured with the jar, his voice teasing, but Will had the feeling that the question applied to more than his ability to drink the powerful Scottish spirit made from malted barley that could put a strong man under the table within an hour.

He pushed his tankard forward and Rufus filled it halfway. "You'll need a few more years under your belt before you can take much more than that, lad," he said, perching on the edge of the table, taking a deep swallow from the jar before putting it beside him. "Right, what could Cato Granville have that he would value above all else?" A bushy red eyebrow lifted.

Will took a cautious sip of the spirit. "I don't know. How could anyone know?"

"He has a daughter," Rufus murmured in an almost musing tone. "Indeed, I believe he has three daughters. . . . He has a beautiful wife . . . ?" He regarded Will with the same lifted eyebrow.

Will was beginning to feel befuddled, but he didn't think the condition could be entirely ascribed to the drink. Rufus seemed to be talking in riddles. He kept silent, regarding his cousin warily.

Rufus picked up the jar again. "It's simple enough, lad. Cato will yield Rothbury revenues to me in exchange for his oldest daughter." He tilted it to his mouth while Will stared aghast, Rufus's plan finally making sense.

"A hostage . . . you would hold the girl for ransom, as a hostage."

"Precisely." Rufus set down the jar and wiped his mouth with the back of his hand. "In exchange for Rothbury—for the revenues of *my* rightful inheritance. His father betrayed mine for those revenues, and now I will bargain for their return with a coin he will not be able to refuse. They are mine, Will," he said with soft savagery. "*Mine.* And I will not endure that they be used by a Granville sewer rat."

Will gulped at the contents of his tankard and choked violently, doubling over as his eyes and nose streamed and the fire scorched his gullet. Rufus thumped him on the back with controlled vigor. "Small sips, Will, small sips," he advised, and the intensity had left his voice, which was once more light and amused.

Will looked up through his fiery tears. "How are you going to do this?"

"I'm not sure yet, but it'll come to me. Now, get you to supper. I've a deal of thinking to do."

Will left his cousin alone with his thoughts and the stone jug. Rufus built up the fire and sat beside it. The spirit infused his body with warmth and relaxation but did nothing to tamp down the surging rage in his mind. Of all the injustices done the house of Rothbury, the hardest to bear was that the marquis of Granville had been given in perpetuity the stewardship of the confiscated Rothbury estates.

And now this, the final humiliation. That Rothbury revenues should be used to support Granville's allegiance in this civil strife.

Rufus drank steadily and deliberately as the fire in the hearth died down, and with it his fury. Cold commitment,

clear planning took its place. And when he finally cast aside
the almost empty jug and made his way up the stairs to his
solitary bed, he had a plan as perfectly formed in his mind as
it was possible for it to be. He had learned quite a few useful
facts during his brief—and surprisingly entertaining—visit to
Castle Granville.

6

$\mathcal{T}$*he men, wavery shadows in the flickering light thrown*
by horn lanterns, just seemed to melt into the wall of Castle
Granville. The whicker of a mule rose from the flickering
darkness far below Portia's spy hole. She couldn't see the animal or animals, who were standing somewhere beyond the
circle of lantern light waiting to have their panniers unloaded,
but she could see the men, bent double beneath their loads,
emerging from the darkness, heading for the secret door, visible in the thick stone only to those who knew what to look for.

The secret entrance was approached from the moat beneath the drawbridge and, as she'd discovered on one of her
daylight reconnaissances, was too low to admit a man standing upright.

There was no other sound, not a whisper or a rustle from
the silent workers. She could make out the brawny figure of
Giles Crampton supervising the operation, but as usual could
identify none of the others.

No one knew she was here, not even Olivia, who was presumably tucked up in bed. But Portia had always had the
habit of familiarizing herself intimately with her surroundings. Such familiarization was best done at night, and unobserved. And it was amazing what one discovered—the scene
on the moat below her being a case in a point.

"We have something in common, you and I." Damn the
man! Why did he keep intruding on her thoughts? Portia
swore vigorously to herself. The problem was that it was true.
She was spying, just as Rufus Decatur had been doing. She
was creeping around at night trying to learn things about an
environment where she didn't really fit. She was an outcast
looking out for herself in exactly the same fashion as the infu-
riating Rufus Decatur. And he'd seen this and she hadn't.

With another vigorous oath, she forced her attention back to her present observation.

She was looking down on the scene from one of the ancient privies set into the battlements. This one overlooked the drawbridge. Installed when the castle was first built some three hundred years earlier, the garderobe had not been used in a generation, but the chute still gave a clear straight shot down into the moat. Lying on her belly, she had a bird's-eye view of the activity below. And it was most intriguing.

It was the third night in a week that she'd witnessed the same scene. The mules arrived just after midnight, to be met by waiting men from the castle. The unloading was swift and silent, and even as she watched now, the last man disappeared into the castle wall with his lantern and the night was returned to absolute darkness and silence.

Portia pushed herself backward until she was sitting on her haunches. The tiny space was damply malodorous, moss growing on the walls and between the flagstones. But it was an excellent spy hole and there was a series of them set into the battlements hanging over the moat, so one could have a bird's-eye view of any number of spots encircling the castle.

What was she seeing? Some cargo was arriving regularly at dead of night, and judging by the haste and secrecy with which it was brought in, not even the castle's inhabitants must know of its arrival. And most certainly not the earl of Rothbury! Although, judging by his past activities, very little of Granville affairs remained unknown to Rufus Decatur.

Portia yawned and unfolded her skinny angularity until she was standing upright. Did he have spies in the castle? Maybe he was watching this scene just as she was. She found herself constantly expecting to see him. Catching a shadowy glimpse of someone vaguely familiar from the corner of her eye, watching newcomers to the castle, trying to penetrate a possible disguise that would reveal Decatur. It was a ridiculous preoccupation, and it irritated her enormously, but she couldn't seem to get rid of it. And the worst of it was that she didn't know whether she was afraid to think of him exposing himself to such danger, or whether she gained some thrill of vicarious excitement at the thought of his reckless bravado.

It was a question without answers and one better not asked. She slipped from the garderobe and made her way around the battlements, hugging the parapet, hoping to be invisible to the sentries in the watchtowers.

However, she reached without incident the narrow flight of stone stairs that would take her down to the bridge that connected the family floor of the donjon with the external castle walls. It was rarely used, although Olivia had told her that in the summertime she would sometimes walk on the battlements when she could get away from Diana. But in general, the family used the gardens and orchard attached to the donjon for their outdoor recreation within the castle precinct.

She gained her own chamber without meeting anyone and, now yawning prodigiously, stripped off her outer garments and jumped into bed. The room was a lot warmer now that she'd ensured herself a plentiful supply of seasoned wood, but it still took a while before she stopped shivering.

She lay in bed, her head resting on her linked hands, contemplating this mystery of Castle Granville. Presumably what she'd been witnessing was connected to Lord Granville's part in the war effort. It might be worth investigating what lay behind the door that opened onto the moat.

She awoke early the next morning, aware to her delight that the sun was shining. A faint diffused yellow light showed through the oiled parchment over the recessed window. A chilly light, but still much more invigorating than the uniform grayness of previous days.

She sprang out of bed, flinging on her clothes even as she poked the dying fire back to life, then went to the nursery to perform her morning tasks at Janet's beck and call.

It wasn't long, however, before Olivia stuck her head around the door. "Father wants to know why you aren't at b-breakfast, Portia."

Portia looked up from the breechclout she was changing and said in surprise, "But I always break my fast in the kitchen."

"Father doesn't know that."

Portia pulled a face. "And her ladyship, I suppose, didn't tell him it was her idea." She had barely seen Lord Granville since the morning after her arrival. He had been absent from the castle for days at a time, and even when he was in residence had rarely put in an appearance in the family quarters, so Diana's rule had been absolute.

Olivia shook her head. "Will you come?"

"Of course." Portia readily handed the baby to Janet and linked arms with Olivia as they made their way down the passage to the dining parlor.

Olivia couldn't remember when she'd last been as happy as she was now. Portia was like sunshine, she often thought. A yellow glow that spread over the dreary pattern of life at Castle Granville, penetrating the shadows, throwing a blanket of warmth over the damp, dank chill of this castle stronghold. Even the servants were different. They seemed to smile automatically when Portia appeared among them, and fell easily into a friendly and often ribald banter with her. Olivia, who had been taught to view the servants only in the light of their duties, found being with Portia a series of revelations. Now she saw the person behind the composed and dutiful expressions of each of those who waited upon her. She learned about their families, about their ailments and their daily pleasures.

As they entered the parlor, Cato was surprised to see an expression on his daughter's face that reminded him of the open, happy child she had once been. He frowned, wondering why it should be so unusual to see her smile, to hear her laugh.

Olivia curtsied and took her seat at the table. Portia in her turn curtsied, murmured a "Good morning," and sat down.

Diana regarded her with covert distaste. The girl was so scrawny, so unappealing with her white face and unfashionable freckles and those sharp green eyes. Yet she vibrated with an energy, a purpose, that Diana found somehow threatening. She knew it was ridiculous to imagine that this ill-favored bastard could pose a threat to her own peace, but life at Castle Granville, while never exactly stimulating, had taken a serious turn for the worse since Portia Worth's arrival. Not that Portia could be blamed for the marquis's unthinkable change of allegiance, but Diana in her present jaundiced frame of mind needed to blame someone.

"Maybe you'd care to share your amusement, Olivia," she said spitefully. "It's the height of ill manners to enjoy a private jest in public. Portia may not know this, but you most certainly do."

The merry glint died out of Olivia's eyes. She murmured, "There's no jest, m-madam."

"Well, something seems to be pleasing you," Diana pressed. "Pray do tell us."

"The baby, madam, produced her first smile this morning," Portia said, buttering a slice of barley bread. "I believe we both found it infectious."

Olivia glanced up from under her eyelashes and caught Portia's mischievous wink from across the table. She had the urge to giggle, and Diana's malice lost its bite. She helped herself to the compote of mushrooms and kidneys, took a sip of her ale, and composedly continued her breakfast.

Cato was fond of his infant daughters, but they barely impinged on his present preoccupations. However, he could see how a baby's first smile might interest women. He smiled with vague benignity around his warlike table and remarked, helping himself to sirloin, "I trust you're finding life in Castle Granville to your liking, Portia."

"I am most grateful for your kindness, my lord," Portia responded.

"You are managing to occupy yourself pleasantly, I trust."

Portia's green gaze flickered toward Diana before she said, "Delightfully, Lord Granville."

"Good . . . good . . ." he said briskly. He hadn't expected anything else, after all. He drew a packet of letters out of his coat pocket. "A letter from your father, my dear," he said to Diana. "And one from your sister, Phoebe, addressed to Olivia, I believe." Here he smiled at his daughter as he handed her the wafer-sealed sheet of paper. Olivia always brightened at correspondence from Diana's sister.

Portia saw Olivia's eagerness as she broke the wafer, and waited curiously to hear the contents of the letter. She remembered Phoebe as being rather round and refreshingly blunt. A soft pretty face with light blue eyes and hair the color of summer wheat. It would be interesting to see how much she'd changed in the three years since their encounter in the boathouse.

Cato broke the seal of his own letter and immediately frowned. It was from his stepson, Brian Morse, the son of Cato's first wife, who had been a widow, nine years older than Cato. Theirs had been an alliance of convenience, and Elizabeth had come with a ten-year-old child in tow.

The marriage had lasted barely six months before Elizabeth had succumbed to typhoid fever. On the death of his mother, the boy had been claimed by his father's family, and Cato had seen nothing of him until a few years ago when the young man had descended upon Granville Castle, claiming his stepfather's hospitality after he'd been sent down from Oxford for unpaid gambling debts and his father's family had refused to take him in.

Cato did not like Brian Morse. The young man appeared to be personable, friendly, amusing, a good sportsman, altogether well versed in all the arts of a noble gentleman with a sizable inheritance awaiting him. But Cato felt there was something shifty about him, something not quite true.

And now Brian was writing to tell his stepfather that he had business with the Cavalier army in the north and would visit Castle Granville at the earliest opportunity. He had obviously not heard that his stepfather had turned against the king's cause.

Cato folded the parchment again and looked up. Diana was rather pale and her long fingers were trembling slightly as she held her father's letter.

"Is something the matter, madam? Is your father well?"

"I don't know," Diana replied.

"May I see the letter?" He extended his hand, the request a mere polite form. A man had every right to read his wife's correspondence. Diana handed it to him and he read it in comprehending silence. His father-in-law, it seemed, was beginning to have his own doubts about the divine rightness of the king's cause. He had not yet declared himself for Parliament, but he was withdrawing from the court at Oxford for a spell to think matters over. Poor Diana, a passionate devotee of the court, and of King Charles and Queen Henrietta Maria, had barely recovered from the shock of her husband's defection, and now she had to contend with her father's.

He handed the letter back to Diana without comment and said matter-of-factly, "And how is Phoebe, Olivia?"

Olivia immediately passed her letter across to her father, who cast a brief eye over it before handing it back. "Not exactly easy to read, but Phoebe at least is delighted to be leaving Oxford and the court," he observed.

"My sister has never possessed the least social grace," Diana declared. "She has no sense, no conduct, no idea of when she's well off . . . of how *very* lucky she is."

Diana rose from the table. "If you'll excuse me, my lord, I have matters to attend to."

He nodded affably, refusing to notice her angry flush or the fiery darts in her eye, and Diana left the parlor, closing the door behind her with something remarkably approaching a slam.

Portia was reading Phoebe's letter, considerably amused by the helter-skelter rambling as the lines were crossed and recrossed. The haphazard, enthusiastic style of the letter perfectly matched her memory of the writer. She became suddenly aware that Olivia was sitting bolt upright across the table, her great black eyes fixed on her father.

"You remember Brian, of course, Olivia," Cato was saying. "It seems he's coming to visit us again . . . at least that *was* his intention. He may change his mind when he discovers Castle Granville is held for Parliament. I don't know . . ." He broke off, looking startled at his daughter. "Is something the matter, Olivia?"

"No, sir," Olivia said, but her eyes were curiously blank. She pushed back her chair. "P-please would you excuse me, sir."

Cato looked disapproving, but he gave permission with a small nod and returned to his letter from Brian.

Olivia cast Portia a look of entreaty and then hurried from the parlor, leaving the door slightly ajar in her haste.

Portia half rose, with a questioning look at Cato, who after a second said with clear displeasure, "You had better go to her. I assume she's unwell. I can't imagine what else could cause her to behave so oddly."

Portia whisked herself from the parlor, and Cato regarded the deserted breakfast table with annoyance, wondering just why he found himself alone with the bread crumbs.

*O*livia's *bedchamber was empty. Portia stood in the door-*way, tapping her teeth with a fingernail while she tried to think where Olivia could have gone. Her cloak was still hanging on its hook behind the door, her gloves lying carelessly on a low armless chair beside the window, so she didn't seem to have gone out. As Portia turned to leave, she heard a faint sound coming from the deep fireplace, almost like the scuffling of a mouse.

"Olivia?" She stepped up to the fireplace. The fire was contained in a basket in the middle of the stone hearth, and on either side stone benches were set into the recessed walls.

Olivia was curled up in the farthest corner of one of these recesses, her whole body scrunched into a tight ball, her head turned away, buried in her hands against the wall.

Portia slipped onto the bench beside her. It was very hot, the stonework holding the fire's warmth, and she had a fleeting moment of envy. If her own hearth had been so constructed, she'd have slept right inside it and maybe been really warm for once.

"So, what is it about this Brian fellow that's upsetting you, duckie?" Portia asked cheerfully, laying a hand on Olivia's averted shoulder.

"How d'you know?" Olivia raised her head and half turned toward Portia, although she remained hunched into the corner.

"Shrewd deduction," Portia said. "One minute you're eating your breakfast, merry as a grig, and the next, at the mere mention of this Mr. Morse, you're beating a retreat as if all the devils in hell were on your heels."

"He is the d-devil," Olivia stated with clear, unadulterated loathing. A shiver went through her and she leaned forward to the fire.

"What did he do?"

There was a moment's silence, then Olivia said, "I c-can't tell you. I c-can't find it."

Portia pursed her lips, trying to make sense of this. "You mean you can't remember?"

Olivia nodded. "I just have this t-terrible *dread* when I think of him."

"Nasty," Portia muttered with feeling. "I've met a few men who've made me feel like that. Nasty, slimy creatures."

"*Yes!*" Olivia sat up straight, bringing her body forward again. "Exactly. He's a nasty, slimy *snake*." Then she hunched over again and said in a near whisper, "I won't b-be able to bear it if he c-comes."

"But I'll be here," Portia said bracingly. "I've learned a trick or two when it comes to dealing with the snakes of this world."

Olivia managed a watery smile. "I c-can't imagine how I ever lived before you came, Portia. I've never had a friend b-before."

"Well, you have one now," Portia said with a grin. She slipped off the seat and stepped back into the chamber, which seemed like an ice box after the heat of the inglenook. "Come on," she suggested impulsively, "Let's go skating. The sun's shining. The ducks'll be hungry and it's far too beautiful to be cooped up inside."

Olivia's throat felt hoarse and scratchy as if she'd been screaming at the top of her lungs for the last half hour, but the nameless dread was receding. *Maybe Brian wouldn't come after all.* Her father had thought it a possibility. *Maybe he wouldn't come. Wouldn't come, wouldn't come, wouldn't come.* She repeated it to herself like a mantra until the words filled her head and banished the last tendrils of fear.

"We'd best creep out in c-case we meet Diana," she said. "She's in such a foul mood, she's b-bound to think up something horrible for me to do this morning if she catches me."

"And if you lend me a cloak, then I won't have to go and fetch my own and risk bumping into Janet." Portia went to the door and opened it a crack, peering out with an exaggerated conspiratorial air that made Olivia chuckle despite herself.

"Have this one." Olivia unhooked her cloak from the back of the door. "I'll wear my b-best one." She fetched it from the armoire and clasped it at her neck; her hands were now perfectly steady when she drew on her gloves.

"Ready?" Portia drew up the hood of her cloak.

Olivia nodded.

They hurried along the passage, took the bridge to the battlements, and climbed down a flight of stone stairs that took them safely into the outer ward, where neither Diana nor Janet Beckton would be likely to venture.

The outer ward was busy, troops hurrying between the stables, the armorer, the blacksmith, the farrier. A wagon full of supplies was being unloaded outside the granary, another with kegs of ale and barrels of wine stood before the ramp leading down to the cellars.

"Why is my father b-bringing in so many supplies?" Olivia asked.

"Probably preparing for a siege," Portia replied as they entered the stables to pick up their skates and stuff their pockets with grain for the ice-bound ducks on the moat. "There's not much fighting in dead of winter, but once spring comes, the fun really will begin. And Castle Granville is such a powerful fortress, and your father has raised such a large militia, it might well suit the king's men to besiege it . . . keep your father and his army out of the fighting."

"Oh." Olivia absorbed this. She hadn't really come to terms with the idea of the war, let alone its reality. It didn't really touch her in the family security of the donjon, except that she was forbidden to leave the castle to ride or go hawking, or even visit the village of Granville that nestled at the base of the hill. But the weather had been so foul, she hadn't really noticed the restrictions too much. Come spring, she would.

She hurried after Portia onto the drawbridge, her bone skates clutched beneath her arm. Skating on the moat had become perforce their favorite outdoor activity, since anything else outside the battlements was forbidden.

Portia was already halfway down to the moat, climbing down the iron ladder from the drawbridge. She sat on the ice to strap on her skates, then rose easily, much more surefooted now than she had been a short while ago.

She skated into the middle of the moat while Olivia fastened her own blades, and tried an experimental twirl, her eyes seeking and finding the darker line in the stone beneath the drawbridge that indicated the secret door. Maybe tonight, if there was no delivery, she would see if she could open it from the outside. It must connect with some passage within the walls, but her chances of finding that from within the warren of the battlements were not good. There must be a catch or lever in the stone . . . unless, of course, it couldn't be opened from the moat. . . .

"*There* they are. *Just the same as yesterday.*" George pointed down to the moat. The eyes of his two dark-cloaked companions followed his finger. They were concealed in a thicket of bushes on a small knoll across from the drawbridge, and they were all aware of how dangerous was their position, a few hundred yards from Castle Granville, on a bright sunny morning.

"But just 'ow are we to pluck the lassie off the ice under the eyes of them there watchtowers?" mused a short, thickset man with a grizzled beard.

"Watch and see, Titus," George instructed with something approaching a grin. "If they do like yesterday, they'll be skatin' aroun' t' moat to feed the ducks on the island. An' on t'other side of the little island they'll be out of sight of the towers fer a few minutes. We can lift 'er off the ice there easy as pie."

"Which one's ours?"

"Lassie in t' blue cloak. Master watched 'em on the moat when 'e went in to the feast. . . . Ah, there they go! Let's get on wi' it now." George was impatient. Every minute they hung around put them in danger of a noose on the battlements of Castle Granville.

The three Decatur men moved stealthily forward, keeping within the concealment of the bushes, following the skaters as they circled the moat.

The island on the far side of the castle was a small, tree-strewn rock sticking up out of the ice. Ducks gathered on the edge, looking mournfully at the frozen surface of the water. When the skaters came into view, they launched themselves skittering onto the ice, their raucous squawking filling the air.

George and his men were close to the edge of the moat now, in the lee of the island. The noise of the ducks would drown any sound of their approach, and, as George had noted, at this point they were shielded by the island from the castle sentries.

The two girls were surrounded by ducks as they scattered grain on the ice. They had their backs to the shore, and when the three men darted, crouched low and utterly silent, across the moat, Portia and Olivia were aware of nothing but the excited waterfowl.

Until something alerted Portia, some atavistic warning of danger. She whirled around just as the thick blanket fell over her head, plunging her into a suffocating darkness, tangling her limbs, throwing her off balance, so she would have fallen had she not been grabbed up off the ice, the blanket wrapped securely around her, trapping her in a tight cocoon. She heard Olivia's scream somewhere outside the stifling blackness, and then she was aware only of being carried at a loping run.

She fought but it was impossible to break free of her swaddling bands. She tried to shout but her mouth became full of lint and hair from the blanket. A hand grasped her head and forced her face into the chest of her abductor. Her nose and mouth were instantly pressed against something hard and unyielding, and she could barely breathe.

She could hear branches cracking, undergrowth crashing beneath booted feet, then someone else took her as if she were a well-wrapped parcel. The skates were unstrapped from her boots as she was held aloft, then she was lifted high in the air and passed over yet again, cradled tightly, turned once more against the iron-hard chest. The horse beneath her leaped forward and the arms holding her tightened, cushioning her against the violent pace of the galloping steed.

Her head was pounding as she tried to grab for air, tried with her tongue to get rid of the sticky fibers filling her mouth, tried to fight down the panic of complete incomprehension. What was happening was unbelievable. There was no rhyme or reason for such an abduction. No one bore her any ill will. She had neither friends nor enemies in this part of the world outside the walls of Castle Granville.

And she was going to faint. Her head swam, her heart raced, cold sweat pricked her skin. And then, mercifully, her head was turned away from the chest, the stifling blanket was loosened and a cold gush of air fanned her face.

She gasped eagerly, turning her face up to the sky that raced by as the horse galloped flat out across the hillside. She could hear other hoofbeats, but she was held in such a way that she could only look upward at the sky.

"Take it easy, lassie," a gruff voice said from above her. "We've a long ride ahead an' if ye'll promise to sit still an' keep quiet, I'll let ye sit up a bit."

Portia was not at all sure she was prepared to keep any promises she made in this situation, but she made a gesture with her captured head that could have been interpreted as agreement. The half nod was instantly rewarded by a merciful change in position. She was hitched up until she was half sitting on the saddle in front of her captor. Her arms and legs were still trapped in the blanket and she had to rely on the man to hold her securely on the horse, but at least her head was free and she could see.

Her abductor was a burly man with a red face and a cheerful eye that struck Portia as insultingly incongruous in the circumstances. His cloak blew back in the breeze and she saw what had been so hard against her face. He wore a steel breastplate—serious armor for an abduction.

Two men rode alongside them, their horses matching the breakneck speed of her captor's. They too wore breastplates beneath their dark cloaks, and they kept their eyes on the path ahead, not once glancing with even mild curiosity in her direction.

"Who are you?" she demanded.

"Never ye mind, lass," her captor said comfortably.

"But I *do* mind! Of course I mind!" she protested, more astonished than indignant at such a ridiculous instruction. "How could I not mind being abducted like this?"

"Settle down," he advised in the same friendly tone. "It's not my place to say anythin', so if ye want to ride comfortably, ye'd do best to keep a still tongue in yer 'ead an' enjoy the scenery."

Portia's jaw dropped and she was momentarily silenced. Then recovering herself again, she demanded, "You could at least free my hands so that I can get this mucky stuff out of my mouth."

"And what stuff would that be?" he inquired curiously.

"From that filthy blanket," Portia almost spat.

" 'Old on." He rummaged in his pocket and produced a large kerchief. " 'Ere, stick out yer tongue, lass."

"Let me do it myself!"

He shrugged and made to replace the kerchief, and Portia thought better of her refusal, sticking out her tongue with bad grace. But it was a relief to have the bits of fiber and lint removed and even more so when he held a water bottle to her lips.

After that, there seemed little point in further conversation, so she sat apparently reconciled, but her mind raced and her eyes darted from side to side, watching for an opportunity, however slight, to escape. Even if her limbs were free, it would be suicide to jump down at this speed, but something might happen.

Something did. The horse veered abruptly to avoid a curled hedgehog in its path and stumbled sideways into a ditch concealed by grassy undergrowth. His rider drew back on the reins, trying to steady the animal to help him recover his balance. His grip on Portia was momentarily loosened, and instantly she kicked out with her trapped legs joined together like a mermaid's tail and twisted out of his grasp, falling hard to the ground just clear of the horse's flailing hooves.

"Hey! Grab 'er!" her captor bellowed to his companions, who'd reined in their own animals when the other had stumbled.

Portia scrambled to her feet, kicking off the blanket, and ran, heading instinctively for a tangle of bushes where she might find concealment. Shouts filled her ears, shattering the silence on the deserted hillside, but she closed her mind to the thought of pursuit and concentrated on reaching her goal. Her heart hammered in her ears and the frigid air pierced her aching lungs.

She plunged into the middle of the bushes and realized her mistake. Thorny branches whipped out at her, snagging her cloak, tearing at her exposed face. She covered her face with her gloved hands and fought to push her way through. But the thornbushes grew denser and with a sinking heart she realized she was going to be trapped in this vicious impenetrable thicket. Her gloves and cloak were ripped to shreds, her face was bleeding, her hair an impossible tangle where bits of lint and fluff mingled with twigs and dead leaves.

She could hear the men pounding behind her, slashing at the thorns with their swords. Her own small knife, nestled as always in her boot, was too puny to cut through the wicked thorny branches, but she had it in her hand when she was finally forced to stop and turn at bay.

The men crashed through the underbrush, cursing as they slashed at the branches. "God's bowels!" George exclaimed. "Will ye look at that. The lassie 'as a knife. Give it 'ere, lass." He extended his hand. "It won't do no good against three of us."

Hemmed in by the thornbushes, facing three men with swords and breastplates, Portia was lost and she knew it. She bent and slipped the knife back into her boot, then shrugged, turning her palms upward in a gesture of resignation.

"Lord love us, but look what ye've gone an' done to yerself," George said. "All bleedin' an' scratched. Come on, then." He stepped up to her, lowered his shoulder and tossed her unceremoniously over his back.

Portia let out a howl of indignation and pummeled his back with her fists but he took not a blind bit of notice, merely strode phlegmatically out of the thicket behind his two companions who cleared the way with their swords.

"That was right foolish of ye, lass," he declared when they reached the horses, now quietly cropping the grass in the ditch. "Now y'are goin' to be uncomfortable, and I'm sorry fer it, but it can't be 'elped."

Portia thought to protest, to plead, to promise even, but pride kept her tongue still as she was swaddled securely once again in the blanket. But this time they tied strips of canvas webbing over the blanket around her ankles, her waist, and over her arms, so she was trussed like a goose for the market. They pulled up the hood of her cloak and fastened it tightly over her head, but at least her mouth and nose were left free.

The rest of the ride was interminable. Portia was sitting sideways on the saddle, held securely against the hard, burly frame of the man they called George. She was miserably uncomfortable because her wrappings made it impossible to twitch a muscle, to adjust her position, to scratch the itch that developed on her calf and rapidly spread all over her body in a maddening prickle.

The three men spoke occasionally to each other, but nothing that was said gave Portia a clue as to where they were going, let alone why she'd been kidnapped. The landscape was desolate, harsh bare heath giving way to barren hills. There were sheep and a few hardy fell ponies, but no sign of human habitation, not even a stone crofter's cottage.

Finally her manifold discomforts gelled into one wretched fact. Her bladder was bursting and the horse's steady canter did nothing to take her mind off the situation. "I need to stop," she said finally. "I need to go behind a bush."

"Bless ye, lass, we'll be there soon enough," George said in his infuriatingly friendly tone. "See the fires up ahead?" He gestured with his whip.

Portia swiveled her head. It was late afternoon now, and still sunny, but she could see the smoke of a fire rising in the clear air from the top of the hill they were presently climbing. "That's where we're going?"

"Aye."

"I don't think I can wait," she said deliberately.

He glanced down at her white set face. "Yes ye can, lass." He put spur to his horse and the animal bounded forward, tired though it was, for the last uphill effort in the direction of stable and oats.

Portia gritted her teeth and forced herself to think of anything but her need for relief. She looked around, searching for some clue as to their whereabouts. The smell of the fire grew stronger, and at last they breasted the top of the hill and she saw a small sentry post, with a lone guard, pike and musket in hand, standing at watch.

He raised a hand in cheerful greeting. "All well, George?"

"Aye, Tim." George acknowledged the wave. If the sentry had been a less senior member of the band, or if Rufus or Will had been there, he would have insisted on giving the password, but in broad cloudless daylight, when a man could see for miles around, it seemed foolish.

"Is the master below?"

"Aye. Don't think 'e's ridden out today."

"See ye in the mess fer a jar later, shall us?"

"Aye. I'm off in 'alf an hour."

They rode down the other side of the hill, but Portia was now so desperate for the privy that she had only a vague impression of a cluster of buildings along a riverbank. She noticed that the men they passed wore soldiers' buff leather jerkins, and their stride was closer to a march than a walk. The buildings looked more like military structures than the cozy cottages of a hamlet, but she identified a blacksmith's, a granary, and a fairly substantial building with an ale bench outside. The mess presumably. Beyond that, she registered very little except an atmosphere of brisk purpose.

George drew rein outside a house at the far end of the village, set a little apart from the rest. He swung down. Reaching up to the saddle, he neatly tipped Portia's wrapped body forward over his shoulder. She bit her lip hard as her bladder was pressed against his shoulder.

The front door opened as he reached it, and he stepped over the lintel with his burden and carefully placed her full length on the floor inside.

"God's bones, George, was it necessary to bundle her up like Cleopatra in the carpet?"

7

Portia knew the voice. She had heard it in her mind so many times in the last weeks.

"Beggin' yer pardon, m'lord, but the lassie's a mite tricky," George said in his affable tones, bending to untie the canvas webbing.

"You do surprise me," Rufus Decatur said with amusement. "I'd have thought such a milk-fed, silken-clothed maid would have caused no more difficulty than a mouse."

The ties were undone and Portia, forgetting her urgent need for a minute, wriggled free of the blanket with an almighty heave. She jumped to her feet, fingers fighting to unloosen the strings of her hood that was still tied so securely under her chin. "Why have you done this *again?*" she cried, shaking her head so that the hood fell back.

"Good Christ, George!" Rufus exclaimed. "What the *hell* have you brought me?" He stared at the white-faced, green-eyed, carrot-topped scruff in complete disbelief.

George said uncertainly, "Why, 'tis the Granville lass, sir."

"Oh, Blessed Mother," Portia muttered. "You were after Olivia." She crossed her legs with sudden urgency. "I have to use the privy."

Rufus gestured wordlessly to the door behind him, his expression that of a man who has found something nasty in his birthday cake.

Portia raced for the outhouse.

"Is it the wrong one, then?" George asked hesitantly.

"Yes, it's the wrong one!" Rufus tried to contain his incredulous anger. "How could you get the wrong one, man?"

"You said the lassie we wanted was wearin' a blue cloak, sir. T'other one 'ad on a brown one." George looked stricken.

"Oh, God in heaven!" Rufus stared at George, the whole ridiculous situation slowly beginning to make sense.

Hearing a step behind him, he whirled to face the unwanted hostage on her return from the privy. "The blue cloak?"

Portia frowned, wondering what he meant. Then her face cleared. "It's Olivia's," she responded matter-of-factly. "She lent it to me."

"I see," Rufus said flatly. "All right, George, you may go."

"I'm right sorry, m'lord."

Rufus waved him away with a gesture of resignation. "How were you supposed to know?"

George hesitated. Decatur men didn't make mistakes. And if they did, they paid for them themselves in guilt and self-reproach.

"Go," Rufus said a little more gently. "You are not to blame, George."

"It's a right nuisance though, innit, m'lord?"

"You have a talent for understatement, my friend," Rufus declared with a short and utterly mirthless crack of laughter. He turned his searching gaze upon Portia, and demanded suddenly into the moment of awkward silence that followed his acid laugh, "Just how did she get so scratched?"

"Lassie took off when me 'orse stumbled," George offered, still standing uncertainly by the door. "Straight into a thorn thicket."

"Running away seems to be a habit of yours," Rufus observed tartly.

"Yes, I developed it when people developed the habit of abducting me," Portia snapped. She felt horribly like weeping and it took all her determination to keep the threatening weakness at bay.

"It would have been better for all of us if you were rather better at it," Rufus declared without a vestige of humor. He turned back to the disconsolate man by the door. "That's all for now, George. Go and get some food and ale inside you. If you see Will, send him to me."

George bobbed his head and slid out of the door. Rufus turned back to Portia, who was standing grimly by the table, clutching its edge with a white-knuckled hand.

"Now what the hell am I going to do with you?" he demanded of the air in general and in a tone of stinging exasperation. "I can't imagine his brother's by-blow is worth much to Cato Granville."

The tears she had been fighting sprang into Portia's eyes and broke loose, trickling maddeningly down her cheeks. She dashed a hand furiously across her eyes, but the tears continued to fall.

For a moment, Rufus was nonplussed. He realized that of all the reactions he might have expected from Portia Worth, weeping wasn't one of them. He had thought her combative and tough, with a cool, realistic view of the world, and this collapse was a complete surprise. He took a hesitant step toward her. "What on earth's the matter?"

"What do you think's the matter?" she demanded with an angry sniff. "I'm exhausted and hungry and my face is all scratched and sore and my clothes are all torn, and all for nothing. You never wanted me in the first place." It was a ridiculous thing to say and she realized it even in the depths of her mortifying weakness, but for some reason the knowledge of being unwanted, something she had absorbed with her wet nurse's milk, was the last straw in this entire wretched confusion.

"You certainly weren't the object of this little exercise," Rufus agreed calmly. "And I'm sorry that you've been so uncomfortable. But if you'd simply done as George told you, you would have suffered little or no discomfort."

"How could you say that?" Portia's tears dried miraculously. "Olivia would have done as she was told because she would have been paralyzed with terror. She's not like me . . . she's gently bred, she's been sheltered all her life. She would have been petrified. You call utter terror little or no discomfort!"

Rufus was relieved to see a return of the Portia Worth he knew. "George isn't a frightening person," he pointed out. "That's why I most particularly chose him for the task. He has a very fatherly air about him."

Portia stared, unable to believe her ears. "Fatherly air!" she exclaimed. "*Fatherly air!*"

"He's the most respected elder in our community," Rufus said a mite defensively. "I value his advice and assistance above anyone's. He knew to treat the girl gently, and he would have done so."

"Oh, I'm to believe that you would have treated the daughter of Cato Granville with decency?" Portia demanded, scorn dripping from her tongue. "You hate the man and I don't believe for one minute that you wouldn't have made his daughter suffer that hatred."

Rufus paled beneath his weathered complexion, and his eyes were blue fire. "Be careful," he said softly.

Portia thought that perhaps she would be a little more circumspect, at least until the fire had died out of his eyes. "You cannot blame me for thinking so," she said, her tone milder.

"I can," he asserted. "I can most certainly blame you for thinking that I would cause an innocent girl pain and suffering for something that is no fault of hers."

"And just what are you doing to me? Am I not an innocent? And am I not suffering at your hands for no fault of my own?"

Rufus looked at her in silence, then suddenly he laughed ruefully and the tension in the room was shattered like crystal. "I suppose you have a point, lass. Sit down." He put his hands on her shoulders and pressed her down onto a stool.

Portia resisted the pressure, looking up at him with clear challenge as he towered over her. The shoulders beneath his hands were so thin, he could feel every bone as if it were a twig that would break between his fingers.

"Sit down," he repeated. "Surely you'll allow me the opportunity to redress some of these ills you say I've inflicted upon you." A red-gold eyebrow lifted in a challenge to match her own. "Are *you* afraid, Portia?"

"No." She sat down on the stool beside the table. "Should I be?"

"No." He shook his head. "But I have an uncertain temper, as I believe I once told you."

He filled a basin with hot water from the kettle hanging on a hook over the fire, and brought the basin to the table. Dipping a towel into the water, he took Portia's chin in one hand and began to dab at the scratches, wiping away the dried blood and dirt.

"I'm not much of a nurse," he muttered, shaking his head. "How could you possibly have done this to yourself?"

"I didn't know I'd run into a thicket of thornbushes until I got there," Portia retorted, wondering why she felt so hot suddenly as his large, powerful hands turned her face around with a curious and incongruous gentleness.

"Just as a matter of interest, what were you going to do if you *had* escaped?" Rufus inquired as he satisfied himself that he'd cleansed all of the visible scratches. He perched on the end of the table, the damp, blood-streaked towel in his hands. "You were in strange territory, miles away from anywhere."

"I didn't think that far ahead."

"Are you ordinarily so impulsive?"

"I am not ordinarily required to try to rescue myself from a kidnapper." Her slanted eyes were narrowed as she looked up at him from beneath the tangled red halo of her hair.

She was such a scarecrow, so thin and seemingly so frail, her freckles standing out against the extreme pallor of her countenance, that Rufus found her plucky bravado peculiarly moving.

"This is a veritable bird's nest," he murmured with an unconscious smile, picking out a twig from her hair. He began to comb through the curls with his fingers, plucking out foreign bodies.

Portia's eyes widened and a slight pink tinged her pale cheeks. He disentangled a clump of blanket lint from a particularly tight knot of orange curls and continued almost to himself, "Somewhere, I believe I have some salve." He dropped the towel onto the table and made his way to the small stone-flagged pantry at the rear of the cottage.

"Ah, here it is. Smells dreadful but it works like a charm." He reappeared, unscrewing the lid of a small alabaster pot. "Keep still now. It stings a little." He dipped his fingertip in the strong-smelling ointment and painted Portia's scratches with it.

She flinched. He wasn't fooling about the sting. Her whole face felt on fire as if a swarm of bees had settled there.

"It'll cool down in a minute," he told her, turning her face from side to side with a hand under her chin as he looked for untreated hurts. "That'll do, I think." He screwed the lid back on the pot. "Now, what else must we remedy . . . ah, yes, hunger. It's a damnably long ride from Castle Granville; you must be starved."

The calm, matter-of-fact way he moved about the kitchen and pantry, setting bread, cheese, and cold meat on the table, somehow belied the contained power of the soldier's body. Everything about him shouted of battlefields, and yet he seemed perfectly at home in a kitchen. Portia found herself fascinated by his deft efficiency, by the sense that he was a man of so many contrasts.

"Try that first." He poured thick creamy milk from a copper jug and set the beaker in front of her.

"I haven't drunk milk since I was a little girl," Portia protested, even as she realized to her astonishment how inviting it looked.

"How old are you?"

"Seventeen." She took a deep gulp of the milk.

"Is that all?" It wasn't that she looked so much older, it was just that her attitude bespoke a wealth of experience.

"The life of a vagabond bastard tends to be aging," Portia observed sardonically.

Rufus contented himself with a raised eyebrow and a shrug. He reached for the stone jar of whisky on the shelf above the fireplace.

"So, what are you going to do now?" Portia demanded through a mouthful of bread and beef.

Rufus seemed to consider the question. "Laughing like a madman is a possibility. Screaming like a banshee is another."

Portia was about to ask exactly what Olivia's ransom was to have been when there was a loud bang at the door. Will burst into the cottage as if Lucifer's hounds were on his tail. "Hell and the devil, Rufus. George says it's the wrong one!" He stared at Portia. "Is it?"

"So it would seem, Will," Rufus agreed, spearing a piece of cheese on the point of a knife and carrying it to his mouth.

Will stepped farther into the room, his eyes still on Portia. "What happened to her face?"

"Scratches and salve." Rufus drank from the stone jar. "Sit you down, lad, and have a mug of ale."

Portia clapped both hands to her still-burning cheeks. Her

face felt swollen as well as sore, and she couldn't imagine what she looked like, but judging by the newcomer's expression it must be pretty dreadful. Maybe the salve had been some horrible trick to disfigure her even further.

"It's all right. The burning will die down soon," Rufus said, correctly reading her expression. "You'll be right as rain in an hour." He sliced more sirloin and forked it onto her platter. "More milk, or would you prefer ale now?"

"Ale, please." There seemed no point responding to this hospitality with sulkiness, although the entire situation felt so unreal that Portia was beginning to wonder if she was going to wake up soon.

Will was still looking at her in disbelief. He'd barely moved from the door. "But who's this one?"

"Portia Worth," Portia snapped, no longer willing to be referred to by this idiotic man as if she were a stuffed dummy. "And if you have questions concerning me, why don't you address me directly?"

Will blushed to the roots of his sandy hair, and his eyes, a paler blue than his cousin's, were filled with dismay. "My apologies, ma'am. I didn't mean any disrespect."

"Disrespect?" Portia exclaimed. "After I've been abducted, and carried off wrapped up tight as a sausage in its skin, and bumped and tossed about for hours . . . you talk of disrespect!"

Will looked helplessly at Rufus, who stood with his broad shoulders against the thick oak mantelpiece, holding the stone jar easily with a finger hooked into the handle.

"But . . . but will Granville pay—"

"I very much doubt it," Rufus interrupted. "But it might be interesting to see how he responds. The ransom message was delivered after the girl was picked up. He'll need some time to deliberate."

"And if he doesn't respond?"

The lingering amusement vanished from the bright blue eyes, and the earl's expression hardened. "Then we'll have to find another way, Will."

"But . . . but I still don't understand who she . . . I mean who you are." Will tried to direct his questions at Portia, who, her hunger appeased, was listening intently, hoping to learn at last exactly what the earl of Rothbury wanted of the marquis of Granville.

"Jack Worth was Cato's half brother. The lass is his daughter."

"Oh." Will continued to stare at Portia, who stared back.

"Bastard daughter," she said deliberately. "Not worth a farthing to anyone . . . now that Jack's dead."

Silence stretched between them, then Will said, unconsciously following the train of thought, "Oh, that reminds me. The boys, Rufus. They were following me but they must have been sidetracked." He wrenched open the door and shouted into the night. "Luke . . . Toby . . . where are you, you little devils?"

Portia shivered as the wind gusted through the open door. Then two bundles rolled past Will's legs and entered the kitchen like a pair of dervishes. They were so well wrapped in coats and jerkins that they were as round as they were tall. Two pairs of blue eyes raced around the kitchen.

"We're back," Toby announced.

"So I see," Rufus observed gravely.

"Who's that?" Luke pointed at Portia.

"My guest," his father replied in the same tone.

"Like Maggie?" Toby inquired with intelligent interest.

Will choked and Rufus said, "Not exactly. Mistress Worth will be staying here for a few days."

"*Oh, will I?*" Portia muttered sotto voce. Who were these two lads, and just who was Maggie when she was at home?

"Shall I put them to bed, then?" Will gestured to the boys, who had quite suddenly collapsed in front of the fire, where they sat rubbing their eyes and swaying slightly.

"Take Toby and I'll take Luke." Rufus bent to pick up one of the children. He carried him behind a curtain in the corner of the room, followed by Will with the other child. Portia listened, now completely astounded. Was there no end to the surprises with this man? Mumbled childish protests came from behind the curtain, but they seemed to receive no encouragement and within a couple of minutes Will and Rufus reappeared.

"Did you put them to bed in their clothes?" Portia couldn't help the question.

"They were too tired to undress," Rufus said casually. "You'll meet them properly in the morning."

"They're yours?"

"My natural sons," he said deliberately. "And they're beyond price."

Portia felt her cheeks warm. She picked up her tankard and drained the contents.

"Anything else you want me to to do, then?" Will fiddled with the clasp of his cloak.

"No. Just stop George from drinking himself into a stupor of recrimination. It wasn't his fault, but he'll take some convincing."

Will nodded and made his way to the door. He paused, glancing over his shoulder at Portia, who was staring into her empty tankard. Rufus made a brusque dismissing gesture with one hand, and Will left without a further word.

Portia looked up. "Where were you intending to keep poor little Olivia? But I suppose you have prison cells in a thieves' den."

"We have a prison," Rufus agreed with a deliberately amiable smile. "But I believe you'll be more comfortable abovestairs. There's an apple loft that's been prepared."

"I'm sure Olivia would have appreciated your consideration, sir."

"I would hope so," he responded, the smile not faltering. "And I hope you'll be as appreciative, Mistress Worth."

Portia stood up, suddenly too tired to fence any longer with such a deft opponent. "Much as I enjoy your company, Lord Rothbury, I think I prefer my own at the moment."

"That is your prerogative," he said gravely. "Come, I'll show you to your bed."

Portia followed him up the narrow wooden staircase and into a large, well-appointed chamber. She looked around at the big bed, the sturdy oak furniture, the fire in the hearth, the rush mats on the clean-swept floor. There was nothing luxurious about the furnishings, but the atmosphere was one of solid farmhouse comfort. "Who sleeps in here?"

"I do." He opened the door onto a small, neat chamber. "And this has been prepared for you."

Portia hesitated.

"You're quite safe from me," Rufus said.

"In my experience, men who say you're safe from them usually mean the opposite," Portia retorted.

Rufus shook his head. "If I want a woman in my bed, lass, I have no difficulty finding a willing one. And I do assure you that unwilling women have never appealed." He stepped aside and gestured that she should enter the small chamber.

Portia could see no reason to disbelieve him, and she could lock the door for good measure anyway. She entered the room.

"I think you'll find everything you need. A nightrobe, towel, soap, water in the ewer, chamber pot beneath the bed." Rufus ran a checking eye over the contents of the room, rather in the manner of an experienced housekeeper. "If you need anything, just call."

"Quite a pleasant little prison," Portia observed, her eye immediately taking in the very small window that was securely barred.

Rufus ignored the remark. He said only, "I give you good night, Portia," and left the room, closing the door softly behind him.

Portia darted to the door. There was neither lock nor bolt. She couldn't lock herself in, but by the same token neither could she be locked in from the outside. She turned to examine the chamber. It was small but adequate and one wall backed onto the fireplace in the bigger room so that some heat was reflected in the bricks from the blaze on the other side.

She sat on the bed and contemplated her situation. The wrong hostage, worth nothing to either side in the ransom negotiations. Rufus Decatur could cut her throat and bury her on the hillside and no one would be any the wiser. Somehow she couldn't see Cato sending out armed troops prepared to do battle for his niece's return. He had far too many important things to concern him in this war than the well-being of his brother's ill-favored and penniless bastard.

And what of Olivia? What must she have made of that violence on the moat? It must have terrified her. So sudden, so meaningless, so savage. It would have terrified anyone, and

Portia knew that Olivia would be wondering what she could have done to help . . . she'd be castigating herself for standing dumbly aside, watching the entire brutal episode. And there was no one in the castle to reassure her. Her father was too preoccupied, and as for her stepmother . . . !

Portia twisted an orange curl around her forefinger. There was nothing she could do for Olivia at this point either. It seemed more than likely that the Decatur's hatred of anything remotely connected with Granville would prevent his tamely sending her back and thus admitting defeat. All in all, her position looked distinctly unpromising.

"*There's not a trace . . . not even a goddamned footprint!*" Cato was speaking even as he entered his wife's parlor. "I just don't understand how she could have disappeared . . . without a trace." He flung himself into a carved elbow chair by the fire and glowered into the flames.

Diana rose gracefully and went to the sideboard. She poured wine into a pewter goblet and brought it to him. "The girl has been nothing but trouble since she arrived," she said. "And I've been against these skating expeditions all along."

Cato drank his wine, his frown deepening. "I saw nothing amiss. They were in sight of the battlements while they were on the moat."

"But not, it seems, for the whole time," Diana pointed out gently, resuming her seat.

"No, so it would seem." Cato rose to his feet and began pacing the room. "How's Olivia now? Has she been able to say what happened yet?"

"Nothing coherent." Diana laid aside her embroidery. "But that's only what you would expect, really. She's not particularly coherent at the best of times, poor dear."

"It was not always so." Cato strode to the window and stood, his hands clasped behind his back, looking down on the inner ward. It was three hours since Olivia had raced screaming into the castle, babbling something about three men and Portia, but it had been impossible to calm her sufficiently to make sense of the story, except the one incontrovertible fact—Portia had disappeared.

"The physician gave her something to help her sleep," Diana said now. "I thought she might be able to speak more easily when she's rested."

"Mmm." Cato swung impatiently away from the window. "I'll go and talk to her again."

Diana rose immediately. "I'll come with you."

Olivia was lying in bed, her eyes wide open despite the physician's sedative. When her father and stepmother came quietly into the room, she closed her eyes tightly and lay very still, praying that they would go away.

Cato stood looking down at her, a puzzled frown in his eye. "Olivia, are you awake?"

Olivia debated. She would have to speak sometime, but it would be so much better if Diana weren't there. She allowed her eyelids to flicker. "Have you found her?"

"You must tell us what happened, my dear. There's little I can do until I know what happened."

There was something unusually reassuring in her father's voice, and Olivia opened her eyes properly. She forced the words out very slowly, trying to control her stammer. "We were s-*skating* and feeding the d-*ducks*. And three men c-came and took Portia." She struggled up onto her pillows and regarded her father intently, ignoring Diana.

"Did Portia know them?" Cato's voice was still gentle.

Olivia shook her head. "They threw a b-blanket over her head and c-carried her off."

"Did they say anything?"

Olivia shook her head. She remembered the whole dreadful scene as a blur. There'd been no noise that she was aware of. One minute Portia had been standing beside her, throwing corn to the ducks, the next she was being carried away. The senselessness and the speed of it all had been terrifying. And Olivia had done nothing. She thought she had screamed, but only once. And it had been a futile gesture. It had brought no help.

"Did they try to catch you?"

Another headshake. "I don't know what I c-could have done," she whispered.

"There were three men, you said before. What could you have done against three men?" He frowned down at her, but he was lost in his own thoughts. It didn't make any sense to him. Why would anyone want to kidnap Portia? And then it occurred to him that it was the second time someone had made off with her in the last few weeks. It was very curious. She'd escaped the last abduction unscathed, but this sounded very different. It sounded planned. The kidnappers had known which of the two girls they wanted and they'd gone about the business with careful deliberation. And with a calculating violence that chilled him. Did they intend harm to Jack's daughter?

It could so easily have been Olivia. Absently, he reached out and stroked a strand of hair from Olivia's forehead. Her eyes, wide and dark, regarded him in surprise, and he realized that it had been a very long time since he had made such a gesture of affection.

"Try to sleep," he said, and was about to kiss her brow when he became aware of Diana's rigid figure at his side. Instead he stepped away from the bed, saying in his usual tones, "You'll feel better after some rest."

"Will you find her, sir?"

"I have men scouring the countryside," he replied. "If she can be found, they will find her."

"B-but will they hurt Portia?" Olivia's voice was urgent, her dark eyes huge and pleading in her wan face.

"I hope not," was all the reassurance he had.

"Come, my lord. The child needs to sleep." Diana laid a hand on his arm, urging him to the door. He glanced once again at the bed. Olivia had slipped down again and closed her eyes. She was lying still as a statue beneath the tightly tucked white sheets.

"I am doing everything I can, Olivia," he reiterated, wishing there was more he could say. Then he followed his wife from the chamber.

"My lord . . . my lord!" Giles Crampton's urgent hail came from behind him as he turned toward his own bastion room.

Cato paused. "What is it?"

"This." Giles flourished a rolled parchment. " 'Twas just delivered, m'lord."

Cato took the paper and immediately felt a tremor of premonition. "Who delivered it?"

"A shepherd's lad, sir. Said it 'ad been given 'im by a man in armor who told 'im to wait till sunset afore he brought it."

Cato clicked his tongue against his teeth. "No sign of the girl, I suppose?" He turned to the door of the bastion room.

"Vanished like she was never 'ere," Giles said. "No one saw 'ide nor 'air of any of 'em."

But Cato didn't appear to hear him. He was staring at the seal on the rolled parchment. It was the eagle of the house of Rothbury. That earlier quiver of premonition lifted the fine hairs on his nape. He broke the seal and unrolled the paper. The missive was short and to the point. Granville's daughter, Olivia, was held hostage. The price of her ransom: all the Rothbury revenues held by the marquis of Granville, together with a full accounting of all such revenues since the steward-ship of the Rothbury estates was given into the hands of George, Marquis of Granville.

Cato began to laugh. He laughed and laughed, flinging himself in a chair and giving himself up to the utterly glorious contemplation of his enemy's total rout. Instead of Olivia, they held a nameless bastard orphan—a relatively inoffensive girl, to be sure, but with no redeemable value to anyone.

He became aware that Giles was watching him uncomfort-ably from the doorway, clearly wondering if his master was having some kind of seizure. Cato told him the situation in a few words, and Giles grinned.

"Wonder what the murderin' bastard'll do, sir." Then his expression changed, his eyes narrowing. "Quite a coincidence that 'tis the second time 'e's grabbed 'er, wouldn't ye say, sir?"

Cato frowned. "The first time was an accident and this time he wasn't after her, he was after Olivia."

"Aye, mebbe so. But 'e didn't do 'er no 'arm last time. 'Ap-pen he'll not this time." Giles shuffled his booted feet. "Who's to say she weren't in league wi' 'im, m'lord? Mebbe she was to decoy Lady Olivia to where they could grab 'er, but summat went wrong."

Cato stared at the sergeant. Giles had a suspicious mind and he'd certainly hinted darkly about Portia's last encounter with Decatur. But it was impossible to believe she'd been sucked into some Decatur plot . . . or was it?

What did he know of her? She had no money, no visible

means of support, except his charity. Maybe she had fallen under Decatur's spell when they'd met on the road. She wouldn't be the first woman to do so.

He strode to the window as the door closed behind Giles, and stood looking out into the darkness. His mind showed him the rolling hills and the undulating path to the Decatur stronghold as clearly as if it were broad daylight.

One of these days, they would have the final reckoning, Decatur and Granville. Cato's eyes hardened as he stared out into the night.

8

$\mathscr{P}$*ortia heard the front door close about half an hour after* she'd been left in the apple loft. She was still wrapped in her bedraggled cloak, sitting on the end of the bed, vaguely aware that the heated soreness of her face had abated, but somehow unable to make the necessary moves to put herself to bed. It was as if the shocks and events of the day had paralyzed her and she could do nothing but sit numbly, unable even to order her thoughts.

But the sound of the closing door below galvanized her. She jumped up and went to the chamber door, opening it gingerly. There was complete silence. Rufus Decatur had gone out and left her alone.

He must think her safely tucked up and fast asleep after the excitements and hurts of the day, she thought. Unless, of course, he assumed that she would be far too intimidated to take advantage of the unlocked door. In which case he was much mistaken.

She tiptoed across the large bedchamber and descended the narrow wooden stairs. The remains of her supper had been cleared away, the fire had been banked, and a fresh candle lit on the mantelpiece. Perhaps he didn't intend to be gone long.

She glanced toward the curtain across the corner of the room and then, unable to smother her curiosity, tiptoed over, drawing it aside. The children were sleeping like puppies, curled around each other under a mountain of covers. They still had their coats and jerkins on, she noticed with a flash of disapproval. Janet Beckton would have forty fits. The idea, despite her predicament, made her grin. This tumbled cot in Rufus Decatur's brigand cottage was a far cry from the neat nursery at Castle Granville.

She peered down at the sleeping faces beneath their identical thatches of fair hair. She remembered the bright blue eyes and thought they bore a strong resemblance to their father. There must be a mother somewhere—a woman not granted the dignity of a wedding ring.

Her lip curled as she stepped away, letting the curtain fall back. Women were apparently accorded little honor in this place.

But where did that leave her? An unwanted hostage . . . a lone woman in this isolated brigand encampment? She had her knife, but it would be a puny defense against a determined attack. A flicker of fear crawled up her spine, contracted her scalp. She'd said to Decatur that she wasn't afraid, but bravado was an inadequate shield, Portia now realized.

Her heart was fluttering as if a flock of butterflies had taken up residence in her chest. She ran to the door and opened it a crack, peering out into the deserted lane. The sky was as cloudless as it had been all day, brilliant starshine and moonlight flooding the village, glittering on the icy surface of the river. She could hear voices, laughter, music, coming from the building with the ale bench, the place she had decided was the mess. If they were all drinking themselves into a merry stupor, she might have a chance at escape.

She slipped into the deserted lane, hugging the wall at her back. She would need a horse. There was no way she could escape on foot, not over the harsh and desolate landscape she'd seen on the journey here.

It was bitterly cold, and the thick, comforting smell of wood smoke hung in the air. She glimpsed golden light behind shuttered windows and occasionally the fragrant aroma of cooking as she hurried along the lane, keeping to the shadows. In those warm and cozy cottages, there were people sitting by fires, eating supper, sharing jokes, secure in their own place, in the camaraderie of their own kind.

Portia had grown up knowing herself to be an outsider, with no place of her own, no family to define her in the world. There was Jack, of course, but Jack wasn't family in the way it was generally understood. He was simply the cause of her existence. She had tagged along behind him in exchange for a haphazard affection and a vague means of support . . . until she was old enough to support both herself and Jack's addiction. Now, as she flitted alone down the darkened lane, imagining the scenes behind the shuttered windows, her usual sense of isolation rose with renewed force. She was trying to escape from a place where she didn't belong, to return to a place where she didn't belong. The irony of the various situations in which she found herself usually amused her. It was a good defense against unhappiness. Tonight it failed her.

She was listening for a horse's whicker, her nose twitching for the smell of a stable. And she found it soon enough.

Not one stable but an entire block of them in the center of the village, a neat, swept, cobbled yard in front of the building. But she saw immediately that her chances of taking a horse without detection were nonexistent. Light showed from both ends of the block, and the tack room door stood open. She could hear voices, the rattle of dice, and as she clung to the shadows, she saw a man emerge into the yard, unbuttoning his britches. He relieved himself against the wall and returned to the tack room.

Portia slipped back into the lane and disconsolately turned her step toward the river. She didn't know why, except that it was a destination and she was not yet ready to accept defeat and creep back to her prison.

But when she stood on the bank, backed against the dark trunk of a leafless oak tree, excitement stabbed her. The frozen expanse meandered through the village, snaking away beyond the village boundaries, starlight glittering on its surface way into the distance. Way beyond the Decatur stronghold.

Rivers went places. Rivers were thoroughfares. There would be habitation, other villages even, along the banks of this one. If only she still had her skates . . .

Then she saw it. A sledge beached on the bank, its wooden runners curved and smooth as silk. Portia darted across, bending low to the ground although there was no sign of human activity here, no lit windows pouring sound and illumination. The riverbank was utterly deserted.

The sledge was piled with skins. It couldn't have been better. If she couldn't find other shelter, she could curl up in them until daylight, once she'd left the Decatur boundary far behind. Her heart surged. She knew now that she was going to succeed. This sledge and its perfect cargo had been put there by fate. She was destined to escape.

But how to propel it? Did they use dogs or ponies? Or did they pull it themselves? They'd need skates to do that.

Then she saw the pole, propped against the rear of the sledge. It was like a barge pole and presumably operated in the same way. One pushed oneself along the ice with thrusts of the pole. So simple . . . so wonderfully convenient.

Portia glanced nervously behind her, suddenly thinking this was all too good to be true. Maybe it was a trap, some devilish trap of Decatur's to catch her trying to escape. She had no reason to trust him . . . to believe him when he said he wouldn't hurt her. Prisoners of war were treated well enough unless they tried to escape. Then all the rules of safe conduct went by the board. If she was caught, what would they do to her? She would be fair game . . . if not for Decatur, then for his lawless band of savages. Sweat pricked on her forehead despite the cold. *She had to escape*; it was as simple as that. She would *not* be caught.

The sledge was heavier than it looked, and Portia was breathless by the time she'd managed to heave it down the bank and onto the ice. She was continually looking over her shoulder, expecting at any minute to see someone racing out of the darkness to challenge her. But the riverbank remained deserted and quiet, although strains of music and voices drifted through the still and icy moonlit night.

Once on the ice, the sledge became as light and maneuverable as a child's boat. Slipping and sliding, Portia pushed it into the middle of the frozen stream, then climbed in and took up a position at the rear, the pole clasped firmly between her hands. She pushed off and the sledge with astonishing power shot away, gathering momentum across the ice. It was miraculous. She barely needed to push at all once it was moving. It occurred to her that of course she was going downstream, out of the high hills, so there was an advantage in the slope of the riverbed. Pure jubilation made her heart sing as the craft sped beneath her and the houses and lights of Decatur village whistled past. *It was going to work.*

The watchman at the first bend of the river saw the sledge when it was fifty yards away, a darkly moving shape on the bright white surface of ice. He gave a little grunt of satisfaction. He needed something to enliven the long, cold hours of his watch in the blind built into the topmost branches of a copper beech tree. His watch point was one of six that covered the river over a ten-mile distance from Decatur village. He lit a flare that would be picked up both by the watchmen in the hilltop sentry posts and his comrades along the river, and huddled closer into his fur-lined cloak as he kept watch on the approaching craft.

The sledge slid beneath his tree and he observed that the figure who drove it had acquired the knack of the pole. The sledge was fairly skimming along, singing over the ice. He recognized the vehicle as belonging to Bertram, the trapper, who sold his skins in Ewefell, some twenty miles downriver. Bertram wouldn't be best pleased at losing both his sledge and a week's worth of work.

Not that the sledge and its driver would get very far. The hilltop sentry's torch had already flared in acknowledgment of the signal, and the master would be alerted within ten minutes.

It took less than ten minutes for Rufus to be informed of the illegitimate traffic on the river. And it took no time at all for him to guess who had given his sentries a little excitement in their customarily dull night watches.

He was in the middle of his supper, good food, wine, and company going some way to assuage the irritations of the day, and this piece of news did nothing for his temper. "God's grace! How far does she think she's going to get?" he demanded of the company in general. "Surely she can't imagine she can dance out of here on a stolen sledge without anyone being any the wiser?"

"Seems that she does," Will commented. "Shall I fetch her back?"

"No, dammit, I'll go." Rufus swung his leg over the bench at the long table and cast his napkin aside. "I was enjoying that lamprey pie," he remarked with another surge of irritation. "The devil take the girl! I'm damned if I'm going to ruin my supper." He swung back to face the table and took up his fork again.

"Jed, fetch my horse. I believe I'll let her get to the third watch before we stop her. Let her think she's getting away with it," he said, adding with a degree of savagery, "the shock'll be all the greater."

Jed, who'd brought the message, saluted and left the mess for the stables to saddle Ajax.

Rufus finished his lamprey pie, but Will could see that his cousin was no longer enjoying his supper and he could find it in his heart to feel a little sorry for Mistress Portia Worth.

"Right." Rufus pushed aside his empty platter and stood up. "I'd best get this over with." He strode to the door, swinging his cloak around him, his expression grim. For two pins he would have let the girl go. She was no use to him. But something wouldn't allow him to let her get the better of him. When he was ready to let her go, he would do so. But he wasn't ready yet. And besides, she had stolen a sledge, not to mention what was on it. Theft was one of the deadly sins among Decatur men.

Jed was holding Ajax at the door. He held the master's stirrup as Rufus vaulted into the saddle. "I sent a runner to the watchmen, m'lord. They'll not stop 'er till ye gives the order."

"Good." The great chestnut plunged forward under the nudge of his rider's heels.

The third watch was three miles from where Portia would have started from. Rufus rode away from the bank, parallel to the river. He had plenty of time. It would take a strong-muscled man the best part of an hour to accomplish that distance poling the sledge. Against all inclination, he caught himself almost admiring the dauntless spirit of the girl. She must have had no idea how far she'd have to go before she was safely out of Decatur territory.

He rode up to the third watch and drew rein beneath the hide. He called softly upward. "How far away is she?"

"About two hundred yards, sir."

Rufus rode Ajax to the riverbank and sat there, motionless in the moonlight, watching the approach of the sledge.

Portia didn't see him immediately. The effort of poling was consuming all her attention. What had seemed easy at the beginning was now arduous, her arm muscles and shoulders aching, her hands sore, even through her gloves, as they gripped and pushed the pole. She raised her head wearily, wondering whether she was far enough from Decatur village to risk stopping and resting. The great horse, his immobile rider, filled her exhausted vision. They stood there on the bank a few yards ahead of her like accusers from the Day of Judgment.

She felt sick. Her palms were suddenly clammy. She could think only of how unfair it was. She had been so sure she would succeed, and now there he sat, waiting for her. *Triumphant.* She could almost have screamed with frustration, but she was also dreadfully afraid.

Could she pole past him, gather enough speed to skim away? But she knew she couldn't outrun the stallion. It would be futile to try. Futile and undignified . . . if there was any dignity to be salvaged from this hideous situation. Paradoxically, her fear gave her some kind of courage. She would not show him she was afraid.

Portia raised her pole from the ice, and the sledge came to a gentle stop in the middle of the river. She sat down on the pile of hides and waited.

Rufus dismounted and stepped onto the ice. He walked carefully, deliberately across to the sledge and stood looking down at her. "Just what do you think you're doing, Mistress Worth?"

"Running away," Portia replied with a snap. "What did you think?"

"I had rather come to that conclusion myself," he agreed with a deceptively amiable smile. "Once again, I'm forced to note that you don't seem very good at it."

Portia folded her hands in her lap and shivered, aware of the sweat of effort drying on her skin beneath her torn cloak and bedraggled gown. Now that she was still, the cold air knifed her and she wished he wouldn't just stand there looking at her with that shark's smile on his mouth and the speculative consideration in his eyes. He was angry; she could feel it as she could feel the stabbing gusts of icy wind. He'd told her he was a man of uncertain temper . . . she'd seen the shadow of that temper several times already. And now he was just torturing her with this ghastly suspense. His eyes glinted at her, chips of blue like the moonlight sparking off the icy surface of the river.

"What are you going to do?" she demanded.

"Do?" Rufus raised an eyebrow. "What do *you* think might be appropriate action, Mistress Worth?"

Portia compressed her lips. "Just get it over with," she muttered, wishing now that she'd chosen to remain on her feet. Sitting here with him towering above her wasn't helping matters in the least.

"The sledge and the hides belong to Bertram." Rufus tapped the back of one gloved hand into the palm of the other, making a rhythmic slapping sound in the quiet night. "He'll expect to see everything back where he left it in the morning, so you'd better get moving."

"Get moving?" Portia regarded him with dawning horror as she began to have an inkling of what he meant.

He nodded. "Take it back, Mistress Worth. We don't tolerate theft in Decatur village."

"But it's upstream!"

"Yes, I believe it is." He stepped away from the sledge. "I'll ride along the bank beside you . . . just in case you get any other foolish ideas." His teeth flashed white within the shadow of his beard, but it was still a far from friendly smile.

Portia glanced down at her hands. The leather in the palms of her gloves was splitting, and her palms stung. Grimly she stood up, took the pole to the back of the sledge, and pushed off. The craft moved barely a foot. It was as if the runners had been blunted or wrapped in rags. She bit her lip and pushed again.

From the bank, Rufus stood watching her efforts for a minute, then he swung astride Ajax and set the horse to a slow walk, keeping pace with the sledge's laborious progress. Slowly his punitive anger died. The girl had been exhausted before she'd begun this mad enterprise, and what she was enduring now must be unadulterated torture. Once again, he was stirred to reluctant admiration by her indomitable spirit. He remembered telling her in Castle Granville that they were alike, he and she. That recognition now vanquished his anger. He would have done just what Portia Worth had done in a similar situation.

It was still damnably irritating, though, to have to spend the shank of his evening chasing after her. His irritation rang in his voice as he called out to her, "Portia, leave the sledge and come over here."

Portia ignored him, setting her teeth, thrusting the pole against the ice. If she stopped, she would lose what little momentum she had. She could see no lights ahead of her now and guessed that the village had retired for the night. Thoughts of the little bed in the apple loft, of fire and candle-light, danced in her head. She closed her mind to everything but the need to drive the sledge across the ice.

Rufus's irritation grew closer to anger again. "God's grace, girl! Will you do as you're bid?" His voice roared across the river.

This time she looked up and saw that he'd drawn rein and was standing in the stirrups, hands cupped around his mouth to amplify his words.

"Why?" she demanded, still pushing.

Of all the obstinate creatures! "Because I say so," Rufus bellowed. "Now come over here at once!"

Portia flung aside the pole and stepped out of the sledge. She no longer cared what further torments the master of Decatur had in mind. She was half dead with cold and exhaustion and decided that the other half would be a welcome relief. She slipped and slithered to the bank and stood there, hands on her hips, glaring up at him. "Now what?"

Rufus leaned down from the saddle. "Give me your hand and put your foot on mine."

Still Portia hesitated, warily examining his countenance. It was not particularly reassuring. Could he really have relented and be offering her a ride back to the village?

"If I have to dismount, Mistress Worth, one of us is going to regret it," Rufus declared. He clicked his fingers impatiently.

It seemed she was damned if she went and damned if she stayed. Portia scrambled up the bank and took the large hand, her fingers curling painfully around his. With her last vestige of strength, she managed to lift her foot high enough to gain purchase on his boot in the stirrup, then she was sailing upward without much help from her own muscles to land on the saddle in front of him.

"Are you just going to leave the sledge there?" she demanded. "I thought you said Bertram, or whatever his name is, will expect to find it where he left it."

Rufus was astounded. Did nothing squash her? Then he felt her shiver, felt the rigidity of her thin frame. She had half turned to look up at him as she threw her challenge, and the moonlight caught her white face, and he saw the strain in the slanted green eyes, and the fear beneath the defiance. Without thinking, he raised his hand and lightly cupped the curve of her cheek in his gloved palm. Her eyes widened. The fear receded and something took its place. Puzzlement that yet contained a flicker of anticipation. And he knew she was remembering as was he that teasing kiss in the court of Castle Granville. It hadn't meant anything. Of course he hadn't meant anything by it.

His hand dropped from her cheek, and with a brisk gesture, he wrapped his cloak around her thin, shivering frame and urged Ajax into a canter.

Portia tried to hold herself upright, to deny her fatigue. Her cheek was still warmed by that strange little caress, but every instinct told her it had been as much an aberration as the stroking paw of the tiger. He had teased her and manipulated her in the castle ward, and he was just doing the same now. It obviously pleased him to taunt her, and she couldn't understand why she had for a minute allowed herself to believe that it was a genuine gesture. He must have seen her gullibility in her eyes.

"Sit back, for pity's sake!" Rufus pulled her backward against him with an impatient movement. "I'm not a porcupine." He held her so tightly she had no choice but to slump against his broad chest. She could feel his heart beating strongly against her ear and her own seemed to slip into the same rhythm, sending her into a strange daze.

In less than ten minutes they were riding into the darkened village, and Portia from within her numbed trance thought with a shudder of how long it would have taken her to propel the sledge, in the unlikely event that she'd been able to do it.

Rufus drew rein outside his cottage and lifted Portia from the saddle, lowering her to the ground. "Go inside and get ready for bed. I'll be back as soon as I've taken Ajax to the stables."

A man clearly accustomed to the habit of command, Portia thought with a twinge of derision that heartened her. It meant she hadn't quiet lost her backbone. She let herself into the cottage. The warmth was blissful. She huddled over the banked fire, stretching her white numbed hands to the glow, wracked by convulsive shivers. A snuffling mumble came from behind the curtain. She froze, listening, but all was quiet again. One of the boys must be dreaming.

Rufus quietly let himself into the cottage five minutes later. He frowned at her. "I thought I told you to get ready for bed."

"I was too cold to go upstairs."

"It's warm enough. Come." He gestured to the stairs. "I hope you've learned a few things tonight about the nature of a military compound, but just in case you're still not completely clear, we'll take certain measures to ensure we both spend what's left of the night in relative peace." He put a hand in the small of her back and pushed her firmly ahead of him.

In the big bedchamber, Rufus said brusquely, "All in all, this has been a very tiresome day, and I find myself very short of patience. You, I know, are exhausted, so let's do each other a favor and get to bed without any more tedious discussion."

He drew off his gloves and unfastened his cloak, tossing them over the chest at the foot of the bed. His buff jerkin followed, then he sat on the chest to pull off his boots and stockings. Portia watched him with a sort of horrified fascination as he unbuckled his belt and kicked off his britches.

"For God's sake, girl, don't just stand there like a moon calf!" In his white linen shirt and drawers, he regarded her impatiently. "Do you wish to sleep in your clothes? If not, I suggest you put on that nightrobe in the other chamber." Turning away, he bent over the washstand, splashing water on his face, running his wet hands through his beard and hair.

Portia turned and went into the apple loft, firmly closing

the door. She hadn't the faintest idea what he'd meant about taking certain measures, but it seemed as if she was finally going to be able to get out of her torn and filthy clothes and sink into bed, and the prospect was far too enticing to waste time probing riddles.

The bang at the door so shocked her as she was fastening the ribbons of the nightrobe that she jumped half out of her skin. "Come out, Portia. I'm ready for you."

"*What?*" She stared at the closed door, her fingers quivering.

The door opened and Rufus Decatur's blue gaze surveyed her through the gap. He crooked a finger in an unmistakable gesture of command. "I am really *very* tired," he repeated wearily. "Come out!" His tone was one that brooked no argument, and Portia found herself moving forward as if drawn by a magnet.

"What are you going to do?" All her previous fears rose to the surface. She was alone with this half-naked man in his bedchamber. There was no one to hear her, and even if there were, no one would interfere with the master of Decatur taking his pleasure.

"Sleep," he said succinctly. "As are you. But since I've had enough running around for one night, I'm going to ensure you stay in one place until morning." He reached for her wrist, drawing her inexorably into the other chamber.

Portia felt as if she had lost all will of her own. She stared, shocked into stunned silence, as he looped his belt around her waist, running the leather through the buckle without fastening it, continuing to hold the free end loosely in his hand. What kind of perversion did he have in mind?

"Fortunately you're skinny enough to leave enough slack in the belt to move around comfortably," he muttered, bending to fling aside the covers. "You may sleep under the quilt, and I'll sleep on top under a rug. That way we shall preserve the proprieties." Suddenly he laughed with such genuine amusement that Portia wondered if the master of Decatur was of sound mind.

"Conventional proprieties don't exist in the Decatur village," he explained. "But we tend to be considerate of the foibles of others. Would you get under the quilt, please?"

Portia was rendered speechless.

"In!" He lifted her and deposited her willy-nilly in the middle of the bed. "Lie down." He tossed the quilts over her, then lay down beside her, pulling up a thick fur-lined rug over himself. Taking the free end of the belt, he tied it one-handed around his own wrist in a complex knot that looked completely undoable to Portia's horrified gaze.

"There. Now I shall be sure to wake up if you get any further fugitive ideas before the morning. Pleasant dreams, Mistress Worth."

And to Portia's indescribable amazement, Rufus Decatur yawned and fell instantly asleep.

She lay rigid for a minute, barely daring to breathe. A minute ago she'd been expecting a rape, and now she was tucked up in bed as cozily and safely as if it were Jack sleeping soundly beside her. She'd shared chambers and beds, blankets and quilts with Jack over the years, listening to his stertorous breathing, sometimes holding her own breath, waiting in terror when she was very little for him to take a breath when it seemed as if he'd ceased to breathe altogether. She could remember vividly the incredible relief of the moment when the shuddering rattle had started up again, and how his drunken snores had provided the only certain lullaby that would send her to sleep.

Tears pricked behind her eyes and tentatively she brushed them away, anxious not to awake her companion. The warmth of the bed began to creep along her cold, tired limbs and the deep featherbed nestled around her. She was vaguely aware of the constriction at her waist, but it was not uncomfortable and when experimentally she turned on her side the maneuver was easily accomplished.

A small snore rumbled from her companion, and now her own eyes were so heavy Portia didn't think she could have stayed awake another minute even if she were still on her feet instead of curled in this nesting warmth. . . .

*R*ufus *awoke a few hours later, just before the first cock* crow. He was always an early riser, regardless of how short the night or how convivial the preceding evening. His companion was curled on her side away from him, her breathing deep and regular. He hitched himself on one elbow and examined her sleeping countenance. It felt a little like voyeurism, watching an unconscious sleeper, but their dealings had been so tempestuous so far he hadn't the chance for a leisurely assessment. And for all her exasperating facets, Portia Worth inspired his curiosity.

Fate had dealt the cards from the bottom of the pack when it came to allocating fortune and favor to this section of the Granville family, he reflected. Not even the most partisan description could apply russet or auburn or copper to the orange flame of hair springing forth from her pale, angular countenance. Her eyes, presently closed, were her best feature, but as counterweights in the scale of negatives they were lamentably light. But then, her physical attributes were probably the least interesting aspects of Mistress Worth. A man face-to-face with that indomitable, challenging spirit was unlikely to give her features a passing thought. She'd grown up in a hard school, he reflected, but it hadn't crushed her. Self-pity was definitely not one of Mistress Worth's failings, although Lord knew she had sufficient reason to indulge in it once in a while.

He caught himself smiling and thought somewhat acidly that it was an addled response to the temperament of his accidental hostage. Not only had he acquired a completely useless bargaining counter, but instead of a docile, meek child, he found himself saddled with a creature who didn't know how to surrender to the inevitable. It definitely added insult to injury.

He unfastened the belt at his wrist with one quick tug on the knot, then slipped a hand beneath the quilts to free the buckle at Portia's waist. His hand immediately encountered skin, the softest, smoothest skin he had ever touched. So amazingly delicate was it that his hand lingered, even as he realized that her nightrobe must have become entangled around her waist and he was presently tracing the bare curve of her bottom. Wisdom told him to abandon both belt and bed without further ado, but his fingers seemed deaf to such sage dictates.

They slid in a delicate voyage of exploration, the exquisite softness of her skin sending little tremors of arousal through his loins. It was a delightful sensation, one he was loath to bring to an end, but Portia stirred suddenly and muttered, pushing at his hand as if it were a buzzing insect. Reluctantly he let his hand fall away and forced himself back to the reality of the cold morning.

He slid out of bed, prepared to abandon the belt, then, without conscious intention, found himself very gently inching back the covers, listening almost guiltily to the continued rhythm of her breathing. The long, pale legs were curled, her arms were crossed over her breast, and Rufus caught himself thinking that there was something remarkably endearing about the slender, vulnerable line of her backside.

What the hell was he doing? He almost jumped back from the bed, feeling like a rapist. Needing a reason now for his actions, with grim concentration and extreme caution, he eased the belt through the buckle and slid it out from under her.

Miraculously, Portia slept on. Rufus pulled the covers over her again, dressed swiftly, and tiptoed downstairs. There was no sound from his sons' bed, and he let himself out of the cottage into the gray dawn, making his way through the village and up to the sentry points to check on the night's reports. The cold air cleared his brain and cooled his recalcitrant loins, and by the time he reached the sentry post, he was almost able to believe the whole episode had been the tail of an erotic dream.

9

There were no reports of untoward movement across the barren landscape during the night. The approaches to the De-catur village offered no concealment from the ring of watch-men on the surrounding hilltops, and the moonlight had been exceptionally bright. As Rufus returned to the village the sun was coming up over the low-lying hills to the east, fingers of pink and orange reaching across the pale sky. It would be another brilliant winter day.

He turned into the mess, ducking his head beneath the low lintel. An elderly man looked up from the range where he was stirring cauldrons of porridge. "Mornin', master. After breakin' yer fast, are ye?"

"Aye, Bill." Rufus stripped off his gloves, surprised to find he was ravenous. "I'm the first, it seems."

"Oh, the littl'uns were in a minute past." The cook ladled porridge into an earthenware bowl and set it before the mas-ter. He brought a pitcher of cream and a bowl of thick, dark treacle.

"They're up already?" Rufus poured cream and spooned treacle, stirring the contents of the porringer with hungry an-ticipation. "Did they eat?"

"Took some bread 'n' drippin' out wi' 'em," Bill observed comfortably. "They was all excited about them puppies."

"Oh, don't tell me Tod's bitch has whelped already?" Ru-fus sighed. "They've been agitating about having a pair of the puppies ever since Tod told them."

"Reckon ye'll 'ave a fight on yer 'ands," Bill said with a grin. "Fancy some sweetbreads?"

Rufus nodded through a mouthful of porridge, swallowed, and said, "Josiah's gone to the cottage already?"

"Aye, about 'alf an hour ago. Said he'd look in on the lass an' see if she needs aught." Bill glanced slyly at the master as he sliced sweetbreads into a skillet. A gently bred woman in the Decatur stronghold had never happened before, and speculation was rife among the lower echelons of the command, who were not in their commander's confidence.

"Good" was all the response he got for his pains. Rufus continued calmly with his breakfast. Expecting his hostage to be a scared and innocent child, he had instructed Josiah, who ordinarily was relegated to helping with the mess and caring for Luke and Toby's basic needs when their father was otherwise occupied, to take care of Olivia. Josiah was elderly, with a gentle and reassuring manner, and Rufus had reasoned that his young hostage would find him a less menacing male caretaker than anyone else in the military compound. Whether the hostage he had inadvertently acquired would need such consideration on his part was another matter.

The mess had filled with other men in search of breakfast by the time Rufus had finished his own meal. He left the noisy building and ducked back out into the crisp morning in search of his sons. He heard their voices before he reached Tod's barn, the excited gabble sounding for once in harmony. As he entered the barn, they bounded over to him, two pairs of bright blue eyes radiating wonderment.

"See the puppies, Papa!" They grabbed his hands, dragging him across to the nest of straw where the red setter had settled her new litter.

"They's blind, Papa," Luke squealed, swinging on his father's hand. " 'Cause they's too small to see."

"Was we blind too?" Toby asked curiously, as he knelt in the straw, expertly soothing the bitch's head with one dimpled fist.

"No, human babies can open their eyes as soon as they're born." Rufus squatted beside his sons to admire.

"When they's big enough, we're havin' two of 'em," Toby informed his father. "Tod said we could."

"We got to choose which ones!" Luke squawked. "Eenie meenie minie mo . . ."

It was too early in the morning to deal with tempests, but their father couldn't afford to give the impression of tacit approval. "You're not old enough yet to have your own dogs." Rufus captured Luke's pointing finger before one of the soft brown bundles could be accidentally jabbed.

"But we *want* 'em!" Toby announced, his voice rising several notches.

"Yes, we *want* 'em!" his little brother added. "Tod said we could!"

"Not until you're seven," Rufus said firmly, rising to his feet and drawing the boys up with him. "Seven is the proper age to have a dog. That's when I had my first puppy."

"Then I'll have mine 'afore Luke!" Toby yelled, prancing on the tips of his toes. "See, Luke. I'll have mine first."

"But that's not fair!" Luke wailed, his voice trembling with tears. "He can't have one first . . . he *can't*."

Too late, Rufus realized what he'd stepped into. Whatever he did now, one of them would consider it unfair. "The issue isn't going to arise for another three years," he said, frowning at them. They looked more than ordinarily disheveled, their jerkins only half buttoned, their eyes still sticky with sleep, crumbs of toast and shiny spots of dripping adorning their small round mouths. They must have rolled out of bed in the very instant they'd awoken. It was their usual habit, one reason why they preferred to sleep in their clothes.

It probably wasn't a very good habit, Rufus thought with some surprise, remembering that Portia, even in her own difficulties the previous evening, had sounded disapproving. He'd never before given it a second thought, but they really did seem remarkably unsavory.

"You both need to go under the pump," he declared, scooping a child under each arm.

The prospect drove all thoughts of puppies from their heads and brought instant alliance. Shrieking in protest, they were borne out of the barn, their squirming bodies dangling beneath their father's arms.

*P*ortia's *eyes opened slowly. It was full daylight and the* memories of the preceding day and night came back in a hot rush of mingled mortification and outrage. She was now alone in the bed she had shared with Rufus Decatur. She moved her hand over her body. The belt was no longer around her waist.

"You awake then, lass?" A man's voice spoke from the far side of the room, and Portia struggled up onto an elbow, blinking blearily.

An old man turned from the washstand where he was placing a jug of hot water beside the ewer. He had a pink face adorned with fluffy white whiskers and an equally fluffy white tonsure around a shiny bald head. Faded blue eyes regarded Portia with benign interest.

"Who are you?" Portia demanded.

"Name's Josiah. Master told me to see t' yer needs. There's 'ot water 'ere fer washin'." He gestured to the washstand.

"How considerate of Lord Rothbury," Portia said acidly. "What time is it?"

"All of eight o'clock." Josiah seemed unperturbed by the acid tone. "Summat wrong wi' the bed in the apple loft, was there?"

"Your master seemed to think so," Portia said as tartly as before. She sat up and yawned, stretching her arms above her head, linking her fingers as she did so.

"Ah, wanted a bedmate, did 'e?" Josiah nodded sagely.

"Not in the way you think," Portia snapped. She pushed aside the covers and swung her legs over the side of the bed. "Lord Rothbury merely kept me prisoner on the bed because he was afraid I'd run away again."

"Oh, aye, I 'eard about that." Josiah said. "Took Bertram's sledge an' all. 'E wasn't best pleased this mornin', I can tell you. 'Ad to go an' fetch it, 'e did."

"Oh, well, remind me to beg his pardon," Portia said with a sardonic smile. "I'm sure I didn't mean to cause a thieving brigand any trouble."

"Eh, someone got outta bed on t' wrong side," Josiah observed placidly. "Mebbe a good wash'll sweeten yer temper." He bustled back to the washstand and poured hot water into the ewer. "There's a nice piece o' lavender soap, too." He looked expectantly at Portia.

"I'm not about to strip naked in front of you," she said. "Or has the master decreed that I'm not to be granted any privacy?"

"Lord bless ye, lass, the master never said nothin' o' the kind. Not that ye needs to worry about me. I've seen all an' more than you've got to show." Josiah chuckled and went to the stairs. "Skinny little thing, aren't you?"

"Very." Portia untied the ribbons of her nightrobe.

The door below banged open and the sounds of shrill, squealing protest rose up the stairs. Rufus's voice cut through the childish trebles. "Josiah?"

"Aye, m'lord. I'm 'ere. What's all that caterwaulin'?" Josiah hurried down to the kitchen where Rufus had set the boys on their feet but was keeping a tight hold on their collars.

"These children need to go under the pump," Rufus announced. "Just hold Toby while I get these filthy clothes off Luke."

Portia heard him in astonishment. Was the man completely mad or just totally heartless? She yelled from the top of the stairs, "For pity's sake, Decatur, you can't put them under the pump. It's freezing!"

Rufus, still clutching the boys, came to the bottom of the stairs. He looked up and saw a pair of bare feet and long white legs. "Aren't you dressed yet?"

"My clothes aren't fit to put on, thanks to you." She hastily retreated from view, grabbed a coverlet from the bed, wrapped it around her like a toga, then made her way downstairs.

The boys ceased their wailing and regarded her with hope. "It's too cold for the pump," Toby declared. "*She* says it is."

"Yes, of course it is," Portia reiterated firmly. "Of all the cruel and absurd ideas. It's January, for God's sake."

Rufus looked both annoyed and nonplussed. "There's no reason for wild accusations," he said stiffly.

"Oh, you mean cruelty?" Portia regarded him with cold scorn. "My experiences in this den of thieves, my lord, make such an accusation perfectly reasonable. And when I think how this *hospitality* was designed for Olivia, I'd like to cut out your heart!"

Rufus released his hold on the boys. "All right, Portia, let's not get carried away here. You have in no way been treated with cruelty, although you're entitled to your own view on the matter. But don't confuse your experiences with the way I treat my children. You know nothing about it. However, I concede that it is too cold to wash them outside. I wasn't thinking clearly. It's just that I always put them under the pump when they get unsavory."

There was a warning snap in his eyes.

"Well, they're certainly unsavory." Portia examined the boys with a critical frown. "I haven't had much experience with children, but surely you could bathe them in a tub or something."

The snap in Rufus's eyes vanished. "They won't keep still," he said gloomily. "And they splash water all over the place. The kitchen's a lake by the time they're finished."

Portia wanted to laugh. There was something so absurd about the master of Decatur defeated by a pair of toddlers. She sat on the bottom step, resting her chin on her linked hands. "Take all their clothes off, sponge them down and put clean things on them, and then they won't look nearly so unsavory."

Rufus seemed to consider, then he said, "I'll strike a bargain with you. If you and Josiah will deal with these two, I'll find you some clean clothes. How would that be?"

Portia regarded the boys, who had retreated to the far end of the kitchen and looked ready to fly out of the back door at the first move against them. "I think you would have the best of the bargain," she said.

"Please yourself. If you want to stay wrapped in a quilt, it's all the same to me," Rufus said airily. "In fact, on reflection I think it would be a very good thing. It would keep you within doors as effectively as any restraints. I withdraw the offer."

"You are an unmitigated son of a bitch," Portia said softly, realizing that they had just come dangerously close to a moment of affability.

"Eh, watch yer tongue!" Josiah exclaimed, for once shocked out of his customary placidity. "You don't use language like that to the master."

"Ah, but Mistress Worth acknowledges no master," Rufus said. "Isn't that so?" He raised an interrogative eyebrow at Portia. "Isn't it so?" he repeated when she made no answer.

"I've yet to meet someone worth the title," she said frigidly. "And I don't expect to . . . not in this life." She rose to her feet, preparing to return upstairs.

Rufus moved swiftly, catching her around the waist and

lifting her down into the kitchen. He held her shoulders and smiled down into her furious face. "Come, Portia, I was merely jesting. Let's call a truce. Help Josiah with the boys, and I'll find you a change of clothes. It's a beautiful morning, and if you promise not to quarrel, I'll take you out for a walk and show you around the village."

It was such a volte-face Portia was momentarily speechless. His vivid blue gaze danced with laughter, his mouth curved in a smile of unexpected sweetness. "Truce?" He pressed the tip of her nose with a forefinger.

God, how she hated him! He was manipulating her again, teasing her with all the deceit and arrogance of men the world over. How could he know that when he touched her and looked at her in that way it made her blood sing? Her loathing of the man just seemed to slide away under a smile that seemed to imply some deep knowledge of the world, of herself, even. But he did know and he was using it for his own ends.

The sheer force of his personality, his physical presence itself, was somehow dictating how she was to respond to him, overpowering her own sense of what was rational and legitimate in the circumstances.

Rufus let his hands fall from her shoulders, and Portia stepped away from him, her hands half lifted as if to ward something off.

"Truce," she said in a voice that didn't sound quite like her own. Then she turned abruptly to where the boys still stood at the back of the room and lunged for Luke, catching him up in a shrieking tangle of limbs. Josiah caught Toby as he dived between the legs of the table.

Rufus stood for a minute, unaware that he was smiling as he wondered what it was about his accidental hostage that was so appealing. She was all spikes and sparks, and yet there were moments when he saw beneath the antagonism, and what he saw he found utterly delightful.

It was disturbing. He turned on his heel and left the shrieking chaos of the cottage.

When he returned half an hour later, it was to find his sons in clean clothes, astonishingly subdued, damp curls clinging to their scalps, cheeks scrubbed shiny. They were sitting by the fire, shivering intermittently like newly bathed puppies, and regarded their father with large eyes filled with recrimination.

"I'm cold," Toby said reproachfully.

"We're both cold," his brother chimed in.

"They're only cold because their skin isn't used to fresh air and water," Portia said. "We almost had to scrape the grime off them."

"Well, I've fulfilled my side of the bargain. See what you think of these." Rufus handed her a bundle, with a strange gleam in his eye that put Portia immediately on her guard.

"I'll be off, then, master." Josiah headed for the door, Luke and Toby on his heels, as Portia took the bundle gingerly, almost as if she were expecting it to conceal a sharp-toothed ferret.

"What are these?" Portia gestured to the parcel.

Rufus grinned. "Take them upstairs and find out. I think you'll be surprised."

"Good surprised or bad surprised?"

"I don't know. But they were all I could find. We have a rather limited supply of spare garments in the compound."

Portia, now convinced that it was going to be an unpleasant surprise, carried the bundle upstairs. Presumably he'd found her some peasant woman's rough homespun gown and holland petticoat. But beggars couldn't be choosers, and if they were clean she'd not complain.

She laid the bundle on the bed and untied it. She stared in astonishment and then lifted up the garments one by one, shaking them out. A pair of doeskin britches, woolen stockings and garters, a shirt of unbleached linen, woolen underdrawers, a sleeveless jerkin of dark worsted, and a frieze wool cloak. There was even a belt, and a new pair of gloves to replace the split ones. Rufus had thought of everything.

Astonishment gave way to delight. She'd always wanted to shed the irksome trappings of femalehood. Here was her chance.

The water Josiah had brought her earlier was tepid now, but she washed herself thoroughly, shivering but resolute. Then, with almost languid pleasure, she dressed, relishing the strange feel of the garments. She sat on the bed to pull on her own boots, then slowly stood up, running her hands down the unfamiliarly delineated length of her body. There was a wonderful sense of freedom in these garments, and they seemed warmer than gowns and petticoats. The woolen underdrawers helped, of course, and the leather britches seemed to resist the cold better. It was, Portia decided, a vast improvement on her previous incarnation, but there was no mirror in Rufus's bedchamber, so she had no way of telling what she looked like.

Rufus had his back to the stairs as she came down, but he turned at the sound of her step. He raised an eyebrow at the sight of her. "How do you like them?" He regarded her over the rim of his tankard as he took a sip of ale.

"I've always believed I was supposed to have been born a boy," Portia said. "I'm not formed like a woman. I don't have any curves or anything."

"I wouldn't say *no* curves," Rufus murmured consideringly. "Turn around."

Portia obeyed.

Rufus's gaze ran slowly down the slender frame. Her legs in the britches seemed even longer than usual. The jerkin sat on her hips and was buttoned tight into the indentation of her waist cinched by the belt.

"It suits you," he pronounced finally, his eyes alight with appreciation.

Portia's smile was involuntary and so full of delight that Rufus was strangely moved. He had the feeling she hadn't received too many compliments in her life. Unless, of course, other hands had come into contact with that exquisitely fine skin, or some other man could appreciate a spirit so unyielding, reflected in a pair of widely spaced, slanted, pure green cat's eyes.

"Now you're dressed, we're going to take a tour of the compound," he said, his tone crisp as he returned to business. He handed her the frieze cloak. "Put this on."

"I can't think why I would wish to tour a thieves' den," Portia retorted, automatically taking the cloak. "You may well think it's the duty of a courteous host, but I do assure you it's a courtesy I can forgo."

The moment of truce was clearly over.

Rufus regarded her steadily, his eyes hard as diamonds.

"Make no mistake, Mistress Worth. This tour has a very straightforward purpose. It's by way of saving myself further trouble. I wish you to understand that any other attempt to leave this compound will be utterly futile. You cannot escape from here undetected."

"And how long do you intend to keep me here?"

"I haven't as yet decided," he said shortly.

"But Lord Granville isn't going to pay any ransom for me. You already know that."

"My decision will not necessarily be based on Cato's actions."

Portia's mouth was a little dry. "Are you going to kill me?"

"What on earth would give you that idea?" Rufus frowned at her.

"You're a thief and a kidnapper. You hate Granvilles, and I'm a Granville," she stated, trying to ignore the blue fire now enlivening his gaze, the little pulse beating rapidly in his temple.

There was a moment of tense silence. Then Rufus said with cold finality, "I am beginning to resent these accusations. Be a little careful. You don't know anything about me. And I suggest that until you do, you keep a still tongue in your head." He took her elbow and propelled her outside into the lane.

He walked fast, almost pulling her along so that she had to skip to keep up with him. In flat tones that did nothing to disguise his continued anger, he imparted information, every detail related to the impregnable nature of the stronghold and the absolute authority of its master.

He didn't stop once, didn't even slow his speed, acknowledging the half salutes from men they passed with a brusque nod—men drilling, sharpening pikes, oiling muskets. The place hummed with martial activity. Portia was disconcerted to find that after the first slightly curious glances, she drew no more attention than if she were a dog accompanying the master of Decatur on his rounds. Did no one here ever question the master's actions?

She made no attempt to interrupt the flow of instructions and against her will began to understand why the men of Decatur viewed their master with such unquestioning awe.

A lawless outcast he might be, the leader of a band of brigands he might be, but he had a fearsome authority and Decatur village was run with superb military efficiency. She remembered how Jack, whenever he'd mentioned Rufus Decatur, had always implied that he was a worthy enemy. Despite his contempt for brigandage, her father had had an unwilling respect for the man whose vengeance could not lightly be dismissed. And she'd heard the same note from Cato, lurking behind his interest in her past encounter with Decatur, his need for the finest details.

She'd have a good few interesting details to impart to Cato after her forced march through Decatur village, she thought suddenly. And that chill of fear rose anew. Surely Decatur wouldn't reveal so much to someone from the enemy camp if he intended to release her unharmed?

"We're going up to the sentry post now." Her escort's clipped tones were for once a welcome interruption to her chain of thought. He pointed up the hill to where smoke curled from the watchman's fire. "You were brought in through the eastern section of the valley. There are posts at every compass point overlooking the Cheviots and all the way to the border. Just as there are along the river for ten miles either side. I believe you discovered that last night."

Portia didn't dignify that with a response, and Rufus continued in the same tone, "My cousin Will has charge of all the sentry dispositions and all the reports. You met him last night."

As they climbed upward Rufus found himself noticing that Portia had begun to walk in a different way, swinging her hips as her stride lengthened. She was obviously adapting to the freedom of britches. In his present mood it annoyed him that he'd noticed.

Will, when they reached him, stared at her with a deal more open interest than his fellows in the village. "That's a novel costume," he observed.

"It was all we had in the stores," Rufus told him. "Her own aren't fit for anything after last night."

Will nodded as if this made perfect sense, and Portia maintained a stony silence. Clearly Will, like Josiah, knew all about her humiliating forced return. It was probably the talk of the village.

Rufus took Portia's elbow again and led her away from the fire. "Now look around. Do you see that on every hilltop there's a watch fire?"

Portia folded her arms across her chest. "You've made your point. More than once."

"Then I trust you've taken it," he said coldly. "You may make your own way back to the cottage. I've wasted enough time on you for one morning, and I've more important matters to attend to." He turned on his heel and began to stride back down to the village.

Portia's jaw dropped at this abrupt dismissal. All her earlier fears vanished under a wave of fury. How dared he snub her with such insulting indifference? She began to run after him, picking up speed on the slippery ground, intending to return insult for insult.

She jumped a small pile of rocks, caught her foot on a patch of ice, fell onto her rear, and slid with a yelp down the path, cannonading into the back of Rufus's legs. His legs shot out from under him and he fell in a helpless sprawl, his limbs mingling with Portia's as they slid together inexorably downward.

Rufus rolled sideways, caught her hard against him and dug his heels into the ice. Her head was tucked beneath his chin, his arms encircling her body. He could feel her ribs, was aware of the rapid patter of her heart against his chest, her long legs tangled with his. She pushed against him, trying to free herself, even as she cursed him for an arrogant, clumsy bastard. Her face, glowing with indignation, was turned up toward him, so close to his gaze that he could see only a pale blur and the bright anger in the brilliant eyes.

His grip tightened, resisting all her efforts to escape. "Did you do that on purpose?" he demanded incredulously as the eloquent tirade of her fury continued to break over him.

"What if I did?" she threw at him, breathless and seething.

There was an instant of silence. Portia saw his eyes narrow, something leap into them, something dangerous and yet it sent a thrill of excitement to jolt the pit of her stomach. The silence seemed to expand until it contained them, suspended, waiting. . . .

Then his hands loosed their encircling grip of her body. He grasped her head between both hands, his fingers twisting in the tangled orange curls around her ears. He shifted his body slightly, his legs scissoring hers, so he was holding her pinned to the ground beneath him. She could feel every line of his powerful frame pressing against her, imprinting himself upon her. She could feel his heat, the warmth of his breath.

"There is such a thing as retribution, Mistress Worth," he murmured, and then he took her mouth with his. This was no light brushing kiss to tease. It was a hard possessive statement. Without volition, her mouth opened for the insistent demand of his tongue, and she felt the sinuous muscular presence plundering the warm, soft cave, tasting her. And then their tongues danced and she was tasting him back, exploring the contours of his mouth, running her own tongue over his teeth, into the hollows of his cheeks. Her eyes were closed on a red darkness and her blood raced with excitement. She could feel the hard jut of his erection pressing against her loins; her hands went around his back, kneading his taut buttocks. His fingers curled deeper into her hair, gripping her yet more firmly, and then slowly he raised his head.

Rufus gazed down into her flushed face, taking in her reddened lips, the dazed look in her eye. He still held her with his body and his hands in her hair, and for a minute he didn't move. "Whatever made me do that? I wonder." The smile that played over his mouth contained both surprise and a degree of bemusement. "It was not at all what I intended to do."

Portia touched her swollen lips with her tongue. "What did you intend doing?"

"Something rather less pleasant," he responded, still with the same smile. "But for some reason, in my dealings with you, you unruly gosling, I keep taking myself by surprise."

He released his grip on her hair and swung himself off her. He stood up, brushing off his cloak and britches. "Get up now." He leaned down to take her hands and haul her to her feet.

Portia pushed back her hair with both hands, trying to subdue the tangled halo, trying to order her senses. The world seemed to have tilted off its axis, and she seemed to be having difficulty standing straight against the steep pitch of the hillside.

Rufus's gaze was still somewhat perplexed as he looked at

her. "You really are a gosling," he murmured. "All leggy and ruffled feathers." He glanced up the hill, wondering if anyone had witnessed that mad moment, and as he did so a trumpet blast from the northern hilltop resounded through the valley.

All thoughts of dalliance, all vestiges of perplexity, were instantly banished. The call meant only one thing. Something of more than ordinary interest had been spied by a sentry. He set off at a rapid pace, climbing back up the hillside.

Portia stood on the path for a minute, still trying to order her senses. Then the trumpet shrilled again and without further thought she began to clamber up after Rufus. There was something so urgent, so elemental, about that call that it couldn't be resisted.

Will, terse with excitement, handed Rufus a spyglass as the master reached him. "Troop of soldiers, to the north, at four o'clock."

"Granville men?" Rufus wiped the glass with his gloved thumb before putting it to his eye. Neither man acknowledged Portia's swift and silent arrival.

"Don't reckon so. They're not flying the Granville standard."

Rufus examined the troop of horsemen moving across the barren landscape some five miles distant. "Looks like Leven's standard," he said. "Cavalry—fifteen or twenty of 'em. Wonder where they're going?"

"We going to stop 'em getting wherever that is?" Will was grinning ear to ear as he asked what was clearly a rhetorical question.

Rufus lowered the spyglass. "Well, now," he teased. "I'm not sure about that."

Will's grin widened. "How many of us?"

"Thirty. Pikes and muskets. Breastplates and gauntlets, but tell 'em to keep their cloaks tight. We'll keep our warlike aspect hidden until we're upon them."

"Right. Shall I sound the call to arms?"

"By all means." Rufus turned and seemed to see Portia for the first time. "Don't get in the way," he commanded, as crisply authoritative as if that moment on the path had never taken place. Then he set off down the hill, without undue haste this time, while behind him the trumpet shrilled two notes that sent another shiver of excitement down Portia's spine.

Portia followed, keeping back so as not to draw attention to herself, and if Rufus was aware she was following him he gave no sign. He strode through the village where men were crowding the lane, strapping on breastplates, shouldering muskets, as they hurried to muster on the bank of the river.

Will appeared as if from nowhere, moving among the men, sending some of them back to work, ordering the others to form a group beneath a bare willow tree.

Rufus walked up to the group of thirty men, and their excited chatter died down. They regarded him expectantly. Portia hung back, fascinated.

"Who's for a foray against Leven's men?" Rufus inquired genially, standing feet apart, hands resting on his hips. His eyes were electric and Portia could feel the energy pulsing from him in waves that drew the men toward him even as they yelled an exuberant affirmative.

"We'll prick his tail a little," Rufus said. "We'll take the Morebattle track and circle them, meeting them head-on this side of Yetholm. Any questions?"

"We takin' prisoners, m'lord?"

"All prisoners will be escorted to royalist headquarters at Newcastle," Rufus stated crisply. "Anything else?"

There were headshakes in response. "Right, gentlemen, let's get moving."

The men broke up, heading for the stables at a run, barely hampered by their armor and weapons. Rufus turned and saw Portia, who was half hiding behind another willow tree. He beckoned her across and there was no sign now of the man who had kissed her with such passion such a short time ago.

"You'll stay here. You know where the mess is; they'll feed you there. You have the use of my cottage." He caught her chin on a gloved hand and said with unmistakable menace, "If you cause any trouble while I'm gone, Mistress Worth, I promise you will regret it. Do I make myself clear?"

"As crystal," Portia said, refusing to lower her eyes.

He still held her chin in silence for a minute, then he released her and strode home. Portia kept pace with him.

In the cottage she stood leaning against the door, watching as he lifted a massive sword, sheathed in leather, from a hook on the far wall. He buckled it to his thick swordbelt, and strapped on a steel breastplate over his buff jerkin. He ran a gloved finger over the blade of a wickedly curved dagger before sheathing it, then slung his cloak over his shoulders, clasping it at the neck.

"Remember what I've said." He gave her a short nod, then moved her aside and left, taking some current of energy with him, leaving the kitchen feeling deserted and lifeless.

Portia huddled deeper into her cloak, gazing sightlessly at the glowing coals in the hearth. With a sudden unplanned movement, she drew the hood up to cover her blazing hair. She left the cottage, not sure exactly what she intended doing but infused with a sense of excitement and daring that seemed to propel her along a path of its own choosing.

10

The stable yard on the surface was a scene of chaos. Men and horses milled, grooms raced to and from the tack room with equipment, while others were scurrying around filling saddlebags with provisions from the mess. Rufus stood head and shoulders above the throng, holding Ajax's bridle and issuing orders to Will, who stood beside him.

It was clear to Portia after a minute's observation that beneath the apparent chaos was a steady, well-ordered process with which everyone was thoroughly familiar. No one had time to notice her, and even if they did they would see only an unremarkable figure in britches and frieze cloak who could be any one of the young men rushing around the yard.

She slipped into the stable, knowing exactly which horse she was looking for. A dainty mare called Penny, who had caught her eye on her earlier visit to the stables during her tour with Rufus. The horse was still in her stall at the far end of the stable block, saddle and bridle hanging conveniently on the crossbar at the rear of the stall, and it was a matter of minutes to saddle her in the deserted building.

Casually, with what she hoped was an air of authority and familiarity, Portia led the mare out of the stable and into the yard. Men were mounted now and the horses stamped and blew, sensing the excitement.

Portia swung herself up onto Penny and unobtrusively edged the mare into the group of mounted men. Rufus mounted the magnificent Ajax, cast a glance over his troop of men, then raised his hand and gestured forward. The young men who had been left behind looked enviously at their luckier fellows as the chosen group clattered out of the yard and turned along the riverbank.

Toby and Luke tumbled into the lane as the cavalcade approached. They clambered onto a gate shouting, "Papa . . . Papa!" at the tops of their voices.

Rufus drew rein and leaned down to scoop them off the gate, setting them on his saddle in front of him. It was a position they were used to, but one that awed them. Their ecstatic shrieks were abruptly cut off. They gazed around wide-eyed in mingled terror and pride as Ajax climbed the hill at the head of the troop of horse.

At the top of the hill, Rufus lifted his sons down into the waiting arms of the watchman. "Send them back when we've gone."

"Aye, m'lord." The man grinned, settling a child on each hip. "Good luck, sir."

They passed through the sentry post and trotted across the hillside, no one as yet aware that Lord Rothbury's little troop contained not thirty but thirty-one members.

Portia realized with a startled jolt that she had succeeded in escaping Decatur village. She had acted without conscious motivation, not really believing that she would pull it off. But here she was, lost in this knot of men, unnoticed by their commander, and presumably a moment would come when she could lag behind, slide into a clump of trees, vanish from sight. She'd be free and clear, despite Rufus Decatur's complacent lectures on the security of his stronghold.

She couldn't help grinning, and then her grin faded as she wondered how Cato would receive her return. Surely he'd be interested in her information? Diana, of course, had probably been singing good riddance since Portia's abrupt disappearance, but Olivia, at least, would be pleased to see her.

The men around her rode in silence, and only the clink of a bridle, the jingle of a spur, competed with the plaintive calls of a plover or the sudden joyous heartpouring of a blackbird.

It was too soon to make her bid for freedom, the countryside too open and still too close to the hilltop watchmen. She managed to remain inconspicuous by casually changing position. There seemed no particular order to the procession, men rode singly or in twos and threes, and Portia moved Penny around the little knots of riders, never in one position long enough to draw attention to herself. However, she kept well back from the head of the cavalcade, where Rufus Decatur rode with Will.

They soon left the open countryside and turned into a narrow, rocky defile that threaded between two folds of hills. The craggy sides rose high, almost meeting overhead at some points. There was never more than a thin sliver of blue sky, and the air was cold and dank, the continual drip of moisture down the rock face adding to the gnarled pendant shafts of ice.

They rode in single file now and in complete silence. It was as if the brooding quality of their surroundings had infused their spirits, and there was no sign of the earlier exhilaration. Penny picked her way delicately between a raw-boned gray gelding and a handsome black mare. She seemed perfectly comfortable, as if she'd taken part in many such expeditions in the past, but her position sandwiched between two other horses precluded Portia's escape from the narrow pass. She'd just have to bide her time until the bottleneck opened.

The cavalcade was still within the defile when Rufus drew rein and signaled a halt. Portia couldn't see what was happening at first, then she noticed one of the men scrambling up the rock face, as nimbly as if he was on a ladder. At the top, he clambered over on his belly and slithered away.

"They should be gettin' close b'now," the man in front murmured to Portia, turning in his saddle to address her as he drew out a packet of provisions from his saddlebags. "The master 'as a right gift fer estimatin'."

Rufus must have based his calculations on how fast Leven's men were moving. But how could he have known that from such a distance with only a spyglass to help him?

Despite the grimness of their surroundings, the men were all now unwrapping provisions, obviously stoking themselves for the battle to come—a prospect that didn't seem to affect their appetites any. Portia was ravenous, but there was nothing she could do except sniff hungrily and pretend indifference.

The man came scrambling back down the cliff and raced to where Rufus was calmly eating bread and cheese atop Ajax. They had a hasty whispered colloquy and then the word came down the line. "They're approaching the mouth. Get in position."

Provisions were put away, muskets came out. The men rode forward to a point where the defile opened out like the mouth of an estuary onto a patch of open ground surrounded by leafless trees and moss-covered boulders as big as small knolls. It was a natural enclosure and the perfect site for an ambush.

The Decatur men were forming rows of five, one line behind the other, holding to the shadows of the hidden pass. Portia couldn't see how she could fail to be discovered if she stayed around. There was no place for number thirty-one in the five-man rows. But now was her chance for escape. She edged Penny backward down the defile. If no one looked behind, she would be able to back around a corner and retrace the path to the open hillside with no one any the wiser. From there she would find her way back to Castle Granville somehow.

Miraculously, no one looked over a shoulder; no one seemed aware of the lone horseman backing away. Once around the corner, Portia turned Penny in the constricted space. Behind her she could hear nothing, not even the shuffle of hooves or a soft whicker, but she could feel the tension like a tight band around her chest as the little troop of Decatur men waited to pit their lives and skills against the enemy.

Suddenly Portia knew that she couldn't ride away from the approaching action. She had to see what happened. She told herself she could easily leave afterward. In the post-engagement chaos she could be out of there and safely on her way without fear of detection. She dismounted, tied Penny to a spur of rock, and clambered up the cliff face. The Decatur man had made it appear easy, and there were hand- and footholds in the crevices, but it was still an arduous climb and she hauled herself onto the top of the cliff panting for breath.

Lying on her belly on the cold ground, she found she had a perfect view of the ambush point. When Lord Leven's patrol trotted through the bare trees, her heart skipped and jumped like a grasshopper.

The attack when it came was so swift and silent that Lord Leven's men were surrounded before they realized it. The Decatur troop rode from the defile, row after row of them, fanning out around the square until they had their quarry encircled. To the watcher above, there seemed to be a moment when it was inevitable that the Scots would lay down their arms without a fight, but then a roaring skirl of sound emerged into the strange flat silence and Leven's men rose in their stirrups with a shout of defiance.

Portia had not at first noticed the piper, but now as the bagpipes blared their martial call, Leven's Scotsmen hurled themselves into battle. Muskets cracked, swords clashed, and above it all the great sound rose ever louder, ever more defiant, ever more urgent.

Portia shivered. The pipes always made her shiver. She loved the sound, she loved to dance to it. It filled her with a wild exuberance when she was aware of nothing but the thrill of her blood in her ears, racing in her veins. It was elemental and savage and she responded to it as if it were a deep and essential part of herself.

It was all she could do to stop herself from leaping to her feet to join the fray. But how could she join the fray when she didn't know which side she was on? And yet she found herself drawing her knife from her boot. Her physical being was operating now without any conscious rational intervention from her brain. She inched forward on her belly until she was lying on a slab of rock directly over the battlefield.

Leven's men were outnumbered and they'd been taken by surprise. But they fought like demons. And the fighting was soon hand to hand. Muskets were useless in these conditions once they'd been fired. There was no time for the cumbersome process of reloading when a man was pressed on all sides. Swords and daggers flashed; a horse screamed and went down on one knee, throwing his rider.

Portia saw Will on the ground. He was on his feet in a trice, sword in hand, as his horse staggered upright, bleeding from a gash in the neck. One of Leven's men turned and rode down upon the unhorsed man. His horse reared, hooves flailing, as he leaned down, swiping his sword in a great arc at the disadvantaged Will.

Portia hurled her knife. Only when it lodged in the sword arm of Will's attacker, arresting the deadly sweep of his sword, did she realize that she'd chosen her side. Her aim had been instinctive and utterly true. Will had time to duck and grab for his injured horse. He scrambled into the saddle just as Rufus, appearing from nowhere, brought his own sword down hard on the enemy's, disarming him with an almighty clash of steel on steel that made the man scream as his already wounded arm was jarred unmercifully.

Only then did Rufus glance upward, his eyes searching for the origin of the knife that had saved Will. Portia still lay on her rock. She knew she was now in full view; she knew that a minute earlier she could have wriggled out of sight and been safe from detection. The knife would have remained a puzzle until the engagement was over. Then Rufus would probably have recognized the knife as Portia's. But by then it would have been too late. She would have been long gone.

And yet she didn't move. His roaming eyes found her, his bright gaze locked with hers, then he wheeled his horse and returned to the fray. Portia, now weaponless, looked around for something with which to contribute her mite. There were rocks and stones aplenty. A catapult or sling would have been ideal, but lacking either, she'd have to make do with manpower. She began a steady bombardment of Leven's troops.

Her aim was mostly accurate and the rain of stones and rocks began to take a toll, men trying to dodge the missiles that seemed to come from nowhere, their concentration constantly disturbed, leaving them open to the more deadly assaults of the Decatur men. And above it all, the pipes continued to skirl.

It was over within fifteen minutes, although to Portia time seemed to be standing still, the scene below her acting itself out in a constant repetition of noise and violence. But Leven's men were outnumbered, disarmed, unhorsed in a steady attrition until only their colonel and two of his men still sat their horses, swords still in hand.

The colonel glanced around, then slowly raised a hand to the piper, who immediately began to play the retreat. The colonel turned his sword hilt forward and offered it to Rufus.

Rufus shook his head. "Nay, man, keep it, if you'll give me your parole. That was well fought."

"Colonel Neath of Lord Leven's Third Battalion gives his parole and that of his company," the man intoned formally, but with a slight question in his tone as he examined his captor for identification of rank if not company.

"Decatur, Lord Rothbury, at your service, sir." Rufus bowed from his saddle, a slightly malicious glint in the blue eyes.

"Rothbury, eh?" Neath looked surprised as he sheathed his sword. "Your name is well known across the border, my lord."

"And reviled, I daresay," Rufus said with the same glint.

"Y'are known as a moss-trooper, an outlaw, certainly," the colonel said in his soft drawl. "But 'tis said most of your unlawful activities have to do with the marquis of Granville and his property. There are those who say you have good reason to prey upon him."

Rufus's smile was ironic. "I'm grateful for the popular understanding, Colonel. But, in my present guise, I fly the standard for Prince Rupert on behalf of his most sovereign majesty, King Charles. We'll be escorting you and your men to Newcastle, once we've tended to the wounded."

"You'll give me permission to talk with my men?"

"I have no objection." Rufus gestured to where his own men were disarming the colonel's, and Neath with a formal salute turned and rode over to them.

Rufus looked up to where Portia still lay on her belly overlooking the battlefield. She met his gaze with an air both rueful and puzzled. Slowly he sheathed his own sword, then rode over and drew rein immediately beneath her.

"So where did you spring from, gosling?" he inquired pleasantly, his gloved hands resting on the pommel of his saddle.

Portia sat up on the rock, letting her legs dangle over the side of the cliff. "I was with you all along," she said. "Right from the stable yard."

"I see." He nodded. "And why didn't you make good your escape?"

"I couldn't until the engagement began, and then I wanted to see what happened."

He nodded again. "That seems reasonable. What doesn't seem reasonable is why you would then announce your presence in such dramatic fashion."

"I'd have thought you'd be grateful."

"Oh, believe me, gosling, I am. And I'm sure Will is even more so. But . . . uh . . . forgive my confusion." A bushy red eyebrow lifted. "Just why would you weigh in on *my* side?"

"I really don't know," Portia said in a tone of such disgust and bewilderment that Rufus couldn't help a crack of laughter.

He held up a hand. "Come down now . . . easily so you don't startle Ajax."

Portia took the hand and slid down from the rock until she was sitting on the saddle facing him. He was very close and she could smell the earthiness of his skin, the tang of sweat, the leather of his buff coat. She could see the tracery of laugh lines around his eyes and in the corners of his mouth, and the pale frown furrows on his forehead against the weathered complexion.

"I presume you have a horse somewhere?" Strong white teeth flashed from within the red-gold beard.

"I borrowed Penny."

"Borrowed?" His eyes lifted again. "You truly intended only to borrow her?"

"No," she stated flatly. "I intended to steal her. And why I didn't is as much a puzzle to me as it is to you."

Rufus appeared to consider. Then he said, "Well, I'm glad you didn't, since theft is not something we tolerate, as I attempted to make clear last night in the matter of Bertram's sledge. Where is the mare?"

"In the defile. And, Lord Rothbury, I think a lecture on the moral principles of a band of outlaws is out of place," Portia retorted in an effort to take her mind off its overwhelming awareness of his body, so large and powerful, and so very close.

Rufus made no response. He lifted her bodily from the saddle, clearly finding her weight no more than a kitten's, and leaned down to deposit her on the ground. "Fetch Penny." He turned Ajax and rode over to where both sides in the battle were assessing the wounded.

Portia fetched the mare and rode her out of the defile. She dismounted again and hurried over to Rufus, who was talking with Colonel Neath as amiably as if they hadn't just fought a pitched battle.

"There's a house of somewhat doubtful repute in Yetholm," Rufus was saying. "But there's nothing to complain of in the hospitality. We'll stop there and tend to the wounded before continuing to Newcastle. That man of yours looks as if he's broken his leg, but we can get a bonesetter in Yetholm for him. Ah, Will . . . what's the damage?"

Will was staring at Portia. "What's *she* doing here?"

"Making herself remarkably useful," Rufus said dryly. "You owe her a debt of gratitude as it happens. Mistress Worth has an assassin's way with a knife."

Will's stare grew wider, and Portia, unable to resist, opened her own eyes as wide as they could go in mimicry. Will's expression snapped back into focus. "That was your knife?"

"Yes, and I'd like it back," she said. "Did the man manage to take it out of his arm?"

"We thought it best to leave it in . . . until he can see a surgeon." Will gave up the puzzle of Rufus's hostage. There were too many practical issues to occupy his mind. "He might bleed to death if we pull it loose here."

"Perhaps we can fashion a tourniquet. I'll go and find him," she said.

Will looked inquiringly at his cousin, who merely repeated his first question with visible patience, "How much damage, Will?"

"Oh . . . apart from the colonel's man with a broken leg and the man with the knife in his arm, it's not too bad. Ned's lost a fingertip. He's looking for it now. He's convinced it can be sewn back on again."

"Ned always did have strange notions," Rufus said. "Let's fashion a litter for the broken leg, put everyone else back on their horses, and we'll head for Yetholm."

Rufus went over to Portia, who was bending over the man who had taken her knife in the arm. "Are you skilled in battlefield surgery?"

"I had to patch Jack up on more than one occasion when he'd been in a brawl and we couldn't afford a surgeon," she returned. "Injuries worse than this, too." She had used her own kerchief as a tourniquet when she'd pulled free the knife and was now fashioning a sling from a checkered napkin that she'd liberated from Ajax's saddlebags. "You'd finished your provisions, so I thought you wouldn't mind lending this."

"Not at all. Anything I have that can be of service," he said amiably. "Did I detect a slight note of envy on the subject of food?"

"Yes, you did. No one thought to put up provisions for me too."

"I daresay it was because the cooks didn't realize you were coming with us," Rufus observed. With a tiny chuckle, he strolled away.

They didn't reach Yetholm until after sunset. By then a hard frost was forming and the horses were quivering and stamping, and the injured man in the litter could no longer control the moans that emerged from his violently chattering teeth.

Portia, riding in the rear of the column, felt colder than she'd ever been, although rational memory told her that wasn't so. But hunger gnawed at her backbone and she could not stop shivering. So locked in misery was she that she didn't at first notice when Ajax surged up out of the shadows. Rufus's voice, sharp with concern, brought her head up with a start.

"Come here . . . take your feet out of the stirrups." He leaned over and swung her out of the saddle and onto Ajax. He pulled off his own cloak and wrapped it around her, then drew her against him. The breastplate was hard at her back, but even so she could feel his body warmth. "Will, take Penny's rein."

Portia hadn't noticed that Will had accompanied Rufus. The younger man took Penny's rein immediately and followed Rufus as he returned to the head of the column.

"How did you know I was so cold?" Her teeth chattered unmercifully.

"An informed guess," he responded wryly, conscious of how the bitter wind was cutting through his leather jerkin now that he no longer had the protection of his cloak.

The village of Yetholm straddled the cart track, and on its outskirts stood a two-storied thatched building. Light spilled from its parchment-covered, unshuttered windows, and smoke curled thickly from two chimneys. Raucous laughter and shouts of a generally genial nature found their way out into the night through the cracks in door and window frames.

"Thank God!" Rufus muttered, nudging Ajax to quicken his pace at the sight of sanctuary.

"Aye, I doubt that poor fellow would survive much more of this," Colonel Neath said, riding beside him. " 'Tis the kind of cold that's no' fit for man nor beast." He cast a curious glance at the tightly wrapped figure huddling close against Lord Rothbury's chest. Soldiers didn't ordinarily cuddle up to their commanders.

If Rufus noticed the look, he offered no explanation, observing merely, "It's too cold to snow though . . . for which we might be thankful come morning." He drew rein before the door that opened directly onto the track.

Will had jumped from his horse, but before he could reach the door it was flung open with a wide expansive gesture.

"Well, well, and who have we here on such a night?" a light voice called merrily. A woman held a lantern high above her head. "Eh, if it's not Rufus. It's been too long since you graced my door, Decatur."

"I know it, Fanny. I've wounded here. Will you send for the bonesetter?" Rufus swung Portia to the ground and then dismounted behind her. He turned to Will, issuing rapid-fire instructions as to the disposition of their own men and their prisoners.

"He's naught but a horse doctor, but I daresay he's better than nothing," Fanny observed, her shrewdly assessing eye taking in the large party with a degree of calculation. "You been scrappin', Rufus, or on the king's business?"

"The latter," Rufus said. He gestured to Neath, who had dismounted and stood quietly by his horse. "May I present Colonel Neath. He and his men are prisoners en route to Newcastle, but we're all in need of warmth, food, and wine."

Colonel Neath bowed. "We'll be grateful for any hospitality you can offer us, mistress, in the circumstances."

Fanny nodded. "We don't trouble ourselves too much with

politics in my house, sir. And it's a slow night, this night. No one's venturing far from home in this cold, so you're all right welcome. Come you in. It'll be a squeeze, but it'll be all the cozier for that."

"Get inside, Portia. Someone'll see to Penny." Rufus urged her toward the door and Portia scuttled in, guiltily aware that she was not going to object to someone doing her dirty work for her.

She found herself in one large room furnished with long tables and benches, two massive fires burning at either end. Women and a few men lounged at the tables among pitchers of ale and flagons of wine. A staircase led up to a gallery that ran the width of the main room. Lamps hung from the rafters and tallow candles burned on the tables. The air was thick with wood smoke and the acrid smell of tallow and oil over-laying spilled wine, stale beer, and roasting meat. But more than anything it was warm.

Portia threw off Rufus's cloak and then the frieze one be-neath. Her hair blazed orange in the lamplight.

"Lord above, 'tis a lass in britches!" Fanny exclaimed. "Is she prisoner or doxy, Rufus?"

"Neither," Rufus replied, taking his cloak back. "Give her a cup of wine, Fanny, she's half dead with cold." He spun back to the door. "I'll be back in a minute. Neath, let's get that man of yours off the litter."

The two men went back outside and Portia found herself the object of a calculating examination from Fanny and the other women in the hall.

"Well, get to the fire, lass. Y'are white as a ghost . . . never seen anything like it." Fanny gave her a push. "Lucy, give her a cup of that burgundy. It'll put color in her cheeks."

"I doubt that," Portia said. She took the wine with a grate-ful smile. She felt oddly at home and a wave of nostalgia hit her with the first sip of wine. She could almost hear Jack's voice, rising with the drink, as he toyed with some deep-bosomed harlot and every now and again remembered to di-lute his young daughter's wine with water as she sat beside him, gazing at the scene with sleepy indifference. Portia had spent many a night in establishments like this one, huddled before the fire or curled under a table while Jack amused himself. She'd been befriended by more than one of Mistress Fanny's profession and had resisted a good few offers in the last couple of years to join their girls, who, compared to Portia's condition, were more often than not enviably well dressed, well fed, and comfortable.

"Scrawny thing, aren't you?" Fanny observed. "Y'are not kin to the Decaturs?"

"No." Portia drank her wine. Her frozen toes and fingers were thawing, and she grimaced with the pain as the circulation returned to their numb tips.

Any further questions remained unasked as the door burst open and Rufus and Neath came in carrying the litter. Behind them men poured in, some supporting the walking wounded, others exclaiming in vivid language at the contrast between the freezing conditions without and the warmth within.

Portia was struck by the easiness they all seemed to feel with each other—a camaraderie that transcended political differences. They all came from the same sphere of society. Civil war had torn them all from the farms and workshops of ordinary life, and on the long ride they had battled the miseries of midwinter campaigning together. Tomorrow they would separate again into prisoners and captors, but for now they were just men grateful to find themselves out of the deadly cold. They took up wine and ale, eyes lighting up at the sight of the women who moved forward eagerly.

"Eh, Doug, ye've need of this to wet your whistle after all that playing!" One of Neath's men thrust a foaming tankard into the piper's ready hand. " 'Twas a brave sound you made, man."

"Aye," the piper said complacently, once he'd downed his ale. "An' there's more where that came from when I've had a bite. I'm fair clemmed."

"You're not the only one," Portia muttered.

"Girls, to the kitchen!" Fanny snapped her fingers. "They'll be no good to you wi'out food in their bellies."

Laughing and chattering, the women surged toward the doors at the rear of the hall just as the bonesetter entered, bringing the icy blasts with him. The injured man on the litter was plied with brandy until his teeth ceased chattering and his moans grew faint while the bone was set. The horse doctor bandaged a sprained wrist, examined Portia's tourniquet and pronounced it sufficient until the man could get to a surgeon in Newcastle . . . so long as the wound didn't mortify, and then he settled before the fire with a cup of wine in his hand, prepared to enjoy his evening.

Portia fell on roast goose, roast potatoes, baked apples. Food hadn't tasted this good since she'd fetched up at Castle Granville. It wasn't that the fare at Cato's table was poor, but the atmosphere at the table was so tense under Diana's harsh and critical stare that one couldn't enjoy a mouthful. The misery of mealtimes explained poor little Olivia's frequent bellyaches, Portia was convinced.

But now she ate with single-minded concentration and wholehearted enjoyment, not looking up from the platter except to take deep draughts of wine. She was unaware that Rufus, sitting opposite at the long board, was watching her.

Rufus himself was unaware that he was watching her. Will noticed it, though, and Fanny, whose sharp eyes and alert brain missed nothing that went on under her roof, was most curious. The look in his eye was one she hadn't seen before. It was almost startled.

"Music, piper!" someone bellowed as the platters were pushed aside and flagons refilled. " 'Tis time for a dance."

Doug got to his feet with an obliging grin. "Och, just keep m' tankard filled an' I'll play all night." He adjusted the strap across his shoulder and launched without further ado into "The Gay Gordons." With cries of delight, couples leaped forward to form the procession of dancers.

The music pulled Portia to her feet like the strings of a marionette. She needed a partner and her eye fell on Will, whose foot was tapping. She seized his hand and whirled him into the dance. He was surprised, but then the music caught him and he was twirling and prancing with the rest of them.

Rufus swung his legs over the bench and leaned back against the table, his tankard held loosely between his hands. She was like a candle, he thought, that long, lean body surmounted by that impossibly orange flare. But she could dance. The piper swung into an eightsome reel and she and Will flung themselves into one of the eights.

Rufus began to feel left out. He considered himself a respectable dancer and, like all inhabitants of the borderlands, could dance a Scottish reel with the best of them. He set down his tankard and entered the eightsome, nudging Will aside. His cousin shot him a startled look, then backed out with an accepting grin.

Portia was in the circle, dancing to her partner. For a few steps they danced opposite each other, then Rufus joined her in the circle, clasping her elbow as she clasped his and twirling with her to the stamping, clapping accompaniment of their fellow dancers.

It was hot and the music grew ever wilder. Portia was indefatigable, her hair clinging damply to her forehead. She cast aside her jerkin in one whirling movement, and Rufus did the same. Not once did she miss a step, even when the piper launched into some of the more obscure reels with their sometimes complicated maneuvers, and it was only when Doug, momentarily exhausted, played a final skirling note, red faced and desperate for ale, that she stopped and collapsed onto a bench, laughing.

Rufus wiped the sweat from his face and flung himself down beside her. "God in heaven, but the music's in you, gosling."

"It was the same for Jack," she said, gasping for breath. "He could outdance anyone. And I do love the pipes."

"An acquired taste, some would say," he commented, taking up his tankard.

"Then I acquired it at birth." She pushed her hair off her forehead and wiped the sweat from her face with the back of her arm. "We haven't really stopped dancing, have we?"

"I doubt it." He reached over and dabbed with his fingertip at a drop of moisture on her nose, observing after a second, "Oh, I think it's only a freckle." But he didn't move his finger. Her slanted eyes, fixed upon his face, were like green fire.

Portia's breath seemed suspended. She couldn't move her eyes from his. She could almost hear her blood coursing through her veins, every sense seemed intensified, and yet she was aware only of the small space that contained the two of them. The world seemed to have shrunk to this taut circle, the noisy crowd around them no more substantial than dream images. Something very strange was happening and once again she felt the disorienting sensation of not being in control of her responses, that those responses were being somehow brought forth from deep inside her by the man whose gaze held her own.

And then the moment was shattered as platters and crockery were suddenly swept off one of the tables with an almighty crash. Rufus's finger dropped from her nose and at last his eyes released hers.

Three men were dragging the table into the middle of the hall. "Come on, ladies. How about a dance to choose your customers?" a massive black-haired man bellowed, as he took up the role of master of ceremonies. "Doug, you play from the gallery. Ladies, take your places on the table. Gentlemen, pick your partner, and if she can outdance you, she demands her own price. If you outlast her, she's yours for the night, no charge. Anyone who falls off the table loses. How about it?"

A surge of laughter greeted the suggestion. The women leaped onto the table, executing a few steps of a reel in invitation. Men jumped forward, pointing and shouting as they picked their partner. Under orders from the master of ceremonies, each woman jumped down to stand with the man who had chosen her, and then one couple took the table.

Doug launched into a caber dance. The man was not as surefooted as his woman, but he did his best, prancing and twirling, flinging his arms wide, while the spectators clapped the rhythm and cheered. The man took a step back, his foot slipped off the edge of the table, and he fell backward, just managing to land on his feet on the floor.

The cheers reached the rafters as the woman jumped down into his waiting arms and whispered something in his ear. He grimaced good-naturedly but nodded, then carried her away up the stairs to the gallery.

Couple after couple danced and the music grew ever faster. Portia was laughing and clapping with the rest, but her blood was pounding in her veins and her excitement was all consuming. It spilled over from that fantastical, intense moment, seemed bound up with it, but all she knew for certain was that she wanted to dance. She needed to dance. Her skin was on fire, whether with wine, excitement, or the wild swirl of the dance she didn't know and couldn't care. With a sudden cry of jubilation, she leaped onto the table as a couple jumped off it together. The piper hurled himself into the fastest, wildest tune he had, and she kept up with him, a whirling dervish on the broad table, hair flying, eyes blazing, her body a blur as she and the piper now engaged in a battle of endurance.

She came closer and closer to the edge of the table where Rufus stood, caught up with the rest in the frenzied magic of her dance. Without faltering, she leaned forward, hands extended toward him, then danced back, beckoning. The crowd roared and stamped. Rufus leaped onto the table. Portia tossed her head, hands on her hips as she danced, and she offered him a smile of such challenge and invitation that no man could resist.

He joined her, his feet flying, as he caught her up and tossed her into the air, sending her twisting away from him down the table, then catching her back again. She was laughing now, but with a strange wild intensity as she matched him, trying to second-guess his movements.

The stamping, shrieking audience was almost drowning out the piper. Rufus suddenly leaped backward off the table, then reached up and caught her around the waist. He held her high above his head as if he were about to toss the caber, then adjusted his hands and slung her around his neck like a shawl.

He picked up a candelabra in one hand, a flagon of wine in the other, and made for the stairs. Portia, still lost in the blood-heating power of the dance frenzy, was barely aware that Rufus was carrying her, his prize, up the wooden stairs to the gallery to the stamps and shouts of approval and a final ululating note of the pipes.

Rufus knew where he was going. He always used the same chamber in Fanny's house. Taking the flagon between his teeth, he flung open the door to a chamber at the very end of the gallery, stepped inside, and kicked it shut.

He set the candelabra on the mantel, the flagon on a small round table, and with a flourish unwound his trophy, setting her on her feet.

"I won," Portia said breathlessly, pushing her hair out of her eyes.

"A moot point," Rufus said, catching her chin on the palm of his hand. He kissed her mouth, his lips hard and yet pliant, his beard silky against her skin. It was as it had been that morning, and yet there was an added dimension . . . a sense of absolute inevitability, of destiny. Portia kissed him back with a fervor that matched the beat of her blood. The music, the shouts, the exultant cries came up from below so that she could feel the rhythm and the passion in the soles of her feet.

She was aware of nothing now except the thrilling of her blood, the scent of his skin, the feel of his mouth against hers, the taste of wine on his tongue and hers. His hands ran down her body and she rose on tiptoe, her arms sliding around his neck as she leaned into the caress.

Rufus laughed softly against her mouth. He moved one hand up to palm her scalp, holding her head steadily as with his free hand he pulled his shirt out of his britches, roughly tugged at the buttons, dragged it out of his waistband and shrugged it off his shoulders. All the while he held her mouth captive with his, and Portia's hands ran up his back, kneaded his shoulders with hungry intensity.

He stepped back from her to kick off his boots, and she followed him, laughing, her mouth swooping and darting against his. And he laughed back, grabbing the back of her neck, pulling her face to his. His tongue plunged and plundered, raiding the soft, sweet corners of her mouth, and she opened her mouth to him, drawing his tongue deep within, refusing to let him go even as he pushed his britches off his hips and had to dance on one foot and then the other to kick them off.

Then his fingers were working the buttons of her shirt, his hands sliding inside, running over her breasts, down over her rib cage, then up to her shoulders beneath the shirt, easing the garment off and away from her. Her breasts pressed against his chest, and her nipples ached and tingled with a new and wonderful sensation. She leaned back as he unbuckled and unlooped her belt. It fell to the ground. Her britches and drawers slid over her narrow hips in one movement, and her skin jumped beneath his brushing hands.

A light touch sent her tumbling back onto the bed, the britches tangled around her knees, caught on her boots. Rufus lifted her legs high as he pulled off the boots, tossing them over his shoulder to thump against the andirons. Her stockings, drawers, and britches were dismissed in the same swift, cavalier fashion, and only then did Portia realize on some far-off periphery of consciousness what was happening.

It was a fleeting realization. It contained the knowledge that if she wanted this to stop, she had only to speak. It contained the knowledge that she had issued this invitation and that the man who was about to take her virginity had no way of knowing he was about to do so.

And then it was gone. His flat palms moved up her legs, from her ankles to her thighs, spreading them gently, stroking the silky inner skin. Her core, the most secret places of her body, pulsed, open, vulnerable, aching with a need that she couldn't form. She looked up into eyes as clear and as bright as a summer sky. They held a soul in their depths. A questioning that was both tender and demanding. And she knew, although she knew nothing of this business, that he wanted to see her response to his body, to feel it within him.

She touched him instinctively, felt his flesh leap against her palm, then he was pressing against the cleft of her body, pressing ever more deeply. She read the flash of surprise at the innate resistance of her untouched body, then she saw comprehension leap into his eyes, but before he could react, she gripped his buttocks urgently, pulling him into her. With a little sigh, he thrust deep and she was aware only of a miraculous opening, of a fullness, a pressure that filled her to the depths of her being.

Then, just as she began to feel the very beginning of some glorious cataclysm of sensation, he withdrew from her body. He fell heavily on top of her, his breathing harsh and ragged, his skin slick against her own dampness, and Portia was left with a curious and aching sense of a void that should have been filled, but was instead gaping and empty.

Rufus slowly rose onto one elbow. He looked down at her as she lay sprawled on the coverlet, her eyes questioning, the hurt of her emptiness as easy to read as a child's picture book.

"Why didn't you tell me?" His voice was quiet and flat.

"It didn't matter. It wasn't relevant," Portia said, her voice low as she struggled with a disappointment that seemed to penetrate to the very heart of her being. She wanted to weep with the anticlimax, with the familiar and this time overwhelming sense that she would always disappoint in the same degree that she would always be disappointed.

"Are you angry?" The question was thin, bloodless.

"If I were, you wouldn't need to ask the question," he replied aridly.

"It didn't matter," she repeated, wretchedly aware that her voice was thick with tears.

"Believe me, Portia, it mattered." Rufus fell onto his back, one hand resting on her belly as if it had been forgotten there. "I do not make a habit of deflowering virgins. And if I did, I would . . ." He sighed. "How was I to know?"

"You weren't." It was only natural that in the face of her blatant invitation he would have assumed that she was experienced in the sexual world. He knew how she'd lived. He knew her parentage.

She swallowed the lump of tears in her throat and surreptitiously turned her head aside to wipe her eyes on a corner of the coverlet.

Rufus sat up again. "Had I known," he said deliberately, "I would have done things a little differently."

"How?" Portia was suddenly intrigued despite her wretchedness. "I thought there was only one way."

"There is," he said, leaning over her and drawing a finger down between the small, pale mounds of her breasts. "But there are various refinements."

"Oh." She was aware of a quickening of her blood as his eyes held hers. She couldn't read his expression, didn't know what he was talking about, but a little thrill of anticipation nibbled at the edges of her unfulfillment.

"Tell me what you felt." He laid the palm of his hand over one breast, covering it completely.

Portia frowned, trying to find the words, to be utterly honest, even while her breast beneath his palm began to tingle and she could feel her nipple hardening. "That . . . that something should have happened that didn't."

He laughed softly. "I thought as much. Poor gosling." He lowered his head to her other breast, his lips trailing over its softness. He was overpoweringly aware as he had been once before of the incredible softness of her skin. It was like the most delicate tissue, impossibly white in the candlelight. His tongue flicked at the crest of her breast and she trembled.

He raised his head and saw the wonderment in her eyes. The wildness of the dance had gone, the frenzy that had brought them both to this place, and now he read only eagerness and the slow mounting of desire. He moved his hand down.

The hand on her bare belly, pressing as it stroked, made her gasp. She turned her head on the pillow, bewildered by the rush of sensation, the storming tumult of the blood in her veins. His hand flattened between her closed thighs, and her legs parted for him even as she drew breath on a little sob of anticipation. Her body cried out for the intimate knowing invasion of his fingers, and this time the tears in her eyes were of a confused pleasure.

He took her mouth again with his, even as the relentless trespass brought her ever closer to the pulsing joyous moment of annihilation that she had sensed before. The skin of her belly rippled, the muscles beneath growing rigid; her thighs tightened around his hand, her buttocks clenched hard with the impossible desire to postpone what she knew was coming and the hopeless need to lose herself in the inexorable joy.

And then when she could hold on no longer, he withdrew his hand. Her body screamed for completion. She cried out with the pain of loss, and then he slipped a hand beneath her bottom, holding the compact muscled roundness easily on one palm as he guided himself within the aching portal of her body. The moist, tender flesh closed around him, and he touched the corner of her mouth with his tongue, murmured a word of reassurance that she hardly needed.

He kissed her eyelids, the tip of her nose, one hand still supporting her bottom while his other caressed her breast. Her buttock muscles hardened in his hand and her nipple crested against his palm. Her skin was damp and hot, her lips parted on soft female sounds of joyous anticipation. He eased deeper within, listening to her body with his own. And when her eyes and her body told him she was ready, he increased his pace, driving deep to her core. Her hands gripped the corded muscles of his upper arms as he held himself above her, and with a cry she yielded herself to the maelstrom.

Rufus held her tight as the storm ravaged her, tossing her high before tumbling her down and down into the still waters of annihilation. He was in no hurry for his own climax this time and waited until her heavy eyelids swept up, showing him the green gaze, drowned in wonderment. She reached up and touched his mouth, then smiled. And he was astonished at how beautiful she looked in this moment of complete abandonment.

Leisurely he began to move again and her body stirred around him, little flutters like a sparrow's wing. She touched his mouth again, then moved her hand down to his belly, surprising him with the knowingness of her caress. His stomach muscles jumped beneath her touch, and with a soft moan of pleasure he withdrew from her body the instant before he too was lost to joy.

She clasped his head to her breast and held him. His body slumped heavily into the mattress and slowly his breathing steadied and they lay quietly, while the noise from below continued unabated, the crashes and yells sounding more abandoned than ever.

After a while Rufus opened his eyes and hitched himself onto an elbow. He traced the curve of Portia's high cheekbones and smiled lazily. "Better?"

"Wonderful," she said with a wicked little chuckle.

Rufus swung off the bed with a laugh and went to the table to fetch the flagon. He took a gulp and held it to Portia's lips. She drank thirstily, then fell back again against the pillows.

"I wonder if I've just broken the pact," she said with another smug chuckle.

"What pact?" Rufus found the throaty little sound as delightful as it was infectious.

"Olivia and Phoebe and I had a pact," she said with mock solemnity. "We even mingled our blood as we swore an oath never to be ordinary. I know that included not getting married, but I'm not sure whether it also included not losing one's virginity."

Rufus raised an eyebrow, a frown ridging his brow. "Who's Phoebe?"

"Diana's little sister. The three of us met up at Cato's wedding to Diana." Portia's smile now had a touch of acid to it as she remembered what had brought the three of them together. "We were all feeling out of place . . . unwanted. And for a few minutes one sunny afternoon, we connected. Three social disasters playing a childish game of fantasy."

In the last hours, Rufus had forgotten all about Cato Granville. He'd forgotten why this girl had come into his life and the question of what he was to do with her.

"What is it?" she asked quickly, seeing the darkness come into his eyes, the sudden set of his jaw.

He shook his head in brisk dismissal. "We've a long journey tomorrow. Let's try to sleep, if we can manage to drown out the racket."

A shadow had fallen across them, and Portia's exuberance died, leaving a cold empty space in the pit of her stomach. She guessed that her careless remarks had reminded Rufus that she was a Granville. And now she too remembered it.

She was a Granville and she'd just betrayed her Granville heritage in Rufus Decatur's bed. Would Jack consider she'd betrayed him? Maybe not. He'd pursued pleasure himself without too much thought of principles and consequences.

But the shadow now would not be thrown off. What was to happen to her now? Had this changed anything? What did she *wish* to happen now?

"I'm not in the least sleepy," she said, jumping from the bed, hiding the chill of her reflections under the mantle of her previous exuberance. "And the piper's still playing. Let's go back down again." She bent to pick up her discarded britches and drawers.

Rufus hesitated. But in the chaos of noise and revelry below, he could postpone reality for a while longer. So he said only, "You're tireless," and began to dress.

It was close to dawn when silence fell over Fanny's house of doubtful repute. The hall was a disaster area—tables and benches overturned, drink spilled, dogs searching out bits of food among the debris, moving stealthily among the bodies that were sleeping where they'd fallen.

Rufus was among the last to succumb and he found Portia curled in the inglenook, finally defeated by sleep. He scooped her out of the embers and carried her upstairs, rolling her beneath the covers before collapsing beside her. Two hours was all he would allow any of them before they resumed the journey. But they were grown men and could take the consequences of their excesses.

Cato Granville *looked up from the pile of dispatches at* the tentative knock on the door to his bastion room. "Enter."

To his surprise, his daughter slid into the room. He couldn't remember when Olivia had last sought him out. With conscious effort, he smoothed away his frown.

Olivia curtsied and stood in silence for a minute. She was wearing a rather drab gown, Cato thought. The dull yellowish brown didn't suit her dark coloring. It made her look sallow. And then it occurred to him that he couldn't remember when he'd last seen his daughter in a dress that *did* suit her. He made a mental note to ask Diana to direct her stepdaughter to a more attractive wardrobe.

"I was wondering about P-*Portia*, sir." Olivia finally spoke. "When is she c-coming *back*?" Her black eyes had a painful intensity, and her hands were screwed tightly together against her drab skirt.

"The business is very complicated, child," Cato said dismissively. "I don't know what will happen."

"B-but it's not fair!" Olivia protested, her eyes intently focused on the inner landscape where she formed her words. "It was supposed to be *me*. Not P-*Portia*. You *owe* it to her to bring her *back*."

Cato was as displeased as he was astonished at such a challenge from his normally reticent daughter.

"This business does not concern you, Olivia," he said sharply. "And I do not appreciate your discourtesy. You may leave."

Olivia flushed. In silence she curtsied again and backed out of her father's sanctum. She stood leaning against the closed door, gathering herself together. That interview had required a great deal of courage, and it had achieved nothing except a show of her father's anger.

The clock in the bastion tower struck four, and she remembered with dull distaste that she was supposed to be attending Diana in the stillroom. Some jars of preserves had gone missing, and Diana was interrogating the stillroom maids. Her stepdaughter was supposed to be learning the arts and skills of household management.

She pushed herself away from the door and trailed grimly down the corridor toward the domestic part of the building. As she rounded the corner at the end of the passage, a voice said, "Well, if it isn't the little Olivia. My own little sister."

Olivia raised her eyes. Her stomach churned. Brian Morse, her father's stepson, barred her way. He'd come after all. And Portia was not here. She had promised to be here, and she wasn't.

Brian Morse was a slight man, with an elongated face, small brown eyes like pebbles, and a startling white lock of hair growing back from his narrow forehead.

Portia would not be afraid. "I am n-not your sister," Olivia managed in a voice that was almost steady.

"Oh s-s-such a f-f-fierce little th-thing, aren't we?" he mocked. He stretched out a hand and made to grab her shoulder.

She jumped back, her face white, her eyes great black holes of disgust and fear. "Don't t-*touch* me!"

He laughed with the same mockery. "You've changed your tune, little sister."

"*No!*" With a sudden movement, she ducked sideways and raced past him, for the first time in her life desperate for Diana's company.

Brian Morse watched her go, a smile on his thin lips. She was growing up, turning into quite the young woman. Tall for her age and with a nicely emerging bosom. Mind you, from that little encounter, she appeared to be still such a pathetic creature that it was barely worth the effort to tease her. He'd always liked a little challenge to his sport.

But then again . . . His smile grew. It might be very amusing to see how far he could push that emerging womanhood on this visit. Four years ago, as he recalled, it had been remarkably easy to drive her to near hysteria. Like taking cake from a baby.

He went on his way to Cato's sanctum, knocking briskly on the door and entering at the command.

Cato half rose from his chair when he saw his visitor. "Brian, I hadn't known whether to expect you or not, under the circumstances."

"There are many families torn apart in this war, my lord." Brian shook the extended hand. "I respect your decision even if I cannot accept it."

"Mmm." Cato gestured to a seat and resumed his own. Brian's sentiments were always appropriate, but glib.

"Oh, forgive me . . ." He remembered his duties as host and got up again. "Wine?" He poured from the flagon on the sideboard into two pewter goblets and handed one to his guest. "Your attendants are being looked after, I trust?"

"I came alone."

"Oh?" One mobile eyebrow lifted in surprise. "The countryside is not conducive to solitary travel these days."

"I'm on a private mission for Prince Rupert." Brian's smile was smug as he took the scent of his wine.

"Then you'd best keep it to yourself," Cato said shortly. "How long do you intend staying?"

Brian looked momentarily discomfited. "If my presence is unwelcome, I trust you would say so, my lord."

"As a supporter of the king's cause, your presence here is inconvenient," Cato said deliberately. "As a member of my family, of course, you are welcome to stay as long as you wish."

"My visit is of a purely social nature. I came to pay my long overdue respects to Lady Granville. I deeply regretted being unable to attend your wedding."

Cato sipped his wine and gave a noncommittal nod. He was aware, although Brian probably didn't know, that his stepson had been absent from the wedding because he had been detained in a debtors' prison in Paris.

"I bumped into Olivia just now," Brian continued. "Such a young woman she is now. Hardly a trace of the little girl I remember from my last visit."

"No," Cato agreed somberly. "Hardly a trace." He reached for the bellpull. "You must be in need of rest and refreshment after your journey. . . . Ah, Bailey, escort Mr. Morse to a guest chamber and have someone attend him during his stay."

The servant bowed and stood aside for Brian to pass through the door.

"I'll escort you to Lady Granville when you've refreshed yourself," Cato said.

The door closed behind his unwanted visitor, and he flung himself back into his carved oak chair, crossing his legs, long fingers playing with the quill on the table. What exactly was Brian doing here? Was he spying for Prince Rupert? He would be able to gauge the size of the Granville militia and its readiness for war. But those were no secrets. It would do no harm for the royalists to know what was easily available to anyone in the area.

But they must not know of the treasure piling up in the vaults of Castle Granville. They must not know how much Cato had collected for Parliament. When the time came to send it on its way, Brian Morse could not be in the castle.

A slight smile touched Cato's mouth as he reached for his

goblet. It was not a particularly pleasant smile. The treasure was going to kill two birds with one stone. Rufus Decatur was prepared to go to outrageous lengths to claw back his family revenues for the king. What would he not do for such a hoard as Cato held in his vaults? It was sweet bait for a trap that would lead Rufus Decatur straight to a noose on the battlements of Castle Granville. And if Jack's daughter was an innocent pawn in the game Decatur played, then her abductor's capture would bring her release.

12

"*We'll not make Newcastle tonight,*" Will observed, looking up into the dirty gray sky.

"No, you'll have to bivouac along the road." Rufus glanced behind him at the procession of horses. The animals were fresher than their riders, who were for the most part red eyed and hungover, clinging to the reins, swaying in their saddles, half asleep.

Portia was riding beside him. She was heavy eyed and languorous. She said very little, out of deference to Will, he thought. The young man hadn't known where to look that morning when Rufus and his bedmate had emerged into the gray dawn. Since Will had found his own solace from among Fanny's young women, his prudish discomfiture struck Rufus as somewhat comical, but then again Will had never come across anyone quite like Portia Worth before.

Portia's silence, had Rufus known it, had very little to do with Will. In the cold light of morning, the question she had struggled to ignore in the riotous games of the night rose hard and cold as crystal. *What was to happen now?* Would she now be a happy prisoner? Cheerfully resigned to captivity in the bed of her captor? She didn't feel either cheerful or resigned. She kept glancing covertly at Rufus and could read nothing in his expression. There'd been little opportunity for private speech since they woke. Rufus had been far too occupied getting his drunk and debauched troops back into military formation. He hadn't been very kind about it either, she'd noticed. But no one seemed to have resented the vigorous curses heaped upon them by their irritated commander.

Colonel Neath rode up from the back. "Och, but I've a head on me to rival Thor's hammer." He cast a wan look skyward, as Will had done. "Looks like snow."

"Aye," Rufus agreed shortly. "You'll find a sheltered spot to bivouac. You've tents?"

"Aye," Neath said. "We've what's necessary. But are you not coming with us, man?"

Rufus shook his head. "No, I'll leave Will and half the men to escort you to Newcastle. The rest of us will peel off at Rothbury."

Portia looked up at this. It was the first she'd heard of this plan. Not that it made much difference to her situation where they went next.

Penny was so accustomed to keeping her place in a troop of horses that she barely required riding, and Portia was almost asleep when the cavalcade suddenly halted. She jerked upright in the saddle, shaking herself awake, and saw that they'd reached a crossroads.

"This is where we part company, Colonel." Rufus leaned forward to shake Neath's hand. "I wish we could have met in other circumstances."

"Aye, me too." Neath grimaced, taking the hand. "I'll wish you Godspeed, man, but not good fortune."

Rufus laughed and raised a hand in salute. "God keep you, Neath. And may you live to fight another day. . . . Will, I'll expect you back within the week. If you're going to dally in Newcastle, send word."

"Why would I dally?" Will asked innocently.

"There's bound to be many opportunities in headquarters," Portia pointed out with blunt truth.

Will blushed and his horse shifted restlessly on the path, aware of his rider's discomfort.

"I didn't mean to embarrass you," Portia said quickly. But the apology only made matters worse, and Will's flush deepened.

Rufus took pity on him. "You'll have enough to do, Will, and little time for dalliance," he declared and turned his horse on the lefthand path. "Godspeed."

"Godspeed, Will," Portia echoed, as Penny without prompting followed Ajax onto the narrow path, together with the fifteen men returning with them.

They rode a short way, then Rufus stopped at the top of a small rise to watch the procession of prisoners and their escort wind its way along the narrow path and out of sight in a grove of saplings. Then he turned Ajax and set off again.

Portia was wide awake now, and she remembered what he'd said earlier. "This place is called Rothbury? Are we passing through your family land?"

Rufus didn't answer for a minute, and when he did speak it was barely audible. "Was."

The bitter tone silenced further questions. As they rode, Portia felt the darkness settling over him like a black mantle. She lost all desire to talk. Behind them, George's familiar sturdy figure rode in the front line of the cavalcade snaking its way along the path. Nobody seemed inclined for speech, and the only sounds were the rhythmic clopping of hooves and the jingle of harness.

Rufus fought the dreadful compulsion. He had known what he risked by taking this route, but it was the quickest way back to Decatur village, and he had been feeling strong, buoyant after the success of his foray against Neath's troop. He had thought he would be safe from the madness. But as they drew closer to the place, the black tendrils of obsession wreathed around him.

When he drew rein at the place, he knew that he could do nothing about his obsession but yield to it. In his father's name . . . in honor of his father's memory. He must not forget. And he *would* not forget.

He turned in his saddle and spoke to George, his tone flat. "I'm leaving you here. Carry on to Decatur and I'll join up with you later."

George's sharp glance was both compassionate and troubled. He knew where they were. "Y'are sure, sir?"

Rufus nodded curtly.

"Where are we going?" Portia inquired.

"You'll stay with George," Rufus stated. Without a further word, he turned Ajax aside and set him up to jump a small stile onto a stubble field.

"Let's keep movin', lass." George came up beside Portia. "T' master'll be along later."

Portia in frowning silence allowed Penny to trot on peacefully. After a few minutes she said, "I'm going to fall back for a minute."

George nodded easily. Nature's calls were answered simply enough in the countryside.

Portia drew aside and allowed the troop to pass her, then she galloped Penny back along the path to the stile.

The stubble field sloped upward and as Penny crested the summit, Portia saw Rufus a short way over the lip of the hill. He sat his horse, gazing down into the valley immediately below. He was utterly immobile and there was something so forbidding about his shape in the lowering afternoon, she began to wish she'd stayed with George.

She was about to turn back when he swung round suddenly in his saddle. His eyes, staring at her across the space that separated them, were like empty holes. The blackness of a terrible rage seemed to envelop him.

She knew nothing about him. He'd told her so only yesterday . . . was it only yesterday? And she hadn't realized how true it was until now. The fragile intimacy of their night together was shattered like crystal.

"Come here, then, and see what you've come to see," he called, his voice bitter and mocking.

Portia didn't want to go and yet she had to. She was drawn toward him as if by some devil's enchantment. She walked Penny down the slope until the mare stood alongside Ajax. The chestnut was trembling, his hide rippling along his neck and over his flanks.

"So, you've a mind to look upon Granville work," Rufus said. "Well, look, then!" He pointed with his whip.

Portia looked down into the valley and saw a blackened ruin. What had once been soft red brick was charred; tumbled walls, their edges jagged, still showed the form of the mansion that had once stood there. Toppled chimney pots lay in the weed-covered grassy courtyards. Between scattered blue-gray slates of roof tiles, shards of window glass still glimmered in the grass. Parkland, once fenced and planted, was now an overgrown wilderness of ragged bushes, and the once neat gravel sweep that had led to the great Elizabethan front door was choked with weeds.

Portia gazed at this stark destruction in stunned silence.

"I was born in that house." Rufus began to speak, his voice savage, his eyes pitiless as they rested on her white face. "I was eight years old when the Granvilles murdered my father as he stood in his own front door. Eight years old when they put a torch to a house whose foundations had been laid on that land before the Conquest. I was eight when the Granvilles drove the Decaturs into the hills like wild beasts."

"Jack told me your father killed himself," Portia said, her voice so parched she could barely form the words. "George Granville didn't kill your father, he killed himself."

"Yes, he killed himself to avoid the dishonor of a traitor's death," Rufus stated. "He killed himself so his son wouldn't see his father beheaded on Tower Hill for a crime he did not commit. And the man whose hand he had shaken in friendship over twenty years as surely killed him as if he'd fired the pistol himself."

Portia glanced once at his face and then looked away, staring down at the ruined house. It was impossible to look upon his countenance and not be terrified by its expression. He didn't seem to know she was there anymore.

"George Granville, as reward for his betrayal, received the stewardship of all the revenues of the Rothbury estates." He continued to speak into the air around her. "I had thought to force Granville to return those revenues in exchange for his daughter. Instead of which . . ."

He stopped and glanced over at Portia, his eyes unreadable, before continuing with a softness that belied the savagery of his words, "I swore to take my father's vengeance, and so help me God I will do it. I will see that sewer rat crawl for his father's treachery."

In horror, Portia knew that he meant every word. But with aching empathy she understood what he had lost. From the age of eight, fatherless, thrust out from his birthright to grow in the harsh world beyond the law, beyond society. A young boy who had seen his father die a dreadful death.

"Your mother?" she said tentatively.

"Died giving birth to my sister, five months after we were driven out." His tone was bleak, distant. "She died because no one would come to the aid of a hunted outcast, the widow of a condemned traitor. The child died within hours."

"Oh God." Portia tried to push away the images of the boy

watching his mother, listening to her screams in the agonies of childbirth, helplessly watching her suffering and the death that left him a homeless orphan.

But it was wrong. There would never be an end to it while Rufus remained enslaved to vengeance. It diminished them all.

"Cato did not kill your father," she said. "He was a boy like you. You cannot hold him responsible for his father's actions."

"So speaks a Granville," Rufus said softly. "How curious that once or twice I've managed to forget what you are."

"I cannot help it," she said. "I cannot help my blood, Rufus."

He made no response, just continued to sit Ajax, staring down again now at the ruins of his home. Portia gathered Penny's reins and spoke the only truth there was. "I cannot help it and you cannot forget it, Rufus. There's no place for me in Decatur village. I'm no good to you as a hostage, and I cannot be anything else to you. I will always be the enemy."

He looked across at her, his eyes now bleak. "You're an hour's ride due south to Castle Granville. Go back home, back to the Granville hearth where you belong."

Portia set Penny down the hill, back to the lane, then turned due south. She didn't look back, but she could still see in her mind's eye the man sitting his horse at the top of the rise, alone with his vengeance.

While she was simply alone. Returning to an uncertain welcome, to be tormented always by the memory of those moments when she had, however briefly, belonged.

The journey from Decatur village passed in a daze. Portia had to ask the way several times, but found herself very quickly on Granville land. It was not much more than a hour after leaving Rufus that she saw the great gray bulk of Castle Granville on the hill across the valley. She didn't know how to describe to herself how she felt. Her wretchedness had increased with each mile she put between herself and Rufus Decatur. It was as if she'd been thrust out into the cold, like a baby bird thrown from its nest. It didn't matter that she told herself she had forced the issue herself . . . that she had left of her own accord. It didn't help at all. None of the many and varied miseries of her girlhood had prepared her for this sense of desolation.

She rode up to the wicket gate and the sentry peered at her suspiciously. She identified herself and it had a galvanizing effect. The gate swung open and the sentry grabbed Penny's reins, yelling over his shoulder, "Fetch Sergeant Crampton. The girl's back."

Portia wearily dismounted and stood in the gatehouse, waiting for Giles. It seemed a less than ceremonious welcome for a miraculously returned hostage.

Giles bustled in. He'd been in the middle of his dinner and still carried a checkered napkin. He stared at her, his jaw dropping, and it was a minute before he demanded, "Where'd you spring from?"

"I escaped," she said. "Why am I being kept here, Sergeant?" It was an attempt at hauteur and it had some effect on the sergeant.

"Lord Granville's at dinner," he said huffily. "But we'd best get along. Come wi' me."

Portia refrained from telling him that she knew her way to the dining parlor perfectly well, and submitted to being escorted like an escaped prisoner.

Within the dining parlor, Cato was wearily trying to entertain Brian Morse. Diana had been transformed from the first moment of their visitor's arrival. Brian had brought with him the sanctified odor of the court. His dress was fashionable, his manner elaborately courteous, with more than a hint of flirtation to lend it spice. Diana was in her element, radiant and glowing. Cato was not.

"If you care to go hawking, Brian, I could—" Cato broke off at the sound of voices outside the oak door. He recognized Giles Crampton's vigorous tones and was on his feet with an unabashed eagerness as the door opened.

The sergeant filled the doorway. "Beggin' yer pardon for disturbin' yer dinner, m'lord, but—"

"No matter, Giles." Cato cast down his napkin. He couldn't see Portia's cloaked figure behind the sergeant's bulk. "Come, let's go to my chamber. If you'll excuse me, my dear." He offered his wife a hasty bow and strode to the door. Then he stopped in astonishment.

"Portia! Good God, girl! How did you get here?"

"She just turned up, m'lord," Giles said, before Portia could speak. "Just turned up at the wicket gate wi'out a word of warnin'."

"I would imagine a warning might have been difficult," Cato said slowly, trying to take in this extraordinary reappearance, and what it could possibly mean. "Are you well, child? Not hurt?"

Portia shook her head but said in perfect truth, "No, but I own I'm weary, sir. It's a long story."

"Yes, of course. Come, we'll discuss it in private."

"What is it, my lord?" Diana's curious tones came from the table behind him.

"Portia has returned," Cato said. "A most extraordinary thing . . . but until she can tell me what happened, I can tell you nothing, my dear." He closed the door firmly at his back. In almost the same movement, he swept Portia ahead of him down the corridor toward the bastion room, Giles marching a step behind.

Inside, with the door firmly closed, Cato surveyed Portia with the same puzzled astonishment. "What happened?"

"I wasn't the right hostage," she said. "But I expect you knew that."

"Yes, I gathered the bastard Decatur was after Olivia." His eyes narrowed. "You were not molested in any way?"

Portia shook her head. "The abduction itself was rough, but I had nothing to complain of in my treatment once we reached Decatur village." She met his gaze steadily.

"She said she escaped, m'lord." Giles was regarding her sharply.

Portia hesitated and Cato's eyes narrowed. "That's right," she said. How could she possibly have explained the truth?

"She was ridin' a blood mare, m'lord," Giles commented. He was still looking at Portia, and it was with clear suspicion.

"A Decatur horse?"

"Yes." It was Portia who answered.

"Did you steal it?"

"I suppose you could say that." She swayed slightly and grabbed the back of a chair. She wasn't up to this interrogation. Not tonight. "I thought of it as merely borrowing."

"Escapin' from Decatur village ain't easy," Giles put in. "Mebbe they was lookin' the other way."

Portia looked at him in confusion. What was he implying?

"The horse must go back," Cato declared. "I'll not give Decatur the opportunity to accuse *me* of theft."

"We could lead 'er most o' the way there, then let 'er find 'er own way back, sir."

"Yes, together with a message for friend Decatur," Cato said grimly. He turned back to Portia. "What happened to your clothes?"

Portia glanced down at her unorthodox attire. "My own were ruined during the abduction," she explained. "These were all that were available in Decatur village. There aren't any women there," she added.

Cato nodded. "I had heard that." He regarded her closely. "Did you learn anything useful while you were there?"

"I don't know what you would consider useful, my lord."

"Did you have the sense of a military encampment?"

"A very efficient one, sir. And they're flying the king's standard."

Cato stood frowning at Portia in her indecorous garb, her hair a wind-whipped tangle. Was she telling him the truth about her escape? There had been that telltale hesitation. Could this surprising return be part of some deeper plan of Decatur's? How could a slip of a girl manage to escape the Decatur stronghold? *And* steal a Decatur blood mare. He couldn't fathom the girl. She was his brother's child, and she looked at him now with his brother's eyes. Could he trust her? He didn't know.

He noticed her white knuckles as she gripped the back of the chair, and the great dark rings beneath her eyes. Whatever had brought her back, she was utterly exhausted.

"We'll talk at length later," he said, waving her to the door. "Olivia will be glad to see you. She's been worried about you, and I understand from Lady Granville that she's been ailing and is keeping to her bed. Why don't you go to her now."

"Certainly, sir." Portia, unable to curtsy in her britches, offered a slightly awkward bow.

The minute she opened Olivia's door, she forgot her own unhappiness.

Olivia lay with her eyes closed, her face whiter than the pillow, the sheet pulled neatly up to her chin. She was as still as if she were laid out in her coffin, and Portia's heart missed a beat. Cato had said she was ailing. But she looked at death's door.

"Olivia?"

"*Portia!*" Olivia shot up in bed and Portia's anxiety receded. Olivia was clearly not at death's door.

"Is it you? Is it really you?" Olivia's eyes widened as she took in Portia's unconventional costume. "You're wearing britches!"

"Yes, it's me . . . and yes, I'm wearing britches." Portia closed the door and came over to the bed. "Why are you in bed? Your father said you were ailing."

"I am." Olivia reached for Portia's hands and clutched them painfully. "Oh, I am so g-glad to *see* you. What happened to you? Why are you in those clothes?" Her black eyes were now bright with interest, and her cheeks had pinkened.

Portia perched on the end of the bed. "It's a long story, duckie."

"*Tell me!*" Olivia demanded, squeezing her hands even tighter.

Portia was silent for a minute. The urge to pour out her heart and her misery was suddenly overwhelming. Then Olivia repeated, "Tell me," and Portia found herself speaking.

She tried to make light of it, but Olivia heard the unhappiness beneath the self-mockery and the ironic tone. And she realized that Portia, whom she'd always thought of as so strong, so funny, so fiercely independent, was wounded. The girl who had been such a steadfast friend to Olivia now needed a friend of her own.

Olivia felt a rush of warmth, of purpose. "D-do you love him?" she asked as Portia fell silent.

Portia's laugh was mirthless. "Love? I don't know what that is, Olivia. I suppose I loved Jack . . . but maybe I just depended upon him because he was all I had. No, I don't think love came into my brief encounter with Rufus Decatur."

"Then what was it?" Olivia persisted, still holding Portia's hands tightly.

Portia gazed into the middle distance, aware of the warmth and strength of Olivia's grip and wordlessly comforted by it. *What had it been?* Passion, excitement, curiosity? All of those things. And if there had been something else, if she *had* felt the beginnings of something deeper—the possibility of something deeper—it was clear that Rufus had not. She would always be the enemy. Always tainted by her blood.

"It certainly wasn't love, duckie," she said with a little shrug. "I don't think love of any kind has a place in my life."

"*I* love you," Olivia said fiercely, leaning forward to hug Portia's thin frame. "*I* love you."

"Oh, Olivia!" Portia swiped at her eyes as tears began to spill down her cheeks. "Now look what you've done!"

"It's good to c-cry sometimes," Olivia said through her own tears.

Portia yielded for a minute and then drew out of Olivia's embrace. "I'm just tired and hungry," she said with a pallid smile. "I don't cry."

"You just d-did," Olivia pointed out with her own wan smile.

"What a pair we are." Portia laughed, this time with a hint of her old self. She examined the contents of the tray that lay neglected on a side table. "Is this your dinner? Can we share it?"

"I'm not hungry," Olivia said, pushing the tray toward Portia.

"Are you sure?" Portia broke a drumstick off a roasted pigeon. She cast a shrewd glance at Olivia. "I've told you my tale of woe; now you have to tell me why you're hiding in here, pretending to be ill."

"B-Brian," Olivia said, falling back against the pillows. "He's here."

"What's the matter with him?" Portia stripped the flesh from the drumstick with her teeth, discarded the bone, and selected a wing, waiting patiently as Olivia stared sightlessly into the middle distance.

Olivia struggled to find something concrete with which to

answer Portia's question. But it was the same as always. There was only this disgust and terror at the mere thought of him. And as always when she tried to penetrate the confusion, she shrank away from it. It wasn't something she wanted to know.

She shook her head. "I can't tell you. I d-don't know. All I know is that I'd like to *kill* him." She looked helplessly at Portia, who did not seem at all shocked by her sentiments. There was something so *solid* about Portia. Nothing seemed to surprise her.

Without noticing what she was doing, Olivia reached out and took a piece of manchet bread from the tray.

Portia merely offered her the crock of butter and took a fork to a dish of pickled beetroot. They ate in silence for a few minutes, then Portia said, "I won't kill him for you, but I know a trick or two to make life quite uncomfortable for him if you like."

Olivia's eyes lit up. "What t-tricks?"

Portia grinned. Her own eyes were still a little red, but the old glint was back. "I'll tell you. But first you have to get up and be sociable. We can't do much to this Brian person if you're skulking in here."

Olivia ate a mushroom tart. Could Portia possibly be a match for Brian Morse? She herself felt so helpless in his company, an already wounded mouse with the cat. But perhaps, with Portia there, she could be strong, could somehow keep herself from his vileness. "All right," she said. "I'll get up in the morning."

"Bravo!" Portia applauded.

Portia had long learned the valuable lesson that in action lay relief from misery, particularly the soul-deep misery of the spirit. She could do nothing to alter her present situation, at least not for the moment, but she could throw herself into Olivia's problems, and if a little mischief was involved in the distraction, then so much the better.

13

Portia would have disliked Brian Morse on sight even if she hadn't known of Olivia's loathing for the man. When she was introduced to him in Diana's parlor later the next afternoon, he took one look at her and dismissed her instantly as beneath his notice. A poor relation with neither countenance nor bearing to recommend her.

"My husband has a very generous nature," Diana said in an undertone that was nevertheless intended for Portia's ears. "I know of few men who would offer houseroom to their half brother's bastard."

"Such an ill-favored wench," Brian murmured, glancing to where Portia stood with Olivia in the window. The last lingering light of the afternoon caught her orange hair and fell across her angular countenance, throwing her nose into harsh relief, illuminating her freckles.

"Olivia," Diana called sharply. "Come over here and converse with Mr. Morse. I don't know what's happened to your manners just recently. It's most unbecoming to huddle in a corner with Portia, who, I am sure, has duties to attend to."

"My father said P–*Portia* should keep me c–company," Olivia declared, jumping to Portia's defense, flushing as much with anger as with the effort of speech.

"My dear, I'm sure your father expects you to show his *guests* the attention due them from a daughter of the house," Diana said, her tongue acid-tipped. "Mr. Morse wishes to visit the mews. I suggest you escort him. Portia is needed in the nursery."

Olivia's eyes, desperate in their appeal, flew to Portia's face. Portia dropped one eyelid in a slow wink and moved casually to the door of the parlor.

"Lord Granville most particularly asked me this morning to remain with Olivia, madam. I believe he wishes me to act in some sort as a companion for her . . . just until she's quite recovered her strength. I'll fetch a cloak for her at once, if she's to go outside. Although it's a very raw evening and I wonder at the wisdom of venturing—"

"Very well." Diana broke irritably into this sweet commentary. "I hadn't realized how late it was." It occurred to her that Cato might well have given the girl his own instructions, and she couldn't set herself up against his wishes without discussing it with him first.

"If it's too cold for outside, perhaps my little sister would take a walk through the gallery with me," Brian suggested. "I'm anxious to renew our acquaintance. It's been such a very long time. You were little more than a baby, as I recall."

He had a particularly oily smile, Portia thought with distaste. Oily and utterly untrustworthy. And he was needling Olivia, she could feel it. For whatever reason, Olivia feared him and he knew it. And he was enjoying himself, toying with her.

"What a good idea," she said, turning back to link her arm through Olivia's. "Let's show Mr. Morse the gallery, Olivia."

This was not what Brian had intended. He considered it beneath his dignity to keep company with this scarecrow, whose status in the household was somewhat less than that of paid nurserymaid. But the temptation to amuse himself with Olivia was too great, and he was confident that he could squash the pretensions of Jack Worth's bastard once he was alone with the two girls. Olivia after all had never given him any trouble.

In the narrow corridor, he took Olivia's free arm and drew her firmly beside him, so that Portia was forced to drop behind. Portia promptly slithered sideways between Olivia and the wall and walked crablike with her back to the wall.

Brian ignored her completely. "S–s–so, little s–sister," he said mockingly, "I w–was hoping f–for a much w–warmer w–welcome."

Portia's anger rose as she felt Olivia's distress. She plunged into battle, drawing his attention forcibly away from Olivia.

"Why don't you pick on someone your own size, you nasty little man?"

Brian looked so astounded that Olivia forgot her terror for a minute and almost laughed.

"You look like some kind of dung beetle in that black velvet," Portia continued. "But I imagine you're so accustomed to occupying the dizzying heights of a dung heap that it feels like protective coloring. Did no one ever tell you that when you have particularly scrawny shanks, black velvet is a mistake. It exaggerates the—"

She broke off and ducked as he swung at her, his face almost purple with astonished fury. "You'll have to be quicker than that to catch me, Mr. Dung Beetle," she taunted. "Mr. Slubberdegullion Whoreson, who's too much of a coward to pick a fight with someone who can give him one back." She danced backward down the corridor, giving him an obscene gesture, as Brian gobbled for words.

"Cat got your tongue? See, Olivia, this piece of gutter slime is going to swallow his tongue in a minute." With impeccable timing, she reached behind her and opened the door onto her own chamber. Deftly seizing Olivia by the wrist, she pulled her in behind her and kicked the door shut, throwing the bolt.

Olivia laughed and laughed. She collapsed against the door as it shivered beneath a violent onslaught from the apoplectic Brian Morse.

"How could you?" Olivia gasped, wiping her streaming eyes. "How did you dare to say those things?"

"Oh, that's nothing," Portia scoffed. "I have a much broader vocabulary than that. Just listen to this." She went to the door and whispered through the keyhole. It was a penetrating whisper but the words were not ones Olivia had ever heard. She didn't need to be told they were unimaginably indecent, however, and hugged herself as silence fell outside. It was an astonished, incredulous silence and into it Portia continued to speak, softly and utterly fluently, ending with a flourish as she likened the unfortunate Mr. Morse's male organ to that of a particularly runty piglet's.

There was no response. Olivia had ceased laughing and

merely gazed in awe at Portia, who leaned back against the door, arms folded, grinning. "That silenced him," she declared after a minute. "And in future maybe he'll be a little careful whom he decides to mock."

"He'll never forgive you," Olivia said.

"So I should hope," Portia said cheerfully. "I'd rather roll in a muck heap than have that bully's forgiveness. Anyway, I've only just started on Mr. Morse. By the time I've finished with him, he's not going to know his arse from his elbow."

Very softly she drew back the bolt and opened the door a crack. The corridor was deserted. "Do you know which is his chamber?"

"We c–can't go in there." The terror was back in Olivia's eyes again and her voice shook.

"He won't catch us, don't worry. But do you know?"

Olivia shook her head. "But Bailey will."

"Good, then you can ask him. Now, come on. We have to go to the privy." She grabbed up her cloak, slinging it around her shoulders.

"What for?" Olivia asked before she realized how idiotic a question it was.

"Not the usual." Portia slipped out of the room. "Come." She beckoned her, took her hand, and ran with her down the passage to the kitchen stairs.

The kitchen was as usual a hive of activity, and no one paid attention to the two girls as they slid through and out into the kitchen yard. The outhouse was at the far end of the kitchen garden, where its product could be put to good use. Olivia, cloakless, shivered as they ran down the path toward the glow of lamplight that hung above the door, but she didn't ask further questions, merely waited for Portia to reveal her plan.

Portia lifted the lamp off the hook at the door and entered the noisome shed. She handed the lamp to Olivia. "Hold it up high."

"But what are we looking for?"

"Spiders," Portia said. "They like the corners of privies. There are some big red spotted ones sometimes, and they bite."

Olivia had no idea what Portia intended, but she couldn't

help a little giggle, shivering as a gust of wind banged the door shut and the lantern flickered.

"Ah . . . here we are. Oh, aren't you a beauty," Portia murmured lovingly, as she knelt on the hard-packed earth. "What lovely big spots you have," she crooned, taking a handkerchief out of her pocket. "There we go, in you pop." She folded the handkerchief over her treasure. "Now let's see if we can find another."

Olivia didn't care for spiders, but she was utterly fascinated and leaned forward to watch Portia's painstaking examination of the darkest corners of the privy.

"Someone's coming," she whispered, hearing a footstep on the path.

"So what? No one's going to question what we're doing in the privy." Portia scooped a second and particularly juicy specimen into the handkerchief.

"I always use the chaise percée in my chamber," Olivia said doubtfully.

Portia only shook her head and continued with her collecting. When she had half a dozen in assorted sizes, she straightened carefully. She laid a finger on her lips and opened the door. A kitchen maid stood on the path. "Evenin', miss." Her eyes widened as Olivia followed Portia, holding the lamp.

"Evenin', Lady Olivia."

"G–good evening, Mary." Olivia handed her the lamp with what she hoped was aplomb and followed Portia's blithe step back up the path to the lights of the kitchen.

"Find out which chamber the snake has," Portia instructed, holding her hand carefully against her skirts beneath the folds of her cloak. "And hurry. Because they're getting restless and I don't want to get bitten myself."

Olivia nodded and wandered over to the servants' table, where Bailey was addressing a platter of sirloin and a tankard of ale. Portia left the kitchen and waited for Olivia at the head of the kitchen stairs. "Well?"

"In the east bastion. But Bailey doesn't know if he's in there now."

"Mmmm." Portia frowned, nibbling her lip. "That could be awkward." She examined Olivia carefully. "If he's in there, we'll have to decoy him. It'll only take a minute. Could you do that?"

"Be alone with him?" Olivia shook her head vigorously.

"It'll only take a minute," Portia urged, realizing on some level that Olivia needed to face down whatever demon was embodied in Brian Morse. "I won't be far away, I swear it."

Olivia swallowed, squared her shoulders. "You p–promise?"

"I promise. Come on. They're doing spidery things all over the place." She set off down the corridor, and after a hesitation, Olivia followed.

They stopped outside the door to Brian Morse's chamber. Portia flattened herself against the wall behind the door and gestured to Olivia that she should knock.

Olivia simply stood there, staring at the door, paralyzed, unable to raise her hand. The silence lengthened, then Portia leaned round and banged loudly on the door. Olivia jumped back, white faced.

The door flew open. Brian Morse surveyed his visitor with his little pebble eyes. "Well?"

"D-*Diana*." It was such an effort it came out more like a screech than anything resembling normal speech. Olivia pointed wildly in the direction of Diana's parlor, standing with her skirts gathered up, ready to flee if he made a move toward her.

Brian didn't bother to engage her further, merely banged the door closed at his back and strode away. Olivia stepped back so that she was blocking any view of Portia should he for some reason look back, but he didn't, and as soon as he'd rounded the corner of the corridor, Portia darted out from hiding.

"Here, take these and put them in his bed! Be quick. I'll stay here and keep watch. I'll whistle if someone comes." She held out the handkerchief with its wriggling occupants as she opened the chamber door with her free hand.

"Go on!" she urged as Olivia still stood there.

Olivia swallowed, grabbed the handkerchief, and darted into the chamber. Portia stepped into the doorway, her eyes darting up and down the corridor. "Pull back the covers at the bottom of the bed," she instructed softly.

Olivia's heart was thumping so violently she could barely breathe. But she followed Portia's instructions and untucked the sheets at the foot of the bed, lifted them, and shook the wriggling contents of the handkerchief onto the bottom sheet.

"Now tuck the sheets in again tightly," Portia directed.

Olivia deftly retucked the sheets, then she gave the bed a little pat for good luck, giggling with a mixture of nervousness and excitement, and rejoined Portia.

"There, that should do it. They'll settle down in the warmth, and when the toad gets into bed they'll gravitate to the warmest, most humid spot available. And guess where that'll be." Portia grinned wickedly. "He'll wake up in the morning covered in great red bites in all the most inaccessible places."

"Are they poisonous?"

"Not lethal," Portia replied solemnly. "I did say I wouldn't kill him."

"Oh, I wish I could see it." Olivia hugged herself.

"Watch him at the breakfast table." Portia grinned.

*B*rian *paused outside Diana's parlor and automatically* straightened his doublet, readjusted the fall of lace on his shoulders. He still hadn't recovered from his experience with Jack Worth's bastard. No one had ever insulted him in such fashion before, not even during his sojourns in the vilest taverns, and he didn't know what to do about it. He couldn't imagine reporting the incident to Granville or Diana. How could he possibly admit that a bastard guttersnipe had so routed him? How could he possibly repeat what she'd said? And the worst of it was that Olivia had heard. That pathetic brat had witnessed his defeat. Somehow, he would be avenged upon the bastard, but in his own time and in his own fashion. He was good at vengeance. He had a long memory and when it came time to strike it was all the sweeter.

He knocked and opened the door to the parlor, bowing low. "Lady Granville . . . how can I be of service?"

She looked up from the letter she was writing and smiled in some surprise. "Why, how delightful of you to keep me company, Mr. Morse. I own life can be a little dreary these days. We have so few visitors. Who would pay social calls to an armed camp?"

She made a little moue of discontent. "Of course, my husband must do what he thinks best, but I do so long for civilization sometimes. A little stimulating conversation, the opportunity to dabble in fashion again. Why, you know I have no idea what the latest court fashions are." Her hand passed in self-deprecation over the skirts of her elegant gown. "I dare swear you must think me a positive dowd."

"Why, no indeed, my dear Lady Granville." Brian took a seat on the sofa beside her. "You are the very picture of elegance. No one at court could hold a candle to you."

Diana laughed musically. "You flatter me, sir. But pray don't stop." She touched his hand. "Give me news of the court. How is the dear queen managing in this adversity? I do so wish I could be with her to lend her my support. And the poor little princess, Henrietta. Such a fragile child. She must be feeling it very badly."

"I was at Oxford two months ago," Brian said. "Their Majesties' courage is an inspiration to all who serve them." He didn't think it necessary to add that although he had certainly been in the city of Oxford, he had not once attended the court-in-exile and his only view of the king and queen had been from the street when they'd attended church one Sunday.

"I wish I could persuade my husband to . . ." Diana stopped, lightly dabbed at her eyes with the corner of a perfumed handkerchief. "Forgive me, Mr. Morse. It's not for me to offer criticism of my husband's decisions, but I feel so . . . so dishonored. My duty, my loyalty, is to my sovereign, and to find myself in this invidious position . . . forgive me," she repeated and buried her face in her handkerchief.

Brian patted her knee, his little eyes sharp. He scented the possibility for mischief here. Very useful and productive mischief. "Sometimes, my dear madam, one must follow one's conscience even if duty dictates otherwise."

Diana looked up. Her countenance bore no disfiguring signs of distress. "What do you mean, sir?"

Brian coughed delicately. "Personal loyalties . . . matters of personal conscience . . . I don't believe that even your husband would expect you to abandon your conscience simply because his own takes him along a different route. And you and I know, dear Lady Granville, that Lord Granville is gravely mistaken in his decision. To stand against the king is to stand against God himself. The king has a divine right to rule. He is God's anointed representative."

This gravely sententious speech was music to Diana's ears. "I do so fear for my husband," she murmured. "What will happen to him . . . to all those . . . who have stood against the king when this rebellion is put down, and they must face the king's wrath?"

"It's a grave prospect indeed," Brian said. "And Lord Granville cannot have considered that his own family will share his fate."

Diana shuddered. "My own father is thinking of declaring for Parliament also. There will be nowhere to take shelter."

"Perhaps . . . but, no, I couldn't . . . couldn't suggest such a thing." He rose and began to pace in apparent agitation around the warm, firelit room.

"Oh, yes, pray do speak your mind," Diana begged.

"It seems so . . . so ungrateful when Lord Granville has welcomed me with such generosity . . . and yet . . .and yet I cannot endure to see you suffering so, my lady." He came back to the sofa and knelt before her, taking her hands. "If you would trust me."

"Oh, but of course I trust you." She squeezed his hands. "What is it you would say to me?" Her eyes shone with eagerness.

"Why, that maybe you could with your own actions mitigate your husband's offense in the eyes of the king."

"Work against my husband?"

"Not exactly. But perhaps if you could find a way to help the king's cause without your husband's knowing . . ." His tongue flickered over his lips. This was dangerous ground, but Diana was regarding him with such open wonder that he could already taste his triumph. What a coup. To subvert the wife within the very confines of a rebel stronghold.

Cato was a powerful man. An honorable man whose

support for Parliament would make an enormous difference to the cause . . . would legitimate it in the eyes of many waverers. If he could be undermined on his own territory, from within his own walls, he would lose all credibility. And Brian Morse, the instrument of his downfall, would receive the immeasurable gratitude of a sovereign once more restored to his rightful throne.

"How?" Diana whispered, no less aware than Brian of the danger. But before he could answer, the door opened.

"Good God, man, what are you doing on your knees?" Cato demanded. "I assure you my wife is already spoken for."

Brian scrambled to his feet. "Oh, my lord, I was . . . was . . ."

"Mr. Morse was helping me look for a particular shade in my embroidery silks," Diana said calmly.

"I see." Cato bent over the basket of silks. "Perhaps I can help."

Diana merely smiled at him. "Come now, my lord, you know you have no interest in anything not connected with this dreadful war."

Cato shrugged. "Perhaps so." He reached for the bellpull.

"Has something occurred to upset you, my lord?" Diana rose and fluttered across to him, laying a concerned hand on his arm.

"Just this damn war," he said shortly. "Ah, Bailey . . . bring wine."

"Anything in particular troubling you, my lord?" Brian inquired, bending to poke the fire.

Your supremely annoying presence, and a whole hornets' nest of suspicions about Portia Worth. "Where're the girls?" Cato asked, seeming to ignore the question. "It's suppertime, isn't it?"

"I don't know," Diana said. "Should I send for them . . . or for Olivia?" She smiled up at her husband, continuing with all sweet concern, "I've been thinking, my lord, that we are perhaps too ready to include Portia in the family. I don't think her influence on Olivia is really to be encouraged . . . particularly after this latest escapade . . . such a terrible business. I know you don't wish to slight your brother's child, but . . . but

I think she would be happier taking her place more with the servants."

Cato tried to control his irritation. He had no intention of taking Diana into his confidence. "I disagree, madam. She seems to have persuaded Olivia to leave her bed, at least. And that can't be bad. I have my own reasons for wishing her to remain within the family circle . . . at least for the time being."

Diana looked most put out. "Am I to know those reasons, sir?"

Cato shook his head. "There's no need to trouble yourself about them, my dear. I have matters well in hand. Ah, Bailey . . ." He turned as the butler returned with the wine. "Tell Lady Olivia and Mistress Worth that we'll be taking supper in ten minutes."

"Yes, m'lord." Bailey bowed himself out.

Diana compressed her lips but held her tongue, and when Olivia and Portia entered a few minutes later, she smiled warmly at Olivia and kissed her. "I'm so happy to see that you're feeling better, my dear child."

Olivia smiled faintly and surreptitiously wiped her cheek as she turned away.

Cato appeared abstracted at the supper table, leaving the conversational burden to Diana and Brian. But he was watching Portia. She behaved with perfect decorum, saying very little, answering politely when spoken to. There was nothing in her demeanor to suggest he had a Decatur spy under his roof. He had sensed that she had not been telling him the whole truth about her sojourn in the Decatur compound. He had had the same conviction when he'd questioned her about her first meeting with Decatur. Perhaps Giles was right. The sergeant was convinced that there was something wrong about the girl's dealings with Decatur.

He wasn't aware of how closely he was watching her, until Portia suddenly raised her eyes from her plate and boldly met his gaze. That challenge was there again. Perhaps she could no more help it than his brother had been able to. And perhaps she was mocking him with it, just as Jack had done . . . thinking she was making a fool of him.

He determined to talk with her again. Probe a little more deeply.

After supper he summoned Portia to his bastion sanctuary. She sat demurely facing him across the big table, trying to hide her unease. She was under no illusions about Cato. He was sharp as a needle. And he must not—*could not*—know the whole truth of her encounter with Rufus Decatur.

"How many conversations did you have with Decatur?"

Portia considered. "Only one really. When I first arrived and he realized I was not Olivia."

"Did that anger him?"

"At first, but then he seemed to realize that his men had made an understandable mistake. I'd borrowed Olivia's cloak and they were told to take the girl in blue."

Cato had learned about the borrowed cloak from Olivia. So far their stories were consistent. "How exactly were you treated?"

With humor; with lust; with passion? Or just simply teased and manipulated by the Granvilles' bitterest enemy? She answered Cato levelly, "I was kept in an apple loft for the most part. I tried to escape by stealing a sledge and going down the river, but his sentries picked me up." She met his gaze.

Cato frowned. "And how did you escape in the end?"

"Some men went out on an expedition, and I managed to mingle with them, and then when we were well outside De-catur village I slipped away." The knowledge that that had been her intention and it could have worked gave conviction to her words.

Portia realized that she'd made no conscious decision not to help Cato in his war with Rufus Decatur, but there'd been no decision to make. She wasn't going to give him anything useful.

Cato stroked his chin, beginning to feel a flash of optimistic relief. So far he couldn't fault her. His gaze fell on a dispatch that had reached him that morning. "While you were there, did you hear anything of an attack on a party of Lord Leven's men just outside Yetholm?"

"Lord Rothbury and some men were absent from the village when I escaped," she responded carefully. "I didn't hear anything about their plans while I was in the apple loft." *Which was undeniably true.* "Has there been such an attack, my lord?" she inquired.

"Apparently," Cato said with a dismissive gesture, as if it were not important. He rose and began to pace the small room. "Did you discover what ransom Decatur was demanding for Olivia's safe return?"

"No." Portia lied directly for the first time. She saw in her mind's eye Rufus's face, a rictus of pain and fury, looking down on his house. She heard his voice, harsh, savage, describing what had been done by Granvilles to his father and his home . . . telling her what he had hoped to gain by abducting Olivia. How could she talk about that horror with Cato when she couldn't bear to remember it?

Cato glanced sharply at her and knew immediately that she was lying. It was in her eyes, in the tension of her mouth. And why would she lie if she had nothing to hide?

He stopped before the fire and stood resting one foot on the fender, his arm along the mantelpiece as he regarded her carefully. "Decatur knew the color of Olivia's cloak. That bespeaks an intimacy with our life here that's hard to credit. And I'm wondering how he would know to look for her on the moat. How would he know you were in the habit of skating together?"

"I don't know," Portia said.

"I'm wondering if perhaps there's a spy in our midst," he said in a musing tone, his eyes resting on her face.

Portia felt as if she were treading on stepping stones across a racing torrent. All she could think of was Rufus eating Cato's meat in the outer bailey, eavesdropping on his enemy's conversations, watching her skate with Olivia on the moat. Risking his neck in a deadly game that only amused him. His eyes had been laughing the whole time . . . it had been the first time he'd kissed her. . . .

Her eyes dropped to her hands knotted in her lap. "I suppose it's possible, my lord."

Cato smiled suddenly and said, "Well, there's no need for you to concern yourself anymore. I'm only glad that you're back, safe and well. And Olivia, I know, is delighted. She has need of a companion. You may go to her now."

When she'd curtsied and left, Cato resumed his pacing. The smile had vanished the minute the door closed behind her. He was certain now that Portia was hiding something.

She hadn't been able to meet his eye. But if she was a spy in his camp, maybe he could turn her to his own use. So long as she didn't suspect his suspicions, she could be fed information. Disinformation that would draw Rufus Decatur into the trap that would bring his downfall.

And what in the devil's name had Brian been playing at with Diana that afternoon? They had certainly not been selecting embroidery silks. The sooner he got rid of Brian Morse, the easier he would be.

Had he known it, unexpected forces were at work to rid Castle Granville of Brian Morse. Brian fell into bed much the worse for Cato's fine cognac and was soon snoring. The nest of red-spotted spiders greeted the expanse of bare flesh disturbing their peace with vicious indignation. They scuttled over him, insinuating themselves into the nooks and crannies where the flesh was at its most moist and succulent. Brian tossed and turned, drawing up his knees, plagued in his drunken dreams with pinpricks of discomfort.

He awoke when the servant assigned to him opened the shutters and the bedcurtains. "There's 'ot water for shavin', sir. An' the boot boy cleaned all your boots."

Brian sat up, blinking at the harsh light. His head was throbbing. He pushed a hand beneath the covers to scratch his thigh and then his groin. Something brushed against his fingers and he threw off the bedclothes. The squiggling red-spotted creatures exposed to the light were like some nightmare of delirium tremens. An involuntary screech emerged from his lips.

The servant stared in astonishment. "Where'd they come from? Them's spiders, them is."

"I know it, you fool!" Brian leaped to the floor. "Kill 'em." He examined his legs. Great red welts showed up against the flesh. He turned his thigh out and saw the line of them creeping up into the dark pubic nest. He shuddered with revulsion as the servant began to thrash at the spiders with the poker.

"Can't think where they come from, sir," the servant declared, chasing a particularly succulent specimen scuttling to safety into the rumpled bedclothes. "You must've brought 'em in wi' you."

"Fool! Of course I didn't." Brian began to scratch and as he scratched the itch grew worse, the welts grew larger, and seemed to spread. "Bring me a bath . . . hot water . . . scalding water!" he bellowed and the servant fled.

In the corridor, the man bumped into Lady Olivia and Mistress Worth. They were strolling casually along the passage, arm in arm. "Good morning, Peter. Is something the matter with Mr. Morse?" Olivia inquired.

"Oh, Lord love us, Lady Olivia. But fair crazed, 'e is." Peter was grinning. "Shouldn't laugh, I know, but Lord, it was funny. 'E's got spiders in 'is bed. An' they've bit 'im all over. Wants scaldin' water now. Fair scratchin' 'isself to death, 'e is." And Peter went off chuckling.

"Oh, Portia, you're so clever!"

Portia's smile was smug. "It's quite a nice little trick, isn't it?"

"And I have another one," Olivia said, her dark eyes alight with excitement.

"Oh?" Portia stopped in the corridor, intrigued. "You're going to play your own trick on the toad! Well done."

"Yes, I am." Olivia flourished a small twist of paper, her face flushed at her own inventive daring. "I paid a visit to the stillroom this morning. I thought I might give him a little surprise in his morning ale."

"What?"

"Wait and see."

Portia chuckled, delighted at the idea of Olivia's taking matters into her own hands. It was the best way to banish spectral fears.

Olivia could barely contain her excitement. When Brian appeared in the dining parlor, she tried not to look at him too openly, but it was very hard to keep secret her laughter and the delicious thrill of anticipation.

Brian responded to Diana's greeting and apologized for being so late at the breakfast table and barely glanced at Olivia when she murmured a stammered "Good morning." He shot Portia a look of pure venom. She responded with a demure half curtsy.

Olivia watched him closely, and every time he wriggled, every time he moved a hand down below the level of the table and she could guess he was scratching between his thighs, she had to stifle her laughter. His expression grew increasingly pained as the dulling effects of the hot bath faded and the full raging itch returned.

At one point he jumped up from the table as if stung, and when Diana looked at him in surprise, he flushed to the roots of his prematurely thinning hair, coughed, and went to the sideboard, lifting the lids of chafing dishes as if inspecting the contents, but all the while he was rubbing his thighs together desperately, shifting from foot to foot.

Olivia glanced at Portia, her eyes glowing with laughter, then casually she leaned over Brian's ale tankard to reach for the salt cellar. As she did so, her closed hand opened over the lip of the tankard, then she sat back in her chair once again and buttered her bread.

Oh, wicked girl, Portia thought to herself with a barely subdued chuckle. She had no idea what Olivia had put in Brian's ale, but guessed it was a choice doctoring.

Brian returned to the table, offered a casual remark to Diana about the weather, and sat down.

"Is everything all right, Mr. Morse?" Diana was genuinely concerned.

"Yes, indeed, Lady Granville." He laughed, but it was a hollow and unconvincing sound. "In such delightful company, a man couldn't have a care in the world." He took up his tankard and drained the contents in one.

Portia was aware of Olivia's utter stillness as Brian drank. Only when he set the tankard down empty did she resume her breakfast.

Cato entered the parlor a few minutes later. He greeted his family and helped himself to veal collops from the sideboard. He'd been up for hours and brought the cold morning on his skin and the distraction of an army commander in his manner. But even he was astonished when Brian suddenly leaped to his feet and ran from the room.

"Good heavens, what ails the man?"

"I d–don't think Mr. Morse is too well, sir," Olivia said with apparent concern. "He seems in p-pain."

Portia choked on a crumb.

"He was well enough yesterday," Cato observed.

"Perhaps I should go to him." Diana rose from the table.

"Oh, I shouldn't do that," Olivia muttered in a voice that only Portia heard.

"I beg your pardon, Olivia?" Cato looked inquiringly.

"N-nothing of significance, sir."

Diana reached the door just as it opened again and a very pale Brian reappeared. "Forgive me," he murmured, resuming his seat.

"Are you quite well, sir?" Portia asked in a voice to rival the music of the spheres.

Brian opened his mouth to reply, then he pushed back his chair with such violence that it toppled to the floor. A groan escaped him as he ran from the room.

Cato was beginning to look alarmed. "Perhaps you should send the physician to him, Diana."

"Yes. Yes, I'll do so right away." Diana hurried from the parlor.

Portia said, "If you'll excuse me, Lord Granville, I believe I'm wanted in the nursery to help Janet with the babies."

Olivia jumped to her feet and excused herself in Portia's wake, leaving her father alone at the breakfast table.

"What did you put in his ale?" Portia demanded in a laughing whisper, dragging Olivia into a window embrasure in the corridor.

"A mighty dose of senna," Olivia told her with a whoop of laughter. "He'll b-be purging on his close-stool all day."

"Oh, clever girl," Portia said with approval. "Brilliant."

Olivia glowed with pleasure.

"I imagine he'll be leaving very soon," Portia said. "People rarely like to stay in places where they've made fools of themselves . . . or where they've been made fools of," she added thoughtfully. "I'd better go and be pleasant to Janet."

She went off with a little wave, and Olivia slipped a hand up to the locket at her neck. She opened it and took out the ring of braided tricolored hair. Friendship was a most powerful force. It could even shatter demons.

14

*W*hat were they bringing into the castle? *Portia squiggled* forward to get a better view down through the privy chute to the moat beneath. She was looking at the same scene she had witnessed before—men unloading pack mules, disappearing with their burdens beneath the drawbridge and through the hidden entrance to the vaults. The operation, as before, was conducted in absolute silence and under the supervision of Giles Crampton.

Portia wriggled backward and stood up in the cramped space. She was fascinated by what she had seen. Fascinated and intrigued. It obviously had to do with the war. Cato was collecting something for the war effort. But what?

Her regular nightly spying expeditions had become all-absorbing since her return to Castle Granville and the igno-minious retreat of Brian Morse. She knew that she was always looking for some sign of Rufus or his men. Some familiar fig-ure flitting in the shadows . . . a familiar voice whispering in the dark. *An old man with a hunched back shuffling along in a peasant's homespun.* If Rufus could spy in the very heart of Cato's domain, it was not impossible to imagine that he or one of his men would be around, watching, in some shape or form. She had no idea what she would do if she did catch sight of one of them . . . or of Rufus himself. Confront them? Offer to help with the spying?

Ridiculous. She was the enemy. Rufus would not accept her help.

She told herself this bitterly, many times over, but it didn't change her actions. Sometimes her abduction seemed like a dream, and the need to remind herself that it had really hap-pened—that everything it had led to had really happened— was like an itch that had to be scratched.

So she crept around the castle, imagining she was gathering information for Rufus Decatur—information that she would never be able to pass on. But it gave her a purpose, made some kind of warped sense in the midst of her confusion and hurt.

Drawing her cloak about her, she flitted out of the cubbyhole and along the battlements. She flew down a narrow flight of stone stairs cut into the curtain wall, emerging into the outer bailey. Pitch torches in sconces along the walls flared in the night wind, throwing eerie shadows across the cobbles.

Portia crept around the walls, hugging the dark pools of shadow, until she reached the wicket gate. It was open and she could hear the sounds from the moat below. The sentry was working with Giles's men unloading the mules.

She slipped through the gate. The bank between the walls and the moat was a mere grassy ledge, a bare six inches wide. Portia flattened herself against the wall and tiptoed sideways until she was safely away from the torchlight illuminating the drawbridge. Then she stood immobile, flat against the wall, and listened. Voices rose soft but distinct from the working party below.

"That's the last mule, Sergeant."

"Right. Close up the vault behind you."

"Aye, sir."

There was a creak as of hinges in need of oil, then a soft thud, and the torchlight vanished. A jingle of harness came out of the darkness, and Portia guessed that the unloaded mules were being led away. She heard steps on the drawbridge, then the wicket gate closed and she was standing alone outside the castle.

Now what?

She sat down and slithered on her bottom down the bank to the ice-covered moat. It was pitch black, the great bulk of the drawbridge looming above her. She felt her way along the wall, the thick stone damp and icy cold, until she was standing directly beneath the drawbridge. Somewhere in the wall here was the hidden door. Without light, the faint outline was not visible, but she'd seen it before and knew that it was no more than three feet up from the surface of the moat. She took off her gloves, her fingers immediately freezing, and felt along the wall.

Ah, there it was. An infinitesimal line in the stones. It was too straight to be a random crack. She traced it along its horizontal top and then down the vertical sides, feeling for a knob, a lever, something that would open it from the outside.

Nothing. The stones were hard, unyielding blocks of ice. And she was stranded outside the castle at two in the morning!

Biting her lower lip, Portia expanded her search, running her flat palms over the stones alongside the line. Still nothing. Her hands were so cold now she couldn't feel anything. She pulled on her gloves again, shivering violently, and leaned back against the wall, wondering what to do next.

The wall opened behind her. It was so sudden she fell backward. There was no lintel and she stumbled into a black void, her hands flailing for purchase. She just managed to keep her feet by grabbing hold of the slab of stone as it swung heavily inward.

She was inside the castle, looking out onto the moat. Behind her it was pitch black, ahead the grayish dark of the night. Once she closed the door, she would be utterly blind.

She stood still, her ears straining into the darkness behind her. She could hear her blood roaring in her ears, her heart hammering against her ribs. Were the men long gone? Was there any danger she might run into them? She looked behind her and could see only a low narrow tunnel disappearing into darkness.

There was silence. A silence so complete it was terrifying. Pulling the door closed took more courage than Portia thought she possessed, but she managed it. The same creak, the same dull thud, and then she was standing in utter darkness and silence. She turned, placed her hands on the walls on either side, and began to walk, her head and shoulders bent low. But gradually the ceiling lifted and she could soon stand upright. The darkness grew less absolute as her eyes accustomed themselves, and as she peered ahead she thought she detected a grayness in the black.

And then she saw a flicker of light. Torchlight. She froze,

pressing herself against the wall even as her heart lifted at this sign of approaching habitation. There was no sound and the light remained in one place, flickering as if in a breeze. She slid forward again, keeping to the wall. The tunnel began to open out and she saw the mouth just ahead. And then she heard the voices. Cato's voice. And Giles Crampton's.

"I think we're done now, Giles." Cato's voice rang with satisfaction.

"Aye, m'lord. It's quite a haul." Giles chuckled. "I doubt there's a silver chalice left between 'ere an' York. When do we send it on?"

"Next Friday by the Durham road . . . now that my stepson's safely out of the way. . . ."

"Left in summat of a 'urry, I thought," Giles observed. "Looked right peaky, 'ardly able to sit 'is 'orse."

"Mmm," Cato agreed dryly. Brian's abrupt departure had not been very amicable. In fact Cato had the uncomfortable feeling that his stepson harbored a distinct grudge against Castle Granville. There had been something most unpleasant in his sallow brown eyes . . . something almost menacing if one were given to fancies. Which Cato was not. He had much more interesting matters on his mind than Brian's petty malice.

"When the treasure leaves on Friday, we shall make sure Rufus Decatur knows exactly when it leaves and by what road." Cato's voice was now cold but the earlier satisfaction was still there.

"Don't quite follow you, sir?" Giles sounded tentative. "Stands to reason 'e'd snatch it fer the king soon as look at it."

"Precisely. But he'll walk into a trap when he does so," Cato declared with the same chill certainty. "He'll attack the shipment and we'll be waiting for him. I shall see Rufus Decatur hang from my battlements before the month is out, you may depend upon it, Giles."

"Eh, 'tis a good plan, sir, but 'ow d'we draw 'im in?" Giles was a man of limited imagination, and his puzzlement was obvious to the listener in the tunnel.

"We spread the word about the shipment," Cato said patiently. "The countryside is crawling with Decatur spies. The information will get to him . . . and . . ." He paused.

Portia crept closer, forgetting the danger in her anxiety not to miss a word.

"And I believe we have a spy right here. If I'm right, Mistress Worth will pass on the information through whatever channels she's been instructed to use."

Giles whistled. "Ye do reckon she's gone bad, then?"

"I don't know whether she's bad so much as gullible," Cato said. "If I'm right, then she'll pass on this information as soon as she hears it, and if I'm wrong, then we'll make sure he hears it anyway."

Portia felt sick. Her hair seemed to lift as her scalp contracted.

She became aware that the voices were fading, then the light was extinguished, but she remained pressed to the tunnel wall until complete silence fell again. When she was certain she was once more alone, she stepped forward out of the tunnel and found herself in a large vault. She could smell the oil of the extinguished lamp. It was very dark, but she could make out the shapes of coffers stacked against the walls. She opened one and stared at the bright glitter of silver, the duller glow of gold, the sparkle of gems, that seemed to throw light into the darkness.

She touched the objects. Candlesticks, chalices, silver plates. There was jewelry too. Rings and broaches. A treasure-house of altarpieces, domestic chattels, personal jewelry. All of precious metals and gems. And all intended to enrich Parliament's coffers. Maintaining an army in wartime was a hugely expensive business. The king was as strapped financially as the rebels. This hoard would give either side a huge advantage once the spring fighting began.

Rufus Decatur would give anything to get his hands on this. And Cato knew it.

Portia let the lid of the coffer fall. The thud in the vast chamber sounded like a drumbeat, and her heart speeded. But silence fell again. She could make out the shadow of an opening in the far wall and went toward it. Another tunnel stretched ahead, but it was wider and higher than the one from the moat. She followed it, thinking furiously.

She had to warn Rufus of the trap. Cato was right. His enemy would have eyes and ears on the alert across the countryside. Nothing that Cato Granville intended escaped the notice of Rufus Decatur. He'd attempt to capture Cato's treasure, and he'd be captured himself.

The tunnel ended at the bottom of a flight of steep stone stairs. At the head was an oak door. Portia felt a chill of anxiety as she laid her hand on the latch. What if it was locked from the other side? But the hasp lifted smoothly and she slipped through, finding herself in one of the sculleries leading off the kitchen.

There was no sound but the loud ticking of the tall case clock in the kitchen and the hiss of a flaming log in the great hearth. Portia made her way via the back stairs to her own chilly chamber, where she sat on the bed behind the closed door, hands knotted in her lap, her mind racing.

So Cato believed she was a spy. A gullible naïf who didn't know what she was doing. A wave of indignation washed through her at the thought of how Cato intended to use her. She was to bait his trap! Well, blood ties or no, she was going to do the opposite.

But how? Unfortunately she didn't have the channels of communication with Decatur village that Lord Granville assumed she had. And it wasn't as if there were friendly postmen willing to take such a charged message across the wintry landscape of the Cheviot Hills in the middle of a war. She had no way of discovering one of Rufus's spies, and she couldn't wander the countryside dropping hints in the hopes that they'd fall on fertile ears.

The answer, of course, was simple. She would have to go herself.

The cold thought rose in her brain that once she'd left Cato's roof on such an errand, she'd never be able to return to it. She would be utterly adrift.

But she knew she had no choice. She couldn't stand aside and watch Rufus go to his death.

She crawled under the covers and shivered through a fitful doze. In the harsh gray light of dawn, she rose and began to move about the chamber, packing up her few belongings. She would have to go on foot. A daunting prospect, but she couldn't take one of Cato's horses, and Penny had been sent back to her owner as soon as she'd been bated and rested. Cato had not imparted to Portia the content of the message he'd sent back with her, and Portia had preferred not to know.

It was a four-hour ride to Decatur village, so it would be around a twelve-hour walk. And once she reached the bleak featurelessness of the Cheviot Hills, she would have no landmarks, only whatever prods her memory might give her. But she could look for the sentry fires. That ring of fire high on the hilltops would guide her from a good distance away.

She would need wine and food. Water she could find along the way. She had very little money left over from what Giles had given her in Edinburgh, but conscience forbade her using that for this purpose. Reluctantly she laid the two silver shillings on the washstand. Then she went to the kitchen to scavenge. It was still very early and only a sleepy scullion was about, poking at the fire and yawning his head off. He didn't acknowledge Portia's presence.

It seemed too short a time from the moment of decision to the point when she was ready to leave, but for such a momentous undertaking her preparations were minimal. She had a flagon of wine and a package of bread, cheese, and cold meat wrapped in a cloth. She was wearing britches under her riding skirt. Two pairs of stockings. A thick woolen cloak and gloves. Her few keepsakes were distributed throughout her various pockets.

Now all she had to do was bid farewell to Olivia and manage to get herself out of the castle without drawing attention to her departure.

The second task was going to be the easier, Portia knew as she made her way to Olivia's chamber.

Olivia was still asleep, but she awoke when Portia shook her shoulder gently. "What are you doing so early?" She sat up blinking, regarding Portia with puzzlement. "Why are you all dressed to go out?"

Portia sat on the side of the bed. "I have to go back to Decatur village," she said. "Your father has set a trap for Rufus and I can't let him fall into it."

"No, of c-course not," Olivia said, her gaze fixed wonderingly on Portia's face. "But what trap?"

Portia explained and Olivia listened, her brows drawn to-gether over her deep-set eyes.

"Will you c-come back?" she asked, but the bravery in her voice, the pain in her eyes, told Portia that Olivia knew the answer.

"You know I won't be able to. Your father will never wel-come me again." Portia leaned over and kissed Olivia's cheek. "But this isn't goodbye. Somehow I know it isn't. I don't know where I'll go after I've warned Rufus. But I'll try to get a mes-sage to you, to let you know what happened."

She frowned in thought, then was struck by an idea. "I tell you what, I'll leave messages on the island in the moat, under that boulder where the ducks gather when it rains. Look for something there whenever you can. Promise?"

"I promise." Olivia forced a smile. "*Go!*"

Portia kissed her again quickly and stood up, swallowing the lump in her throat. "Just one more thing." Her voice was urgent, eyes intent. "Olivia, you must pretend to know noth-ing about me . . . about why I've left or where I've gone. Can you do that?"

"Of course." Olivia sounded indignant that Portia should have doubted it. "Now go before I start c-crying."

Portia hesitated for a second and then left before she gave in to her own threatening tears.

She left the castle through the wicket gate in the north keep, telling the guard that she was going to feed the ducks. It was such a common occurrence that the man merely nod-ded, exchanged a few words about the weather, and let her through.

It was full daylight now. The sky was clear and there was very little wind. It seemed auspicious weather for the trek that lay ahead. The path dropped steeply into the valley, then wound its way for several miles along the valley floor before climbing up into the first series of hills leading into the Cheviots.

Portia walked briskly, swinging her arms, humming to herself to keep up her courage. When she could, she walked parallel to the roadway, concealed behind hedgerows. A lone woman was easy prey for anyone with hostile intent, not to mention the troops of soldiers who regularly crossed her path. Fortunately, tramping feet, the fluting of martial pipes, and the steady beat of the drum heralded the latter's approach in plenty of time for her to seek concealment.

She ate some of her small store of food at noon and rested for a while, but it was too cold to sit for long on the hard ground, even with a hedge as windbreak at her back. She passed a few hamlets and several isolated cottages, gradually becoming aware that the shadows were lengthening as the light was slowly leached from the sky. She'd been walking since eight that morning, and each step was becoming an effort. She had no idea how much farther she had to go, and once it was dark, not only would she never find her way but the already freezing temperature would plummet. She would have to find shelter. Some cottager would surely take her in.

The countryside had so far borne few signs of war, but that changed just after Portia had reached her decision to seek shelter. She had been walking down a narrow lane with high hedges on either side. A faint smell of lingering smoke was in the air, but she put it down to a farmer's bonfire or late stubble burning, until the hedge suddenly gave way to open fields on either side of the lane.

The fields were burned to the bare earth; trees, so painstakingly planted as windbreaks against the vicious gusts blowing off the hills and the moors beyond, were scorched skeletons against the darkening sky. The skeleton branches had rags dangling from them, and as Portia approached she saw that the rags were corpses, hanging from nooses, twisting in the freshening wind. They had been there for several days, and they bore the insignia of Lord Newcastle's royalist troops.

Portia turned aside, retching in disgust at the stench of corruption, the eyeless sockets, and the great flocks of black crows circling and cawing around their carrion feast.

A pathetic whimpering came faintly from the ditch alongside the gallows field as she stumbled away from the atrocious sight. She tried to ignore the sound but it went on, pathetic and yet insistent with a kind of last-chance desperation, and finally she turned back, averting her eyes from the gallows as she tried to trace the sound.

Its source proved to be a puppy, not more than five or six weeks, Portia judged. Not old enough to be motherless, certainly. It lay in the ditch, liquid brown eyes staring up at her from beneath a matted curly fringe. Its coat, in a most improbable shade of mustard, was a tangle of burrs and knotted curls.

"Oh, what an unprepossessing little thing you are," Portia murmured, feeling an instant bond with the abandoned waif. She bent to pick it up. It shivered against her, all skin and bone and wet hair. A scrap of material fluttered around its scrawny neck. It was a piece of a royalist flag.

Portia glanced involuntarily to the killing field. Had this puppy been a troop mascot? It seemed likely. A mascot left behind to starve in the aftermath of atrocity.

"Come on, then, pup. For some reason, I get the impression you and I are two of a kind." She tucked the creature under her cloak, against her heart, and felt the rapid fluttering of its own heart and the involuntary tremors, which slowly died down as the puppy warmed up.

Now she had to find shelter for the two of them. It was almost full dark, and what little warmth there had been in the day had fled under the rising wind. Portia trudged down the lane, even more wary now. The barbaric troop of parliamentarian soldiers who had committed that atrocity could still be around, and even if they were long gone, the local inhabitants would be afraid and more than ordinarily suspicious of a stranger.

She came to a hamlet about two miles farther down the road. The cottages were shut up tight, only the thin plumes of smoke from their chimneys indicated habitation. She chose the cottage nearest the small church and, with a boldness she didn't feel, knocked on the door.

There was no answer. She knocked again and waited. No sound, no sense of life. And yet she knew someone had to be sitting before the fire whose smoke curled from the roof. She knocked again and called softly, reassuringly. Maybe if they heard a woman's voice, they would open up.

Nothing. She walked back into the lane and surveyed the house as it squatted in a bare vegetable patch. The windows were shuttered, showing not a speck of light.

Portia shivered. She had never before felt so completely alone, and she was very frightened. She was as frightened of the cold, of the impossibility of spending a brutal February night without shelter, as she was of human attack. The puppy whimpered. The animal must be starved. Was it old enough to eat bread and meat and cheese?

But first they had to get out of the night. The sky was black with cloud, utterly lightless, and the wind was rising. The church would offer sanctuary. It would be cold and hard, but they would be out of the wind and safe from human interference.

She opened the lych-gate and trod up the path to the church door. It was a small Norman church, a huddle of gray stone, with a rose window over the arched oak door. Portia lifted the latch and pushed, praying that it wouldn't be locked. The door creaked loudly as it yawned open onto the dark, damp chill of the vestibule.

She stood accustoming her eyes to the darkness, and slowly the font, the long rows of pews, the glimmer of the altar, took shape. Maybe there were priest's vestments in the sacristy, something at least that she could wrap herself in. There was the altar cloth, but that seemed somehow sacrilegious.

She approached the altar and sat down on the top step against the communion rail, unwrapping her cloak to lift out the puppy.

"So, what sex are you?" It was too dark to see, but her searching fingers found the answer quickly enough—definitely female. The little creature licked her hand and whimpered again.

Portia set her down and opened the cloth package of food. The puppy scrabbled frantically against her knee as she smelled the meat. Portia took her knife from her boot and cut the meat up into the smallest pieces she could and laid them down on the altar steps. The puppy seemed to sniff and the offering disappeared.

"I have a feeling your need is greater than mine," Portia murmured, cutting some more. She fed all the meat to the puppy and drank the wine, feeling it warm her on the inside at least. She contemplated lighting one of the altar candles but decided that showing a light would not be wise. She had no idea what kind of reception she'd receive from the hamlet's inhabitants, but from what she'd seen of the shuttered cottages, it was wise to assume that it wouldn't be friendly.

The puppy, its belly full, trotted off into the darkness. Portia, guessing what she was after, scrambled up hastily. "Wait . . . you can't be uninhibited in a church." She scooped her up and carried her back outside. In the churchyard, behind the shelter of a yew tree, they took care of nature's needs, then returned to the church.

Portia found a threadbare cassock in the sacristy and wrapped herself in it. She sat with her back against the altar and closed her eyes. The puppy crawled up onto her lap and dived under her cloak and cassock, seeking her warmth.

"It's all right for *some*," Portia said, shivering. The trip outside had undone all the good of the wine and she had only a swallow left.

It no longer seemed sacrilegious to make use of the altar cloth. She couldn't imagine God would be offended if it would save one of his creatures from freezing to death where she sat.

Even with the altar cloth, it was too cold to sleep. She was bone weary, every muscle tensed against the deep ache of the cold. "You know something, Juno, if that ill-tempered bastard of a Decatur is in the least ungrateful after what I've been through, I shall take my knife to his throat," she muttered into the puppy's neck, finding some comfort in talking aloud even to an animal who couldn't talk back.

Why had she decided to call this unprepossessing scrap Juno? The question flitted through her brain without stopping for answer. Her mind began to play tricks. She thought she was back in her bed in Cato's castle. Then she was back in St. Stephen's Street in Edinburgh listening to Jack curse her up hill and down dale because she hadn't brought him enough brandy to keep the demons at bay. Then she was in a sunny meadow along the river Loire. The sun was hot on her back, baking her bones, and Jack was sitting a little way away from her playing dice with a pair of itinerant peddlers who were only just beginning to understand that the man they'd thought would be an easy mark was going to take them for everything they possessed, right down to the boots on their feet.

She brushed at her cheek where a fly was buzzing her, disturbing the glorious lethargy of the sun's heat, the lovely crimson-shot blackness behind her closed eyes. The buzzing continued. Annoyed, she slapped at it and something nipped her finger hard enough to jerk her back to grim reality.

She stared blankly at Juno, who stared back with her liquid brown eyes filled with anxiety. The puppy had been licking her cheek, sensing that she was slipping away into some landscape from which she might not return.

With a violent shiver, Portia leaped to her feet, dragging the altar cloth tightly around her as she began to walk the nave, up and down, up and down, until she was wide-awake and the blood was moving, if sluggishly, in her veins. She was still colder than she ever remembered being, but she was awake and alive.

She went to the door and peered out. The darkness was graying slightly, but the sky remained heavily overcast. "I think we'd do better on the move, Juno. I'd rather face a band of brigands than freeze to death here." She replaced the altar cloth and the priest's cassock, ate the last crust of bread and gave the cheese to Juno, then set her face to the wind, the puppy huddled beneath her arm.

By full dawn it had begun to snow, and she was now threading her way through the trackless wastes of the Cheviots, the only witnesses to her passing a few miserable sheep huddled beneath the scant protection of leafless trees. Thirsty, she made a hole in the ice covering a small stream. Juno drank greedily but the water was so cold it gave Portia a screeching headache. Tears of misery and desperation were falling unbidden and unheeded, freezing on her cheeks. She shivered convulsively, her clothes no more protection now than if she were naked. Only the puppy kept her going, created a small spot of warmth against her chest.

The snow grew heavier and she could barely see a step ahead of her, and now she no longer knew whether she was going in the right direction or merely round and round in circles. Nothing mattered except to keep putting one numb foot in front of the other as she stumbled into the wind-driven snow.

When she first saw the diffused glow through the white veil that smothered her, Portia barely heeded it. She'd forgotten what she was looking for . . . had almost forgotten who she was. There was just the single driving force—to put one foot in front of the other.

But her feet took her upward toward the glow without conscious instruction from her brain. She stumbled in a rabbit hole and fell heavily, wrenching her ankle. And then she lay there, sobbing with pain and cold and terror, knowing that she was going to die where she lay, in a snow shroud.

15

*P*itch torches *flared through the white. Voices came at* her from far above. Hands lifted her, and Portia clutched Juno to her with every fiber of her remaining strength.

Someone was forcing her lips apart, forcing her to drink. She coughed, choked with shock as the fiery spirits burned her gullet. An acrid ammoniacal smell burst through the darkness blanketing her senses, and she opened her eyes with a shudder.

"Lord love us, but if 'tain't the lass from Granville." George's voice was astounded. He pressed the flagon to her lips again. "Drink, lassie. Y'are near perished." Anxiously he passed the vial of ammonia beneath her nose while she was trying to drink, and she choked again, spluttering the rough brandy over her cloak.

A brazier glowed in the small watchman's hut, and it was warm and frowsty with the mingled smells of sweat and frying onions and ale. Juno wriggled out from under her cloak and jumped to the ground, making immediately for the brazier, where she nestled close, shaking herself.

"Lucifer an' all 'is angels! What's that?" George exclaimed.

Portia couldn't speak. Her lips were numb, her tongue seemed frozen to the roof of her mouth, her jaw was locked. She looked helplessly at George and his much younger companion, who both stood staring at her as if she'd emerged from the spirit world.

George scratched his head. "Jamie, run down and fetch the master. Tell 'im 'tis the lass from Granville . . . come back fer some reason."

Jamie enveloped himself in his cloak, took up a pitch torch from the sconce on the wall, and set off at a scrambling run down the path to the village. He raced down the narrow lane and stopped, panting, at Rufus's house. He banged on the door and shouted.

"Eh, m'lord! Come quick! Y'are wanted quick up top."

Rufus flung open the door. "What is it? Soldiers? Raiders?" As he spoke he grabbed for his swordbelt hanging on the hook by the fireplace.

"No . . . no . . . 'tis not soldiers, sir." Jamie shook his head vigorously. "No, nor raiders neither."

Rufus buckled his belt, his movements no longer so urgent. "What is it, then, Jamie?" The lad was a little slow, and badgering him only flustered him.

"Mr. George, sir, sent me to tell ye."

"To tell me what, Jamie?" Rufus slung his cloak around his shoulders.

" 'Tis the lass from Granville," Jamie pronounced proudly. "She's come back, but Mr. George don't know why. But she's 'alf perished. Thought she was dead, we did, lyin' there in the snow an—"

He got no further. Rufus had pushed past him and was racing up the lane. He climbed up the hill, his pace barely slowing, and strode into the hut, banging the door shut behind him.

"Holy Christ!" Two strides brought him over to where Portia was huddled on a three-legged stool beside the brazier. Her lips were blue, and he could see where her tears had frozen on her deathly white cheeks. Snow still clung to her eyelashes, and the fringe on her forehead was stiff with ice.

"What have you done?" he whispered. "What have you done to yourself?" He dropped to his knees, brushing the icy fringe from her forehead. He chafed her cheeks between his palms, desperate to see the life and recognition return to the slanted green eyes. She was staring through him as if she didn't recognize him.

He had tried so hard not to miss her. Had tried so hard not to worry about her. He had told himself that a brief and lusty encounter was all that either of them could have expected. She was a Granville. She could never be anything else. She'd defended the Granvilles when he'd been opening his agony to her. She'd ridden off and left him in his pain. She should have understood the desperate rage that had made him say what he'd said, but she'd failed him. She hadn't been able to put aside her Granville loyalties.

He'd nurtured his anger with a fierce flame, but now as he tried with his own breath to return the living warmth to her face, to her eyes, that anger was as if it had never been.

And she had come back. But why?

He wasn't going to get an answer to that question in her present condition. Practical concerns drove the rush of emotion aside. He bent and lifted her to her feet, tightening the cloak around her. "I'll take her down."

The words pierced Portia's numbed trance. "Juno!" she managed to say through violently chattering teeth.

"Oh, that must be the dog, sir." George bent to pick up the puppy. "Clutchin' it like 'twas a lifeline, she was."

Rufus, holding Portia against him as she swayed on her feet, surveyed the disreputable mutt in astonishment. Juno wagged a hopeful tail and panted breathily, tongue lolling.

"She saved my life," Portia said, coherently although her voice was a thread and sounded strange to her ears. "She has to stay with me."

Rufus couldn't make sense of her words, but he was too relieved at hearing her speak to care. He hoisted her up and over his shoulder, holding her steady with an arm at her waist. Then he took the puppy from George, tucking it under his free arm, and set off back down the hill at a steady lope.

Portia was beyond noticing this undignified method of transport. She was aware only that she was safe . . . that sometime soon the deep cold shivers at her very center would cease and she would be able to rest. Beyond that, she couldn't think.

Rufus flung open the cottage door and carried his two burdens inside. He dropped the puppy to the floor and eased Portia off his shoulder and onto a stool beside the fire. She still looked barely alive; even that flaring orange hair seemed to have dulled.

The incredulous thought occurred to him that she must have walked all the way from Castle Granville. And now he felt as he had once done when Toby, racing after a ball, had blithely leaped fully clothed into the river beneath the mill wheel just above the millrace. Rufus's terror, once the child was safe, had yielded to an anger that neither he nor Toby had forgotten.

Portia's body was convulsed with shivers, her teeth chattering unmercifully. "My ankle," she said, reaching down to feel her wrenched ankle through her boot. "It hurts terribly."

Rufus knelt to pull off her boot and then swore. The ankle had swollen and it was impossible to get the boot over it. "What the *hell* did you think you were doing?" He pulled his knife free of his belt and sliced gingerly through the side of the boot. "I cannot imagine what could have possessed you to attempt such a thing unless you've gone stark staring *mad!*"

"Oh, I'm mad all right," Portia stated through waves of pain and misery as he eased the boot over her ankle. "Mad to think it mattered a damn to me whether you swung from Cato's battlements or not."

Rufus held her foot in his hand. He looked up into her white set face with an arrested expression. "Should I know what you're talking about?"

But Portia's horrified gaze was fixed on her ankle. Her foot looked as if it was attached to a pumpkin. A dead white pumpkin streaked with red. She stared dumbly at this repellent sight.

"Seemingly not." Rufus murmured the answer to his own question. He had greater concerns at the moment, anyway. He returned his attention to her damaged foot, considering aloud, "Normally, the only way to bring down the swelling would be to pack your ankle in ice, but—"

"No!" Portia cried, tears welling at such a hideous prospect. "I couldn't bear it."

"If you'd let me finish, I was going to say that your flesh is already frozen, so I don't suppose it would do any good at all." He set her foot down gently and stood up. "I'll bandage it tightly and then we'll see. Right now you need to get out of those clothes."

He strode upstairs, impatience reverberating in every step. Portia tried to staunch her tears. His anger seemed so unreasonable, after what she'd gone through to help him. And she was so desperately tired. Juno crept against her sodden skirts and whimpered in sympathy.

"These should provide some warmth." Rufus reappeared with one of his own thick woolen shirts and a fur-lined robe. "You'll have to try and stand on one leg . . . what is that unsavory mongrel doing?"

"She's cold and tired and hungry," Portia said.

"She's also filthy." Rufus supported Portia with one hand under her elbow while with the other he began to strip off her soaked garments. She swayed unsteadily, but with fatigue rather than lack of balance.

Rufus knew that the most pressing need was to warm her, to get the blood moving again beneath that delicate white skin. He was afraid of frostbite, particularly in her swollen ankle. Brusqueness hid his concern as he unbuttoned, unhooked, divesting her of every stitch of clothing.

As he peeled down her riding britches, he realized that the wet had seeped even through the leather. He ran his hands over her belly, down her thighs, across the flare of her backside. Her skin was deadly cold to the touch. He caught his breath.

"God's bones, girl! You're soaked to the skin! Of all the demented, infantile things to do! Have you completely taken leave of your wits? What did you think you were doing . . . taking a Sunday afternoon stroll in the hills?"

Portia stared down at her thin, shivering body. Her skin was a horrible dead white and she shuddered with distaste. Shuddered that he should be looking at her nakedness, should be handling her body as if it were a fish on a slab. She couldn't bear to be standing naked before him. Her legs seemed like sticks, and her breasts were shriveled and covered in goose bumps, her nipples shrunken.

With an inarticulate imprecation, she shoved him aside and reached for the robe he'd hung to warm in front of the fire. She tore it down. "I can manage . . . leave me alone." In her haste, she accidentally put her bad foot to the ground and reeled back with a cry of pain.

Rufus caught her against him. "Be still!" he thundered, and Juno yelped in fright, cowering against the table leg.

Portia gave up. She was at the very limit of her strength and her will to endure.

Rufus rubbed her body with a towel, roughly as he forced the blood back to the surface so that the dead white became tinged once more with a healthy pink. He turned her around, lifted her arms, parted her thighs, abrading the soft inner skin, leaving not an intimate cranny untouched. His jaw was set with grim determination, and if he was aware on any level that this was a body he had possessed, had played upon, had once brought to the peak of pleasure, he gave no sign. And through it all, Portia gritted her teeth and tried not to think of anything. Her skin began to feel as raw as a scraped potato, but she uttered not a sound.

"Now put these on." He dropped his shirt over her head. It swamped her, reaching to below her knees. He pushed her arms into the wide sleeves of the fur-lined robe, much as he would have manipulated his sons' arms into their jerkins. "Sit down." He pushed her back onto the stool, and once more clothed, her vulnerability tucked away beneath wool and fur, Portia could allow herself to be aware of her surroundings.

"When did you last eat?" He began to bandage her ankle with wide strips of cloth.

"I had a mouthful of bread this morning. I had to give the meat and cheese to Juno; she was starving," Portia replied, her voice dull. She was warm though. A wonderful marrow-deep warmth that went a long way to compensating for the throbbing ankle, now tightly bandaged.

Juno wagged her plumed tail and batted at Rufus's leg with a small paw.

"She's hungry too," Portia explained unnecessarily. "Would you please feed her?"

Rufus looked at Portia on her stool, swathed in garments that completely drowned her. Her head was really all that was visible, an orange tangled halo sitting atop the dark fur collar of his robe. She was regarding him now with the rueful resigned bravado that had always inspired his respect and admiration, however reluctant.

Those slanted green eyes had haunted his dreams ever since she'd left him. That pointed nose. Those high cheekbones. The incredible softness of her skin was embedded in his hands' memory. He had fought it, denied it. Told himself that if their encounter had come to a natural end, he would have felt none of these strange hankerings, no sense of unfinished business. But now, as he looked at her, he acknowledged that he had never felt for another woman what he felt for Portia Worth. Not that he knew exactly what it was that he was feeling. But it went way beyond the simple lust of a convenient, brief, sexual partnership.

The dog scratched again at his boot. He looked down at her, seeing how pitifully small and young she was.

He began to laugh. Portia regarded him for a minute as if he'd taken leave of his senses; it was such a volte-face. But then she remembered that Rufus was given to such rapid changes in mood. Warmth and strength began to stir once more. She smiled tentatively and brushed her hair out of her eyes. "Are you pleased to see me?"

"Yes, dammit!" he said with some exasperation. "Don't ask me why. You turn up in a blizzard, half dead with exposure, scaring the wits out of me . . ." He looked down at the puppy again and his laugh rippled anew.

"What a pair you are! The pathetic creature could be your daemon." He picked up Juno and held her in the air to examine her more closely. "I doubt she's even weaned. Where did she come from?"

Portia told him how she'd found the puppy, and Rufus lost all desire to laugh. "Bastards," he said. "There've been reports of such barbarisms flying around for weeks, but it's the first time I've had an eyewitness account."

"Is it just the rebels who are being so savage?"

"No," Rufus said shortly. "I wish I could say it was, but both sides are as bad as each other and the reprisals grow ever more barbarous." He talked as he poured milk into a saucer that he set on the floor for Juno, who fell on it with an excited yap.

He poured whisky into two cups and gave one to Portia with the injunction that she drink it slowly, then he perched on the corner of the table and considered her closely. "So, what's all this about hanging from Granville's battlements?"

"I came to warn you that Cato's setting a trap for you. I couldn't send a message since I didn't know how to find your spies. Since you consider me to be the enemy, I suppose it's not surprising you wouldn't take me into your confidence." Portia was surprised that she had the energy for challenge.

"You didn't stay around long enough to warrant my confidence," he said quietly.

"I didn't see how I could have stayed after what you said. I still think you're wrong to be ruled by this vendetta. But I'm not part of it, Rufus." She half rose from the stool and then remembered her ankle. Her eyes raked his face.

Rufus stroked his chin, his eyes narrowed as he stared into the fire. Then he looked up, his bright gaze resting on Portia's pale countenance. "So, if you think I'm so wrong, tell me now why you risked your life, abandoned the only home you have, to help me. I should think you'd be delighted to see me swinging from Granville's battlements."

"One would think so," she returned smartly. "Believe me, I fought the impulse. But for some unfathomable reason, I lost."

Rufus grinned. Pure delight fizzed in his veins. Delight and immeasurable relief that she was truly unscathed. "Oh, gosling! Nothing blunts that hornet's tongue! So, tell me about this trap."

"I overheard Cato and his second in command, Giles Crampton. I used to wander around the castle at night." Portia offered the partial explanation with a little shrug. He didn't need to know about ancient privy chutes. She told him what she'd overheard and he heard her out in silence, drinking his whisky, his expression now impassive.

"I had gathered that Cato and his peers were collecting around the countryside," he observed when she had finished. "There should be quite a treasure trove by now." Rufus's smile was grim. "It'll fatten the king's treasury nicely."

Then his expression changed. He stood up and came over to her. He lifted her chin on his palm. His eyes were now grave as they looked down into her own. "I am very glad you came back. I don't know what I can offer you, but since you've been reckless enough to abandon Cato's hearth, then I fear you must accept mine." He ran the pad of his thumb over her mouth.

"I don't need your charity," Portia said, turning her head

slightly away from him. She wasn't certain quite what he was saying. The invitation, if it was one, lacked something. If he was offering her a home just because she had nowhere else to go, just as payment for her information, she knew she wouldn't accept it. "I didn't come here expecting it."

Rufus's hand dropped from her face. He stared down at her. "*Charity!*" he exclaimed.

"I can manage alone," Portia persisted. "I've always managed alone."

"Dear God! If you weren't in such a pathetic condition . . . !" He spun away from her and took one quick turn around the room. Then he came back and stood foursquare in front of her. "Do you *wish* to stay here?"

"Not if you're always going to think of me as a Granville," Portia said. Suddenly there was so much at stake. More than she could yet fully grasp.

"You are," he said flatly. "I don't see how I can forget it."

"But how important is it?"

Rufus sighed. "I have missed you, Portia. Not a Granville. But *you.*"

Portia smiled slowly, feeling the warmth seeping through her veins. "That's all right, then," she said.

Rufus had the strangest feeling that he'd just been routed in a battle he didn't know he'd been fighting.

Then Portia said softly, "I missed you too. I kept looking around for an old man with a humpback, lurking in some corner of one of the courts."

Rufus stroked her face lightly with his palm, feeling his unease fade. He was aware once more of her pallor, of her weakness, of his need to look after her. "I'm going to fetch you some food from the mess. I won't be long."

"Bring something for Juno too."

Alone, Portia sat drowsily in front of the fire, the ache in her ankle dulled by the whisky. She felt for the first time in her life as if she had come home.

Rufus returned within ten minutes, shaking snow off his cloak, stamping his boots in the doorway. A lad carrying a laden tray came in after Rufus. He glanced curiously at Portia as he set the tray on the table and seemed inclined to linger.

"Thank you, Adam," Rufus said pointedly, putting a lidded jug down on the hearth.

"Right, sir." The boy cast one more glance at the figure by the fire and with obvious reluctance went back into the snow.

Portia sniffed hungrily. "What is it?"

"Soup, braised ox tongue, and sack posset." Rufus filled a bowl with vegetable soup, his movements swift and efficient. He gave it to her and stood watching as she ate, like a mother hen with a wounded chick, Portia thought, stifling a smile. There was something wonderfully comforting about that close, concerned regard. It told her that in some way she belonged again. She belonged enough that the most trivial aspects of her well-being mattered to Rufus.

She drank the soup greedily. It tasted like manna from heaven. Rufus replaced the soup with the ox tongue and set a saucer of chicken giblets on the floor for Juno, who attacked it with something remarkably like a growl. Rufus poured himself more whisky and stood before the fireplace in his habitual pose, one arm resting along the mantelpiece, one foot on the fender. He watched, amused by his own possessive satisfaction, as his patients ate with steady concentration. Color was returning to Portia's cheeks and a little bounce to her hair, he noticed.

At last Juno abandoned her dish and came to the fire. She lay at Portia's feet, rolling blissfully onto her back, exposing her distended belly to the warmth, her legs flopping in the air.

Rufus took away Portia's empty platter and took up the covered jug from the hearth. "Drink this and then I'll put you to bed." He filled a tankard with the hot spiced milk curdled with wine and Portia curled her hands around it, burying her nose in the fragrant steam.

"Where're the boys?" His choice of words had reminded her of his unruly and ramshackle pair. She glanced toward the curtained corner with a little start. "They aren't out in the snow, are they?"

"No, of course they're not. I don't let them out in a blizzard." Rufus sounded indignant at such an implication. He was filling a warming pan with embers from the fire. "They'll sleep with Will tonight."

"Do they often do that?"

Rufus shrugged, setting down the tongs. "Quite often . . . if they're with him when they get sleepy." He picked up the warming pan and went upstairs.

Portia drank her sack posset. It seemed a remarkably haphazard way to bring up children, but who was she to talk? She who'd never known a moment's routine in her own upbringing. Not that she'd trumpet Jack's parenting as a model.

When Rufus came back down again and lifted her to carry her upstairs, she felt the most glorious relaxation, a warm and sensuous languor. Lying back in his arms, she lazily lifted a hand to touch his face.

"Don't get any ideas," he said, supporting her against his upraised knee as he turned back the quilts on his own big bed. "Necrophilia has never been a passion of mine."

"I'm not that tired," Portia said hopefully.

"Believe me, you are," he stated, deftly divesting her of the fur-lined robe and inserting her neatly into the bed. The warming pan had been passed over the sheets, and the bed was blissfully cozy.

Juno whined from the bottom of the stairs. The flight might just as well have been a sheer mountain for all her ability to scramble up it on her short legs.

"The dog may sleep below by the fire," Rufus said firmly, seeing Portia about to plead for the puppy. He looked down at her, thinking how pitifully frail her shape seemed under the covers. And yet he knew how robust she really was—at least, when she hadn't trekked for twelve hours through snowdrifts to save his neck.

"I have to talk to George about posting pickets. Will you be all right alone for a little?"

"Mmm." Portia yawned, waves of sleep breaking inexorably over her. "But can't Juno sleep up here?"

"No. She's filthy and probably flea-ridden," Rufus declared. "She'll be warm enough by the fire. Now go to sleep and don't argue." He bent and kissed her, his lips lingering for a minute on hers. He'd forgotten how deliciously soft her mouth was. Soft and sweet and wonderfully responsive.

"More," she demanded, when reluctantly he raised his head.

"Later. You may have as many kisses as you wish," he promised with a light laugh, then left her before she could sing more of her siren songs, and went downstairs, quietly letting himself out of the house.

Juno whined and scratched at the stairs. When Portia didn't come down to fetch her, she began to bark, incredibly annoying little yaps that made it impossible for Portia to sleep even through her exhaustion.

"Juno, be quiet."

It did no good. The yaps grew more high-pitched and impossible to ignore. With a groan, Portia dragged herself up and out of the nesting warmth. She stood on one leg and hopped across to the stairs. "How can I possibly come down to fetch you when I can't put my foot to the floor?"

The puppy took a running jump at the first step and tumbled backward. She yapped again, looking expectantly upward. "And you are filthy," Portia said. Juno whined.

"Oh, Lord!" Portia sat down on the top step and inched her way down on her bottom. The stairs were steep but the descent was surprisingly easy to accomplish using just one foot, while she held the injured one out stiffly in front of her.

At the foot of the stairs she scooped an ecstatic puppy into her lap and tried to lift herself backward onto the step above. The problem was immediately apparent. It was impossible to climb back up in the same way without using both hands. And she was holding Juno on her lap.

Portia groaned again. She swiveled round so she was facing up the stairs and lifted the puppy up three steps. "Stay there." Then painfully she hitched herself upward until she'd reached Juno and could lift her farther up.

The front door opened so softly she didn't hear it, so intent was she on this exhausting ascent. She didn't hear Rufus until he exclaimed from the bottom of the stairs, "I don't believe this! Tell me I'm imagining this, Portia."

"It's Juno," she said, between tears and laughter. "I know you said she couldn't come up, but she was yapping and whining so much I couldn't go to sleep. So I'm trying to get her upstairs so I *can* sleep! I'm so tired, Rufus." The last was almost a wail.

She was so utterly irresistible in her obstinate, dogged persistence against all the odds. Anyone else in such a state of exhaustion would have been able to ignore the puppy's distress. But not Mistress Worth.

Rufus reached up in a leisurely movement and plucked Juno from the step, holding her by the scruff of her neck.

"Oh, please don't put her outside," Portia begged.

"I'm going to bathe her." He held the animal at arm's length. "It's not what I usually like to do at eleven o'clock at night. However, needs must when the devil drives, and you, Portia Worth, wield a damnable devil's pitchfork." He dumped the puppy on the floor and leaned forward to scoop Portia into his arms again.

He carried her back upstairs and deposited her firmly in bed. "This time, would you please stay here?"

"You're not going out again?" Her eyelids were drooping already.

"No." He tucked the sheet tightly around her so that she felt as if she were in swaddling bands. "Now, for pity's sake, go to sleep."

Portia listened for a minute to the comforting sounds of his movements below. She could hear his voice, soft and slightly exasperated, talking to the puppy. She was trying to make out what he was saying when she fell into the deep black hole of oblivion where the scratching and whining and yelping from downstairs could not penetrate.

Juno objected vociferously to hot water and lye soap, but Rufus was ruthless. It didn't take long for the puppy to recognize the hand of a master, and finally she gave up her struggles and merely looked miserable and more akin to a drowned rat than a dog.

Rufus toweled her vigorously. "I know damn well you're going to insist on getting on the bed," he said. "And that mistress of yours is going to turn her slanty green eyes on me and there'll be nothing I can do about it." Juno thumped her tail, sending a shower of drops across the room. "You are trouble!" Rufus stated vociferously. "But I tell you straight, I am not going to sleep with a smelly wet dog, so keep still."

Finally he set her down in front of the fire, poured himself a large dram of whisky, and sat down beside her, stretching his legs to the fire. Juno put her head on his foot with a little sigh of contentment. Rufus glowered down at her but the puppy merely grinned at him.

Rufus gazed down into his whisky and turned his thoughts to the information Portia had brought him. His fertile brain examined and discarded plans as his blood stirred with anticipation. He saw his chance to outwit Granville *and* make off with the treasure, with little or no danger to his own men.

And the treasure would be his perfect bargaining counter.

His lips thinned, making of his fine mouth an almost invisible line. If the king wanted Decatur assistance, he would pay for it.

16

*A*s Portia *swam up from sleep, lingering tendrils of warm* dreams clung to her, drawing her down again to the soft pillowy depths. She lay buried in warmth, her body so heavy she couldn't move a limb, her mind drugged with sleep. For long minutes she was disoriented, images of ice, of closed doors, of cold corpses battering against the shutters of her mind. Then, slowly, full memory returned. She still couldn't move a muscle, but her fogged brain cleared, and she knew that she was lying in Rufus Decatur's bed, that her body was pressed to his side, rolled against him by his weight on the mattress. She was aware that the chamber was filled with a pale light that some part of her brain identified as snowlight. She remembered the blizzard then. She remembered Juno and as she lay still in the uncanny quiet created by the snow blanket beyond the window, she heard the puppy's snuffling breath from the end of the bed.

And then she became aware of something nudging her bare thigh. The shirt was twisted around her waist and something was burrowing, nuzzling against her skin. Indolently she moved a hand down and her fingers closed over the hard shaft of flesh that with a life of its own flickered, grew, pulsed against her palm.

Portia smiled to herself. Rufus was still asleep while his body frolicked, following its own instincts. She played with him, her fingertips lightly stroking, kneading, sliding back the soft hood to feel the dampening tip. The flesh leaped in her palm, like some blind burrowing animal. Her smile broadened, her loins were filled with a delicious languid warmth, and with her free hand she touched herself.

"Let me do that." Rufus's sleepy voice, husky and with a

smile dancing in its depth, caressed her even as his hand moved over her belly, slid between her thighs. His fingers found the little nub of her sex, the moist and tender opening of her body.

They lay side by side under the nesting warmth of the covers, playing with each other, until urgent desire banished the last vestiges of languor. Rufus turned her gently so that her back was to him and fitted himself against her, curling around her bottom. "I don't want to hurt your ankle," he whispered, his beard silky against her shoulder, drawing a surprised chuckle from her. "Bring your knees up."

Her body thus opened to him, he slid within her, one hand at her waist, the other against the nape of her neck, warm and firm. Portia could do nothing but lie still while the waves of delight lapped over her, awakening her muted nerve endings, her sleep-quiet skin. And when he grasped her tightly against him, his breathing swift and hard against her neck, his belly pressing against her bottom, his flesh pulsing deep within her, flooding her womb with his seed, she felt herself drifting away, without form or sinew, a bubble of exquisite sensation.

With a soft exhalation, Rufus fell back, his hands loosening on her body. "Welcome to the day, gosling."

Portia chuckled weakly. "That was a delicious good-morning. Oh, Juno!" she exclaimed as a wet tongue slobbered across her cheek. "But you do smell clean," she murmured with approval, patting the puppy's head. Juno gave a little yap of pleasure and tumbled off the bed, running to the head of the stairs and then back to the bed.

"She'd better go out." Rufus flung aside the covers and stood up. He stretched, and the muscles in his back and buttocks tauntened. He bent to poke the fire into life again, throwing on kindling, then logs as the blaze took.

Portia feasted her eyes on his naked body, noticing how the pale light from the window caught the fine red-gold hair clustering on his shoulder blades, in the small of his back, along the lean, powerful thighs. He was very beautiful, she thought drowsily, regretting the moment when he reached for the robe she'd borrowed the previous evening.

Juno yapped again and Portia sat up, sensual dreaming forgotten. "Oh, Juno, no!"

"God's Grace!" Rufus exclaimed, turning on the puppy, who was squatting by the head of the stairs, a puddle spreading beneath her. "The wretched creature isn't even housebroken!"

"She can't help it," Portia said. "She's so little and she's been on the bed all night. She was probably bursting."

"I was about to take her out," Rufus said grimly. He caught Juno up by the scruff of the neck and carried her at arm's length downstairs.

Portia listened to his voice, calm but undeniably scolding the errant puppy as he deposited her outside the door. He came back with a cloth and pail and mopped up the puddle. He looked less than pleased, Portia thought guiltily.

"Shall I do it?"

"No," he said.

"She can't be expected to know these things yet," Portia pointed out, trying very hard not to hear the puppy whimpering from the snow outside the kitchen door. "She'll have to be taught to go outside."

"I had not expected to add housebreaking a puppy to my list of chores," Rufus said aridly, wringing the cloth into the bucket.

"You won't have to do it. I'll do it."

Rufus got off his knees. "It'll keep you occupied, I suppose."

Portia hauled herself up against the pillows. "Occupied? What do you mean?"

Rufus reached for his clothes on the chest at the foot of the bed. "I've been racking my brains trying to think what I'm going to do with you," he said, throwing off the robe.

"*Do with me?*" Portia felt a faint stir of indignation at his tone. The languorous glow of after-love was disappearing rather rapidly.

Rufus pulled on his drawers and britches. He turned back to the bed. "This is a military camp, lass. There are no women, no friends or confidants for you. Everyone has their own duties . . . including me." He was putting on his shirt as he talked. "I cannot be forever entertaining you or—"

"I don't *need* entertaining!" Portia exclaimed. "You talk as if I'm some flighty flibberty-gibbet who's going to be a burden to you."

"No . . . no, I don't mean that!" Rufus said, tucking his shirt into the waistband of his britches. "But the fact is, this is no place or situation for a woman. And I don't know what to do with you . . . how you're going to occupy yourself."

"Oh, I expect I'll sew on your buttons and clean your house and cook your meals," Portia said dangerously. "That should keep me out of your way."

"Josiah wouldn't care for that," Rufus said seriously. "He'd feel usurped."

Portia gazed at him in disbelief. He had actually thought she was in earnest! "If this is such a problem for you, then I can't think why you asked me to stay," she said.

Annoyance and impatience flashed across his eyes. Then he seemed to make an effort to banish them. He came over to the bed. He bent over her. His mouth hovered, tantalizing, his eyes now teased. "Actually, I know exactly what I'm going to do with you. I'm going to keep you in my bed. The prospect of your lying here with nothing to do but wait for me to come to you is utterly delicious."

For a moment Portia couldn't resist the sensual promise in his voice. She responded with a low chuckle. "Pleasant dreams, my lord." She brought up her knee, pressing it with pointed emphasis against his groin.

Rufus's eyes darkened. His hands lightly clasped her throat, but before he could bring his mouth to hers, Portia wriggled sideways. "To be serious . . ."

"Oh, I am being," he said. "Keep still."

"No!" Portia pulled at his hands. "This is important, Rufus."

He released her and straightened, his expression now dark with annoyance. "I haven't time to argue over such a pointless issue. I have a host of things to do this morning." He sat on the chest to pull on his boots.

"Pointless? It's not pointless!" Portia couldn't understand how he didn't see this.

"There's a war on, Portia," he stated as if talking to a particularly stupid child. "I have an expedition to mount. In the light of those things, it is pointless."

"You're going after the treasure?"

"Of course." He buckled his swordbelt and when he

turned back to her it was clear his mind was elsewhere . . . once more in that dark place where Portia didn't want to follow.

"And with any luck," he said, almost to himself, "Cato Granville and I will meet up in his thwarted ambush." He smiled the cold, mirthless, grim smile that Portia hated. "A neat piece of table-turning to have Cato's head spitted on my sword, don't you think?"

"You know what I think," she said, biting her lip.

Rufus looked at her for a moment, with that same intimidating expression, and she returned his gaze steadily. A series of crashes sounded against the front door as Juno, frantic to be let in, hurled her small body against the oak.

"Damn dog," Rufus said, his expression clearing. "I'll send someone with breakfast for you. Do you want me to carry you downstairs?"

"Yes, please," she said, hearing how dispirited she sounded. She swung her legs over the end of the bed and scrutinized her ankle. It was still swollen and it still throbbed.

Rufus handed her his robe. "Don't let's quarrel, gosling," he said with clear effort. "It's not necessary. We'll find something for you to do."

"I want to be a soldier," Portia stated, pushing her arms into the robe. "I've always wanted to be. If you're going to fight this war, then I'll fight it with you."

To her fury, Rufus burst out laughing, all his tension vanished under the supreme humor of such an idea. "There's no place for a lass on a battlefield!" he exclaimed.

"I didn't do too badly with Colonel Neath," she said crossly, pulling the robe tight around her.

"No, a very creditable imitation of David and Goliath." Rufus was still chuckling. "I don't deny you're very handy with a knife. But women do not make good warriors, lass."

"Some have," Portia said tightly. "Joan of Arc, for instance. Boadicea, for instance. The Amazons."

"Enough!" He threw up his hands in mock despair. "You've windmills in your head, lass."

Portia said no more and Rufus took her silence as agreement to let the ridiculous subject drop. He lifted her and carried her downstairs, set her on a stool at the table, kissed her, ruffled her hair with careless affection, and left, letting Juno in on his way out.

The puppy bounded ecstatically to Portia, jumping up at her lap. Portia stroked her head absently, then, grasping the side of the table, stood up gingerly, wondering if she could make it through the fresh snow to the privy. She probably should have used the chamber pot upstairs, but she didn't like the idea of not being able to empty it herself.

She hopped to the scullery and found a pair of wooden clogs and a stout blackthorn stick by the back door. She stuck her good foot into one of the wooden clogs and with the aid of the stick hobbled out into the backyard. The blizzard had dumped close to a foot of snow, it seemed. The sun on the snow was dazzling and the air could cut glass. Someone in the last hour had shoveled the path to the privy. Someone delegated to take care of the master's comfort, she thought. There were definite advantages to rank.

The smell of bacon greeted her when she returned to the kitchen, blowing on her bare hands to warm them, shaking snow off the hem of the robe.

"I've brought your breakfast." Will turned from the table where he was setting out dishes. He blushed a little as he took in her dishabille. Rufus's robe swamped her, but there was still something sensuous and intimate about it.

Juno bounced around Portia's legs in greeting, as if she hadn't seen her in months, and Will with visible relief turned his gaze upon the puppy. "The devil! What an ugly thing! Where'd it come from?"

"She came with me. She's called Juno." Portia hopped to the table and sat down with a hungry sniff. "Can you keep me company for a few minutes, Will? There are some questions I want to ask you."

"Can't Rufus answer them?" Will looked rather as if he'd wandered into a witches' coven.

Portia took a sip of ale and broke a chunk off the loaf of bread. "What do you have to do to be a soldier in the Decatur militia?"

This was a comfortable subject and Will looked immediately more at ease.

"First, you must be able to draw a longbow of ash and hit a target at twenty-five yards." He counted off on his fingers. "Then you must be able to handle a cavalry sword. Third, you must be able to fire and reload a musket within two minutes . . . and hit a target at twenty paces. Fourth, you must be able to handle a pike."

It was an impressive, not to say intimidating, list of requirements. Portia speared bacon on her fork. "Would it matter if one used a lighter sword than a cavalry sword, and a willow bow instead of ash? As long as one used them properly?"

Will considered this. "I don't see why it should," he said after a minute. "As long as your comrades can depend upon you, then . . ." He paused, looking at her curiously. "Why do you want to know?"

"Because I intend to join your militia," she said simply. "And I want you to teach me what I need to know."

Will's jaw dropped. "I can't—"

"You can if you're willing," Portia interrupted. "I'm a good fencer already. I'm an expert with a knife. And I'm quite a reasonable archer. Of course, I've never used weapons in a battle . . . except of course for the knife . . . but I'm ready to do so."

"Does Rufus know?" Will still looked incredulous.

"Well, he does and he doesn't," Portia said judiciously. "It would be a secret though. I want to surprise him." She regarded Will shrewdly. "I saved your life once. You could say that I'm calling in the favor."

Before Will could respond, excited squeals preceded an energetic thumping on the door. "It's the boys," Will said distractedly. "They were following me." He rose from the table and went to open the door. Two small bundled figures tumbled in, caught off balance as they'd been jumping to reach the latch.

"Papa's comin'," Luke shrieked, righting himself.

"He wants to talk to Will," Toby explained with rather more solemnity. "You've hurt your foot," he stated, pointing to Portia.

"How d'you do it?" Luke inquired, scuttling on his knees to where Portia still sat at the table. He peered intently at her bandaged ankle.

"I tripped in a rabbit hole," she informed him placidly. Neither child seemed inclined to question her presence in their father's house.

"Oh, what's that?" Toby caught sight of Juno, who had retreated behind the log basket and was regarding these strange beings with a somewhat nervous air. "It's a puppy!" he exclaimed, leaping to his feet and rushing forward. "Look, Luke, it's a puppy!"

Juno growled, her hackles up, and backed up until she was almost in the fire as both boys reached for her with their eager dimpled hands, their voices shrill with excitement.

"Don't scare her," Portia said. "She's very little and you seem very big to her."

The boys nodded and dropped their voices to whispers as they waggled their hands, trying to coax Juno out from sanctuary. "Why won't she come?" demanded Luke.

"Because you've frightened her," Will said. "Come away from her and if you take no notice of her for a few minutes maybe she'll feel brave enough to come out."

The boys backed away on their knees and sat on their ankles a few feet from Juno, fixing her with intent bright blue stares.

"We come to c'llect our swords," Toby said without taking his eyes off the puppy.

"They're hanging on the hook next to Papa's." Luke pointed. Portia's gaze flew to the hook where Rufus kept his swordbelt and for the first time saw the two little wooden swords sheathed in felt hanging beside their father's great curved weapon. She grinned, it was such an absurd sight.

"God's grace! You are a pair of Lucifer's imps! You have wings on your feet!" Rufus appeared in the still-open doorway. His face was ruddy with cold and he clapped his gloved hands together vigorously. He gave Portia a quick smile but he was clearly distracted.

"Ah, Will, I'm glad you're here. Granville is sending his treasure out on Friday. They're going by the Durham road." He bent to the fire, rubbing his hands together.

"And we're going to stop them," Will stated with a grin.

"Some of us are." Rufus straightened, his voice crisp. "I'll be leading the expedition. You'll stay here as commander, with George as your second."

Will couldn't hide his disappointment but he didn't attempt to argue. Orders were orders.

"How convenient," Portia murmured so that only Will heard. He cast her a quick glance and she winked at him. He blushed and turned back to Rufus, who was continuing to speak, issuing rapid-fire orders as he paced the kitchen.

"Right, put that in motion, Will, and order a general muster in fifteen minutes," he finished. "Oh, and take the boys with you."

"We want our swords!" Toby announced, jumping up at the hook.

"Here." Rufus took them down. "Now go with Will."

The three of them left and Rufus turned back to Portia. He came over to her, catching her chin on the palm of his hand. "The day seems to have gone off course," he murmured. "Forgive me if I seemed too abrupt, gosling. It's a failing of mine, I know."

"Oh, I quite understand," she responded with a demure smile. "You're such a busy commander. So many lives depend upon you . . . why, even a king's throne and—"

The sweet little diatribe was silenced by his mouth. And this time Portia yielded to the wave of pleasure, her lips parting, her tongue flickering against his mouth, dipping into the corners in insistent little darts like a butterfly on buddleia. She had her plan and she was going to demolish Rufus Decatur's prissy ideas about what a woman could and could not do in his world. Until she was ready to spring her surprise, she could afford to pretend submission.

Rufus held her chin on the palm of his hand as he kissed her, moving his mouth from hers to touch the tip of her nose, her eyelids, the high, angular cheekbones, painting her features with the tip of his tongue and the pliant brush of his lips.

A trumpet blast calling for the general muster brought him reluctantly upright. "Let me put you back to bed, gosling. You still look exhausted."

Portia offered no objection and within minutes she was back in bed, Juno, after another visit outside, curled breathily into the small of her back.

"There now," Rufus said, with a mischievous twinkle. "All tucked up and waiting for me. Just as I like." The clatter of his booted feet on the stairs had faded before Portia could come up with a suitably tart response.

The sensation that awoke her was so delicate, so tantalizing, that for a moment she thought she dreamed it. Then she became aware of the air on her skin. Her robe was opened, the sides spread wide, baring her body. And something was moving over her skin, something exquisitely insubstantial, arousing little flickers of dreamy pleasure in its wake.

Her eyes opened and met the intent gaze of Rufus Decatur. He was naked, propped on one elbow beside her, and he was smiling with pure mischievous delight. "Don't speak," he said softly, and as if to enforce the command, he touched her lips with the soft plume of a quill pen.

Then she understood what had been causing that strange and wonderful sensation. She lay still, gazing up at him in wonderment and surprise. The quill pen whispered on her ear, tracing the shell-like curve, dipping inside so that she squirmed with a sensation so exquisite that it was almost painful and she would have spoken if he hadn't placed a finger on her lips. The plume painted the curve of her cheekbones and then the line of her collarbone.

Portia quivered, a curious tightness building in her belly. Her nipples cried out for the brushing caress even before it came. Before he traced the small mound of her breast and then delicately . . . oh, so delicately . . . flicked at the nipple until it tightened and the spiral of tension coiled ever tighter in her belly. The fluttering touch moved over her stomach, flicked into her navel, and then gently he parted her thighs, spreading them wide on the bed.

The air, cool and yet not cold, laved her heated center, making her feel truly opened, exquisitely vulnerable, and yet not afraid, only filled with a deep and inarticulate longing. The plume whispered over her inner thighs, so that her opened body throbbed, and then the sensation changed. The tip, sharper than the feathers and yet surprisingly soft, pricked her skin as he drew it up her thigh in a long steady line, drawing ever closer to her center. His gaze held hers. She was drowning in the bright blue pools that were so intent and yet so filled with that mischievous delight. She wanted to speak, to urge, to cry out with the anticipation that filled her so completely her mind no longer held sway over her body. Her loins throbbed, were filled with an unendurable longing—and yet she must endure.

With her eyes she begged for release and yet in this sensate world of utter confusion she begged too that this would never stop. He opened her center, the moist and swollen lips that guarded the secrets of pleasure. His touch was so delicate and yet it rendered her utterly exposed, utterly at the mercy of the pleasure only he could bring her. For an eternity, nothing happened. She lay untouched, suspended on the very outermost brink of bliss, and then he wielded the dainty instrument of delight. Her body jumped as the current of unimaginable joy jolted her again and again. She was lost to the world. Mindless. Aware of nothing but the great crimson waves of bliss breaking over her.

And before she came to shore, Rufus smiled and took her mouth with his as he gathered her against him. He slid into her tender opened body, his own flesh now a pulsing throb of need. Her eyes were wide open as she gazed up at him, still caught in the rolling peaks of a climax that had changed shape, had begun to sharpen, to build anew. Rufus knelt up between her thighs and drew her legs onto his shoulders. He drove deep into her, to the very edge of her womb, and he held himself there, sliding his hands down her thighs to cup her raised buttocks. She arched her back with a little sob, trying to draw him even further within her as her inner muscles tightened around him. With a wicked little smile, he withdrew slowly inch by inch until the very tip of his flesh stroked the nerve-stretched entrance to her body. Then, with one swift movement, he sheathed himself within her again.

Portia cried out, again and again. It was unbearable, it was astounding, it was unimaginable. Her fingernails raked his back and she clung desperately to him, clasping him tight in her arms, clinging to him as if he were driftwood in a raging sea.

But at last her hands fell limply from his back. "Sweet Jesus, what was that?" She could barely speak, her mouth pressed into his shoulder, tasting the salt sweat of his skin.

Rufus rolled sideways and lay still, his chest heaving, his

belly glistening with sweat. One heavy hand moved blindly to cover her pubic mound, the fingers tangling in the damp curls, possessing her.

"*La petite mort*," he murmured. "For those lucky enough to experience it."

"The little death." Portia turned her head sideways to look at him, the wonderment still lingering in her eyes. "I could become accustomed to such a dying."

He chuckled weakly. "It doesn't always happen, lass. There are always disappointments in the business of loving."

Portia stroked his nipples with the tip of her forefinger. "Is that a warning?"

He captured her hand with his free one and kissed her palm. "Don't expect the heavens to fall in every time, love."

"All right then, I won't." She grinned at him. "Even something a little less cataclysmic would be worth having."

Rufus laughed and reached over to close the sides of her robe. "You'll get chilled."

"It's quite warm in here."

"It's a furnace!" he corrected with some vehemence. "Before I dared expose that fragile little body to the air, I built the fire up until it was close to setting the chimney afire."

Portia sat up. "So you'd planned this?"

"Not really." He swung to the floor. "It came to me in a flash of inspiration." He stood, hands on his hips, looking down at her on the bed. "We had some unfinished business, if you recall."

"Oh, yes," she said lazily. "I recall." Her gaze sharpened. "When are you leaving?"

"In the morning. We have to prepare our own reception for Granville's men, and the disposition of the treasure. It can't lie around the countryside."

"No," she agreed, managing to sound a little forlorn. "How long do you think you'll be gone?"

"It's hard to say. But at least a week."

"I see," she said with a mournful droop to her mouth.

"Who wanted to be a warrior?" he teased, brushing a lock of hair from her forehead with a finger.

Portia lowered her lids to hide the flash in her eyes.

"I'm resigned to being a left-at-home-to-worry woman," she murmured.

"There's nothing to worry about," Rufus said seriously. "I promise you, lass, that *I* will return unscathed from this little expedition."

And how many wouldn't?

She had betrayed Cato and his men to Decatur vengeance. Or had she simply protected Rufus from Granville vengeance? Maybe it all came to the same thing.

17

Will was as embarrassed on the third day of lessons as he'd been on the first. He stood on the riverbank, watching critically as Portia drew back the slender willow bow, taking aim at the target set into the thick trunk of a leafless oak.

It was the britches, he thought. That was what made her seem so outlandish, so unlike any woman he'd ever met. But then he thought it wasn't just that. Although that was a part of it. It was all part and parcel of her strangeness. And Will was a conventional soul, truly comfortable only with the routines and the people he knew. He liked the excitements of his out-law life, certainly, but they were what he was used to. He knew what to expect, and what to expect of his comrades. And this Mistress Worth was as unexpected and as curious as if she'd descended from the moon.

At first Will hadn't known whether Portia was serious or not about joining Rufus's militia, but after its commander and his men had left Decatur, she'd made it crystal clear that she was in deadly earnest. And Will had found her impossi-ble to resist. He still didn't know why. Oh, it was one thing for her to remind him that she'd saved his life, to say she was calling in the favor, but he still could have refused on the grounds that his commander hadn't authorized it and he couldn't act without orders. But for some reason he hadn't been able to say that.

He'd consulted George, who was Rufus's oldest friend, the man who, on the death of Rufus's uncles, had taken on the role of elder statesman among the outlaw clan. And George, instead of saying Portia's idea was ridiculous, had merely twin-kled at Will in his placid fashion and said, "Why not? Can't do any 'arm to gi' the lass a few lessons. It'll be between 'er an' the master in the end, anyway." And he'd offered to teach Portia the more savage arts of pike and musket, leaving Will with the delicacies of archery and swordsmanship.

George seemed to have no difficulties with his task, but then the older man was not disturbed by his new pupil, unlike Will, who, in Portia's presence, became tongue-tied, argumentative, although he didn't want to be, and stumble-footed.

Will forced himself to concentrate on the task in hand. Having once agreed to take it on, pride would not let him fail. It wasn't going to be his fault if Portia didn't succeed in making the grade.

As he watched her closely now, she was testing her healing ankle gingerly before loosing the arrow, and he knew from three days of this all the telltale signs of nervousness that preceded the moment of firing. The set of her shoulders, the little adjustments of her feet. He waited for her to look up into the sky as she always did the instant before loosing the arrow.

And as always he was aware of reluctant admiration at her determination. If determination alone would get her through, she would succeed. The willow was strong, much stronger than any bow she would have used in sport archery, and it was an effort for her to bend it, but she managed it now with the appearance of ease.

An excited shout came from the lane leading to the river just as she released the string. The arrow flew mortifyingly wide of the mark, to land on the river, skidding across the ice.

"We'll get it . . . we'll get it!" Toby and Luke, still shrieking, materialized from the lane. "We saw you . . . we saw you," they chanted, as they raced past and skidded across the ice to retrieve the arrow. There was a brief rough-and-tumble as they fought for possession, then Toby, triumphant, slid on his bottom back to the bank, waving his prize above his head. Luke, wailing, remained in the middle of the ice.

Will went to fetch him, carrying him back to shore. "You can't be here while we're practicing," he said.

"We'll stand behind," Toby protested. "Way way behind. All the way over here." He bounced back a few yards in demonstration.

"That's not good enough," Will said firmly.

"Apart from anything else, you ruined my shot," Portia

declared, taking another arrow from her quiver. "If you do that again, I could easily misfire and hit you. And then where would you be?"

"Dead?" questioned Toby thoughtfully.

"Hurt, anyway," Portia said. "Go back to the village, and when Will and I have finished, I'll come and fetch you and we'll take Juno for a walk."

"Promise?"

"Promise."

They went reluctantly, looking over their shoulders as they did so.

"I think," Will began diffidently, "that you're not standing quite right. You need to open your legs more." A deep flush spread up from his neck.

"Like this?" Portia braced herself, feet wide apart, as she fitted the arrow to the bow.

"Yes, but your shoulders . . ." Will adjusted her shoulders, his face aflame, silently wishing his cousin to the devil. He stepped back. "Now try."

The arrow this time hit the target respectably close to the center. Will retrieved it. "That was good."

"Not good enough," Portia stated flatly. "I'm damned if I'll leave this bank today before I get a bull's-eye, Will." She took the arrow back and fitted it to her bow. "Tell me what else I'm doing wrong. You must know."

"I think it's the way your fingers are controlling the arrow," he said diffidently. "You're holding it too tightly." Standing behind her he reached around to demonstrate. His arms brushed her breasts and he jumped back as if he'd been burned.

Portia turned to him. "Look, Will, can't you forget that I'm female?"

"Not very easily," he said. "And particularly when you're Rufus's bedmate."

"Oh." She scratched her head in thought. "Can't you think of me like one of the other women who come into the village?"

Will merely stared at her as if she'd lost her wits. She sighed. "I suppose not. Well, let's look at it this way. As far as

I'm concerned, you're Rufus's cousin and therefore almost like a brother to me. Can't you see me like a sister?"

"I suppose I could try," Will said a touch glumly. "But it's not easy. I've never had a sister . . . and I don't think even if I had she would be anything like you."

Portia gave up. Will would get used to her in the end.

Her lessons with George were altogether easier. The old soldier saw only his task, and once he'd decided for himself that his pupil was absolutely serious, he went about teaching her with the prosaic efficiency he employed with any new recruit. It took Portia a while to get used to lunging at a sack of straw with a pike, imagining that the wickedly sharp point was ripping through human flesh and sinew. She wasn't bloodthirsty by nature, and George's lessons in anatomy, while pointing out the most efficacious points of contact, were remarkably graphic.

However, she told herself that this was only an exercise. She had to prove to Rufus and his men that she could do it. That she could be depended on in any situation. It didn't *have* to mean that she would find herself actually trying to skewer someone's guts.

The musket was better. There was some distance involved in firing a bullet, although she was under no illusions as to the damage it would cause. Her long, thin fingers were deft and quick, and she had little difficulty mastering the art of reloading in the time allotted. The weapon was heavy on her shoulder, though, and the recoil jolted her arm badly. Within a few hours she'd acquired a massive bruise, and it took all her powers of endurance to continue practicing without letting George see how painful it was.

The rapier work was the best. Jack had taught her to fence when she was twelve. It was a sport at which he had excelled until brandy had ruined his eye and the tremors prevented him holding anything heavier than a brandy flagon. Will was much more relaxed when they were fencing in Tod's barn. Portia's skill left him little to teach her, and quickly their bouts became enjoyable for both of them.

As the days passed with no news, Portia quelled her anxiety. She told herself that the longer Rufus was away, the better.

She wanted to be absolutely proficient when he returned. She wanted George and Will to be able to say without a qualm that she was skilled enough to stand beside them in the line of battle. Her lessons drew observers. They were amused, skeptical, at first. But then there were subtle changes in their attitude. Their comments became encouraging rather than slightly mocking, and soon they were offering their own advice. Portia began to feel with each day that she was somehow—all on her own without Rufus—forging a place for herself among these men.

Not once did she feel threatened by her position as a lone woman among an infamous band of savage brigands. Experience had taught her to expect the worst of men, particularly in groups, and at first she assumed their restraint was because she was the master's woman and no one would dare to muscle in on their commander's territory. But that wouldn't preclude lascivious looks, insulting sexual innuendos, asides, and degrading jokes. But there were none of those either. It was a pleasant surprise, one that put a few dents in her preconceived notions of the male sex in general.

She was engaged with Will in a fierce fencing match in Tod's barn when Rufus returned. He had ridden into the village a little ahead of his men and arrived without fanfare, wanting to surprise Portia. He was disappointed to find the cottage empty, and went in search of her in the mess.

"Oh, the lassie's usually wi' Will in Tod's barn at this time o' day," Josiah informed him casually from among the cooking pots.

Rufus was intrigued. What possible daily business could take Will and Portia to the barn? He made his way there and paused at the unmistakable sound of steel on steel. Frowning now, he slipped through the half-open door to the barn and stood in the shadowy dimness watching the two lithe figures.

Portia was good, he realized immediately. She was quicker than Will, and maybe a little less accurate in her lunges because of her speed, but she parried his attacks with impeccable precision and her opponent could rarely get under her guard.

God, how he'd missed her! Even in the absorption of planning, in the heat of danger and the excitement of victory, he had thought of her constantly. He couldn't wait to get back to her . . . couldn't wait to hear that she had missed him as he had missed her.

She'd not been sitting moping in his absence, though, he thought wryly. He watched her for a moment, unseen, enjoying this private moment of appreciation. Her grace and enthusiasm on the piste reminded him of her wonderful uninhibited dancing, and of the lithe, sinuous way she used her body in lovemaking. She was laughing with exhilaration as she caught Will's blade with a parry in tierce and Will, looking grimly determined in contrast, dropped his point.

"Bravo, gosling." Rufus stepped out of the shadows, clapping his gloved hands in approval.

"*Rufus!*" Portia tossed her rapier onto a bale of straw, bounded across the barn, and leaped straight into his arms, wrapping her legs around his waist, her arms around his neck, kissing him with unashamed passion.

"You're safe," she declared against his mouth. "I was so worried, although I tried not to be."

"Of course I'm safe," he scoffed, his hands cupping her buttocks.

"But did you get the treasure?"

"It's been transported to Newcastle."

"Any casualties?" Will asked, trying not to sound as awkward as he felt. He didn't know where to look. His cousin's hands seemed so large and Portia's bottom so small.

"Some," Rufus said. "But no deaths on our side."

There was a moment of silence. Portia couldn't bear the suspense. Even if it jeopardized this moment of reunion, she had to find out. Had she betrayed Cato to his death? "Cato?" The one-word question seemed to crash through the silence.

Rufus set her on her feet. "Granville did not take part in his ambush," he stated. "Left it to his minions . . . fortunately for him," he added with a harsh laugh. "We routed them so thoroughly, had he been there we would have had our reckoning, he and I." Then, with almost visible effort, he wiped the darkness from his eyes and said briskly, "So what are you doing fencing with Will?"

Will looked at Portia, who looked at Will. Then Portia took

a deep breath and said, "Will and George have been teaching me all the necessary skills to fight in the militia."

"*What?*" Rufus demanded.

"I told you I wish to join your men," Portia said steadily. "And I can prove to you now that I'm quite capable of doing so. I'm good enough, aren't I, Will?" She fixed him with a gimlet gaze, willing him to speak up.

Will felt the ground shift beneath his feet. Rufus was looking as if he couldn't believe his ears. But Will was no coward. He said, "Her swordplay's better than mine, and she's decent enough with a bow."

"Thank you, Will," Portia said softly.

He glanced at her quickly, then shrugged. " 'Tis the truth. You saved my life once, and I'd not fear if you were beside me again."

High praise indeed! Portia flushed with pleasure. She had the impulse to kiss him, but soldiers did not go around embracing their comrades in arms.

"Are you telling me you dragged George into this ridiculous business?" Rufus demanded.

"Aye, m'lord. I've been teachin' 'er pike and musket." George spoke from behind him. He'd heard of the master's return and had come immediately to hear news of the expedition. Judging from the master's fulminating countenance, it seemed Portia's plan was in danger of foundering. "The lass'll do well enough, sir. The men've been watchin' 'er practice. They're all of the same opinion."

That was something Portia had not heard. Her flush deepened. She said with swift determination, before Rufus could react, "I'll prove it to you, Rufus. You saw me fence just now, but I'll fence with you." She darted to pick up her rapier, drawing it in a swift salute through the air. "And then I'll hit three bull's-eyes on the target out of six arrows, and I'll show you how I can fire and reload a musket in just over a minute . . . and then I'll show you how I can disembowel a hay bale." Her eyes shone with the overpowering need to convince him; the words tumbled from her mouth in an exuberant cascade. "If you'll just let me—"

Rufus held up a hand. "I don't need to see you do these

things," he said, his voice clipped. "If Will and George say you can do them, then that's good enough for me. But it doesn't make any difference, lass. D'you really think I'm going to let you expose yourself to the dangers of a battlefield?"

Portia squared her shoulders and faced him, her chin tilted, her mouth set. "If I wish to expose myself to those dangers, that's my business, not yours, Rufus. I'm good enough to fight under your standard, and it's insulting for you to say that just because I'm a woman you won't permit it. If your own men are willing to have me join them, why should you prevent it?"

At the end of this impassioned speech, the silence in the barn was so thick it would have smothered a conflagration. No one noticed that George had beaten a quiet retreat.

Rufus's expression was unreadable, then he said brusquely, "Will, in an hour, I'll give a briefing on the expedition. General muster in the drill hall."

Will gave a half salute and left the barn with clear relief in his step.

Rufus turned back to Portia, who was still regarding him with an air of fierce challenge. "Must you glare at me like that?" he asked with a slightly quizzical smile. "I've had warmer welcomes from a stone."

Portia hesitated. She saw now how tired he was. He was gray with fatigue, his eyes dark ringed, his fine mouth drawn within his beard. And she felt a surge of guilt at having launched her attack before he'd had time to recover from the journey. The issue was not so vital that it couldn't wait until they'd greeted each other properly.

"I'm sorry," she said with instant remorse. "You look so tired, love."

"An understatement," he said, passing a hand over his chin. "I'm in sore need of a bath and a change of clothes, and a cup of mead wouldn't come amiss."

"I can provide all of those things," Portia said with a smile, taking his hand and leading him out into the lane. She swung on his hand as they walked to the cottage in a silence that was now both contented and anticipatory.

Rufus pushed open the cottage door. "Yes . . . yes, I'm

delighted to see you too, Juno . . . I think." He addressed the puppy, who was prancing on her hind legs and yapping in a shrill ecstasy of greeting.

Portia reached up and lightly touched Rufus's face, running the tip of her finger over his mouth. "I'll bring you the mead." She filled a tankard from the pantry. "Shall I get the bath for you?"

"Please." Rufus groaned as he sat down at the table, stretching out his long legs. "God, I'm awearied. We've been riding for twelve hours straight."

Portia dragged the tub before the fire and hefted the copper kettle from its hook, staggering slightly under its weight, but when Rufus moved to help her she shook her head. "I can draw a willow bow, Rufus, and massacre a bag of straw with a pike. And I can certainly carry a kettle of hot water."

Rufus raised an eyebrow but he said nothing. However, he left her to pour the steaming water into the tub herself while he began to unbutton his buff leather jerkin. He kicked off his boots and rolled down his stockings, before standing to unbuckle his swordbelt and divest himself of his britches and drawers.

Maybe she was being selfish, but without the slightest nudge of guilt Portia threw self-restraint to the four winds. "Are you so tired because you didn't sleep in Newcastle?" she inquired innocently, as he stepped into the tub and eased himself down, his long legs dangling over the end. "Or were you too busy with town amusements for something as dull as sleep?"

Rufus regarded her with narrowed eyes. "Are you perchance trying to pick another fight?"

"This one's as an alternative to loving," she said, kneeling beside the tub. "I feel the need for some excitement." She leaned over and kissed him, running her fingers through his beard, her tongue, sinuous and importunate, demanding entrance to his mouth. Her hand moved down over the strong column of his throat, over his chest, lingering at his nipples, her fingers lifting the red pelt that sprang in energetic curls across his upper body.

Rufus rested his head on the back of the tub and closed his

eyes, yielding to the wicked little caresses, the tantalizing darts of her busy fingers as her hand slid beneath the water, played a tune on the muscle-taut skin of his belly. And then lower, between his thighs, lifting his soft organ, cradling it in her palm, squeezing gently, pulling back the little hood of flesh to find the sensitive tip.

He leaped into life against her palm and she laughed softly, nibbling the corner of his mouth, dipping her tongue into the cleft of his chin.

"God's grace, but you'd tempt a man from the grave," Rufus murmured. "Just what have you been up to while I've been away?"

Portia leaned over and kissed him with her eyelashes, fluttering the golden fans across his lips. "Let me see . . . archery, swordsmanship, murdering sacks of straw, loading muskets . . . oh, and dreaming. I had plenty of time to dream alone in that great bed. And I believe I dreamed to good purpose," she added with a triumphant little crow of laughter, sitting back on her heels. "What say you, Lord Rothbury?"

"I say that it's time I gave you something to dream about," he declared. "Take your clothes off."

Excitement flared in her eyes. "Here . . . now?"

"Yes. Hurry."

Portia stood up to throw off her clothes, and then, naked, she looked down at him, uncertain what happened now.

"Come here." He reached for her hands and pulled her down. "Kneel astride me. . . . That's it. Now guide me within."

Portia followed instructions, her tongue caught between her teeth, a little frown of concentration between her brows. She lifted herself slightly to take him within her body, then lowered herself gently so that she was sitting astride his hips.

"Now you play the tune," Rufus said, his hands clasping her waist. "You move as you wish. Whatever feels right. You're in control."

Portia's eyes widened, but it didn't take her long to realize that he spoke only the truth. And not only was she in control of her own pleasure, she was also controlling her lover's. She laughed delightedly, reading his responses in the bright gaze below her own, feeling every ripple of his body as if it were her own. She wanted to keep them both suspended in this glorious sensate realm and experienced a flash of disappointment when she realized she could do nothing in the end to hold back the tide of passion as it swept aside the dikes of control. But it was a mere flash lost forever in the glorious cascade of pleasure.

A long note of a trumpet, sustained in a thrill of sound, brought Rufus out of his postcoital trance with a jerk. "Hell and the devil! Is it an hour already?" He patted Portia's hip. "Up, love. I have to go."

Portia reluctantly got to her feet and Rufus stood up in a shower of drops. "Mother of God!" he exclaimed. "What the hell happened to your shoulder?" He touched the yellowing contusion spreading from her neck across her shoulder.

"It's the recoil from the musket," Portia explained. "But now I use a pad of rolled cloth to support it, and it's a lot less painful."

Rufus stood frowning as if about to say something, then he shook his head in brusque dismissal of his thoughts and stepped out of the tub. The consequences of her decision were her own, and if she had to learn them the hard way, so be it. She'd made it clear she didn't want to be babied, didn't want any concessions.

"Get dressed," he said, rubbing himself vigorously with a towel. "It's a general muster and you're not exempt."

Portia wasn't sure whether she understood aright. She regarded him almost warily. "Are you . . . am I . . . may I . . . ?"

"Yes, I am . . . yes, you are . . . yes, you may join the militia," Rufus said, in a tone that didn't sound exactly thrilled to bits about his capitulation. "It's against my better judgment, but don't expect any concessions. From me or from anyone, is that clear?"

He glowered at her, but Portia only grinned in delight. She was perfectly happy in this instance to have the commander replacing the lover. "I wouldn't wish it otherwise, my lord." She whipped the towel from his relaxed grip and used it to dry herself before scrambling into her clothes. "How much d'you think Cato's treasure is worth?"

Rufus buckled his belt. He had his back half turned from her and she couldn't see his expression. "Enough," he said.

Enough for a king's pardon. Enough for the restitution of the house of Rothbury. Enough to wrest his birthright from the control of Cato Granville.

18

Portia wriggled forward on her belly until she had a clear view from the top of the hillock down onto Castle Granville. The drawbridge was down, and as she watched, a detachment of soldiers marched out from the castle, the standards of Granville and Parliament snapping in the wind above them.

She could see the ducks' little island in the middle of the moat. It would take her fifteen minutes to climb down, five minutes to leave her message for Olivia, and maybe twenty minutes to get back uphill. How to explain such an absence to Paul, her present partner?

She edged backward and stood up. Paul was sitting on the ground, his back to a rock, placidly eating an apple. Their two horses, tethered to a sapling, were busy with the contents of their nosebags.

"How long d'you think it'll take the others to get here?" Portia inquired casually.

"Will said to expect 'em afore sunset," Paul replied. "I don't reckon 'e thought we'd get done quite so fast." He grinned and tossed aside his apple core. "We wouldn't 'ave been either if you 'adn't picked up them tracks."

Portia unbuckled her saddlebag and withdrew a cloth-wrapped package. "Did you eat all the chicken, Paul?"

"I thought you said you didn't like it."

"I never said any such thing," she protested. "Oh well, I suppose I can make do with cheese." She perched casually on the rock with her bread and cheese.

"Yeah, I reckon if you 'adn't picked up them tracks, we'd prob'ly 'ave missed 'em altogether," Paul said, picking his teeth with a twig.

Portia's smile was a little smug. "They were certainly surprised when we jumped out in front of them." She and Paul had been given the task of following two men, traveling as well-to-do farmers, who Will had heard on his spy grapevine were actually rebel couriers, carrying information from General Fairfax in Hull to Lord Leven, who was camped outside Durham.

Paul chuckled. "Aye, the master'll be pleased wi' what we got out of 'em."

They'd tracked the two men to a hamlet some five miles away from their present picnic spot and had managed to spring an unpleasant surprise on them. With the result that the two couriers were now lodged, bound and gagged, in a henhouse awaiting an uncertain rescue, and the papers they'd been carrying were tucked away in an inner pocket in Portia's saddlebag. They were interesting papers, too, revealing information about troop movements that would be of vital importance to the royalist armies.

Will had sent Portia and Paul off on this errand while he and the rest of the patrol had gone after a small troop of Granville militia, hoping to engage them in a skirmish.

It had been a desultory war in the north border lands during these winter months. One of skirmishes and spies, of sieges and needling harassment. No decisive battles had been fought since Leven had brought his Scots army across the border. The royalist forces still held the north, except for Hull, but spring was in the air, armies would soon be able to move more freely, and the royalist forces under Lord Newcastle were now outnumbered. If the two wings of the rebel armies joined forces, the king's cause would be destroyed in the north.

Rufus would certainly be very interested in the information Portia carried in her saddlebags.

"I'm going for a little stroll, Paul." She slid off the rock.

Paul merely grunted and closed his eyes, arms folded over his chest beneath his cloak, preparing to take a nap.

Portia knew he assumed she was merely going to answer nature's call and left him with that assumption. With any luck, he'd sleep most of the afternoon . . . she might even be back before he awoke.

She moved with all the speed and cunning she had learned in the last weeks, through the small grove of trees that covered the hillside leading down to the castle, darting from trunk to trunk, using the concealment of bushes and rocks. Her britches and jerkin were dark wool, blending with the landscape, and her bright hair was concealed beneath a cap that hugged her head. She had both rapier and knife in her belt . . . and if she had to use them it wouldn't be the first time. She had learned many things in the last weeks, not least that scruples about shedding blood vanished into the wind when one's own blood was threatened.

She inched her way around the moat until she faced the little island. There was a warmth in the March sun now; the vicious bite of the winter wind softened. In a week the ice on the moat would be too thin for Olivia to venture forth on skates. This was Portia's last chance to leave the promised missive beneath the boulder.

She had been agonizing over how to get a message to Olivia, but there had been no opportunities until today. Even if it would have been possible to leave Decatur village without detection, she'd been kept far too busy to make such an expedition.

The master of Decatur had been true to his word, and the new recruit to the ranks had been absorbed without reference to her sex or her relationship with the master. Her position was lowly, and she was regularly assigned to the boring and tedious tasks that went into keeping a full-scale armory in pristine condition. She took sentry duty according to the roster, and if it meant she was absent from Rufus's bed, the commander accepted it without a murmur. And when Rufus went out on expeditions, he didn't always include her among those he chose to accompany him. She'd challenged her exclusion on one occasion, only to be told that he'd checked the roster and seen she was assigned to culverin drill. And Portia had reluctantly come to the conclusion that Rufus genuinely had not considered the possibility of changing her duty to accommodate such conflicts.

Today's little excursion had begun as routine. Will was checking up on the network of spies he had around the countryside and had taken a detachment of ten with him, including Portia and Paul. Ordinarily he would have been content just to pursue the rebel couriers, but the news that a small troop of Granville men was approaching from York had fired his blood. He wanted to conduct an engagement, without either Rufus or George. It would be the first time ever, and it was too good an opportunity to prove his skills as a battlefield commander.

Sending Portia and Paul after the couriers, not a particularly dangerous task since they'd be better armed than their quarry and would have the advantage of surprise, had seemed to Will to be the perfect solution. They had arranged to rendezvous for the ride back to Decatur village at sunset. Which gave Portia two hours to complete her business on the moat. Plenty of time.

She looked up at the castle, the standards flying from its battlements and keeps. On the ice, hidden by the island, she would be out of sight of the drawbridge and the watchtowers, and once on the island she'd be quite safe from detection. Nevertheless, it took a deep breath of courage to force herself to emerge from the safety of the bushes and step down onto the ice. It looked greenish and transparent, and there was a single ominous crack as she walked forward.

"Hell and the devil!" she muttered, and, crouching low, raced across the ice. She had no idea how deep the moat was, but even if it was shallow, she'd be in a pretty pickle if she went through the ice. She scuttled onto the island amid a quacking flurry of ducks and dived into the screen of bushes.

The boulder was there as she remembered. She took the letter out of the inside pocket of her jerkin and slid it beneath the boulder, then prepared to make the dash back across the ice.

She heard the voices the instant before she stepped out from concealment. They were a little way away and it took her a minute to realize that one of them was Olivia's. But who the hell was the other one? It was one thing for Olivia to see her here, but she couldn't afford anyone else to catch her.

There was nowhere to go. The island was little bigger than a large rock, and she was taking advantage of its only concealment. Perhaps Olivia was skating on the moat and would bypass the island. The voices came closer. They were high and intense, both female. Portia frowned, searching errant memory. There was something familiar about the second . . . ah, she got it. It belonged to Phoebe. Diana's little sister. Not dangerous unless she'd changed dramatically. She perched on the boulder and waited.

The girls came onto the island. "The boulder is behind the bushes," Olivia said, her voice somewhat breathless. "She p-promised to leave a message, but she hasn't yet. I'm worried that maybe she didn't get to Decatur."

"I got there all right, duckie," Portia said, relishing her moment of surprise.

Olivia squeaked with shock and delight. She flung up her hands. "Oh, *Portia!*"

Portia hugged her. "I left you a note, but it's a bit superfluous now." She regarded Olivia's companion with a smile. Phoebe hadn't changed at all. Her round face was pink with surprise, her candid gray eyes full of good nature.

"Good heavens, how you startled us," she declared rather obviously. "Olivia was sure you were dead. What extraordinary clothes you're wearing."

"They're very practical for the life I'm leading these days," Portia said with a cheerful grin.

"Olivia thought you were going to be Lord Rothbury's mistress. Does he like you in britches?" The question expressed simple curiosity.

"Not in bed," Portia said wickedly.

"You're wearing a *sword!*" Olivia gasped. "*Why?*"

"Because I'm a soldier," Portia said patiently. "I always wanted to be."

"Yes, that's what you said in London," Phoebe put in. "I remember. When we all swore to be true to our ambitions, and not to be ordinary."

"Well, I don't think I've broken the pact," Portia said. "There's nothing ordinary about being a soldier."

"I haven't got very far with my ambition," Phoebe said a touch gloomily. "I'm trying to write poetry, but I'm not very satisfied with my efforts. There's always something missing, it seems to me. And I can't do good works when we're not permitted to leave the castle because of the war."

Olivia wasn't listening to this exchange. "You c-can *use* the sword?" she demanded of Portia, eyes incredulous.

"Of course."

"Show us, then."

Portia realized how very far she had moved from Olivia's life. "It's not a toy," she said quietly, and changed the subject. "So, Phoebe, what brings you up north?"

"Oh, my father! He's declared for Parliament and so he brought his own militia up here to join with General Fairfax, and he thought I'd be safest in Castle Granville with Diana," Phoebe said in disgust.

"Yes, Portia. And D-Diana hates her more than she hates *me*."

"Lord, that must be hard," Portia said.

"It's *dreadful*," Phoebe stated. "She is such a horrible person. I thought maybe being married and having babies would make her kinder, but it hasn't . . . oh, look, how did I get stains there?" She brushed dismally at a collection of spots on her cloak.

"And your petticoat flounce is torn," Olivia pointed out helpfully.

"Oh God!" Phoebe wailed. "*How?*"

"When you fell on the ice."

"I can't skate properly," Phoebe said with a glum sigh. "I trip over my feet just walking, so how could I possibly expect to remain upright with these on my boots?" She raised one foot with the bone blade attached.

"You won't be able to skate much longer anyway. The ice is thinning," Portia said, thinking to offer comfort.

"Yes, and it would be just my luck to go right through it," Phoebe said. "I'm so fat. Diana says I'm like an elephant."

Portia regarded Phoebe critically. "You're not fat. You're round."

"*I* couldn't wear britches," Phoebe stated. "Can you imagine what I'd look like?"

Olivia gave a little choke of laughter and Portia said, "Why would you want to?"

"I don't," Phoebe said. "Fortunately." Then she went into a peal of merry laughter that transformed her countenance, chasing away the self-deprecatory frown in her eyes.

"Well, I'm glad you're here to keep Olivia company," Portia said. "I've been worried about her."

"I told Phoebe about what you did to Brian," Olivia confided on another choke of laughter.

Portia grinned. "What we *both* did, duckie." Then she sobered. "What did your father say when I disappeared?"

Olivia shook her head. "He was very angry. But I said I didn't know where you'd gone, or why. He seemed to believe me. And then something really bad happened. I don't know what. But I know he blames you for it."

Portia nodded. It was what she'd expected. "I have to go," she said abruptly. "I'm glad you've got Phoebe here, Olivia. Goodbye." She slid past them before they had fully grasped that she was leaving so suddenly. Then with a quick wave, she plunged onto the ice, racing across the moat to disappear into the bushes on the far side.

Portia clambered up the hill. She heard the jingle of bridles, the low murmur of voices, just before she broke from the grove of trees onto the open hillside where she'd left Paul sleeping. She slowed her step and crept forward, her heart banging against her ribs. She must have been away for at least an hour. Had Paul been ambushed?

What she saw, however, made her curse under her breath. Will and his group had arrived earlier than expected. They were all still mounted except for Will, who was deep in conversation with Paul—an agitated conversation judging by the waving arms.

She braced herself for questions and sauntered out of the trees. "It wants an hour to sunset," she observed. "You made good time. Did you have good fortune?"

Will spun round. "Where've you been? Paul said you've been gone for hours."

"Paul was asleep," Portia said, taking a calculated risk. "I've been and gone several times." A quick glance at Paul reassured her. He was now looking uncertain.

"Where did you go?" Will was frowning.

"I must have eaten something that upset me," Portia said. "Surely you don't wish me to go into details."

A couple of weeks ago, Will would have blushed to his

ears, but no longer. He was as comfortable with Portia now as he was with any of his comrades and found it perfectly possible to ignore her relationship with Rufus. His rank within the militia gave him authority over her, and since Portia didn't question it and Rufus clearly upheld it, matters between them had become easy and friendly. He merely retorted, "Well, I hope we don't have to keep stopping for you on the way back. The countryside is crawling with Roundheads."

Portia swung herself into Penny's saddle, bringing the mare up beside Will's mount. She could tell that Will was upset about something other than her disappearance. "Did you find more than you bargained for with the Granville men?"

Will was silent for a minute, then he said reluctantly, "We had them on the run, but a battalion of bastard rebels came over the ridge. We were hopelessly outnumbered, so we had to abandon the chase."

"Oh, I'm sorry." Portia leaned over and touched his gloved hand in a fleeting gesture of sympathy. She had guessed how much this expedition had meant to him. "But you *did* have the first lot on the run."

Will's expression cleared. "Oh, you should have seen them go, Portia! They turned tail like so many rabbits before the reaper. We could have taken 'em all prisoner."

"There'll be another time," Portia comforted. "And a good commander knows when to pull back from battle. Rufus is always saying so."

"Aye, he is, isn't he?" Will looked much happier. "Paul told me you took dispatches from those couriers."

"Did he tell you what was in them?"

"No . . . we were too busy wondering what had happened to you."

"As I said . . ." Portia raised a speaking eyebrow, then leaned sideways to unfasten her saddlebag. She fumbled inside for a second, then withdrew the rolled parchment. "See for yourself."

Will eagerly scanned the parchment, then he let out a low whistle. "Troop movements. This has to go to York immediately."

"That's rather what I thought," Portia said. She could tell

by the gleam of excitement in his eye that he'd forgotten his earlier disappointment in the prospect of bringing such a vital document back to his commander.

It was full dark when they passed the sentry fires and came to a weary halt in the stable yard. Will dismounted and Portia, handing Penny to one of the lads on stable duty, said, "Are you coming to the cottage, Will? I expect Rufus will be there."

Will hesitated. Portia had been responsible for acquiring the priceless piece of information, but he, as leader of the expedition, had the right to take the credit for it. "You take it if you like." He reached inside his jerkin.

"No, you go. I'll go and find the boys. I expect they have Juno with them. It's past their suppertime and I'm sure they're not at home yet." It was an educated assumption. Luke and Toby were only ever to be found at home when they were asleep, and not always then. Rufus didn't seem to feel the need to instill routine in their lives, and Portia couldn't see that it was any business of hers.

Will watched her go, feeling ungenerous and almost childishly petty in the face of Portia's considerate restraint. He knew how anxious she would be to greet Rufus. She always became fidgety as they approached the village after an absence, and he sensed how she was longing to gallop ahead instead of trotting in decorously as part of the troop. And now for his sake she'd postponed the moment she'd been anticipating for the last hour.

But his own excitement soon overcame conscience, and he found himself running toward Rufus's cottage. Rufus was standing in the open doorway, looking down the street, when Will came racing up.

"Where's Portia?"

Will heard the sharp edge to the question and understood that Rufus had been anticipating her return as eagerly as had Portia. He flushed and said, "She went to find the boys and Juno. She said she'll be along in a few minutes."

Rufus frowned, then stepped back into the lit cottage. "You had a successful day?"

"We intercepted couriers." Will handed over the parchment, trying to conceal his bursting excitement. "Details of troop movements!"

Rufus ran his eyes over the message. "How did you get this?"

Will's hesitation was barely perceptible, before he said, "Portia and Paul did." He explained the events of the day and the decisions he'd taken in meticulous detail and with total honesty.

Rufus listened gravely. Once or twice a quick frown flashed across the calm blue gaze, but at the end, he smiled and said, "A thoroughly successful expedition, Will. I congratulate you."

Will beamed with pleasure. "We'll be sending the information to the command in York, then?"

"Yes, it needs to go tonight." Rufus turned to the table to pour ale for them both.

"I'll take it."

Rufus shook his head. "Nay, lad, you've been riding hard all day. George can carry it."

Will looked disappointed but resigned. He drank his ale and set the tankard on the table. "I'll be off, then."

Rufus nodded. "Before you go off duty, take the dispatch to George and give him your instructions."

Will looked gratified. He'd expected Rufus to take over this matter of such vital importance. "He's to leave immediately?"

"Immediately," Rufus affirmed. He leaned over and clapped him on the shoulder. "You did well, Will."

"Yes, didn't he?" Portia's voice chimed in from the doorway. She stood regarding the two men with a slight smile that did nothing to hide the sensual glow in her eyes as they rested on Rufus. "The boys have gone downriver with Silas . . . to visit some friend of his, apparently. And they've taken Juno with them. There's no knowing when they'll be back. I can't help feeling it's late for them to be out."

"Oh, Silas will look after them," Will said airily. He brushed past Portia with a word of farewell.

Portia continued to stand in the doorway, motionless, her eyes still fixed upon Rufus. "Don't you think it's very late for them to be out?" she said.

"I think the absence of both dog and boys is very fortu-
itous." He came toward her slowly, investing each step of his
advance with silent promise. Portia shivered in anticipation,
wondering how it was he could do this to her. How just being
in the same room with him could cause such a melting in her
loins, such a weakness in her thighs, such a jolting current of
lust in her belly.

Rufus stood in front of her without touching her. He
leaned around and pulled the door closed, the latch clicking
like a statement in the fire-warmed, candlelit silence. He was
so close to her he could almost feel her heart beating, and the
scent of her skin filled his nostrils—it was a rich earthy scent
where sweat and horseflesh and fresh air mingled with her
own particular fragrance, a fragrance he didn't think he could
ever tire of. It was youthful, delicate, and yet abundantly
healthy, and it went with the exquisite softness of her skin and
the wild, unruly strength of her hair and the living light in her
eyes.

He raised a hand and pulled off her cap. The bright orange
mass of curls sprang free with a life of their own, and the pale
face was surrounded by a flaming halo. She had a smudge of
dirt on her cheek.

Negligently almost, he traced the line of her cheek with
his forefinger, lightly pressed the jutting tip of her chin, ran
the pad of his thumb over her mouth. All the while she stood
still, her eyes never leaving his face, her lips slightly parted as
if she had been about to speak but something had prevented
the words from issuing forth.

He unclasped her cloak, tossing it aside, then pulled off
her gloves, one at a time. They joined the cloak. He unfastened her swordbelt, hanging the rapier up beside his own
heavy cavalry sword. Then he lifted her, and sat her on the
edge of the table to pull off her boots and stockings.

Portia fell back on the hard flat surface of the table. She
raised her hips so that he could pull off her britches and drawers, lifting her hands way over her head to grasp the far edge
of the table. Rufus, without taking his eyes from hers, unfastened his britches.

Guessing what he wanted of her, Portia wrapped her legs
around his waist. The jutting spike of flesh slid into her body

with the ease of temptation. She gripped the table edge even tighter, lifting her hips, moving against him as he stood, holding her ankles at his back, watching her with that deep smile in his eyes. Portia laughed with pure exultation and the sound was almost shocking, breaking as it did the powerful intensity of their silence.

Rufus chuckled, transferred his grip on her ankles to one hand and brought the other hand around. He ran his thumb in a long, leisurely rubbing caress over the moist and heated opened core of her body, and the hot fire of pleasure made her cry out. Her hips arced on the hard surface beneath her, her eyes closed as the wave of pleasure curled ever closer, and her breath was swift and ragged.

Rufus held her on the edge, feeling the little ripples of her muscles around his flesh buried so deep within her. He watched her face, loving the wonderful translucence of her skin as her climax approached. Her eyes shot open, meeting his intent gaze, and then she was lost. She reached up, pulling him tight against her, feeling the throbbing pulse of his flesh against her womb. Her fingers tugged urgently at the dusting of red curls on his back, as his soft groans of delight were muffled against her shoulder.

"Welcome home, gosling," Rufus murmured, slowly bringing himself upright again. "I give you good evening."

"And I you, Lord Rothbury," she returned with an impish grin, sitting up on the table. "I wasn't expecting such a vigorous welcome, I must say."

"Learning from experience is a sign of intelligence," he observed, refastening his britches.

"Ah, but when I'm with you I forget everything I've ever learned," she said, sliding to the floor. "I'm sure I'm not very nice to know at the moment . . . I must reek of horseflesh and sweat."

In just her shirt, she went to the pantry to fetch a basin. She filled it with hot water from the kettle and, discarding the shirt, set to washing herself with matter-of-fact efficiency.

Rufus leaned against the mantelpiece and watched her. She was as thin as ever, despite a regular and more than ample diet, but he loved the angularities of her body, the sharp bones of her hips, the narrowness of her clearly delineated rib cage, the hollow of her throat within the necklace of her collarbone, the shape of her shoulder blades moving beneath the white skin.

"You had quite an adventure today, I gather," he observed.

Portia paused in her ablutions, the washcloth suspended beneath one raised arm. "What did Will say?"

"Oh, that you and Paul had pursued the couriers alone and had succeeded in lifting their documents . . . vital documents, as I'm sure you realized."

"Of course I did," she said, resuming her washing. "Paul and I set up a neat little ambush for them. Paul pretended that his horse had thrown a shoe in the middle of the lane, and he was positioned across it so they had to stop. . . ." She handed him a washcloth and turned her back.

Rufus obliged while she continued. "And he engaged them in the most wonderfully inane discussion, in the broadest Yorkshire you could imagine, so they could hardly understand a word, and while they were distracted, I came at 'em!"

"Part your legs."

She did so and he drew the cloth down between the cleft of her buttocks, along the inner reaches of her thigh. Her voice faltered.

"You were saying?" Rufus prompted, draping the washcloth over her shoulder and returning to his indolent position against the mantelpiece.

"I fired a shot from my musket which spooked both their horses. And as they reared, Paul jumped up and grabbed both bridles. They were still trying to get their swords out when I rode down on them, took one of them with my rapier and the other with my knife."

"Did you kill them?"

"No . . . it would have been in cold blood. We couldn't have done that," she said flatly. She shrugged on her shirt again, buttoning it swiftly. "We disarmed them and tied them up in a henhouse, which we'd found earlier, and set their horses loose."

"Sounds very neat." Rufus bent and picked up her drawers and britches, tossing them across to her. "And was that your only adventure?"

Portia had her head lowered as she climbed into her britches. "Yes, of course," she said. "Paul and I waited for Will and the others, and we all rode home together." She fastened her waistband, aware that her fingers were suddenly all thumbs.

"I'm starving. Paul ate all the chicken and I've had nothing but bread and cheese."

"We'll go to the mess presently. Will said you weren't at the rendezvous when he arrived." He was watching her very closely, watching the clumsy fumble of her fingers, although his voice was casual, his posture still indolent, as he leaned against the mantelpiece, one arm stretched along its length, fingers curled loosely around the handle of his tankard.

"And did he also tell you that my stomach was upset and while Paul slept the sleep of the just, I spent most of the afternoon behind a bush?" she demanded, combing her fingers through her hair, her face slightly averted.

"No, he didn't mention that." He took a sip of ale, but his eyes never left her face. Pink tinged the pallor of her high cheekbones, and her mouth was unusually taut. "The rendezvous was very close to Castle Granville," he continued casually. "Did you manage to see anything of interest while you were waiting?"

Portia shook her head, still keeping her face averted. "Nothing out of the ordinary. The drawbridge was down and there were detachments of troops coming and going. It all looked very busy, as usual."

Rufus knew with absolute clarity that she was not telling him the truth. He had been perplexed when Will had told him of Portia's unexplained absence so close to Castle Granville. He had thought to press her a little for an explanation, but immediately his puzzlement gave way to unease. Something was not true in her responses. And he was not interested in confronting the issue with finesse. "You're lying," he stated baldly.

The pink flooded her cheeks. "I don't know why you would say that."

"Do not lie to me, Portia." His voice was clipped, dismay yielding to the anger lurking just below the surface calm. "What did you do when you left Paul?"

Portia looked directly at him then. She saw how his fists were clenched, how lightning forked in his eyes. She had the sense that the man who had loved her with such passion only a short time ago was about to be taken over by his demons again, and fear quivered along her spine. She couldn't bear it again.

She swallowed hard, then said with all the courage she could muster, "I wanted to leave a message for Olivia. I'd promised to let her know that I was safe, but I haven't had the chance before."

"You are in contact with Granville?" His voice was now very quiet, but his expression was as terrible as ever.

"With Olivia," she said, hearing the desperation in her voice. "Only Olivia. She's my *friend*, Rufus. She worried about me. I promised to leave her a note. I went to do that, but she and Phoebe came by chance while I was there and we talked. That's all."

"Phoebe?"

"Cato's sister-in-law. She's my friend too." Portia lifted her chin, finding renewed courage and strength in her own words. No one, not even Rufus Decatur, was going to dictate to her whom she could have as friends.

"Granville women," he said flatly.

"Oh, devil take it, Rufus," Portia exploded. "Olivia doesn't give a damn about this feud you have with her father, and neither does Phoebe. I spent five minutes with them, and we didn't talk of it once! That may surprise you, but—"

"Be quiet and come here!" he interrupted, moving suddenly away from the mantelpiece, his eyes glittering. He jerked a hand imperatively.

Portia instead moved back. "I'd rather step between a rutting boar and a sow in heat," she stated, putting the table between herself and Rufus.

"*Come here!*"

Portia shook her head and when he came toward her, his step measured, his eyes filled with purpose, she reached behind her, her fingers closing over the handle of the copper pitcher of ale. "Don't touch me, Rufus!"

He didn't seem to hear her. He came on, shoving the table

aside with alarming ease. Portia hurled the contents of the pitcher. Ale flew in a foaming jet and fell in a cascade over his head, pouring down his shoulders. It worked, stopping him in his tracks.

His expression was so incredulous, he looked so utterly dumbfounded with ale trickling into his boots, that Portia had a hysterical urge to laugh.

And then he lunged for her with something remarkably like a roar. Portia leaped to one side, realizing too late that she'd jumped away from the door, her only possible escape route. There was nowhere to go in the cottage. She ran for the stairs, but he'd darted sideways, reaching them the same instant she did. One arm flew out, blocking her passage upward. Instinctively she ducked beneath the arm and leaped for the first step, knowing that it was futile. There was no safety above.

Fingers closed around her ankle. A determined jerk had her tumbling backward, to be caught against him, his body iron hard and distinctly damp at her back. The reek of ale was overpowering.

"Damn you, Rufus! What are you going to do? Don't you dare touch me." She fought desperately but his grip merely tightened, lifting her off her feet so that she was struggling and kicking like a fly caught in a web, her death throes watched by an interested and hungry spider.

Then he was carrying her upstairs, still struggling. He dropped her face down on the bed and as she wriggled to the edge, he placed a knee in the small of her back pinning her like a butterfly in a display case. "Let me go, you great bully!"

Instead, he swung himself onto the bed and straddled her, sitting firmly on her bottom. Catching her wrists, he clipped them in the small of her back and held them there with one hand. She heaved against him, kicking her legs, even though she knew she was as helpless as a baby.

Rufus waited patiently, until she'd exhausted herself against his strength, then he shifted his position and rolled her over onto her back, still straddling her hips.

"Dear God," he said. "If I'd known you enjoyed a little caveman play, I'd have indulged you sooner."

Portia realized with a shock that not only was he no longer angry, he was actually laughing at her. "Whoreson!" she said. "You are an unmitigated bastard . . . a dung beetle . . . a shiteater . . . a . . . a . . ." Her inventiveness faded. "And you smell like a brewery!"

"Then drink deep," he said, bending over her, lifting her head on his linked hands as he brought his mouth to hers. She was not comfortable and it was not a gentle kiss . . . or even particularly loving. But it had its place in the rough-and-tumble of the last minutes, in the edge of anger that had driven them both.

When he released her, allowing her head to fall back on the bed, Portia's lips felt swollen as if stung by a colony of bees. Her heart was pounding and she could barely catch her breath. She felt as if she'd run a marathon, or as if she'd lost a wrestling match. Which, of course, she had.

"That was what I intended doing all along," Rufus declared. "As you would have discovered if you'd come to me when I asked, instead of behaving as if you'd found yourself in a den of lions." He swung himself off her and began to throw off his reeking garments.

"You were always going to kiss me?" She couldn't help her disbelief.

"I was going to kiss the righteous indignation from your expression," he said. "It was such a wonderfully brave attempt to put me in my place." He shook his head with a rueful grimace. "Just what did you think I was going to do?"

"I didn't know," she said simply. "After the last time."

Rufus turned back to the bed, his expression once more grim. "I suppose I deserved that. I will try very hard not to deserve it again."

"And you don't mind that Olivia is my friend?" It felt like probing a still raw and open wound, but Portia knew this couldn't be put to rest until it was said. She knew her Granville blood still mattered to him, even though she'd given him her unconditional loyalty. Until he could accept her truly for everything she was, she would always be torn in this way between friendship and kinship and love.

Rufus stood silent for a minute, his ale-sodden shirt hanging unnoticed from his hand. Then he said, "Yes, I mind. But I also realize that I cannot remake you. However much I might wish to, I can't rewrite your history, and while I must have your loyalty, I realize that you have other claims upon it, too."

He sounded so sad, so achingly vulnerable, so very much alone. Portia realized that however much love she could give him, however much glorious lust they shared, Rufus's life essentially was still desperately lonely. How could a life driven from his earliest memories purely by vengeance be anything else? A life with no room in it for other emotions, for the gray areas of friendship outside the Decatur stronghold.

She reached for his hand, lifting it to her cheek. "You have my loyalty, Rufus."

He said nothing, only caressed her cheek with the back of his hand.

19

"*There are severe sanctions for sleeping on duty.*"

Portia opened her eyes and yawned. She smiled blearily at the large figure standing over her, blocking the sun. "I'm not on duty."

Rufus nodded solemnly. "As of ten minutes ago, you were."

"Oh, that can't be!" Portia sat up on the mossy grass. "I can't have slept that long." She struggled to her feet, hauling herself up by the tree trunk in whose gnarled roots she had been sleeping so peacefully.

Juno bounded along the riverbank toward them, barking delightedly. She dropped a stick at Rufus's feet and sat on her haunches, tongue lolling, looking up at him with clear invitation. He bent to pick up the stick, then hurled it along the bank. The puppy sped away.

"I don't know why I fell asleep, I only sat down for a few minutes," Portia muttered, shaking out her jerkin, brushing twigs and bits of moss off her britches. It kept happening. An invincible wave of sleepiness would break over her and she'd find herself nodding off where she sat. "Now George will grumble and look reproachful."

"No he won't. As it happens, someone else is taking your duty." Rufus sat down on the grass with his back against the tree and patted the moss beside him.

Portia didn't immediately accept the invitation. She frowned. "Why?"

"I have a more important task than sentry duty for you." He shaded his eyes against the warm May sun as he looked up at her.

Portia glanced around. Her eyes glowed with a lascivious

light, and her tongue touched her lips. "Here? Isn't it rather public?"

"For once, you insatiable wench, that was not what I had in mind," he declared, laughing at her. "Come, sit down, there's something I have to tell you."

Portia regarded him thoughtfully. She sensed some current of excitement in the air. His expression was superficially as calm as ever, but his eyes had taken on that electric hue of summer lightning, and there was a barely restrained tension in his powerful frame as he leaned with apparent nonchalance against the tree at his back.

"What's happened?" She sat down beside him.

"A messenger from Oxford." He closed his eyes, raising his face to the sun, and a little smile played over his mouth.

"From the king? No, Juno, take it away. It's all covered in slobber." Portia picked up the stick the puppy had deposited in her lap and dropped it with a grimace of distaste onto the grass.

"From the king," he affirmed, still with the same smile, still without opening his eyes.

"Am I supposed to guess? Here, Juno, fetch this instead." She hurled a pinecone and the puppy raced after it.

"No, when you've stopped playing with that animal and can give me your full attention, I will tell you."

"Oh, I'm sorry." She leaned sideways and gave him an apologetic kiss on the corner of his mouth. "I am all attention."

"The king, in his infinite wisdom, acknowledges the services of his loyal subject by granting the house of Rothbury a full pardon and complete restitution of lands and revenues." His eyes opened and Portia read there deep jubilation, an inexpressible satisfaction, and something else that gave her a little shiver of disquiet. Triumph . . . the triumph that comes from the utter humiliation of an enemy, from putting a foot on his neck as he lay at one's feet.

Juno returned, shaking the pinecone and growling. But something in the atmosphere made the puppy turn aside and flop on the grass with her new toy between her paws, her eyes fixed adoringly on Portia.

"There's more," Portia stated. "What is it?"

"I have orders to lay siege to Castle Granville," Rufus continued. "After our defeat in April, the rebel army far outnumbers the king's in the north. If we can remove Granville from the equation—permanently prevent him from bringing his militia into battle during the summer campaigns—we'll go some way to improving our odds." His hand moved unconsciously to his swordbelt, his fingers playing over the plain hilt of his great curved sword.

"What better person to entrust with the task of capturing the marquis and his castle than his neighbor and blood-sworn enemy, the earl of Rothbury, the king's most loyal subject?"

The shiver of disquiet became a full tornado. His triumphant words were laced with acid, and it dawned on Portia that Rufus Decatur's loyalty to his king was not based on principle. He was engaged in this conflict purely for his own ends. And she knew that wasn't true of Cato. Cato had chosen Parliament's side out of deep moral conviction. Did that make Cato the better man . . . the more honorable man?

It was not a question Portia wanted to answer. She knew that the king's armies were hard-pressed now, after a stunning defeat at Selby in April. A move to disable Cato and his force was only logical. "When do you invest the castle?"

"We leave at nightfall." He stood up in one lithe unbroken movement and reached down to pull her to her feet. "I intend to be in position at the castle gates when Cato opens his eyes on the morning. Go to the cottage and put your things together."

"I'm to come?"

His eyes narrowed, the color darkening to the blue of midnight. "You are part of this militia. Every able-bodied Decatur man will take part in the siege. It will be long, tedious for the most part, but I intend to have Cato's submission before the summer is out . . . whatever I have to do." His eyes raked her face. His voice was now very quiet as he said, "Do you have difficulties with this, Portia?"

Her pause was infinitesimal but she knew he'd marked it. She shook her head. "No."

He continued to scrutinize her countenance, as intently as

if he would see into her mind, then he said, "I am assuming Granville will be well prepared for a siege. Is that a correct assumption?"

"Yes," she said, her voice low. "He has stocks of grain, his cellars are full. I saw the preparations when I was there."

Rufus's face was expressionless. "But there is one thing he does not have in plentiful supply. One thing that he and his people cannot live without. Do you know what that is, Portia?"

She frowned, thinking. But her impressions of Castle Granville had been of an impregnable stronghold. Run with superb efficiency. Nothing left to chance. She shook her head. "No, I don't."

He smiled but there was no warmth, no humor, no pleasant quality to the smile. "You'll discover soon enough." Then with a short nod he strode away.

In the hole left by his departure, Portia became aware of movement, of excitement. Men were running, calling, the drums were beating the roll call, and trumpets blasted from every watchtower, summoning any who were absent from the village. The time for skirmishes was over. The men of Decatur were going to take part in their first real engagement of the war.

And what of the innocent people in the castle? What of Olivia and Phoebe? The babies? Even Diana? What had they done to be made war on? To face starvation and privation? To see the enemy at their gate? To endure the attacks of battering rams and cannon? The relentless firing over the walls? All the miseries of a siege?

Portia could feel no excitement, only a swamping depression. She had to take part if she was to keep faith with Rufus. And yet she wanted nothing to do with it. And what was this secret he held that would bring the walls of Castle Granville tumbling to the besieger?

She went back to the cottage, her step lacking its customary buoyancy. But Juno made up for any shortage of ebullience as she pranced and darted ahead, investigating scents, disappearing headfirst down rabbit holes, her plumed tail waving in frantic excitement.

The cottage was quiet, the fire in the hearth low, used in these warm spring days only for heating water. Portia went upstairs to gather together her possessions. They were sparse; when laid upon the bed, the little pile looked almost pathetic. A change of underclothes, stockings, her buff jerkin, and two linen shirts. Absently she began to fold the squares of linen she used during her monthly terms, laying them on the pile. Then her hands stilled. She stood looking down at the bed.

Surely she was late this month. How late? She tried to think, to remember. But she'd never paid much attention to this monthly inconvenience. It came when it came, and it was always a nuisance. She knew very little about the workings of her own body, having had few female confidantes in her growing, and no one to take the place of a mother. When she'd first bled, she'd run to Jack in tears, certain some dreadful wound had opened in her body.

He'd been drunk, as usual, but he'd pulled himself together enough to tell her that it was just one of those things that happened to women and she'd have to put up with it. The next day, he'd taken her to see the madam of his favorite brothel in Glasgow. The woman had given the bewildered girl a rough-and-ready education in the facts of life, and Portia had managed her own affairs with very little attention ever since.

But that lack of attention had its disadvantages. She ran her hands down her body. It felt the same. If she *had* conceived, when would it feel different? She felt perfectly normal in herself. Surely if something as momentous as conception had occurred, she would have noticed *something*.

The front door flew open and banged shut below. "Portia . . . Portia . . . Portia!" The excited shrieks of the boys drove the disquieting puzzle from her mind for the moment.

"What is it?" She went downstairs.

"We got to get our things together 'cause—"

"Yes, an' I want to take my soldiers," Luke shrilled, interrupting his brother's more measured speech. "Only I can't find 'em . . . I thought I left 'em with Silas, but he hasn't got 'em." He began to throw bedcovers on the floor, diving and swooping like a demented seagull.

Juno, who'd come in with the boys, joined in the hunt with excited yaps. Toby, bouncing on his toes to reach a wooden trumpet on the shelf above his bed, grabbed at the end of the shelf, bringing it toppling down on him in a shower of toys and wooden puzzle pieces.

"What the hell is going on?" Rufus's voice, very close to a bellow, crashed through the turmoil. "It's a madhouse in here."

"They seem to think they're coming with us," Portia said. "They aren't, are they?"

"I can't leave them here. There'll be no one to look after them," Rufus pointed out above the continued hubbub. "*Be quiet!*"

The roar brought a moment's silence. The children, totally unabashed, stopped and regarded their father inquiringly.

"You can't take children to a siege," Portia said. "It'll be dangerous."

Rufus ran a distracted hand through his hair. "Every able-bodied man is coming with us. You're not suggesting I leave this pair to the care of the infirm, are you?"

That thought did not bear contemplation. "No, of course not. But surely there's someone else. What about with the women at Mistress Beldam's?"

"I'm not leaving them in a brothel."

"I can't see that that's any more unsuitable than an armed camp," Portia said.

"What's a brothel?" Toby inquired.

"A place where women live," Portia answered.

"We don't want to live *there*," Luke said with disgust.

"No . . . not *there*," Toby agreed vigorously, wrinkling his nose. "I got to find my soldiers!" He returned to the hunt with renewed enthusiasm.

Rufus stood frowning as the noise level rose anew. "They have to come," he said finally. "It's not as if we'll be fighting a pitched battle."

"It's your decision." Portia turned back to the stairs. "You're their father."

"But I value your opinion." Rufus followed her, leaving the uproar behind them.

"Then answer me this. You're the earl of Rothbury. No longer an outlaw . . . no longer a moss-trooper. You have your estates back. You will rebuild your house. You'll take your place in the world of law. Where are the boys going to fit into that society?"

Rufus realized that in all his careful, ruthless planning, and now in the flush of triumph, he hadn't given thought to such issues. He hadn't even considered how he himself would fit into that society. He'd left it at the age of eight. He had no practice in its rules or its customs.

"I don't know," he said quietly. "I haven't thought that far ahead . . ." Then with a flash of defensive impatience, "For God's sake, Portia, I only received the news this morning. And we're in the middle of a war. I have other things on my mind."

"Yes, of course you do." Portia turned once more to the clothes on the bed. "I'll see to the boys' packing, and ours. I'm sure you're needed elsewhere."

Rufus hesitated, puzzled by the tenor of the conversation. He had the feeling that he was missing something, that Portia had some point she was trying to make, but it had eluded him. "I really don't see any alternative to taking the boys with us," he said, returning to what had begun the discussion.

"No, I suppose not," Portia said. "I wasn't thinking very clearly. I don't imagine it'll be any different for them there than here, really."

"Except that they'll be living under canvas."

"Well, that'll certainly find favor." She flashed him a smile over her shoulder as her hands kept folding and refolding the same shirt. "You'd best get back to work."

"Yes . . ." Still he hesitated, then with an uncertain shrug he hurried away, his sons' voices billowing out through the door in his wake.

Portia sat on the bed, holding the shirt forgotten between her hands. She'd been speaking of herself, she realized. Or at least, including herself with the children. What place would there be for her in the rehabilitated household of the earl of Rothbury? She belonged to the armed camp, to the outlaw's way of life, just as Luke and Toby did. And what if she was carrying a child? Another of Rufus Decatur's bastard offspring . . .

"Portia . . . Portia . . . we *need* you!" Luke's head popped up at the top of the stairs, his father's vivid eyes aglow. "I can't find my green shirt. An' it's my absolute favorite."

It was also in rags, as a result of one too many encounters with a thornbush. Rufus, on one of the infrequent occasions when he noticed what his sons were wearing, had spirited it away, hoping that out of sight would be out of mind. It had worked for a week. No longer, apparently.

Portia stood up, telling herself firmly that moping about imponderables was pointlessly wearying. There were enough practicalities to occupy her. "I'll see if I can find it, Luke."

$\mathscr{I}t$ was dark when the main body of the cavalcade passed between the sentry fires of Decatur village. Portia rode beside Rufus at the head, Juno sitting on her saddle, upright and alert beneath her cloak. Luke and Toby had gone ahead, riding in the cart that carried Bill and the mess, a pack train of laden mules accompanying them.

Portia, even after five months in the Decatur stronghold, was astonished at the speed and efficiency with which this massive operation had been put under way. And even more by the utter secrecy. Boats laden with arms and ammunition had been dispatched downriver. They'd be met and unloaded onto carts in the dark hours before dawn, just before the river snaked out of the hills into the valley at the foot of Castle Granville. Farmers' carts trundled through the countryside, their burden of culverins concealed beneath bales of hay for cattle feed.

The village had been left with a skeleton guard. There was nothing to steal there, no armed troops to be destroyed. Rufus had reasoned that rebel marauders would not waste their time on a near-deserted village, populated by the elderly and infirm.

There was no conversation in the ranks of riders. They were all dark clad, blending into the moonless night as they rode in close rank through the desolate landscape. But there was a prickle in the air, a quiver of excitement and anticipation to which only Portia, it seemed, was immune. She could sense it in Rufus beside her. He rode without his usual relaxation. His body was taut in the saddle, his eyes darting from side to side, missing nothing . . . not the flicker of grass as a hare loped by, nor the faint crackling in the undergrowth made by some night creature. An owl hooted, an animal screamed in pain, the sound shocking in the still night. Juno trembled and crept closer to Portia.

For the most part, Rufus took a route that kept them away from habitation, but once they rode through a shuttered hamlet, moving their horses onto the grassy verge that ran alongside the gravel lane running through the center of the village.

Portia found it eerie, riding right through these sleeping people, horses' hooves muffled by grass, the wicked glint of sword, dagger, pistol, hidden beneath dark cloaks. They would waken in the morning and have not the faintest idea that an army had passed among them.

At two in the morning, they reached the wooded hillside opposite Castle Granville. Concealed among the trees, the men dismounted, tethered their horses, and ate the provisions they'd carried in their saddlebags. Leather flagons of wine were passed around, but there was little sound . . . nothing that could carry across the valley to the watchers on the ramparts of Castle Granville.

Portia, nibbling a thickly buttered bannock, walked to the edge of the trees and stood looking across at the bulk of the castle, grayish white in the darkness. Rufus intended to make his move just before daybreak, bringing his men up to assault and surround the castle walls before the sentries fully realized what was happening. Once the besiegers were in place, the castle would be sealed tight as a drum.

She turned, feeling rather than hearing the footstep on the mossy ground at her back. Rufus came up beside her. He placed a hand on her shoulder and held a flagon of wine to her lips.

She drank the rough red wine with pleasure, but shook her head when he encouraged her to drink again. "What will you do if Cato sends his men out to fight?" Her voice was barely a whisper, in keeping with the inhabited silence around them.

"He won't," Rufus returned, a glint of satisfaction in his eye. He drank deep from the flagon. "Not without suffering unacceptable losses. He'd have to lower the drawbridge, and we would block it at our end."

"Yes, of course. But will you have enough men?"

"A troop of Prince Rupert's infantry will join us by midday. Infantry and engineers experienced in digging siegeworks. There's no way Granville and his men will be able to leave."

From nowhere the image of the concealed door beneath the drawbridge flew into her head. She could feel the lines in the stone against her hands, could see the low narrow tunnel winding through the vaults, up the stone stairs, emerging into the scullery.

She hadn't mentioned the door when she'd told Rufus of the conversation she'd overheard between Cato and Giles. She'd had only one thought, to warn Rufus of the trap. Extraneous details had been lost in the mists of her exhaustion.

Should she tell him now? But an entire troop couldn't leave by that exit. They would emerge onto the moat within the besiegers encampment, and while one man might evade the sharp eyes of Decatur watchmen, a group could not.

She had no need to tell Rufus of the door. If Cato couldn't use it to evade the royalist siege, then Rufus didn't need to know of it. She could forget it existed.

But if Rufus knew it existed, he could use it to gain entrance to the castle.

The pit of her stomach seemed to drop. Her skin prickled as if she'd walked through a bed of nettles. If she was truly loyal to Rufus, she would tell him what was to his advantage. Surely she would?

"Rufus?" Will's voice came out of the darkness, and Rufus turned away from Portia. She breathed deeply. The moment was passed . . . for now.

"Is it done, Will?" There was a ring of urgency, of anticipation in his voice.

"Aye." Will stepped up to them.

He had not accompanied the cavalcade, and Portia saw now that his face was blackened with dirt, his teeth glimmering white as he grinned. She could see his excitement, feel it coming from him in waves. "It's done. They'll be without water within the week."

"Good man!" Rufus clapped him on the shoulder. "You've set a guard at the dam."

"Aye." Will grinned.

"What d'you mean?" Portia laid a hand on Rufus's arm. "What dam?"

"Ah, well, I told you I had a little surprise for Cato." Rufus smiled the smile that Portia hated to see. "The one weakness of Castle Granville is the water supply. The well is fed from a stream up in the hills behind us. Dam the stream, deny the well." He opened his hands palm up, indicating the simplicity of the tactic. "When Cato finds himself short of water, then we shall see him jump."

Portia knew logically that she couldn't fault the tactic if she didn't fault the siege itself. It was in everyone's interests that it be over as soon as possible. But she hated Rufus's triumph, his gloating satisfaction. He had not gloated so over the defeat of Colonel Neath and his men. He had treated them with respect and honor, friendship even. But Colonel Neath was an ordinary enemy. Cato was not.

She knew she was not going to tell anyone of the secret entrance to the castle.

The figures came out of the dark, swarming up the hill. They came with the crack of musket, the beat of drum, the shrill of pipe, the bright orange flare of torches. The watchers on the battlements of Castle Granville were for an instant frozen with shock and the terror of the unexpected. The night had been quiet. The sentries had paced the ramparts, the guards in the watchtowers had played cards and dice. Only night sounds had disturbed the peace. And now, out of the night, in the hour before daybreak, a shouting horde advanced upon them.

Fire crackled on the narrow ledge beyond the moat, at

the very base of the castle; smoke rose in choking greasy billows. Somehow, sometime in the night, the fires had been laid under the very eyes of the watchmen. Somehow the attackers had carried the kindling across the moat to pile it against the walls. Now the flaming torches arced through the dark to fall among the dry brushwood. The foul stench of burning pitch and tallow wreathed the castle walls, and the clamor from the assaulting force grew fiercer, wilder. A dreadful taunting designed to intimidate, to humiliate.

Cato was aroused from the first deep sleep he'd had in weeks. Diana shot up in bed. "What is it? What's that noise?"

Cato didn't answer. He scrambled into his britches and ran barefoot and shirtless from the chamber. Giles Crampton was racing toward him down the corridor.

" 'Tis a siege, m'lord. They've surrounded the walls, bridged the moat. We didn't see 'em. Didn't 'ear a peep. Christ an' his angels, sir, I swear they must 'ave come up like ghosts." He wrung his hands in distraught defense, but Cato barely heard him and made no response.

He burst out onto the ramparts, heedless of the sharp stones beneath his bare feet, and ran to the watchtower over the drawbridge. "Mother of God!" He looked beyond the smoke and flames to the ranks of men crowding the far side of his moat. He coughed as the filthy, oily smoke filled his lungs. The fire would do no damage to the castle itself. The stone walls would need more than a bit of burning brushwood and pitch to bring them down, but it made observation almost impossible. But it also meant that the besiegers could not see to fire upon them.

He signaled that the men should retreat from the battlements to the outer bailey, where they could take stock. Diana appeared on the steps from the donjon. She was wrapped in a cloak over her nightrail, and she looked terrified.

"My lord, what is it? Are we under attack?"

He controlled the urge to dismiss her. Of course she was frightened, and deserved to know what was happening.

"It rather looks as if we are besieged, madam," he said, trying to make his voice light as he came up the steps toward her. "But there's nothing to worry about. We are well prepared to withstand months of investment. Our cellars and granaries are full. And Fairfax will come to our aid. He'll raise the siege in no time."

Putting an arm around her slender shoulders, he eased her ahead of him back inside. "I must dress. It will be for you to calm the household . . . and the girls, of course. Make sure they understand that there's nothing to alarm them."

He put Diana from him and strode past her. She stared in disbelief, for the first time in her adult life utterly at a loss. The shouts and musket fire continued unabated. She put her hands over her ears, trying to shut them out.

"Diana, what is it? What's happening?" Phoebe came flying toward her, Olivia on her heels. "What's going on? Is it a battle?"

Diana shook her head, her hands still clapped to her ears. Her face was whiter than whey. She stumbled past them, leaving them gazing after her.

"Lord, I've never seen Diana look so sick," Phoebe observed in wonderment. "Never expected to, either," she added.

"Come!" Olivia tugged her sleeve impatiently. "To the b-battlements. We'll find out what's happening." She pulled Phoebe toward the door and began to run.

They reached the outer ward as the sky was lightening, pink and orange streaks appearing on the horizon. Men were racing from the barracks, milling in the court, hefting muskets, drawing swords. Olivia kept to the edge of the court, Phoebe following suit, until they reached the narrow flight of stairs cut into the wall. Olivia darted up to the battlements, then choked, doubling over.

"Filthy!" Phoebe gasped, stumbling to the parapet to look over. "Look at all those men, Olivia. There's thousands of them." It was a serious exaggeration, but in the eerie light of the smoke-wreathed dawn, the apparitions below seemed myriad.

"They're attacking the castle," Olivia said with a thrill of excitement that quite superseded fear. "Just like Portia said would happen."

"What did Portia know about it?" Phoebe was instantly curious.

"Portia knows everything," Olivia said simply.

"I doubt that," the more realistic Phoebe said. "Even though she's joined with the royalists, she can't know everything."

"Well, she knows a lot," Olivia stated, and Phoebe was prepared to let it go at that.

"Whose standard is flying?" Phoebe leaned over the battlements, blinking vigorously in an attempt to clear her watering eyes. "Is it the king's? Yes, I believe it is, but there's another one . . . an eagle, I think. Azure on a gold background."

"*Decatur!*"

The girls spun around. Cato stood behind them, his face a mask of rage, all semblance of his previous tranquility vanished. His enemy was at his gates. And the enemy was not King Charles.

A herald's fanfare blew through the drifting smoke. The light was growing, the fires dying down. Rufus Decatur, astride his chestnut steed, rode forward to the edge of the moat, to the point where the drawbridge, had it been down, would have given him access to the castle.

He sat his horse, the standard of the house of Rothbury planted in the socket of his saddle. He signaled for the herald to sound again.

Cato's own herald responded immediately and the marquis of Granville took a step up onto the ledge immediately below the parapet. The rules of war and of parley ensured his safety.

Rufus stood up in his stirrups and his voice rang out through the hush of dawn. "My lord of Granville, I am come in the name of your most sovereign majesty, King Charles, to demand that you lay down your arms of rebellion and surrender your person and your castle to His Majesty's mercy."

Cato answered, his voice as measured as his adversary's, his words as formal. "In the name of Parliament, I will uphold the cause of the people. Castle Granville will not surrender."

He stepped back off the parapet. The silence was complete. It seemed to Phoebe that no one knew what to do next. Then Cato said harshly, "You two shouldn't be outside. Go in, and stay within doors."

They obeyed without a moment's hesitation.

In the back rank of the Decatur force, in the hush that followed the declaration of battle, Portia was overcome by a wave of nausea. She fought it, but it was invincible. She scrambled off Penny and stumbled behind a bush, heaving up her guts in bleak misery.

20

"*Did* you eat something bad, Portia?" *Luke's worried lit-*tle voice accompanied a dimpled hand on her back as Portia crouched in the bushes.

"Probably." Portia sat back on her heels, wiping her mouth with her kerchief.

"I 'spect it was goosegogs," Toby said knowledgeably, squatting down in front of her, regarding her with his head on one side. His own most recent bout of sickness had followed an extended visit to a gooseberry bush.

Portia smiled weakly but with what she hoped was reassurance. So far she'd managed to keep this gruesome early-morning business to herself, and she didn't want the children running to Rufus with tales of her woes. "It's all over now, I'm quite better," she said. "Have you had breakfast?" The thought of food brought another wave of sickness sloshing through her belly.

"Bill made us coddled eggs," Luke said. "Are you really all better?"

"Yes, really." Portia staggered to her feet, picking up her discarded straw hat. It didn't quite match her soldier's costume, but it protected her delicate pallor from the sun. "Where's Juno?"

"Down a rabbit hole."

Silly question. "Let's go back to the camp." She took their hands and walked back with them to the encampment crowding the foot of Castle Granville, but before they reached the first row of tents the children's attention was caught by a soldier repairing the broken axle of a baggage cart and they darted off to offer their assistance, leaving her to continue alone.

In the two weeks since they'd been in position, siege engineers had built bridges across the moat, sturdy enough to hold the culverins, and the steady boom of cannon was a daily ritual, at dawn and sunset. The castle walls so far had withstood the bombardment with no major breaches, but they were showing signs of wear and tear.

Archers shot their arrows in a fairly relentless harassment over the walls, and Granville men returned the fire, but in desultory fashion causing few casualties. It was too risky for them to stay above the lip of the parapet for long enough to take careful aim. The oily fires were lit under cover of darkness to render the air stifling and foul for both besieger and besieged alike. But at least those outside could retreat, Portia reflected. For the castle inhabitants the nightly suffocation would be torment. There was nowhere they could go to escape it, and the weather didn't help. It had turned hot and thundery, but without the relief of a storm.

The sky this early June morning was steely gray with thunderheads, and the heaviness added to Portia's miseries. It made her head ache and the continual dragging nausea seemed harder to bear, and even harder to conceal. Her duties were not arduous these days. She helped with construction of the bridges and with the light rope ladders that they would use if the opportunity arose to scale the walls. She performed picket duty, patrolling the perimeter of the camp and the moat, on the watch for any undue movement within the castle. And always as she passed the spot, she averted her eyes from the concealed door just above the surface of the moat.

Prince Rupert's battalion had come as promised, and as Portia crossed the beaten-down grass toward the headquarters tent, she heard the prince's voice, ringing with confidence and good humor, addressing his commanders. The prince had just succeeded in relieving the rebel blockade of York and was flushed with triumph and the conviction of success.

Because of the heat, the men had abandoned the tent and were meeting under the shade of a beech tree, gathered around a long table on which a map was spread out. The prince, magnificent in his peacock blue doublet, his scarlet slash, his hair falling in a curled and glowing cascade to the collar of Valenciennes lace spread over his shoulders, pointed with a stick to a place on the map.

"Gentlemen, we must—we *will*—force a decisive battle. The king demands it." He raised his shining face to the sun, flourishing his pointer. "It is the king's will, my lords."

Rufus was studying the map, his expression showing none of the prince's enthusiastic conviction. In fact, Portia thought, observing from some ten yards' distance, he looked as if he were about to burst into vigorous disagreement. She could tell by the set of his shoulder, the line of his mouth. But to her surprise he remained silent, continuing to study the map, a frown creasing his brow.

He looked up suddenly and she knew he'd sensed her presence. With a word of excuse, he moved away from the group and came toward her. "How now, gosling?" He smiled, but the strain remained on his face. "Are you idle this morning?"

"Until noon," she said. "Is there trouble brewing?"

"I don't know. The prince is convinced the men are ready for a decisive action. I'm not so sure."

"Will that mean you'll abandon the siege?"

Rufus looked back at Castle Granville. The pennants still flew from the battlements in brave defiance of the army at its gates. "They've been out of fresh water for several days now. Even if they had stored extra barrels in the cellars, with five hundred people and I don't know how many horses, they can't last much longer."

He glanced down at Portia, the blue eyes raking her face. "That hat isn't going to do any good hanging from your hand." He took it from her and set it on her head, adjusting the brim to a rakish angle. "You're looking peaky. Are you ailing?"

"No. It's just the heat," she said in swift disclaimer. "What will happen to Olivia and Phoebe and Diana and the babies?"

"They'll be given safe conduct to wherever they wish to go. Is that what's worrying you?"

"I worry at how they're suffering now," she said bluntly.

"It is for Cato to bring an end to that suffering," Rufus returned curtly. "He has only to haul down his standards and lower the drawbridge."

"And then you'll hang him," she stated.

"No. He will be the king's prisoner, not mine. I am interested only in his submission." It was said with a cold finality.

Portia said nothing, but her freckled face was set, her angular features standing out against the white skin in the shadow of the hat brim. She didn't believe him. Rufus was using the pretext of war to further his own ends. He had won restitution and freedom, but he still wanted Cato's life for his father's.

Rufus found himself waiting for her to respond, although he knew she would not, could not, give him the response he wanted. He wanted her to say that she understood, to rejoice with him in the prospect of his victory. But he knew he would get nothing more than this silent acceptance of his obsession, and the equally silent loyalty that she had promised him. And he knew that both that acceptance and the loyalty brought her pain.

The silence lengthened and with a brusque gesture he strode back to the men under the tree, turning his back on her pain, and on the fact that he was responsible for it. He could do nothing now to stop the juggernaut, even had he wished to.

Portia turned with leaden step toward the mess tent. She'd had no breakfast and she felt both hungry and sick at the same time. Her entire body didn't seem to know what was happening to it or how to react. Her breasts were sore, her mood swung from wild elation to the depths of depression, she was as likely to snap as to smile without reason for either. This business of reproduction, she decided, was vastly overrated.

And she still hadn't told Rufus. She wanted to tell him, but she wasn't ready yet. She hadn't sorted out her own feelings about it, and she was afraid, too. Afraid that he would not respond as she needed him to respond. He already had children; it wouldn't be such a momentous thing for him. She knew he would not reject the coming child, but it was likely he would simply shrug his acceptance, promise to provide for the infant, and leave it at that. The child would be his bastard. The child's mother was his mistress. They had no claims except those of love and honor. He would fulfil the latter claim, but Portia didn't know about the former.

And she needed more . . . much much more . . . than a dutiful response. She couldn't endure to think of her child growing up as she had done, knowing herself to be unwanted, to be a nuisance, a dependent burden with no established place in the world. And yet she knew with grim certainty that the bastard child of a bastard was doubly cursed.

She wanted to tell *someone*. Needed to confide, to talk through it, to come to some understanding of her own feelings. But apart from Rufus, she had no one else to listen to her on such a subject.

"Eh, lassie, you didn't come fer breakfast." Bill hailed her as she hovered in the entrance to the mess tent. "There's a nice piece of fat bacon 'ere an' a fresh bannock."

"I'll just have the bannock, thank you, Bill," Portia said hastily, averting her eyes from the thick white and highly prized fat around the slab of bacon Bill was preparing to slice.

"Please yerself, lass. But it's a rare treat."

"Just not this morning, thanks. Is there any milk?"

"Aye, in the pitcher out back." He gestured with his head to the rear of the tent where stone pitchers stood in bowls of cold water.

Portia drank deeply, straight from the pitcher. The milk was cool, creamy, new drawn that morning from the small herd of cows at pasture in the valley. Granville cattle, pastured outside the castle. There'd be no milk for those imprisoned within the walls. She replaced the pitcher, dipping a finger into the bowl of cold water. What must it be like to have no water? To ration it and watch the level dropping with the knowledge that there would be no more?

Even if Cato had been able to send men undetected out of the secret entrance, they'd never be able to carry back sufficient water for the whole castle. He must be watching every day, in increasing desperation, for the relief forces to come to his aid. But Fairfax and Leven were too busy after their defeat at York to spare time and men for Castle Granville.

She wandered out of the mess tent and down to the moat. The level of the water was low. It had been close to six weeks since it had last rained, and even the snowmelt had dissipated. The mud and weed at the bottom of the moat were clearly visible through the scummy water. Once in the water, she would be so far below the level of the bank she would only be visible to a man looking directly down into the moat. And the pickets didn't do that. They walked the perimeter of the camp, and the bank along the moat around the castle, and when they weren't looking straight ahead, they looked upward at the battlements or directly across at the castle walls. And the smoke from the fires would provide additional cover.

It would be too risky to climb down into the moat directly opposite the drawbridge. The Decatur guard was heaviest there. But around the other side, around by the duck island . . . It was darker there, the lights of the encampment less obtrusive. Once in the water, if she swam close under the bank, she would have a good chance of being undetected. And the secret door was set into the wall immediately below where the support for the drawbridge jutted out into the moat, even when the bridge was up. She would be in shadow there, able to take the time to find the catch to open the door.

Portia realized with remarkably little surprise that she had formed her plan without consciously coming to a decision. It seemed inevitable that she was going into the castle to talk with Olivia and Phoebe. She needed to find out how they were, and she needed to confide her own condition. Her friends had nothing to do with this damned war and even less to do with Rufus and Cato. She would not be betraying Rufus by simply talking with them. He had understood once before . . . had finally accepted her need to do that. This was no different from the last time.

She made her preparations with the same detached mental efficiency that had created the plan. She exchanged picket duty with Paul, who was only too happy to relinquish the midnight-to-four shift. Rufus thought nothing of her going on duty at midnight, and nothing of her retiring to bed immediately after supper while he was still entertaining Prince Rupert and his officers.

When he came to bed at eleven o'clock, Portia feigned sleep, although she was far too keyed up to sleep. He didn't light the lamp, relying on the dim reflection of the torch kept burning throughout the night in a sconce beyond the entrance flap. She knew he wouldn't disturb her in the half hour before she had to be up, and lay still on her narrow cot, aware of him standing above her as he pulled off his boots, aware of his eyes on her still countenance as he listened to her breathing. Then he moved away from her and she could relax and listen to him moving about the small grass-scented space.

She could see him as clearly as if she had her eyes open . . . see his every gesture with the clarity of love and lust, knowing when he unbuckled his belt, unfastened the waistband of his britches, unbuttoned his shirt . . . see him pull the shirt from the loosened waistband of his britches with both hands in a rough, hasty motion that never varied. Behind her closed eyes, she could see his broad chest now, the small hard nipples, the line of red-gold hair creeping down to the navel in the concave belly, and then down. . . . He was pushing off his britches, kicking them free of his feet, bending to strip off his stockings.

The ropes on his own cot creaked under his weight, and she knew as surely as if he was lying beside her that he was sleeping in his underdrawers. Not that he would be wearing them if he *was* lying beside her. A smile touched her lips. She found deeply pleasing the idea of his sleeping in clothed celibacy when she was not available.

Her eyes were suddenly heavy, her breathing taking up the sleeping rhythm of Rufus's deep, even breaths. Sleep came for her, soft and caressing as swansdown. . . .

She was jerked awake. Rufus's hand was on her shoulder, gently shaking her, and beyond the tent flap she heard the sentry sent to wake her, calling her name in a hoarse whisper.

"You were dead to the world," Rufus said softly. He was leaning across the small space that separated their cots.

Portia groaned. She couldn't help it. The shock of waking from the deep currents of first sleep was too much, and immediately the waves of nausea churned in her belly.

"Go back to sleep," Rufus said. "I'll take your duty."

"No . . . no." She sat up, thrusting the sticky cobwebs of sleep away. "No, it's my duty. I'll do it." She kicked aside the blanket and sat up, keeping her head lowered in the hope that she could master the sickness before she had to stand up.

"Portia, are you ill?" His voice was sharp with concern.

"No . . . no." She shook her head gingerly. "I just don't want to be awake at midnight." She reached for her britches at the bottom of the cot. She had gone to bed in her clothes, except for the britches, and now had only to thrust her stockinged feet into the legs and pull them up and then step into her boots to be ready to go.

Gently she stood up. The world swung around her and her stomach swung with it. She bit the inside of her cheek until the pain made her eyes water as she fastened the waistband and buckled her belt. Rapier and knife lay ready to be sheathed. She held on to the tent post as she stepped into her boots.

Rufus was lying propped on an elbow, watching her in the dim light, his eyes narrowed. Something was amiss. Was it just the disorientation of an abrupt waking? Every instinct told him to insist that she go back to her cot. But to do that would mean denying her the respect she demanded and had earned among the men of Decatur. She expected no concessions, and on the one or two occasions they'd been offered had rejected them with vigorous indignation.

Portia thrust her rapier into its sheath and tucked her knife into her boots. She had herself in hand now and was able to smile as she blew him a kiss before ducking through the small opening.

Rufus fell back on the cot and lay with his hands linked behind his head, now fully awake, disturbed by a deep unease that had no apparent cause.

Portia nodded to the man who had woken her and made her way through the camp away from the castle to the outside perimeter, where the man she was to relieve was walking the picket line. This particular patrol was a lonely one, ideally suited to her purposes. The main activity was concentrated at the castle, but the entire bivouac had to be picketed along its outer perimeters and this stretch of territory was isolated, covering the wooded area at the rear of the camp. No one would come this way. It crossed no other picket line. No one would know if the picket on duty had slipped away from her post for an hour or two. Or only in the most unfortunate of circumstances, and Portia had decided it was a risk worth taking.

Adam greeted her with a grin of relief. "Hell's teeth, but am I glad to see you. I thought Paul was taking the next one, though."

"I exchanged with him. I wanted some time tomorrow afternoon."

"Oh, aye." Adam nodded in easy acceptance. "Well, it's been about as exciting as a spinster's bed. I wish ye joy of it." He raised a hand in farewell and set off with a bounce in his stride to an ale pot in the mess.

Portia realized that she no longer felt sick. Perhaps terror was the antidote. She patrolled her route three times. No one came near her. There were no sounds but the occasional faint noises from the camp below, the usual forest rustles of small animals, and the call of a nightjar. The moon was new, a mere sliver in the dark sky, visible only occasionally when the heavy thunderclouds shifted. The evening star showed now and again, but on the whole the night was as dark as one could expect a night in June to be.

Portia slipped into the trees and found the oak tree she had selected that afternoon. She felt beneath the thick moss covering its roots and pulled out the dark cap that would cover her hair. She took off her boots and her stockings and her white shirt, burying them beneath the moss. Without a shirt, the dark wool jerkin was hot and prickly against her bare skin, but it would enable her to blend with the shadows. Her rapier joined the discarded garments under the moss. She bound the knife against her leg over her britches with a strip of linen, wrapping the sharp blade securely in several folds of material.

She thrust the fruit she had also hidden into her pockets— apples and pears. It was all she could take. Anything more substantial would be ruined by the water in the moat, but she had reasoned that if one was thirsty, the moist flesh and sweet juice of the fruit would be welcome. In final preparation, she tied a kerchief around her mouth and nose. Then, barefoot, she crept forward through the trees, around the castle until she was abreast of the ducks' island.

She slithered down the hill on her belly. The picket was walking his line—a two-hundred-yard stretch between the posts. When he was three quarters of the way back, facing away from her, Portia slithered the last few yards and dropped over the rim of the moat. She stayed there, finding a foothold in the bank so she could hold herself above the water level, clinging to a twisted root poking through the mud just above her head.

The fires were smoldering against the walls, but the kerchief protected her from the worst of the smoke and would muffle an inconvenient cough. She waited until she heard the picket return. When he turned again and passed her, she inched forward, clinging like a mollusk to the bank, hoping to keep herself as dry as possible for as long as possible. There were three patrols between the ducks' island and the drawbridge, and her greatest danger would come when she followed the curve of the moat to the stretch where it ran directly in front of the encampment.

Luck was with her. She seemed to have found a ridge of soil in the bank of the moat, just wide enough to give her toes purchase, and she was able to creep crabwise under the overhang until the shadow of the drawbridge supports loomed ahead. Above her she could hear muted voices now and again as the pickets exchanged comments, but the camp was abed. As was the castle—or so she hoped.

Facing the wall beneath the drawbridge, Portia took a deep breath. If she stopped to think, she wouldn't do it. She slid beneath the surface of the water, feeling the weeds reaching up to twist and twine around her ankles as she swam underwater the short distance to the shadowy safety of the far wall.

She raised her head above the surface of the water and took a gulp of air. It was acrid with smoke but better than nothing. She ducked back beneath the water and waited with bursting lungs, in case anyone on the bank had noticed a disturbance on the water during her swim. Once it had dissipated, they would with luck move on and forget about it.

When she could hold her breath no longer, she slowly raised her head again. The hulking shape of the drawbridge supports was directly above her head. The castle wall where the level of water had dropped was green with slime. Above the green, however, the wall was as clean as she remembered it when she was standing on the ice. She edged closer to the wall, feeling with her toes for a crack or cranny where she could stand and lift herself out of the water and up to the level of the door. Her questing feet found what they sought. It was a bare toehold, but it lifted her high enough to reach up and find the lines of the door.

But where was the lever that opened it? She had found it by accident before. But this time she couldn't stand with her back against it and find the pressure point by the same lucky chance. At least she knew that it was contained within the door itself and not along the edge. She took the top section of the door and moved her hands over the stone, pressing firmly with the heels of her palms. Then she moved down several inches and covered that area.

Despite the warm night, she was rapidly chilled, her wet clothes clammy and clinging. Her hands were shaking, her teeth chattering so loudly she was sure someone would hear. Whether it was with cold or tension she no longer knew, but doggedly she continued her minute exploration of the stone.

And then it happened. There was a tiny click and she felt the stone move beneath her flat palms. Her heart jumped. The slab swung inward just as she'd remembered. She hauled herself up and over the edge into the black tunnel. It seemed darker even than she'd remembered it, and she was now bitterly cold.

She hesitated, the door still open behind her. It was not too late to go back . . . to forget this whole crazy idea. Her teeth chattered unmercifully and she began to shake with cold. If she went back now . . .

Even as Portia thought this, thought of her dry shirt waiting among the roots of the oak tree, she was pulling the door gently closed behind her and moving along the tunnel, holding the walls as she'd done before. The vault opened up ahead. It was empty now. Portia made for the opening in the far wall that would take her to the stairs. She was moving swiftly, silently, without thought.

With barely a whisper, the door opened as easily as it had

done before, and Portia found herself in the familiar scullery. The silence was profound. There was no fire in the range; even the clock was still. She flitted through the scullery to the back stairs. As she crossed the kitchen she heard a sound. A shuffle, a mumble. She froze against the walls, praying her dark clothes would make her inconspicuous in the shadowy kitchen. The sound came again and she relaxed. Someone was snoring. One of the kitchen boys was presumably sleeping on a bench near the empty range.

She slid onto the stairs, as stealthily as any spy in an enemy camp, and flew upward. The stairs opened onto a little-used corridor that intersected the main passage where the family's bedchambers were to be found.

Portia had almost forgotten that she was cold and wet now. Excitement and terror warmed her, kept her moving to Olivia's door. She lifted the latch and slipped inside, and only when she'd closed the door behind her did she realize that her heart was beating so violently it felt as if it would burst from her chest.

21

"*What is it? Who's there?*" Phoebe's alarmed voice broke through the darkness.

"Hush! It's only me," Portia whispered back.

"*Portia!* Is it you?" Olivia shot up in bed, her nightgown a white gleam in the shadows of the bedcurtains.

"Yes. Do be quiet." Portia flitted to the bed, where the two girls sat side by side, staring at her in astonishment.

"It's all very well to say 'It's only me,'" Phoebe declared with some indignation. "How could we possibly expect to see you?"

"No, how could you?" Portia agreed. "But please whisper."

"You're all wet?" Phoebe said. "You're dripping all over the floor."

"I had to swim across the moat." Portia shivered, hugging her arms across her chest. "And I don't seem to be getting much of a welcome for my trouble."

"Oh, Portia, of c-course you are!" Olivia leaped from her bed, flinging her arms around Portia in a convulsive hug. "Oh, you're so cold! You're soaked to the skin!"

"I know," Portia said gloomily. "I brought you some fruit." She took the offering from her pockets and laid it on the bed.

"Take your clothes off." Olivia began to pull and tug at Portia's jerkin. "We can try to dry them."

Phoebe had climbed from the high bed herself and was rummaging in the linen press. "Here's a woolen robe you could borrow."

"Oh, thank you!" Portia flung off the soaked and clammy jerkin and peeled down her britches. "Wet clothes are the most disgusting things."

"Here's a t-towel."

Portia scrubbed herself dry and was suddenly vividly reminded of Rufus scrubbing warmth and life back to her deadened body after she'd been lost in the blizzard. Somewhere, she thought, if she were warm enough to find it, there was a supreme irony in her present situation.

She thrust her arms into the sleeves of the robe that Phoebe held out for her and wrapped it tightly around her body. Her teeth had stopped chattering at last.

"I brought you some fruit," she said again, gesturing to the bed. "It's not much, I know, but all I could carry."

"I don't understand anything," Phoebe said, taking a hearty bite of a pear. "This is good. . . . How on earth did you get in here? No one can get out, so how did you get in?"

"There's a way in," Portia said, seating herself on the window seat. "But I can't tell you about it. I needed to see how you both were. I was worried about you."

"It's horrid," Olivia said, hitching herself onto the bed. "We c-can't cook anything because there isn't any water."

"And there's only ale to drink," Phoebe put in. "And Lord Granville is so angry all the time, and Diana blames him for everything, only of course she doesn't say so, but she takes it out on us. It's most uncomfortable." On this understatement, she tossed the core of her pear into the empty grate and carefully selected an apple.

"And it's so hot," Olivia said. "We c-can't open the windows because of the smoke. And my father won't let us go outside because of arrows."

"Will it soon be over, do you think?" Phoebe regarded Portia shrewdly.

"I don't know," Portia said. "And I can't talk about it." A fierce frown furrowed her brow. It was harder than she'd expected to keep faith with Rufus while offering comfort to her friends. She hadn't anticipated such questions, but of course she should have done.

"You can't talk about it because you're the enemy," Phoebe observed with customary bluntness.

"Portia's not the enemy!" Olivia exclaimed, her voice rising in her indignation. "How c-could you say such a thing?"

"Strictly speaking, Phoebe's right," Portia said. "But I didn't come here to talk about the war. At least, not directly. I wanted to see how you were. And . . . and . . . well, I wanted to talk to you both."

"Is it lonely, being in the army?" Phoebe asked.

Portia shrugged. Phoebe's bluntness verged on the tactless, but she had an uncanny way of fingering the truth. "I didn't expect it to be, but yes, it is a bit."

She realized that she had always been lonely, always dependent only upon herself, even when Jack was alive. But she'd persuaded herself she hadn't needed companionship and so hadn't missed it. But Olivia and Phoebe had given her an insight into what female friends could offer, and it was something that no amount of passion and loving between a man and woman could replace.

"But what of Lord Rothbury?" Phoebe persisted, with the same directness. "Aren't you still his mistress?"

"I'm having his child." Portia found herself blurting her news.

"Oh!" Olivia's eyes were round as saucers. "B-but you aren't married."

"You don't have to be, duckie," Portia said wryly. "As I am the living proof."

"Won't you get married, though?" Phoebe asked. "Before the child is born?"

"I shouldn't think so." Portia's eyes were on her hands, twisting in her lap. "I haven't told Rufus yet, but . . ." She looked up with a tiny rueful laugh. "But I'm not exactly the kind of woman of whom countesses are made. Can you imagine me as Lady Rothbury?"

"But the earl is an outlaw."

"Not any longer. The king has pardoned the house of Rothbury and granted restitution of their lands." Portia reasoned that divulging this piece of information would not be a betrayal. It was no secret, and if Cato didn't know it already, he soon would.

"I think you'd make a wonderful c-countess," Olivia said stoutly.

"But would you wish to be?" Phoebe again asked the

shrewd question. "You've always said you weren't conventional . . . that you wanted to be a soldier . . . that you weren't supposed to be a girl."

"Yes, well, nature obviously didn't agree with me," Portia responded a shade tartly. "Otherwise I wouldn't be finding myself in the ultimate female condition."

The little gilt clock on the mantelpiece chimed three o'clock and Portia jumped off the window seat as if stung. "I have to go! I didn't realize how long it had taken me to get here." She threw off the robe and scrambled back into her wet clothes, shuddering.

"No one knows you're here?"

"Only you two. And you mustn't say anything!"

"Of course we wouldn't!" Phoebe exclaimed.

"Will you c-come again?"

"If I can." Portia buttoned her jerkin. "But I don't know what will happen next." She regarded them helplessly. "I wish I could do something for you."

"The fruit was lovely," Phoebe declared comfortingly, adding with straightforward curiosity, "Do you feel sick? I've heard pregnancy makes people sick."

"Almost all the time," Portia replied with a grimace. "As soon as I wake up until I go to sleep again."

"Oh, how horrid. I'm glad I'm not going to get married," Olivia said, reaching up to kiss Portia.

"But Portia isn't going to get married," Phoebe pointed out. "It's passion that causes the problems, not marriage."

Portia chuckled, her depression lifting. "How right you are, Phoebe. Stay a virgin and then you'll have nothing to regret." She blew them both a kiss from the doorway. "This war can't last forever." Then she asked what she realized now she'd come to ask. "Will you be godmothers to the baby?"

"Of course," Olivia said.

"Send us your ring when the time comes and we'll come to you . . . somehow," Phoebe declared.

For once, Portia didn't find the notion whimsical and unrealistic. She'd given her baby two godmothers and she knew her friends would find a way to stand by that obligation. Even the bastard child of a bastard could have friends in high places. And Olivia and Phoebe, whether they married or remained spinsters, would never lack for worldly comforts.

There was a warm place beneath her ribs that seemed to keep the cold and the fear at bay as she crept back along the corridor, through the scullery, and into the black tunnel. It seemed to take her much less time than it had coming, and within minutes she was at the opening to the moat.

The lever on the inside was not hidden, since obviously there was no need to conceal it from those who would use it. Portia lifted it softly and pushed. The door swung open. It was still night, but it was a grayish darkness after the pitch black of the tunnel. She could make out the tents of the besiegers across the moat, and the flickering torches of the watchmen. The fires at the walls were dying down now, and the smoke was less thick and acrid.

She slid down into the moat, and the water felt almost warm through the clammy cold of her wet clothes. She reached up to pull the door closed, and in that moment, as her body was outlined against the gray wall, a torch threw its light across the still, dark waters of the moat.

Portia felt the light on her back, felt herself exposed like a black dot against white parchment. Her heart hammered. She didn't dare to move. And then the shout came and she knew she was lost as the alarm was raised.

There were excited cries, racing feet, the bright light of more torches. Portia slid into the water, not knowing what else to do. As the surface closed over her head, a musket cracked and the ball smacked against the wall behind her. She swam desperately underwater, trying to get a sense of direction. Was she going toward the bank? Musket balls whizzed over the water and she knew that they were waiting for the moment when her head broke the surface and gave them a proper target. Her lungs were bursting.

When she knew she must breathe in air or water, she raised her head. Someone shouted from the bank and a musket fired again, the ball splashing just by her head. She ducked again, with a lungful of air. That second had given her back her sense of direction, and had also shown her that three men stood on the bank, muskets at the ready. If she could get them to fire all three at once, then she'd have time while they reloaded to declare herself.

Portia had given up all hope of escaping. Now she wanted only to stay alive. She thrust her hand above the water. A musket fired. She raised the other one and was rewarded with another crack. Then she lifted her head and ducked instantly below the water. The third shot landed in the water so close to her head she could almost smell the gunpowder.

She raised her head and yelled the day's password. Then she screamed, "Hold your fire!" as she splashed her way to the bank, making as much noise as she could . . . making it clear that she was giving herself up.

The three watchmen reached down and hauled her up onto the bank. She lay on her belly, gasping for breath, choking with the water she had swallowed in the last frantic moments. They stood over her. She could see their boots. Then one of them pushed her onto her back with his foot. She looked up into unfamiliar faces. These were not Decatur men, they were from Prince Rupert's battalion and they wouldn't know her.

"I belong to the Decatur militia," she got out.

"What's a Decatur man doin' comin' outta the castle?" one of the men demanded, prodding her again with his foot.

"Reckon he'll be answerin' questions soon enough," one of his companions said. "Let's get 'im to the captain." Two of them bent and grabbed her under the arms, dragging her to her feet.

"I can walk," she protested, but they ignored her, dragging her along through the sleeping camp to the tent that housed the captain of the guard.

The guard captain of the prince's battalion was sitting over a pot of ale, throwing dice with his second in command. He looked up with interest as the sentries marched in with their prisoner.

"What have we here?" He pushed back the canvas stool and stood up, coming over to Portia, who had been thrust to her knees on the ground.

"Caught 'im comin' outta the castle, sir. Outta the wall . . . some kind o' concealed entrance. 'E was swimmin' across the moat."

"Scrawny looking lad," the captain observed. He reached down and yanked Portia to her feet by her collar. "So, let's hear your story, m'lad."

Portia shook her head, then reeled as the captain's hand slammed across her mouth, his heavy signet ring cutting her lip.

"Come, come," he said, all persuasive malice. "You'll be singing soon enough. Who are you?"

Portia wiped blood from her mouth with the back of her hand. "I'm with the Decatur militia."

The captain struck her again across her cheek and she reeled and fell to her knees. "Fetch Lord Rothbury," she gasped through the tears of pain that clogged her throat. She had never been mistreated in such a way, and with her terror came a surge of rage that anyone would dare to use her with such uncalled-for violence. "He'll vouch for me."

There was a moment of silence. Then the captain said, "And just what d'you know of Lord Rothbury, fellow-me-lad?"

"I told you. I'm with his militia," Portia repeated doggedly. She staggered to her feet

The man hesitated, uncertain how to proceed in the face of the prisoner's apparent certainty. "All right," he said eventually. "But if this is some kind of trick, my lad, you'll pay for it." He turned to one of the sentries. "Go and rouse Lord Rothbury. The rest of you go back on watch."

$\mathcal{T}$*he sentry's urgent call roused Rufus from sleep.* He had sat up and was out of his cot in one movement, reaching for his britches. "What is it?"

"Captain of the guard sent me, m'lord. We've caught a prisoner, sir, comin' outta the castle, swimmin' across the moat. Captain wants to interrogate 'im, but the prisoner says as 'ow you'll know 'im."

"Sounds interesting," Rufus observed, dressing rapidly. An escapee from Castle Granville was certainly an interesting development.

He followed the sentry through the camp, ducking into the entrance of the guard tent with a cheerful, "So, what have we here, Captain?"

Portia was standing somewhat unsteadily in the center of the tent. Rufus took in her soaked clothes, her swollen and bleeding mouth, the dark swelling on her cheekbone.

"What in the name of sanity . . ." he began, turning angrily to the captain of the guard. "What the *hell* is this?"

The captain found himself blustering under the livid glare of the earl of Rothbury. "We caught him trying to swim the moat from the castle, m'lord. The watchmen saw him come out of the castle by a hidden door." He saw the earl's expression change and said with more assurance, "He says you know him, m'lord."

Rufus ignored the captain. He turned to Portia, his face now carved in granite, his eyes empty. "What were you doing in the castle?"

Portia touched her lip again with a fingertip. It came away sticky with blood. "I went to see Olivia and Phoebe." It seemed simpler to tell the plain truth without protestations and defenses at this point. But she saw with a desperate sinking of her heart that Rufus was already gone from her.

"How did you get in?" There was no expression to his voice or on his countenance. It was as if he had not the slightest interest in the person whom he was questioning, only in the information.

"There's a concealed door," she said miserably. "I discovered it when I was staying in the castle."

Now that deep and apparently baseless unease was explained. Now it seemed to Rufus that everything fell into place. She had known of the door and she had said not one word. The siege could have been ended long since if the besiegers had been able to enter the castle by surprise. She had had that information and she had not divulged it. And there could be but one reason for her silence.

Now he knew that she had been deceiving him all along. She had come to him with information that would convince him of her credentials, but Granville had offered him the treasure only as a means to plant a spy in his camp. It was so simple and he'd fallen for it. He had just once dropped his guard with a Granville, and they'd made a fool of him.

The cold dispassion left him and the dreadful devils of rage that he thought would tear him asunder pulsed in his voice. "You've been using it to gain entry to the castle ever since we began the siege. You've been visiting your family, carrying information, providing comfort. What has Cato to say about—"

"No!" she cried. "No, I have not. This was the first time. I did not betray you, Rufus. I wanted to see my friends. That was all."

"Your pardon, m'lord, but I'm confused." The captain spoke up hesitantly. "This is one of your men, then?"

Rufus leaned forward and plucked the cap from Portia's head. "No," he said distantly. "She's not one of my men, but she travels with us."

"Oh, aye." The captain nodded his understanding. Camp followers were common enough, although it was unusual to see them dressed as this one was. But then, this one had been up to something more sinister than merely following the drum. "But she's been spying, you say?"

"So it would seem," he said as distantly as before. "And not for the first time."

"No, I haven't!" Portia heard the desperation in her voice. She couldn't believe that Rufus had denied her to the captain . . . had relegated her to the status of a whore. "You *know* I haven't, Rufus."

He ignored the appeal. "You do not deny that you entered the castle by a secret entrance?"

"No."

"You do not deny that you knew that by so doing you were consorting with the enemy?"

"Olivia and Phoebe aren't the enemy," she said, her voice dull as she understood that she was not going to convince him of the innocence of her errand . . . not this time.

"You were in that castle. You were among the enemy." He waved a dismissive hand. "You swore allegiance to the Decatur standard and you betrayed that allegiance."

Portia shook her head, her cheek and lip throbbing. "Please, Rufus—"

"Did you take anything into the castle?" The interruption was as hard and rasping as a file against iron.

She looked at him, bewildered. "Just fruit," she said. "I

thought they might be thirsty." And then she heard how she had finally condemned herself.

The captain said swiftly, "That's offering comfort and succor to the rebels, the king's enemies. It's treason and a matter for headquarters."

Rufus looked steadily at Portia. "How could I have been so deceived?" he said. "You are a Granville. You carry the germ of deceit and betrayal in your blood." He turned away with a gesture of disgust.

"It's a matter for headquarters, m'lord," the captain repeated. "She'll be sent there for questioning as soon as it's light."

"Rufus . . ." Portia held out her hand in appeal. He couldn't walk away from her. Surely he couldn't.

He glanced over his shoulder and said with the same cold distance. "I can do nothing for you. You condemned yourself." He pushed through the tent door and was gone.

Portia stared at the tent flap still stirring where he'd roughly thrust it aside. She couldn't believe that her whole world had collapsed, so suddenly, so completely, and so without just cause. But they were binding her hands with thick, rough rope and prodding her forward, out into the night, and the reality of imprisonment, of the horrors of interrogation that awaited her in York, of the spy's noose at the end of the agony, filled her mind. She wanted to scream at the injustice, but her tongue was locked.

They forced her to sit at the base of a tree a few hundred yards from the guard tent, and they tied her securely to the trunk with rope beneath her arms. They used the loose end of the rope that held her wrists to bind her ankles as well, and then they left her trussed, wet and shivering, to await the dawn.

*R*ufus *walked through the camp. He was blind and deaf,* locked into his own world where the rage burned bright as a volcano, and the hurt was a black pit as cold as the rage was hot. But at last something broke through the trance, and he heard his own voice over and over in his head, "There is

nothing I can do for you." It became a chant, blocking out all
else, and finally he stopped walking and turned back to find
Will.

Whatever she'd done, he could not condemn her to what
awaited her in York. The madness of obsession had driven
him to speak as he had done, but he was in control now. Oh,
the rage still burned, and the hurt still froze some central core
of his being, but he was rational again and he could not forget
what she had been to him, what she had meant to him. He
could not stand aside while they hurt her, and he could not
watch her death. She was false, she deserved what they would
do to her, but he could not let it happen.

Will listened in disbelief to what had occurred, but he offered no comment, recognizing that the master of Decatur
was but newly in control of his devils. He heard his orders and
slipped away through the camp.

Portia leaned her head against the trunk of the tree. Her
face burned and throbbed, and she had lost feeling in her
hands. When Will appeared out of the trees behind her, she
merely looked at him, her mouth too swollen to move even
had she thought of anything to say.

He knelt and swiftly cut her bonds. "Come. You must be
away from here before they come to take you."

She managed to speak. "I don't know whether I can walk."
She didn't even know whether she could stand. Her mind
could no longer keep track of what was happening, and her
body seemed simply to have given up.

Will didn't reply. He lifted her easily and at a half run carried her back to Rufus's tent. Rufus was waiting for her, but
his eyes were cold and distant as Will set her down on her cot
and then hurried out.

"Get out of those wet clothes, quickly," Rufus instructed,
indicating the pile of dry clothes he'd set out. "If you're still
here at dawn, I won't be able to save you. *Be quick.*"

In a daze, Portia stripped and dragged on the clean garments and her spare pair of boots. The silence that bound
them was hideous. She couldn't bear to look at his face and

see there the dreadful contempt and the betrayal in his eyes. She sensed that the terrifying rage was gone, but this cold and scornful disdain was almost worse. But she did not venture a word more in her defense.

George entered just as she'd pulled on her boots. "Horses're ready," he said, and seemed deliberately to avert his eyes from Portia.

"You'll need to help her to mount. She's exhausted." It was the first time he had acknowledged her condition, and Portia felt an instant's hope. But when she looked toward him, he merely looked through her as if she were made of air.

George simply lifted her as Will had done, carried her out, and hoisted her up onto Penny. "I'll lead her. Just hold on to the pommel," he instructed.

Portia obeyed. Rufus had not followed them out of the tent, and she couldn't even summon up the energy to ask where George was taking her. As he clicked his tongue and set their horses in motion, Juno barreled out of the undergrowth, yapping excitedly, prancing on her hind legs demanding to be lifted up to the saddle. George ignored the puppy and urged the horses to a trot.

"George, please." Portia could hear the tears in her voice. "Juno . . ."

George swore. "My orders said nothin' about that damn puppy."

"Please."

He looked at her properly for the first time, it seemed, and there was a softening to his mouth. Then he drew rein and when Juno bounded up, he leaned down, caught her by the scruff of the neck, and yanked her upward. " 'Ere." He handed the puppy across to Portia, who managed a painful smile of thanks. She didn't know where she was going, but having Juno was an immediate comfort.

The next hours passed in a daze. She didn't know whether she slept or was just unconscious some of the time. All her being was centered on her hands clinging to the pommel. If she didn't let go, it didn't matter that her eyes were closed, her head drooping, her body swaying. Her mind had ceased to work. She couldn't think of what had happened, or what might happen. She existed only in this moment, this little space in time that contained her body.

She was barely aware when they passed through the sentry posts into Decatur village. The posts were unmanned, the fires unlit. The village was no longer a martial establishment, and its few occupants were content with the small rituals of daily living that provided a threat to no one.

George led Penny to a stone building on the outskirts of the village. It was small and square, its windows barred, its single door of massive oak kept closed with a heavy bar across it on the outside. It was the Decatur prison.

Portia half fell into George's arms as he reached up to help her dismount. She was clutching Juno as if the puppy were her only connection with life. She didn't take in her surroundings, merely stood swaying as George raised the iron-bound bar across the door and opened it. He urged her inside into the dark and musty interior. There were two cells. Small, stone-floored, barred spaces, each containing a narrow cot and a bucket. It was a prison, not designed for comfort.

"In 'ere, lass." George swung open one of the barred doors and gave her a little push into the cell. "I'll fetch ye some water an' some bread. The master says y'are to stay 'ere until 'e's decided what to do wi' ye."

Portia dropped onto the cot. There were two thin blankets and it seemed like heaven. She rolled herself into the blankets and was instantly unconscious, Juno curled tightly against her breast. She didn't hear George return with a pitcher of water and a loaf of bread, which he set down on the floor of her cell, didn't hear the key grate in the lock or the heavy bar fall in place on the outside door.

Juno awoke her hours later. It was dark and Portia for a moment had no idea where she was, or even, for a terrifying instant, *who* she was. The puppy was scratching and whining at the barred door, clearly desperate to go outside.

"Oh God!" Portia sat up, memory flooding back and with it the now familiar misery of waking nausea. Her face felt stiff and sore, her mouth twice its normal size. She stumbled to the bucket and retched, but it was so long since she'd eaten, she brought up nothing. Juno continued to whine.

"I can't let you out." Portia sat back on her heels on the cold stone floor, for the first time fully aware of her predicament. "I can't let either of us out." A faint diffused light came from the barred window high up in the wall and she guessed it was moonlight. There was total silence. Was she to be left moldering here forever?

It was a terrifying thought, almost worse than the prospect of what had awaited her in York. She forced down the panic, swallowed the tears, and broke off a piece of bread. Plain bread sometimes helped the nausea. She nibbled it slowly, feeling her stomach settling. Juno had yielded to the force of nature and was squatting in the far corner of the cell, looking apologetically at Portia.

Then came a sound. The scrape as the heavy bar was raised on the outside door. Lamplight poured into the space and Portia couldn't help a little cry of relief.

"Eh, just what've you been an' gone an' done?"

Josiah's rather creaky voice was the most welcome sound Portia thought she had ever heard. The old man set his lamp down on a table outside Portia's cell. A rich aroma drifted upward from the covered dish he set beside the lamp. Josiah approached the cell, the lamplight shining off his round bald head, giving the fluffy white tonsure a pinkish tinge.

"I'd best take the pup out . . . oh, too late." He spotted the puddle and shook his head with annoyance. "I looked in a couple o' times, but you was both dead t' the world. I'll fetch ye a mop."

"Can you let us out?" Portia stood up and approached the bars.

"Just the pup, George says." Josiah unlocked the door and opened it. Juno raced out between his legs, and the old man closed the door again. "I'll be back wi' that mop." He shuffled out of the building, Juno darting ahead of him.

Portia sat down on her cot and contemplated her situation. It was better than she'd thought a few minutes ago, but it seemed she was to be kept a prisoner in this tiny space.

Josiah returned with a bucket of water and a mop, which he passed to Portia, unlocking and locking the door with great caution. "So, what 'ave ye gone an' done? George wouldn't say."

"Nothing, as it happens," Portia said grimly, cleaning up Juno's mess. "But Rufus thinks I have."

" 'Tain't like the master to be unfair," Josiah stated, clearly not believing Portia's claim. "Not in all the years I've known 'im . . . an' I've known 'im since 'e was nobbut a nipper." He unlocked the bars again to take back the bucket and mop.

"There's no need to keep locking and unlocking those bars," Portia said wearily. "I'm not going anywhere. Where's Juno?"

"Runnin' around outside." Josiah hesitated, looking at the prisoner's wan and battered countenance, then he turned to the table, leaving the bars unlocked. "Ye want some supper?"

As usual these days, Portia's stomach was giving mixed signals, but she knew she needed food. "Can I come out and eat it?"

Again Josiah hesitated. Then he said, "If'n ye promise—"

"I'm not going anywhere," Portia repeated swiftly. She stepped into the main room. "What did George tell you?"

"Just that the master's ordered that y'are to be kept in prison until 'e says otherwise. I'm to take care of ye, since there's only us old folk left be'ind." He lifted the lid on the dish. "There's a spoon fer the stew."

Portia ate standing up because there was no chair. And with the first spoonful she found she was ravenous. "Could you bring me some warm water to wash, d'you think?"

"Aye, I'm to give you anything you need," Josiah said with a nod. "Empty the bucket an' such like . . . bring 'ot water and food. I'll bring ye wine, or ale, when I comes in the mornin'."

Portia set down the empty bowl and returned to her cell. "Can you bring me something to do? Paper, a quill and ink, perhaps, and one of Rufus's books? Any one will do."

Josiah looked doubtful. "Take things from 'is cottage when 'e's not there? I dunno."

"I don't think he'd mind," Portia said. "And if he does, he won't blame you, he'll blame me."

Josiah frowned, his weak, faded eyes examining his charge. She looked desperate in her unhappiness and he could think only of how vibrant and happy and exuberant she had always been. Whatever she'd done, this imprisonment in the near-deserted village was harsh enough without adding to its severity.

"I s'pose I could," he said after a minute. "An' it'll get awful tedious sittin' in 'ere on yer tod."

"Thank you." Portia managed a stiff but grateful smile.

But when Josiah had returned Juno and left, and the bar fell heavily across the outside door, Portia lay down on the cot, assailed by misery.

She could see Rufus's cold eyes, hear the bitter contempt in his voice, and it was unendurable that he should believe what he did of her. She loved him and she had dared to think that he loved her. But he believed her false, and if he had loved her, he would have known she could not have betrayed him. If he had loved her, he would have accepted her . . . accepted who and what she was, and none of this dreadful confusion and wretchedness would have happened.

She was so very tired of steering a path through the obstacle course of his vendetta. So very tired of denying some part of herself in order to satisfy Rufus. It was too high a price to pay for his . . . his what?

Regard? Love? Passion?

Oh, what did it matter anymore? Everything was dust and ashes. Portia curled herself up in the blankets, and sleep brought temporary end to misery.

22

"How far gone are you, then?"

Portia raised her head from the bucket and sat back on her heels, wiping her mouth with her handkerchief. "How did you guess?"

Josiah shrugged. "Not 'ard, when a lassie's pukin' every mornin'. So, 'ow far gone are you?"

Portia struggled to her feet. Josiah was the only person she saw these days and the only person in whom she could confide. "It's embarrassing, but I'm not sure. I can't remember when I had my last terms."

Josiah placed the pot of porridge on the table. "Pukin' usually stops after the first three months."

"You mean I won't be heaving up my guts *forever*?" Portia was more than ready to accept that Josiah had some knowledge of these things.

"Most don't," Josiah replied. "But some lassies do."

"I'll probably be one of those who do," Portia said glumly. She stretched in the cramped space, envying Juno, who was running free outside. Josiah made sure the puppy had three good runs a day. But then, Juno couldn't use a bucket, Portia reflected wryly.

"Does t'master know?" Josiah asked, unlocking Portia's cell.

"By the time I was sure, the right moment never arose to tell him." Portia came out of the cell with a little sigh of relief. Five days of this confinement was becoming tedious. Her legs jumped with the need to walk; her body, filled with suppressed energy, refused to settle into sleep; her mind seethed with "if onlys."

"Josiah, could I just walk a little along the riverbank? I give you my word—my parole—that I'll come back."

Josiah looked uncomfortable. "I knows ye won't be goin' anywhere, but I 'aven't 'ad orders."

Portia was stumped. The Rufus she thought she knew would not have condemned her to this kind of confinement. It made sense to think that in the intensity of those last moments in the camp, he'd given his orders and simply missed specifying the details of her imprisonment. But perhaps not. Perhaps this was what he'd intended. He'd saved her from a spy's punishment, but his own was another matter. Ultimately more merciful, but still dreadful.

"Mebbe I could send—" Josiah's musing was cut off by the shrilling of pipes. The cottage was set away from the village, but they could hear the commotion—racing footsteps, shouts.

"What is it?" Portia moved swiftly to the barred window, her blood racing. She knew the answer in every bone and sinew. Rufus was back.

"I'll go an' see. Eat yer porridge an' I'll be back." Josiah's shuffle was faster than usual as he went to the door, releasing a breath of early-morning-fresh summer air that filled Portia with an aching need to leave her prison.

The door banged shut behind him, and Portia heard the heavy bar drop into place.

She ate her porridge, without enthusiasm or appetite. Inaction dulled appetite anyway, and the diet lacked the kind of variety that might stimulate it. But she was conscious of the life growing within her. A life that had somehow become intrinsic to her own. She lived for this child. Her blood flowed for the child. Her mind thought for it. Her lungs breathed for it. It was as if her body was devoting itself without conscious instruction to the nurturing of a life that had not yet discovered its own importance, or its own needs. She was the child within her womb as that child was her own self.

The simple task of eating also calmed her. The sounds beyond her prison had now changed. Now she could hear the pipes and drums of an army, the marching feet, all the concomitants of a conventional military discipline that subsumed the martial encampment of an erstwhile outlaw.

Rufus Decatur was no longer a moss-trooper, an outlaw.

He was the rightful earl of Rothbury, fighting for his king, and Portia Worth was a traitor whom he was harboring. Whatever business had brought him here, he would have to ignore her presence officially. But surely he would come to her . . . say something . . . send a message through Josiah or George or Will.

Juno's short barks at the door to the jail heralded Josiah's entrance, with the puppy bounding ahead of him. Juno leaped at Portia as if she hadn't seen her for a week.

"Yes . . . yes . . . I love you too." Portia bent to stroke her. Two months ago she could have lifted her easily into her arms. But at six months the puppy was bidding fair to become a large dog, although Juno hadn't seemed to realize that herself and looked disappointed when she was left at ground level.

"Is it Rufus?" Portia tried to keep both anxiety and hope from her voice as she looked up at Josiah while keeping a calming hand on Juno's neck.

"Aye." Josiah's customary tranquility was disturbed. "They're all back, wi' the prince's men, too. They're sayin' there's goin' to be a big battle. T'army's 'eadin' out t'morrow mornin'."

Portia's heart plunged. "Did you see Rufus?"

"Not to speak to. . . . You finished 'ere?" Josiah gestured to the bowl on the table. His old eyes were troubled. "Seems very busy, 'e does . . . what wi' the prince's officers an' all."

"If he wants to talk to me, I suppose he will." Portia sounded as dispirited as she felt. She went back into her cell, Juno at her heels. "He knows I'm here, after all."

"Aye, but 'e doesn't know yer carryin'," Josiah said, locking the barred door before picking up the empty porridge bowl. "I'll be back wi' dinner at noon."

Portia lay back on her cot and listened to the familiar sounds of the door and the bar locking her in. How long was Rufus intending to keep her here? Until the war was over? Until she no longer faced charges of treason? Would he ever talk to her again? Or would Josiah open the door one day and tell her she was free? Free to go wherever fancy and fate took her, so long as she never crossed Rufus Decatur's path again?

Free to give birth to a Decatur bastard who would never know
its father?

*R*ufus *entered his cottage and the emptiness assailed*
him. It had been many months since he'd lived here without
Portia, and something essential seemed to have gone from the
place. Her heavy winter cloak still hung from the hook by the
door, and he knew that if he went upstairs he would see her
nightrobe over the bedrail, and he could even fancy that the
mattress was still imprinted with the slight indentation of her
body. His own body was so much bigger and heavier than Portia's deceptively frail form that she always rolled down into the
valley he made to come to rest against his back, curled
around him like a limpet on a rock.

He had never in his life been as wretched as he was now.
Not even as an orphaned lad, cast adrift with the memories of
his father's last words and the sound of the shot that had killed
him and the reek of the smoke that had burned to ashes the
only home Rufus had ever known. Not even when he'd stood
over the dead bodies of his mother and infant sister and worried about how he was to bury them.

There had still been a future then, a terrifying, unknown
future, but the knowledge of a future was essentially hopeful. Now he felt as if something vital to his continued existence had been cut out of him. There was nothing to look
forward to, nothing to plan for. For the one and only time in
his adult life, he had given himself—his trust, his loyalty, and
his love—to another person. He had loved . . . no, *still* loved
her . . . with such an overwhelming power that that emotion
contained all others. And she had deceived him, used his love
to betray him. And the knowledge of that was unendurable.

"Is she here? Is Portia here?" Luke and Toby pushed against
his legs in their hurry to get inside. They tumbled headlong
into the kitchen and righted themselves, looking around the
barren room.

"She's not here?" Luke said, his voice forlorn.

"She's not *anywhere*," Toby stated flatly. He looked up at
his father. "*Where* is she?"

Rufus had thought they'd accepted Portia's disappearance as easily as they usually adapted to their lives' constantly changing circumstances. Now he realized it had been wishful thinking. The fact that they hadn't questioned her absence meant only that they had put their own construction on it, and had simply assumed she would reappear in familiar surroundings. Now they were both looking up at him with a mixture of accusation and trepidation, and he cursed himself for being such a blind fool. Portia had become as indispensable a part of their lives as she had of his. He'd been too absorbed in his own wretchedness to look at his sons and see how they were dealing with her sudden and unexplained absence.

And now in order to answer his children, he had to face the question he'd pushed aside in the last week. He couldn't keep Portia imprisoned forever. So what was he to do?

"I don't know," he heard himself saying, almost absently answering his own question, not Toby's.

The boys stared up at him incredulously. "Where is she?" Toby repeated with a strangely adult air of patience, as if he believed that his father hadn't properly understood him the first time.

"When's she coming back?" Luke demanded, a quiver in his voice as he stared up at Rufus.

"I'm not quite sure," Rufus said, forcing a note of brisk reassurance into his voice. "She had some things to do."

"But she didn't even say goodbye. I felt sure she'd be here," Toby said with the same strange maturity that covered a wealth of confusion.

"She had to leave very suddenly and she didn't wish to wake you," Rufus said. "I've explained that already. Now, you're going to stay at Mistress Beldam's for a couple of days, so hurry up and get anything you want to take."

Once he'd told Portia with some indignation he wouldn't consign his children to the care of a brothel, but while he could take them to the relatively placid scene of a siege, he could not have them on a battlefield. And Rufus was under no illusions about the nature of the coming battle. Prince Rupert was insisting that the king's men were ready to fight, that it was time to force the decisive battle of the war. But Rufus suspected . . . no, he knew . . . that the prince was mistaken. The king's men were not ready to fight a decisive battle. And if they lost this one, then Charles might as well surrender to Parliament.

His short acquaintance with the prince had convinced him that the man, for all his reputation as a supreme commander, was far from levelheaded. It would have been sensible to have seen the siege of Castle Granville through to its conclusion. To walk away from it when it was so close to success had been rash and fatal for morale.

The king's army had been losing steadily since the winter, and they needed some clear success. The surrender of Castle Granville would have afforded them that. Rufus had seen how dispirited the king's men were, but Prince Rupert refused to acknowledge it. And Rufus had had no choice but to obey the orders of his supreme commander. Rufus had committed himself to the king for the present, and he was subject to the orders of Prince Rupert, whether he agreed with them or not. After this battle was fought . . . if he walked whole from the battlefield . . . then he would reassess his position.

How it had maddened him to walk away from Cato's castle, to leave the man triumphant when Cato had been so close to surrender! But Rufus held close the conviction that their final confrontation would come another day. In this coming battle they would meet on the field. He knew it in blood, bone, and sinew.

"Beggin' yer pardon, master . . . ?"

Josiah's voice, sounding almost apologetic, brought him out of his reverie. He spun round with a smile of greeting.

"Could I 'ave a word in private, m'lord?"

Rufus had known he would have to discuss his prisoner with Josiah as soon as he returned to Decatur village, and he had prepared himself for the conversation. "Of course." He gestured to the stairs. "Lads, get your things together. Bill is going to take you in the cart as soon as you're ready."

"We got everything already," Toby declared, and there was a note of accusation in his voice. "When Portia was here, before we went to the siege. We got everything then."

"Yes, there isn't anything we want left here," Luke put it, butting his father's knees with his head.

"Then go outside and play." Rufus propelled the boys firmly outside the door and came back in, closing the door at his back. He leaned against it, ignoring the shouts of protest. "So, how is she?"

Josiah stroked his chin and looked grave. Rufus experienced a wave of pure terror. "What is it?" he demanded. "Is she all right?"

"Oh, aye, m'lord. The lass is as well as could be expected," Josiah replied slowly. "But she needs some exercise . . . a walk along the river now an' again. I didn't 'ave no orders, so . . ." He looked inquiringly at the master.

Rufus, from the dreadful depths of his hurt, had thrust aside all images of Portia herself . . . all recognition of her as a person. Now she came back to him in all her warm and restless liveliness. Her long-legged energy, the wild halo of orange hair, the slanted green cat's eyes so filled with laughter and mischief and shrewd intelligence. And his own body reverberated with the sense of her confinement, of the dreadful inaction, the hours of boredom.

Five minutes' walk along the river would take him to her.

And then he thought of what she'd done to him, and the bitterness flooded back in a corrosive wave that ate into memory and destroyed all softness.

"I don't want the boys to know she's here. Once Bill's taken them away and we've left in the morning, you may give her her freedom," he said distantly. "Tell her she's not to be here when I return." With a brusque gesture, he moved past Josiah and went abovestairs.

Josiah listened to his pacing along the wooden floor above. There was no purpose to his steps, it was as if he was pacing because he couldn't bear to be still. Josiah had seen the anguish on his face a moment earlier. He had seen the same on Portia's face many times in the last week. No two ways about it, two people were making each other very unhappy for some reason . . . a reason that Josiah, from a lifetime's experience, was certain couldn't be worth such pain. There was a child coming, too. And if Rufus cast the lass aside as completely as he seemed to intend doing, then he'd never know it.

Josiah gave a brisk little nod of decision and quietly let himself outside. The children were sitting in the dirt, idly scratching patterns on the ground with a stick. They looked up as Josiah emerged, and the flash of hope in the pair of blue orbs was replaced with a look of such disappointment that Josiah's old heart turned over. "Eh, lads, you want to come an' 'elp me collect the honey from the 'ives?"

It was an invitation that would normally have sent them into transports of delight. Now, however, they went with him in a dispirited silence, dragging their feet.

Portia spent the long hours of the day listening to the sounds that drifted muted through the high barred window of her cell. Pipes, drums, marching feet, shouted commands. She was aware of a curious atmosphere that was borne on the air, it seemed. A sense of fear, an edge almost of desperation to the sounds of an army preparing to do battle.

For a few hours she paced the stone-flagged floor of her cell, under Juno's puzzled eye, her ears straining to catch the sound of a footfall on the path outside. She knew she would sense his coming as soon as he was within a hundred yards of the prison, and hope buoyed her until past noon. Then somehow she knew he wouldn't be coming. He was going to go off to battle without seeing her. Without a word of reconciliation, he was going to face his death, willing to leave her to spend the rest of her life carrying the burden of this severed relationship, of the knowledge that he had died hating her, believing her false.

She fought the tears in grim silence as she waited for Josiah. But it was midafternoon before the outer door opened and the old man entered, breathing hard as if he'd been hurrying.

"Lord bless us! But it's all go today." He set a covered basket on the table. "I 'ope you didn't think I'd gone an' forgotten you." He unlocked Portia's cell, his eyes taking in the prisoner's extreme pallor, the set of her mouth, her eyes glistening with unshed tears.

"No, I didn't think that." Portia stepped out into the main room as Juno raced to the door, wagging her tail expectantly. "What's happening in the village?"

Josiah let Juno out, then turned back to the table to unpack the basket. "Army business . . . folk marchin' around
lookin' important. . . . Come an' eat now. Y'are eatin' fer two,
remember."

"How can I forget?" Portia ate listlessly, all her energy consumed with the effort of not asking about Rufus . . . not asking
if he'd said anything about her.

The army left at dawn. Portia heard them go in the gray
early light, the steady tramp of boots, the clatter of hooves,
jangle of bit and bridle. For once, there was no martial music,
no pipe or drums, and the absence lent a somber note to the
departure, so that Portia wondered if they were even flying the
standards with the brave show of an army who believed in itself, in the rightness of the cause and the certainty of victory.

Rufus had always been open with his doubts about the
wisdom of the king's high command. Their bravery was un-
questioned but their tactics and their assumptions were often
less than rational. Now Portia wondered if he was feeling they
were on a fool's errand. She wondered what had happened at
Castle Granville. Had Cato capitulated in the week she'd
been absent? It was possible but unlikely. And if he hadn't,
then how had Rufus reacted to being given orders to abandon
the siege?

It was dreadful to be so ignorant. Josiah had volunteered
no information, and pride, useless and pointless, had kept
Portia from asking directly what he might have gleaned about
the siege, the army's plans, and the mood in the camp.

She paced her cell, tormented with her ignorance, tor-
tured with images of Rufus dead, dying, mutilated, screaming
in agony. And then she heard the soft clop of hooves, the faint
jingle of a bridle, a small whinny, and her heart leaped with
hope. She ran to the barred door of her cell and stood there,
holding the bars, listening for the familiar footstep.

Juno whined and stood on her hindlegs, putting her
forefeet firmly on the door lock. Footsteps meant release.

"Rufus?" Portia could barely speak his name as she heard
the bar lift on the outside door. Her hands were clammy, her

heart pounding so hard it hurt. "Rufus . . ." Her voice died. Her disappointment was so great she didn't think she could bear it.

Josiah came in, his arms laden, a glint in his faded eyes. "Come along, now, lass." He set his burdens on the table and unlocked the cell door.

"The rear'll be no more than 'alf an hour ahead of you. And they're not Decatur men. Decatur men are in the van . . . where'd you'd expect 'em to be." He nodded with a hint of pride. "You'll be able to mingle wi' the stragglers easy enough, 'cause they'll not know you."

"What're you talking about, Josiah?" Portia stepped out of her cell. There was an unusual energy emanating from Josiah. And she felt the first stirrings of a nameless hope.

"You must go after 'em, of course," Josiah declared. "I've brought yer rapier an' musket, an' the knife George took off you. An' 'ere's yer breastplate, an' 'elmet, an' jerkin. Penny's all saddled an' ready to go. The army's 'eadin' fer Marston Moor, just beyond York. There was plenty o' talk in the mess last night. So, off you go, lass."

Suddenly, Portia knew what was happening. She saw her way clear. Josiah was giving her her freedom and the means to be once more in command of her own destiny. She was no longer helpless.

She was too much a soldier now herself to have any more illusions about the coming battle than she knew Rufus would have. From the most optimistic viewpoint, he was as likely to die upon the field as to walk away from it. She wanted only the chance to put things right between them before he fought on that field.

As she pulled on her buff leather jerkin and strapped on her breastplate, she refused to allow the thought that Rufus wouldn't listen to her, would still be so locked into his rage, that obsession-fueled rage of vengeance, that he would not hear her. She would *make* him listen to her. *Make* him hear.

Josiah handed her her weapons and she sheathed her rapier, thrust her knife into her boot, slung her musket and bandolier across her chest. Immediately she felt as if she'd reentered the world she knew. These were the tools of her trade. She tucked her telltale hair into the knitted black cap and put on her steel helmet. Only those who knew her well would recognize her for what she was.

"Will you take care of Juno, Josiah?"

"Aye. Don't you worry about the pup," Josiah replied. "Just get on wi' what ye've got to do."

Portia went to the door and whistled for Juno. The puppy came scampering along the riverbank toward her, wagging her tail and bouncing on her large paws. Portia picked her up with some effort, and Juno licked her face ecstatically. "You're going to stay with Josiah," Portia told her and carried her into the jail.

"Can you hold her while I make my getaway?"

Josiah received the wriggling bundle placidly. "Away wi' you, then, lass, and God be wi' you."

"With us all," Portia said somberly. Then she kissed Josiah soundly on both cheeks. "I'll never forget this."

"Eh, I'm an old man, lass, an' I can't stand to see folks makin' themselves un'appy fer no cause. You go after him, an' you put things right. The master's a stubborn wite at times an' 'e makes mistakes like the rest of us." He waved her away with his free hand.

Penny was cropping the grass, reins knotted at her neck. She whinnied in greeting as Portia stroked her neck and pulled her ears in her own customary greeting, inhaling the rich scent of horseflesh and leather.

It was the last day of June. Portia swung into the saddle and breathed deeply of the soft morning. It was still early, but the air already held the promise of another hot day. She turned Penny toward the hills and the mare trotted briskly upward and out of the Decatur stronghold through the now-deserted sentry post.

They took the York road. The sun came up, hot and dazzling, and the earth was hard, the grass smelling almost scorched. Penny seemed anxious to move quickly, her ears twitching with the knowledge of the army ahead of her, in whose ranks she knew she belonged. But Portia was in no hurry to catch up with the army. Their route would be easy to follow, and she wanted to run no risks of premature discovery, so she held the mare to an easy trot.

The hillside was yellow and purple with broom and heather, and Portia's heart was singing as jubilantly as the larks hovering over the fragrant heath.

Rufus would listen to her. He *would*.

23

The two men walked through the trees down to the river.
Behind them rose the smoke of cooking fires in the afternoon
air and the sounds of a large army making camp. Portia shad-
owed them, flitting soundlessly from the concealment of tree
and bush, keeping them in sight but never coming close
enough to risk detection. In the last two days, since they'd left
Decatur village, she'd followed Rufus whenever the opportunity arose. Sliding in and out of crowds, her eyes hungrily pursuing him, her ears straining for the sound of his voice. It was
an agony to be so far from him, and yet the sweetest torment
to observe him in this way, unobserved herself.

During the march that had brought them to this place, the
mounted Decatur men had stayed in the van, Prince Rupert's
infantry marching behind, a small cavalry force bringing up
the rear. They had bivouacked for the night outside the walls
of York, and throughout that night they were joined by the
rest of the royalist force, marching in from the countryside
under their individual commanders.

Portia had mingled with the newcomers, safe from recognition. It was simple enough to escape attention — she was
experienced enough now to know how to conduct herself in
a company of soldiers, and no one questioned her claim to
belong to some company positioned at another point along
the line.

Whenever she saw Rufus, her stomach quivered, her body
plunged forward under a spur of longing. She needed to run
to him, to feel his arms strong around her, to smell his skin
and hair, to run her fingers through the silky red-gold beard,
to bask in the warm living light of his eyes. They had been so
cold, so dreadfully distant, the last time they'd looked upon

her, and she could barely contain her need to banish that memory, to put in its place the loving, humorous, tender gaze that alone made her feel whole.

Each time she observed him, she was afraid that even across the distance that separated them he would feel the heat of her gaze, would sense the power of her need, which was so strong she felt it must pulse in the air around him, a current that flowed from her to him in ever stronger waves. Sometimes she thought it was impossible that he couldn't feel her presence with every breath he took. But not once did he look in her direction, and her fear of confronting him, her terror that he would reject her again, kept her procrastinating, observing from afar, satisfying her need only with her eyes.

And even as she waited and planned and postponed in apprehension the moment when she would reveal herself to him, a different dread threaded black and cold through her every waking minute. She had to confront him before dawn, before the coming battle. Otherwise it might be too late.

As she moved through the throngs of men, always on the outskirts of any group, she heard the disaffection of soldiers who hadn't been paid in months. Men who were beginning to see no point in sacrificing themselves for a cause that had little or no relevance to them. And her own dismay, she knew, would mirror Rufus's. These men would not fight with a whole heart. Whenever they looked upon their beribboned, belaced commanders on their magnificent steeds, they felt no identification, no pride, no loyalty. No reason at all to give their lives so that these men could continue to live their own lives of wealth and privilege.

Now they were camped at the place that Prince Rupert and his commanders had designated as the battlefield on which the king's decisive victory would be won. A few miles to the north of York, Marston Moor was a bleak expanse of moorland where two armies could maneuver in the rigid formations of pitched battle.

It was midafternoon when Portia followed Will and Rufus down to the river that flowed at the base of a small tree-studded knoll. They had left the Decatur company preparing their dinner in camp with the rest of the royalist army at the end of a short day's march. The standards of Parliament's forces could be seen with the aid of a spyglass, fluttering among the tents at the far side of the moor. The atmosphere in the king's camp was edgy, and Portia wondered how the enemy were feeling as they prepared to face the hideous reality of the coming dawn.

Will and Rufus didn't seem to be speaking much, although Portia was too far away to hear even if they had been talking. They reached the bank of the river, and Portia crept close, ducking behind a holly bush. She was close enough now to hear them, but they said nothing to each other, merely threw off their clothes and together waded into the river.

Portia watched with the unabashed delight of a voyeur. It had been so long, it seemed, since she had seen Rufus naked. Now she wondered if he had grown thinner. She fancied his ribs were more pronounced, his back leaner. But his backside was as taut and smooth-muscled as ever, his waist as narrow, his hips as slim. She felt her loins quicken with desire when he bent to splash water over his face and his buttocks tensed and the muscles in his thighs rippled. Will, too, was a fine figure of a man, with the lean suppleness of youth, but no one could compare with Rufus. With his power, his strength, the contained authority of his body.

The two men swam for ten minutes, racing each other across the river, and it seemed to the watcher on the bank that there was a joylessness to the exercise. It was as if it were something they both needed to do for purely mechanical, practical reasons. When Rufus strode from the water, his body rising above the surface with each pace, the water flowing from him, Portia took inventory of his body, of everything that had given her so much pleasure, had filled her with such transcendent delight.

She loved his flat belly, the sharp bones of his hips, the soft pelt on his broad chest. And she adored his navel. Her tongue flickered as she relived the memory of sipping wine from that wonderfully deep indentation in his belly, her tongue delving, stroking, tickling. He would squirm beneath the tickling strokes of her tongue, his thighs would tense, the muscles of his stomach jump. She could taste on her tongue even now the salty tip of his penis, could feel the muscular hardness as she drew him into her mouth, curling her tongue around him.

And as she crouched in the concealment of the holly bush and watched Rufus dry himself carelessly with his shirt, Portia was suddenly swept with a near ungovernable lust, so that her hands trembled, her knees were like water, and she sat down abruptly on the damp mossy undergrowth where the sun rarely reached.

Will came splashing out of the water, much more noisily than his cousin, and flung himself down on the grass. His voice carried easily to Portia.

"If you're so pessimistic about the outcome of tomorrow's battle, Rufus, why would you fight it?"

There was a moment's silence before Rufus replied, "Two reasons. I pledged myself and Decatur men to the king's cause, and for this battle at least, I'll stand by my pledge. . . ." He paused, then said, "I will release any Decatur man from his loyalty to my standard if he chooses not to risk his life."

"You know no one would do such a thing," Will objected with some heat. "They'll give their lives for you."

"Yes, but why should they give their lives for a lost cause?" Rufus shrugged. "There're men on both sides must feel that."

"And the second reason?" Will prompted.

Rufus spoke without expression. "I intend to meet Cato Granville on the field."

"And killing him will make you happy." There was no question in Will's voice.

Rufus lay back on the grass, hands linked behind his head. "It will be duty done."

"Duty done? No more than that?" Will now sounded incredulous.

Rufus turned on his side, gently encouraging an ant onto a blade of grass. "I seem to have lost my ability to care about anything, Will."

"Because of Portia?" Will spoke hesitantly. The subject had been taboo, but he sensed something akin to an invitation now.

Again Rufus was silent. Then he sat up and reached for his

damp shirt. "I've come to the conclusion, Will, that a man can only give himself once to a woman . . . give himself heart and soul. And if that gift is spurned, it leaves him with very little interest in the future."

He pulled on his britches. "Come, it's time we went back to camp." And his voice was now matter-of-fact, completely without emotion, and utterly forbidding.

Will took his cue and dressed, and the two of them walked back to the camp in much the same silence they'd held on the way to the river.

Portia stayed huddled beneath her bush for a long time before she too made her way back to the campfires.

"*So*, what d'ye think?"

Cato lowered his spyglass and turned to the man who had spoken at his elbow. Oliver Cromwell was a stocky man with shorn hair and a general air of dishevelment. His collar was stained, his jerkin spotted with grease, his hair clinging lankly to his skull.

"There's a good four hours of daylight left," Cato responded thoughtfully. "And judging by the cooking fires, we'll catch 'em on the hop."

"Precisely." Cromwell rubbed his hands together in satisfaction. "What d'ye think, Fairfax?"

Lord Fairfax raised his well-bred nose and appeared to sniff the air. "It seems a trifle unchivalrous," he observed. "Descending upon the enemy when they're snug around their fires, about to sit down to dinner. But it'll surely give us a decisive advantage."

"Aye, and war's hardly a chivalrous business," Cato returned. He raised his spyglass again and looked across the expanse of moor to the enemy fires. Was Rufus Decatur among the royalist force? It was likely, and if so, if both of them survived the vagaries of battle, there was a chance they would meet on the field. A meeting that would bring an end one way or the other to the feud of their fathers. If he himself died today, either at Decatur's hands or on the battlefield, he had no heir to perpetuate the feud. It was not a burden to be carried by daughters. And by the same token, Rufus Decatur had no legitimate heirs to bear the burden of vengeance for the house of Rothbury.

Cato was unaware that his lips were tightly compressed as he returned his concentration to the conversation continuing around him.

"They'll have their glasses trained on us as we have ours on them." Lord Leven pursed his mouth in thought. "They'll observe any overt preparations for attack."

Cromwell's eyes sparkled with enthusiasm, and when he spoke with conviction and authority, it was clear to his listeners that his battle plan had been made long since. "But if Fairfax brings his force to make a flanking attack to the right, their approach will be concealed by the wood . . . and if the Scots take the left flank, they'll be hidden for the first hundred yards by that hill." He gestured with his whip to the small rise in question. "The main body of the army will make a frontal attack as soon as you've surprised the enemy."

"Aye, they'll be far too occupied wi' us to notice ye." Lord Leven rubbed his hands and chuckled. "I reckon we'll have won the day by sundown."

It was unusual for the generally somber Scot to sound so optimistic, but all three men felt a surge of confidence as they envisaged the peaceful scene of an army at its evening campfires thrown into panic and disarray by an unexpected fullforce attack.

"Let's do it, then." Cromwell spoke decisively, and with a brief handshake the four men parted to see to their dispositions.

*P*ortia *was squatting on her heels beside a campfire, eat-*ing a sausage pierced on the tip of her dagger while throwing dice with two farmers' lads from Cumbria, both of whom were terrified at the prospect of the upcoming battle, their first experience of being under fire. Portia's idle chatter and the fact that she was steadily winning on the throw of the dice served to take their minds off their fear, and she reflected that she was performing a useful community service while lining her empty pockets.

The conversation she had overheard between Rufus and Will sent her alternately to the peaks of hope and into the pits of despair. Rufus had said he loved her. But he'd also spoken with utterly flat finality about the destruction of that love. And time was running out. Tonight she had to find him. She told herself she would finish this game, and then she would go.

The first confused sounds—shouts, the crack of musket fire, the pounding of hooves, the clash of steel—came just as she was scooping up a handful of coins amid the vigorous oaths of her fellow players. The group of men around the campfire leaped to their feet, casting aside food and ale tankards, bemusedly grabbing for their weapons lying carelessly on the grass beside them. Pandemonium ensued, men running hither and thither like headless chickens until their sergeant bellowed for order and they came to a shuffling halt while the sounds of attack continued from beyond the small copse where they had made their bivouac.

Portia unobtrusively slipped away into the trees. She had not come to Marston Moor to fight to the death on the battlefield . . . to expose her unborn baby to a pointless danger. She found that her mind was crystal clear, her body moving fluidly through the trees as she approached the fighting.

It was clear to her that the rebel army had launched a surprise attack, and her thoughts now were concentrated with a deadly precision upon the Decatur men. She knew they were bivouacked on the right flank of the line, and she could hear the fierceness of battle coming from that direction as she made her way toward their position.

A horse came crashing through the underbrush, and a magnificent black destrier reared above her. The cavalry officer on his back was resplendent in silk and lace, flourishing a curved sword.

"Hey, you there!" He stood up in his stirrups, as his horse plunged and reared at the end of a short rein. "What battalion?"

"Decatur," Portia said.

"Then why aren't you with them?" His sword cut through the air in a sweeping arc that would have parted Portia's head from her shoulders if she hadn't jumped back. His face was red with a furious panic, his eyes bloodshot and wildly ferocious.

"I was visitin' another bivouac, sir," she gasped. The man was taking her for a deserter. "I'm on me way back to me company. But what's 'appenin', sir?"

"Get back to your company. Your sergeant will tell you what you need to know." He wheeled his horse and galloped back through the trees.

Portia pulled off her helmet and knitted cap, shaking her hair loose. It was time to discard the trappings of a soldier. She unstrapped her breastplate and cast it aside into the underbrush and then crept forward to the very edge of the copse. Now she could smell the gunpowder; the clash of steel and the crack of musket fire were very close. Shouts and screams rent the air; frantic yells mingling terror with exultation sent shivers down her back.

Portia shinnied up an oak tree, her blood pounding in her ears, her mouth parched with her own fear. A fear that was not for herself. Halfway up the tree, she settled herself into the crook of the trunk, her legs straddling a wide branch. Parting the screen of leaves in front of her, she had a clear view over the moor.

At first she couldn't tell what was happening. The scene was anarchical, straight from the pits of Chaos. She couldn't distinguish royalists from rebels amid the surging, swaying lines of men. The smoke of musket and cannon obscured whole sections of the field, clearing suddenly to reveal the ground littered with the writhing bodies of men and horses. Riderless horses galloped panicked across the field, trampling dead and wounded alike beneath their iron-shod hooves; infantrymen wandered dazed in circles amid the fighting, looking for their own companies, seemingly unaware of the target they presented for the massive chargers bearing down on them, and the swooping swords of the cavalry bringing death from above.

Portia watched in a sick and ghastly trance, her nostrils assailed by the dreadful smell of blood, her ears pierced with the screams of the wounded, the blood-curdling shrieks of attack. She watched as a royalist officer, blood streaming from his face, his lace jabot torn, his buff jerkin ripped from neck to waist by some forgotten and maybe barely noticed sword cut, rallied a group of pikemen, forming them into a ragged line. They ran, yelling, pikes at the ready, straight for a line of rebel infantry, who immediately discharged their muskets, and when the smoke had wafted away, the bodies of the pikemen lay like crumpled dolls upon the red ground, the headless corpse of the officer who had led them lying a few feet in front.

Now Portia was able to distinguish the opposing sides. And now she could see with dreadful clarity how completely the royalist army was overwhelmed. They would have been outnumbered anyway, but taken by surprise, they had no chance to rally, no chance to push back the overwhelming attack of superior numbers.

And Portia had a view of only one portion of the battlefield, the sector where the Decatur men were stationed. From her aerie she couldn't distinguish individual men, but she knew Rufus and his men would be down there, fighting on that bloody field.

And then she saw the Decatur standard, the proud eagle of the house of Rothbury rising high above the carnage. And she wanted to be there on the field, fighting with her friends and comrades beneath that standard. She had missed the chance to put things right between them before the battle, and now all that was left was to share this terrible danger, to stand beside her lover, beside the father of her unborn child. And the longing was so overpowering she felt as if it could bear her like a strong wind into the center of the battle without the least assistance of muscle and sinew.

But she remained where she was, in the angle of the trunk and the branch, her hand resting protectively on her belly, her eyes riveted to the carnage, her heart filled with unspeakable dread.

*R*ufus *was aware of men falling around him. He saw* George go down, the man who had taught him so much about the handling of men, of the basics of battle, who had taught him how to face and make his own the harsh realities of a life outside the law.

Rufus fought his way through the scarlet chaos, the hideous brilliance of death, to reach the fallen man. But George was dead, his eyes staring upward into the orange sky, his stoic realism and placid wisdom leaking from him in the blood that congealed beneath his head.

Rufus closed George's eyes and slowly straightened. Ajax stamped his feet, raised his nostrils to the wind, only the whites of his eyes visible. Rufus swung himself into the saddle again. He turned the horse back toward the battle. He saw Paul, who carried the Decatur standard, topple sideways from his horse under the swinging attack of a Roundhead blade. Ajax, under the prod of spur and rowel, burst through the men crowding the fallen man.

Rufus leaned down and swept up the standard as it fell from Paul's limp fingers. Now Rufus fought only for the lives and the deaths of the men who had stood beneath the Decatur standard. Men who had shared his outlawed life, who had taken his quarrel as their own. He had dragged them into this fight for his own ends and now he owed them all—the living and the dead—the final victory of the house of Rothbury.

He rode into the thick of the fighting. He cut down the king's enemies when they were in his way, he joined skirmishes when his assistance was needed, but always he was searching. He rode through the carnage like a man possessed and yet untouchable. Musket shot whistled past his ear, swords flashed so close he could feel the wind rustling his hair, but he and Ajax plunged through the churned mud and blood of the battlefield until finally Rufus saw the standard of the house of Granville.

And he saw Cato, Marquis of Granville, astride a gray stallion, rallying his men with great shouts of triumph, standing in his stirrups as he exhorted them to the final push that would break the king's army once and for all.

"On this field of Marston Moor, the rights of the honest yeoman of England will be secured!" Cato's voice rose on a thrilling peal of conviction, and his men answered the call with a roar. They hurled themselves onto the broken ranks of the royalist force, and as Cato's horse surged to lead them, Rufus Decatur moved Ajax directly into the gray's path.

There was a moment of confusion, but it was only a moment. Then Cato's gaze cleared, he brought his horse under control, and the two men faced each other amid a murderous turmoil that faded into the distance like the bells of cows in an alpine pasture.

"So, Decatur," Cato said in the stillness that surrounded them, closing them off from the world like the thorny thicket of Sleeping Beauty's castle.

"Granville."

The curt greeting was sufficient. Rufus turned Ajax aside and rode away from the fray. Cato followed, both men now intent on the culmination of the personal feud that had colored their lives, their decisions, their emotions, since childhood.

They reached a corner of the field over which the battle had flowed and ebbed an hour previously. With unspoken, mutual consent, they drew rein and dismounted.

Rufus planted the Decatur standard in the soft ground and cast off his helmet and breastplate. Cato removed his own armor and when both men stood in britches and buff jerkin, they turned to face each other.

"Swords?" Cato inquired almost distantly. "Or swords and daggers?"

"It matters not," Rufus said with the same distant courtesy.

Cato said, "Swords only, then." He drew out his dirk from the sheath at his belt and tossed it to the ground a good few feet distant.

Rufus did the same. Then he drew his sword.

They stood facing each other.

Portia didn't know why she chose to climb down from her observation post when she did. There were instincts and presciences that controlled her, and she didn't question them. She understood only that the battle was lost for the king's men. Not an indecisive loss, not a negotiable loss, but a crushing defeat that would bring to an end the king's cause in the north, if not across the land.

And she understood that somewhere on that bloody field

she would find Rufus dead or alive. If he was dead, she would find his body. It was hers. It was all that was left to her. There had been no reconciliation, but she would find his body, would make peace as she could. Once she had had his love. And now she carried part of him within her.

Portia walked out onto the battlefield of Marston Moor. The evening star was pale but visible. The western sky was ruddy. She walked through the bodies, through the injured, through the little groups of skirmishers, as if she were a ghost, invisible and inviolate. She didn't hear the screams of the wounded, the cries for water, the shrieks of broken horses. She didn't smell the blood, was not aware of the sodden earth beneath her feet. She walked until she saw the Decatur standard thrashing in the rising breeze.

She heard sword upon sword. In the eerie quiet of dusk, there was at first only that sound. Then Portia became aware of the breathing, the deep, heavy breathing of laboring men. She heard the muted noise of booted feet moving purposefully over soft ground. But there were no voices.

As instinctively as she had descended from the oak tree half an hour before, Portia moved toward the sounds, her feet noiseless, her body sliding into the dusk shadows.

She saw the two men in their elaborate dance of death. Their swords were like silver fish, weaving, dancing, jumping against the dimming light. Their powerful bodies had somehow lost force and substance for the watcher, but were more like spirits in this dance, deadly but beautiful.

And then understanding burst forth, shattering Portia's strange trance, hurling her back with explosive force into the world of living reality. And she saw how well matched they were, and she understood how this dance must end. One of them would die. Or both of them would die.

And Portia was filled with an anger so fierce it eclipsed all other emotion. Did they not understand how they were loved? Did they not understand how many people depended upon their strength, their compassion, their love? Did they not understand how much they *owed* to the people who loved and depended upon them, upon whose love and understanding they in turn depended?

She reached into her boot for her knife. She held it poised, her eyes narrowed, focused on the twin blades. The two men were not aware of her presence in the shadows; they were aware of nothing but their own battling concerns. But Portia now was as clearheaded as she had ever been. She was a soldier planning an intervention, and coldly, unemotionally, she watched and waited for the perfect moment.

When it came, she knew it. She didn't hesitate. The knife flew from her hand, striking Cato's sword in a cascade of sparks as he thrust beneath his opponent's guard. Cato's sword was deflected. Portia flung herself forward between the two men. She landed on her knees, ducking her head beneath the blades poised above her.

The astounded silence engulfed them all. Rufus stepped back, his point lowered. Cato did the same. Portia raised her head.

Rufus threw his sword from him. He bent and caught Portia under the arms, lifting her to her feet. He held her and shook her. He set her on her feet, took her by the shoulders, and shook her until she thought her head would leave her shoulders.

"How *dare* you! How *dare* you do something so reckless, so unutterably *stupid*!" he raged. "I could have killed you!" He caught her to him, crushing her in the vise of his arms, hurling his fury with liquid eloquence at the top of her head even as he stroked her hair, clasped the nape of her neck, gripped her narrow shoulders.

Portia struggled to free herself. Her own anger was still riding high. She was weeping with rage and remembered frustration and the sheer joy of knowing that Rufus loved her. She felt it in his hands even through their roughness, and she heard it in his voice despite the savagery of his tone. But she couldn't distinguish her emotions, and her anger at what had brought them to this place still ruled.

"How could you do this?" she exclaimed, finally wrenching herself from Rufus's grasp. "Both of you? Hasn't there been enough killing for one day?" She turned on the stunned Cato with an all-encompassing wave of her hand. "What does it matter if your fathers hated each other? What can that possibly weigh in the scale against your own lives? The lives of your children?"

"Just a minute . . ." Cato held up a hand in an imperative gesture for silence, but Portia was unstoppable.

"What will happen to Olivia?" she demanded. "If you die in this pointless feud with Rufus, what will happen to your children? Do you think it matters a whore's curse to them what occurred nearly thirty years ago? They want their father, they need—"

"Hold your tongue!" Cato had recovered his senses and now interrupted her tirade with such force that despite the energy of conviction, Portia stopped midsentence. "I'll not be spoken to in such fashion by a mere chit of a girl!" he exclaimed. "Where in the devil's name did you spring from?"

"How could that matter?" Portia waved the question away as she turned on Rufus. Her eyes were green fire; her hair blazed with an energy all its own; her entire body thrummed with the power of her need to stop this madness.

"What of the boys, Rufus?" she demanded. "Are you prepared to leave them orphaned, as you were? Exiled without place or family? Who will they be? What will they have when you've given your life for some futile vengeance?"

She saw his eyes, saw the demons spring to life, but she ignored them, stepping close to him, raising her face so that she looked him in the eye and faced down the demons.

"And what of this child, Rufus?" Her right hand rested on her belly. "I am not prepared for my child to come fatherless into this world."

The flat statement lay between them. Cato took a step back as if standing aside from something that now excluded him.

Rufus heard Portia's words. He saw her hand resting on her belly. He remembered his mother standing in just that way, protecting the fatherless child she carried. He remembered the infant, his sister, blue, waxen, blood streaked.

"My child?" There was a strange distance to his voice as if he couldn't quite take it in.

Portia heard only a question mark. "Whose else would it be?" she snapped, aware of a thickness in her throat. "Or did you imagine I'd been consorting with the entire Decatur village?"

There was a moment of silence, when it seemed as if all three of them held their breath in the encroaching darkness.

Then Rufus said quietly, "I deserve much, gosling, but not that."

Portia turned away with an inarticulate little gesture.

"How long have you known?" Rufus asked, laying a hand gently on her shoulder, asking, not compelling, her to turn back to him.

"Since the siege . . . just before, I think. But I don't know much about these matters, so I wasn't sure." She half turned toward him again, but her voice still had an edge.

"Why didn't you tell me, love?"

"First I wasn't sure . . . and then when I was, you weren't exactly receptive," she returned, wondering why she couldn't quell this bitterness; why, now that everything was going to be right between them, all the pain of the last two weeks came up to overwhelm her with hurt so that she felt it afresh and she needed to give it back. "You wouldn't have listened to me that night. Would you?"

"No." The single word carried a lifetime of remorse. He wanted so badly to hold her, to smooth the hurt from her brow, to wipe the bitterness from her eyes, to beg her forgiveness, but she was holding herself away from him, sharp spurs of pain and anger like a protective fence around her.

"I went into the castle because I wanted . . . needed . . . to talk to . . ." Portia stopped, ran her hands through her hair, pushing it off her forehead. She had run out of anger, and the protective walls tumbled down in shards at her feet.

"Olivia?"

Portia nodded.

Rufus had no words to express his sorrow, but he knew that now he could hold her. He drew her against him, his hand once more clasping her neck in the way that she knew, that brought her so much peace and contentment. "Forgive me," he said, his voice hoarse with guilt for what he had done to her in his blindness and his bitterness. "I did not know what it was to love until I met you."

Cato had been standing silently to one side, motionless as he listened. There was much he didn't understand about the way things had happened between these two, but the power of emotion that connected his brother's daughter and Rufus Decatur was almost palpable. He sheathed his sword, breaking the intensity with a calm question. "Am I to understand that my niece is carrying your child, Decatur?"

"So it would seem, Granville." The vivid blue Decatur eyes were slightly mocking as they regarded the marquis of Granville over the bright orange halo surrounding Portia's head. "It would appear that more than spilled blood will join us."

"Portia is her father's child." Cato's own smile, slightly sardonic, met the earl of Rothbury's. "And, like her father, seems to have carved her own destiny without regard for the usual forms and customs. I would like to wish you both joy of each other, Decatur, but I doubt you'd accept the sentiment. . . ." He shrugged and now felt for words.

"My father was not a pleasant man. He believed in doing his duty without consideration for emotion or the ties of sentiment. Your father took a stance against the king . . . my father accepted the king's commission to visit justice upon your father."

Cato gave a short laugh. "It seems ironical in our present circumstances. My father would have had no compunction in delivering me to the headsman for the stand I now take against the king.

"But I do know that every sovereign of revenue from the Rothbury estates is accounted for, from the moment of your father's death. I ask you to believe that. I cannot undo whatever wrong my father did your father, whether it was real or perceived. But I can forget their feud in the name of this coming child, if you can do so."

His tone was blunt, the sentiment generous. Rufus felt Portia move against him. He felt the ripples of her skin, the quick little breaths she took. And finally he understood that the demons who had ruled him were not his, they belonged to his father . . . a man of rash and hasty temper, quick to see insult where none was intended, and as quick to suspect treachery.

Two inflexible temperaments had collided close to thirty years ago, but the detritus of their collision no longer needed to litter the lives of their children and their grandchildren. It would be hard to cut out of himself those aspects of his father that had contributed to the tragedy of so many lost and wasted lives. But he would do it.

Rufus took Portia's hand. "Will you give your niece in marriage to the earl of Rothbury, Granville?"

"I'm not sure it's my place to do so." Cato smiled and his face was transformed, giving him an almost mischievous expression. He reached for Portia's free hand. "The lady has a mind of her own. Do you wish for this union, Portia?"

"Yes." The one word seemed quite sufficient.

Rufus felt as if this was the moment toward which all the previous moments of his life had been leading. He felt as light as air. "Then we'll do it now," he said decisively. "Granville, will you fetch a chaplain?"

"A drumhead wedding," Cato mused with that same puckish grin. "Seems appropriate enough for a bride in britches." He strode toward his horse. "I'll be back within the half hour."

"But we can't get married here!" Portia protested. "I don't wish to be a bride in britches."

"My darling gosling, I am not prepared to let another hour pass before we put this ramshackle union of ours onto a proper footing," Rufus said, his tone as decisive as before. "Apart from the fact that you always wear britches anyway, I fail to see that it matters a damn what you wear."

"But I'm not the stuff of which countesses are made." Portia didn't know why she was still making objections, but somehow she couldn't help herself. "I'm the bastard daughter of a Granville wastrel! How can I possibly become countess of Rothbury?"

Rufus swung her toward him. He took her face in both his hands and regarded her closely in the gathering dusk. "What nonsense is this, Portia?"

She shrugged helplessly. "I don't know. *Is* it nonsense, Rufus?"

"Arrant nonsense," he affirmed. "And it will be very much better for both of us if you never indulge in it again."

"Of course, you're not exactly the stuff of which earls are made," Portia observed with a sudden smile.

"Very true." He stroked her face, his gloved fingers tracing the curve of her jaw, and when he spoke again his voice was very soft and intense. "You are the very breath of my life, love. I cannot bear to think of the hurt I have done you, but I swear to you now that I will honor you and love you and cherish you to my dying day."

*A*nd later Portia answered his vows with her own under the direction of a somewhat bewildered chaplain in the flickering light of a lantern standing on an upturned drum. She felt Cato's hand firmly clasping her fingers as he gave her hand to a Decatur, and Rufus took her from a Granville with the same firm clasp. He slipped his signet ring on her finger, with the eagle of Rothbury stamped into the gold. It slid round on her long, thin finger and she tucked it into her palm, holding it with her thumb.

She passed her wedding night with Rufus searching for the men who had fought beneath the Decatur standard, and as dawn broke she fell asleep on Ajax's saddle, held securely by her husband, with Will leading Penny as had happened once before, on a cold winter night when the king's cause had still been strong.

Rufus led his depleted force back to Decatur village, and there, in renewal and inexpressible gratitude, he took his bride for his own, possessed her and was in turn possessed. And when she lay against his chest in the glorious space between sleeping and waking, her skin damp with passion, her body limp in the aftermath of joy, Rufus knew a joy and a certainty that he would never have believed possible.

He smiled in the darkness, smoothing the damp curls from her forehead.

"Why are you smiling so smugly?" Portia murmured, burrowing her cheek into the soft red-gold pelt of his chest.

"How do you know I am?" He stroked the length of her back, reaching down to cup her bottom in his palm.

"I can feel it in your skin." She kissed his nipple, moving

one leg over his in a gesture both languid and inviting. "I'll always know what you're thinking."

"That ought to terrify me," Rufus said, sliding a hand between her thighs. "But for some reason, it doesn't."

"Because you'll never again have thoughts that you won't wish me to hear," Portia predicted with a throaty little chuckle. She moved indolently against his hand, and her chuckle deepened.

Epilogue

"*B-Brian's here.*" Olivia's dark head dipped on the whisper.

"Where?" demanded Phoebe, her step slowing.

"Behind us." Olivia's hand on Phoebe's arm tightened. "I can feel his eyes."

Portia glanced over her shoulder, toward the cloister they had just left. "Oh, yes, there he is," she said cheerfully. "Dung-stinking whoreson."

Brian Morse was standing in an arched doorway opening onto the cloister. He was leaning against a stone pillar, his arms folded, his eyes following the three young women as they walked arm in arm across the smooth grassy quadrangle.

"What's he doing here?" Olivia murmured.

"The same as everyone else, I imagine," Portia replied as they entered a circle of rosebushes in the center of the quad. "He's probably hanging around the edges of the peace talks. I can't imagine he has any kind of important role to play."

"He can't see us in here anyway." Phoebe bent to smell one of the great yellow roses climbing a trellis within the little garden. She jumped back with a cross exclamation, licking a bead of blood from her finger where a thorn had attacked her.

"Now there's blood on my gown." She brushed ineffectually at a smear of blood on her gown of white dimity.

"It'll stain," Portia said, somewhat unhelpfully, standing on tiptoe to see over the rosebushes. "There's Rufus and your father, Olivia. In the far cloister." She frowned. "Who's that with them?"

Olivia, now as tall as Portia, looked across the bushes. Phoebe, rather shorter, was obliged to jump to see over.

"It's the king," Phoebe said with awe. Her sojourn at the

king's court in Oxford gave her a familiarity with the sovereign that the other two didn't have.

"Let's go and greet them." Portia licked her fingertips and smoothed her eyebrows. "Is my hat straight?"

"We can't just b-burst in upon them," Olivia protested. "They're in private discourse. It would be improper."

"My husband is holding my baby, in case you hadn't noticed," Portia said sweetly, adjusting the wide brim of her straw hat. "If that's not unconventional, I don't know what is."

"That's true," Phoebe agreed. She was much struck by the sight. Rufus Decatur was deep in conversation with King Charles and the marquis of Granville. Not an unusual event during these uneasy days of peace talks, except that he was holding a baby in the crook of his arm. A round-cheeked, green-eyed infant with a dusting of freckles across the bridge of her nose and a soft, downy cluster of strawberry blond curls. The child was sucking her fist and gurgling; her other fist was tightly embedded in her father's hair. And the earl of Rothbury appeared to be completely at his ease, completely unaware of the extreme oddity of the picture he made.

"I'm going to be introduced to the king," Portia stated. With an impish grin, she abandoned her more retiring friends and stepped out of the shelter of the rosebushes.

Brian Morse moved away from the doorway, watching the countess of Rothbury as she crossed the grass toward the three men. His mouth curled, his little pebble eyes flattened. Jack Worth's bastard had managed to become accepted in legitimate society. It didn't seem to matter to anyone that her husband had been one of the most notorious rogues in the country, a common thief and brigand, the son of a convicted traitor. The earl of Rothbury had somehow forged for himself a place of high influence with both sides in these peace negotiations. And his scrawny, freckled bastard of a consort, without making the slightest effort to adapt herself, was considered no more than a rather charming eccentric.

But Brian wasn't finished with Lady Rothbury . . . indeed, he had not even started. Her and the brat Olivia. His cold gaze flickered across to his stepfather. He had a bone to pick there, too. Cato must have been responsible for whatever had poisoned Brian on that ghastly visit. Granville had needed to get rid of the royalist supporter under his roof and had chosen a malicious and humiliating way to do it. And Brian was not about to forget it.

He spun on his heel and stalked back into the cool dimness of the abbey chapel.

Portia approached the three men with her usual swinging stride. The smile that the sight of Rufus always engendered tilted the corners of her mouth. Restitution of Rufus's birthright hadn't changed him very much. He still wore the plain, practical dress of a working man; his hair was still clipped short in contrast to the flowing locks of the king and his Cavaliers. He had no time for the formalities and procrastinations that went under the name of court courtesy, and his manner was frequently brusque to the point of curtness. Portia thought, judging by the king's somewhat aloof expression, that Rufus had probably been imparting a few of his uncompromising home truths to his stubborn and beleaguered sovereign.

The three men turned toward her as she came up to them. She curtsied deeply to the king as Rufus introduced her. Charles murmured a greeting but he was clearly displeased about something. Rufus, however, seemed unperturbed. The baby laughed merrily at the sight of her mother and stretched out her arms in eager demand.

"Oh, fickle Eve," Rufus said reproachfully, handing the child to Portia.

Portia kissed Eve's round cheek and the baby chuckled with delight, grabbing a handful of her mother's hair.

"I'll talk further with my advisors," Charles said with undeniable hauteur. "Rothbury, Granville, Lady Rothbury. I give you good day." He inclined his head and strode off, leaving the men to bow and Portia to curtsy to his back.

"I thought *you* were his advisors," Portia observed, frowning.

"Only when we give His Majesty the advice he wishes to hear," Rufus said with a sardonic smile.

Cato shook his head with an unusual air of distraction. "Do you know where Olivia and Phoebe are, Portia? We have to return to Cliveden. I've just received word that Diana is worse."

"I'm sorry to hear that," Portia said truthfully. She didn't care for the woman, but neither did she wish her harm. Diana had been ill for several weeks, remaining at Cato's house just outside London while her stepdaughter and sister accompanied Cato to Uxbridge, where the peace negotiations were taking place in an atmosphere that was intended to be festive. However, things were not going according to anyone's plan.

Cato pulled at his chin. "The flux shows no signs of abating. The physician says she is growing very weak."

"Olivia and Phoebe are in the rose garden." Portia gestured to the middle of the quad. "They wouldn't come out with me because they thought it would be disrespectful."

"You, of course, saw no such impediment to bringing yourself to the king's notice," Rufus observed with a grin.

"On the contrary, it seemed my bounden duty to relieve you of Eve. It seemed the height of disrespect to be conversing with your king while clutching an infant," Portia declared with a lofty air.

"If you'll excuse me . . ." Cato moved away toward the rose garden, too bound up in his own thoughts to pay attention to their badinage.

Rufus gazed across the quadrangle to the far cloister, a frown now in his eyes. "Did you notice a man standing over there a little while ago?"

"Oh, yes, it was the dung beetle." Portia lifted one of Eve's dimpled fists and sucked her fingers. The baby shrieked with delight.

"I remain unenlightened." Rufus's frown had increased.

"Brian Morse, Cato's stepson," Portia explained. "He's Olivia's nemesis for some reason . . . she's not at all clear what it is about him that scares her . . . but he mimics her stammer and taunts her. He's a loathsome creature." She grinned reminiscently. "We arranged for his very precipitate and rather mortifying departure from Castle Granville. I'm sure he bears us a grudge."

"I see." Reflectively, Rufus tapped his teeth with a fingernail. There was something about the man's silent observation that had made him uneasy. He would do a little investigating of Master Morse himself. Then the frown cleared from his eye and he regarded Portia quizzically.

"I think it's time you donned your britches again."

"Oh, don't you care for my gown?" Portia looked down at her gown of apple green silk. "I thought it quite pretty."

"Oh, it's pretty enough," he said. "But I find I prefer the britches."

Portia's eyes sparkled at the sensuous note in her husband's voice. "I can hardly wear britches in the king's presence."

"No, but we're leaving the king's presence. I've done all I can here. The man's as stubborn as an ox. He won't make peace on Cromwell's terms."

"So the war will continue?"

"Presumably." Rufus shook his head impatiently. "But I've had enough of it for the moment. I intend to spend the next few months supervising the rebuilding of my house, the civilizing of my sons, and . . ." He paused and pressed his thumb against her mouth. "And the loving of my unruly gosling of a wife."

His eyes, vivid and filled with promise, held the slanted green gaze beneath him. A shiver ran down her spine as she waited, breathless, for the kiss that would make good the promise . . . for the moment when the enchanted circle enclosed them, the world faded, and she would know again the all-encompassing certainty that her life, her soul, her heart, belonged to this man as his belonged to her.

About the Author

JANE FEATHER is the nationally bestselling, award-winning author of *The Emerald Swan*, *The Silver Rose*, *The Diamond Slipper*, *Vanity*, *Vice*, *Violet*, and many more historical romances. She was born in Cairo, Egypt, and grew up in the New Forest, in the south of England. She began her writing career after she and her family moved to Washington, D.C., in 1981. She now has over two million books in print.

Coming soon . . .

Phoebe's deliciously romantic story in
Jane Feather's second "Bride" book

The Accidental Bride

Look for it in the summer of 1999

But first, a special valentine treat from
Jane Feather

A Valentine for Emma

on sale in January 1999

*Read on for sneak previews
of both romances. . . .*

A Valentine for Emma

"They're gaining on us, Ned." The speaker swiveled in his saddle, one hand resting on his mount's crupper as he stared across the darkening landscape behind them. He could see faintly the rising dust of a headlong pursuit. He cast a despairing glance at his companion. Edward Beaumont, Fifth Earl of Grantley, was leaning heavily over his horse's withers and his back was wet with blood.

"I know it." The words were a mere thread, tailing off in a gasp of pain as Ned dragged air into his shattered lungs. Blood bubbled from his lips. "I can't outrun them, Hugh. You must go on and leave me here."

"No, I will not." Hugh Melton leaned over and seized his companion's rein, urging the horse onward. "I'll not leave you to those Portuguese savages. We'll be in Lisbon by dawn. Come *on*, Ned!"

"No." The flat negative had more force than anything Ned had said since he'd taken the Portuguese sniper's bullet to his back an hour earlier. With his last strength, he hauled back on the reins. His horse whinnied and pranced, confused by the contradictory signals he was receiving. "Damn it, Hugh, you must go on . . . save yourself." He struggled for a minute, fingers scrabbling inside his jacket. "There's more at stake than you know."

Hugh was silent. He had guessed as much . . . had suspected for many months during this Portuguese campaign under Wellington's command, that his oldest friend played a more devious role than his simple title of aide de camp to the duke would imply. And he'd guessed that this supposed jaunt to Lisbon from the lines before Torres Vedras had more than a few days of well-earned leave as its purpose.

"Here." Ned pulled out a thin packet. Blood smeared the protective covering of oiled parchment that enclosed the contents. He swayed violently in the saddle as he leaned over, pushing the packet at Hugh. "Get this on the first ship out of Lisbon."

"What is it?" But even as he asked the question, Hugh understood that Ned would not give him a straight answer. He looked at the packet. It was addressed to Ned's home, Grantley Chase in Hampshire, and it bore the name of Lady Emma Beaumont.

"A letter for my sister," Ned gasped. "For God's sake, Hugh, go. It cannot fall into their hands." The wounded man slumped sideways in his saddle; the reins slid through his fingers. Only his feet in the stirrups seemed to hold him in place.

"God's grace!" Hugh reined in both horses before Ned could fall to the ground.

"Help me down," Ned gasped. "I can hold my seat no longer . . . for God's sake, man . . . quickly. They'll stop for me and give you a few moments' grace. You can outride them." A spark of desperation for a moment enlivened golden brown eyes that were growing dimmer by the minute.

Hugh swung off his horse. He caught his friend as he slipped from the saddle into Hugh's arms. Hugh laid him down on the hard, summer-parched ground that still held the day's heat. He stood looking helplessly down at the man whose blood was seeping inexorably into the earth. He glanced again at the packet he still held. And then he heard the sound of hoof beats, carrying on the still evening air, pounding the dirt.

Ned's eyelids flickered. "For pity's sake, Hugh. Don't let me die in vain."

Hugh hesitated no longer. He remounted with an agile spring. He thrust the packet into the breast of his tunic and kicked his mount into a gallop. He would not, *could* not, think of his friend lying in the dirt waiting for the attentions of those who had been chasing them since early afternoon. If they were after what Hugh Melton now carried, they would not find it. By dawn it would be in Lisbon, on the first troop ship bound for England.

The four horsemen reined in their plunging horses as they came up with the inert body on the ground, the patient steed cropping at a low bush. One of them, whose lavish silver braid and epaulets denoted his leadership, flung himself from his horse with an oath. He bent over Ned.

"He lives yet," he said grimly, his hands searching roughly, tearing at the bloodsoaked garments, rolling the man over onto his belly heedless of his wounds. He swore vigorously as his search turned up nothing. "He hasn't got it. Two of you go after the other one. Pedro and I will work on this one. For as long as he lives, he has a tongue."

Ned heard the words as from a great distance. A strange little smile quirked his lips as they yanked him over onto his back. He looked up at the swarthy face hanging over him. Hard black eyes, a cruel mouth beneath a thick waxed mustache.

"My apologies, Colonel," he murmured in Portuguese. "I may have a tongue, but it's not at your disposal." He closed his eyes, the smile still on his lips. He saw now a different face filling his internal vision. Eyes as golden as his own, a wide smiling mouth. "Em," he said, and died.

GRANTLEY CHASE, ENGLAND. DECEMBER, 1810

"It's outrageous! *Insufferable!* I absolutely will not tolerate it." Emma Beaumont tore at the lace-edged handkerchief between her hands as she paced the elegant salon. The flounced hem of her gown of dove gray crepe swung with every step.

"Oh, Emma, dearest, you cannot talk so," declared a middle-aged lady in a round gown of dark silk. The lappets of her cap trembled against her cheek as she shook her head decisively.

"Oh, can I not, Maria?" exclaimed the infuriated Lady

Emma. "Mr. Critchley, something must be done about this. I *insist* upon it. I cannot imagine what Ned can have been thinking."

An embarrassed silence followed her declaration. Mr. Critchley coughed behind his hand and rustled his lawyer's papers. The middle-aged lady plied her fan vigorously. An elderly couple seated side by side on a sofa with gilded scroll ends stared into space. The man thumped his cane on the Aubusson carpet with monotonous thuds, while his spouse pursed her lips and gave a sour little nod, as if vindicated in some way.

"Emma . . . Emma!" a voice drawled from the far side of the room. "You're putting everyone to the blush." Alasdair Chase was leaning against the wall of bookshelves, hands thrust deep into the pockets of his buckskin britches. His mud-splashed topboots gave evidence of a day's hunting. There was a wicked glimmer in his green eyes, a sardonic quirk to his mouth.

Emma spun around on the speaker. "All but you, Alasdair, I daresay," she said with the same bitter fury as before. "Just what arguments did you use with Ned to get him to agree to this . . . this intolerable *insult*?"

The tapping of the cane grew more pronounced; the elderly gentleman on the sofa coughed vigorously against his hand.

"Emma!" moaned Maria from behind her fan. "Only think what you're saying."

"Yes, indeed, Lady Emma . . . only consider," murmured the distressed lawyer.

Emma flushed and pressed her palms to her cheeks. "I did not mean . . ."

"If you must rail at me, Emma, then do so in private." Alasdair pushed himself away from the wall and crossed the room toward her. He moved with a lithe step; his slender body was supple as a rapier, giving the impression of sinew and speed rather than muscular power. A hand cupped her elbow. "Come," he said in soft command, and drew her toward a door in the far wall.

Emma went with him without protest. Her color was still

high, her fingers still ripped at the now ragged handkerchief, but she was in control of herself again, aware once more of her audience, and the impropriety of her words.

Alasdair closed the door behind them. They were in a small music room containing a handsome pianoforte and a gilded harp. He went to the piano, raised the cover, and played a scale, a vibrant ripple of notes that filled the small chamber.

Emma walked to the window. The winter afternoon was drawing in, the stark leafless trees bending against a sharp northeasterly wind coming off the Solent.

The notes faded and she heard the soft thud as the lid of the piano was replaced. She turned around. Alasdair stood with his back to the instrument, his hands resting on the smooth cherrywood cover behind him.

"So . . ." he invited with a lifted eyebrow. "Between ourselves, you may say what you please. I shall not take offence."

"It would ill become you to do so," Emma retorted. "Your hand is in this, Alasdair. Do you think I don't know how you could manipulate Ned when you chose."

A muscle twitched in Alasdair's lean cheek and his eyes narrowed imperceptibly. "If you think that, you didn't know your brother as well as we all believed," he said, without expression.

"If this was not your doing, then whose was it?" she cried. "I cannot believe Ned, of his own free will, would serve me such a trick."

Alasdair shrugged. "Why do you believe it to be a trick, Emma? Isn't it possible Ned thought such an arrangement would be in your best interests?"

"Oh, pah!" Emma exclaimed, and then was instantly furious that the childish exclamation had escaped her. She resumed her pacing and Alasdair watched her, the glimmer back in his eyes, as she stalked from one end of the small chamber to the other.

Lady Emma Beaumont stood five feet nine inches in her stockinged feet and was built on generous lines. Alasdair Chase, from intimate knowledge, knew that her height masked the rich curves of her body, and he was, as so often, distracted by the mental image of the figure beneath the elegant gown—the wonderful deep bosom, the long slope of her back, the flare of her hips, the taut swell of her backside.

Abruptly he turned back to the pianoforte and raised the cover. He played another cascade of notes.

Emma stopped dead.

Alasdair spoke almost casually over his shoulder as his fingers continued to ripple over the keys. "You know, my sweet, you had better accept it with a good grace. You'll only make yourself ridiculous otherwise."

He saw her wide mouth tauten, her eyes, more gold than brown, burn with another flash of anger. A needle of wind found its way between the glass and the frame of the window. The fire in the hearth spurted and a flame shot up; the wax candles in the branched candelabra flamed on the pier table beneath the window. The light caught her hair. Amazing hair, Alasdair had always thought. Striped hair, where onyx mingled with tortoiseshell amid swathes of pale gold, like summer wheat. When she was a child, he remembered, the paler colors had dominated, but as she'd grown, the darker strands began to predominate.

"Don't call me that," she said with low-voiced intensity.

Alasdair turned once more from the pianoforte with a small shrug. "As you please."

Emma hesitated, then she walked to the door leading back to the salon. Her shoulders were unconsciously squared as she opened the door and reentered the room.

The Accidental Bride

"So, what d'ye say, Granville?" Lord Carlton regarded the marquis of Granville with a touch of anxiety that he tried to conceal.

Cato Granville stroked his chin as he reflected. "I'm very unlucky with wives, Carlton," he said finally. "Or perhaps we should say my wives have been unlucky in their husband." His mouth took a wry turn.

"To be sure, for a man to lose three wives before he's hit his prime is unfortunate," Carlton said. "But hardly unusual, dear fellow."

"True enough. But for a man of five-and-thirty to be considering a bride so—"

"Oh, you're going to say Phoebe's too young for you," Carlton interrupted with a dismissive flourish. "That's nonsense, man. A man of your age could take a fifteen-year-old without remark, and the girl's all of seventeen. Only consider the advantages . . . she's healthy and strong, capable of bearing you a good many sons. And you need sons, Granville. A brood of daughters is all very well, but a man in your position needs an heir. Unless, of course, y'are considering adopting that stepson of yours," he added, his eyes narrowing.

"No," Cato declared flatly. "I have no intention of adopting Brian Morse."

"It would be awkward to do so," Carlton conceded. "The man's for the king, and y'are a staunch Parliamentarian."

Cato merely nodded. That was far from the most important reason why he wished to have no intimate dealings with the son of his first wife. He did not trust Brian Morse.

"And that brings me to the other advantage of the alliance I'm proposing, Granville." Carlton spoke earnestly. "We're in alliance in this civil war and I'd cement that with family ties again. The world's going to be a very different place when the dust settles, and a man's going to need all the allies he can draw. Carlton and Granville will be a powerful force in the new world, and . . ." he continued persuasively, "if you take Phoebe to wife, then Diana's dowry will remain in your charge instead of reverting to her daughters. Phoebe will come with all the Carlton holdings in Cumbria. Close enough to Castle Granville for easy administration, and rich in forest." He paused for effect, then asked again, "So, what say you?"

Cato kicked a slipping log back into the grate. "The girl's my daughter's bosom companion, Carlton. I think of her as I think of Olivia."

"Odd's blood, man! She's not your daughter!" Carlton exclaimed, clearly impatient with what struck him as a ridiculous objection. "Think of the advantages, now. I know she can't hold a candle to Diana. Her sister was a diamond of the first water and my little Phoebe is . . . well . . . not handsome in the same way. But she's well formed, her features are pleasant enough. She may be a trifle scatter-brained, but she'll grow out of that if you make your objections clear. She has no experience of the world. You'll be able to shape her to your own requirements," he pressed. "The younger the filly, Granville, the easier she is to break."

Cato frowned, finding something distasteful in such a turn of phrase. His former father-in-law was a bluff and frequently tactless man. However, his arguments in favor of the match he was proposing were strong. Cato needed an heir. And for a man to wed his late wife's sister was a common practice. It kept dowries in the family, and renewed whatever family alliances had been part of the incentive for the previous connection. And in these troubled times, the political alliance he had with Carlton would be all the stronger for such a renewal.

"Give me some time to think about it," he said after a minute. "I'm fully sensible of the advantages, but with Diana a mere eight months in her grave, this is perhaps premature."

"Not in wartime," Carlton declared. "Such niceties as long mourning go by the board. You need a wife, and when you next go into battle, you need to leave her breeding . . . carrying your heir." He nodded decisively. "You return to the siege at Berringhurst Castle in a week. A stray shot from the ramparts . . ." He shrugged expressively.

"I don't expect to be wed in a week," Cato said dryly.

"No . . . no . . . of course not. But you take my point."

"Aye, I take your point."

Carlton was obliged to be satisfied with this. He picked up his hat and whip from the chair and pulled on his heavy leather gauntlets. "I'm joining Cromwell's cavalry outside Oxford. Send word to me at headquarters when you've come to a decision."

Cato walked his guest to the front door and saw him ride away down the carriageway, then he turned back into the house. The engagements in the civil war had moved from the north of England to the south and west and he'd been reluctant to leave his family alone in Castle Granville without his protection. He had brought them with him and installed them in this pleasant manor house a few miles from the city of Oxford, where King Charles had his headquarters. Cromwell's cavalry were besieging the city and attacking the pockets of royalist sympathizers in the Thames valley, and Cato's own militia had joined with the newly formed New Model Army under Cromwell's ultimate command.

Diana, who had so hated the frozen north and the bleakness of castle life, would have enjoyed this gracious house in the flat mellow countryside of Oxfordshire. It was one of fate's many ironies, Cato thought as he crossed the stone-flagged hallway. Her death had been so sudden, leaving him with their two infant daughters.

"Where are the young ladies, Mistress Bisset?" he inquired of the housekeeper who had held the reins of his household since Diana's death. Cato thought Olivia should probably be more involved in domestic management these days than she appeared to be, but she had never been inclined toward domestic duties—always more interested in her books, to her stepmother's unvarying irritation—and he was so rarely at home himself at present he had not troubled to disturb the status quo.

"In their parlor, my lord." The housekeeper bobbed a curtsy. "Lady Olivia asked for reading candles a while back."

She managed to sound a trifle disapproving, and Cato understood that the woman considered reading candles in the middle of the afternoon a great extravagance. Just as she considered reading in the daytime a great waste of time. The young ladies would be much better occupied with domestic activities that didn't require such a luxury until the light was gone and the day's work over. Diana would have shared Mistress Bisset's opinion. Olivia and Phoebe would not have been indulging themselves while she had been alive.

However, he merely nodded and made his way down the corridor at the rear of the great hall. He knocked on the door at the end of the corridor and opened it without waiting for permission.

Olivia was sitting on the windowseat, her legs drawn up beneath her, her back against the wall. She looked up from her book as her father entered and hastily uncurled herself to stand up and curtsy.

Phoebe was sprawled inelegantly on the floor before the fire. Beside her reposed a pewter tankard and a plate of macaroons. She held a quill in her hand and was engaged in writing on a sheet of vellum. She too scrambled to her feet in great haste and curtsied.

"G-good afternoon, sir," Olivia said. "D-did you wish to see me?"

"You might infer that from my presence," Cato said, aware that he sounded less than pleased. He regarded Phoebe with a frown in his eyes. She had ink on her fingers and a fair amount seemed to have splashed on her lace-edged apron and smudged the white collar of her dark stuff gown. "What are you writing?" he asked.

"A poem, sir," Phoebe responded promptly. "But I cannot get it to scan aright. I am having great difficulty with the second stanza."

"Phoebe is a very g . . . good poet, sir," Olivia put in eagerly. "She writes the prettiest verses."

"May I see?" Cato inquired, holding out his hand.

Phoebe hesitated. "I . . . I don't usually show my verse until it's finished to my satisfaction, sir," she said, glancing down at the parchment on the floor.

"Then when it's finished to your satisfaction may I have the honor of reading it?" Cato was amused now, a smile replacing the frown in his eye. He had the feeling that Phoebe would defend her unfinished poem with all the fervor of a lioness with a threatened cub.

"It is I who would be honored, my lord," she said very properly, with another curtsy.

Cato nodded and turned once more to Olivia, who had fixed him with a fierce stare that he knew meant she had something of importance to say.

"Sir, c-could I please have a tutor?" she said in a rush.

"A tutor?" He raised his eyebrows in astonishment.

"Yes." Olivia nodded firmly. "I need help with my Greek and mathematics . . . and I'm t . . . trying to read Pliny."

"We met a man from Magdalen College at church on Sunday," Phoebe explained. "He said that with the war there are a great many students, and tutors too from the university, who would be glad of some private employment. He and Olivia were talking about Ovid and Pliny for hours."

Cato was silent. It was perfectly usual for a wellborn girl to be lettered, but most unusual for her to be educated in the classics, in the way of her male counterpart. But Olivia was an unusual girl. She always had been, even before her unfortunate stammer had developed and she'd become so shy and withdrawn. She'd always preferred books and study to the more ordinary pursuits favored by young women.

But he could see no real objection. There were indeed many unemployed members of Oxford university in these troubled times. Men for whom politics meant little but whose course of study had been interrupted by the war.

In the considering silence, while Olivia waited with bated breath, Phoebe surreptitiously bent and picked up the mug of milk and a macaroon from the dish on the floor. She dipped the little cake in the milk and popped it into her mouth, then drank deeply from the mug. She'd missed breakfast that morning because she'd been out in the village helping an old widow dig up the cabbages that had been buried at the beginning of winter in a trench in her cottage garden to guard against frost.

Phoebe was a well-known figure in Woodstock and the surrounding countryside. She put her energy and her robust enthusiasm to work among the women left to fend for themselves by their men who had gone for soldiers. She was as ready to turn her hand to digging cabbages and pressing apples for cider as she was to caring for a sick grandfather or minding a brood of children while their mother did what she could to put food upon the table.

"I suppose I could make inquiries for a suitable tutor," Cato said after a minute. He was rewarded by his daughter's shy smile and the quick excited flash in her dark eyes.

He glanced again at Phoebe, reminding himself why he had come into this room. A pained frown furrowed his brow.

Phoebe realized that Olivia was gesticulating at her from behind her father's shoulder. She frowned in puzzlement, then comprehension dawned and her hand flew to her mouth, then down to her ink-stained apron as she looked for a handkerchief.

Cato could bear it no longer. He drew out his own pristine handkerchief and caught Phoebe's chin on the palm of his hand, tilting her face up. His fingers were warm and firm against her jaw as he wiped the milky moustache from her lip. Her eyes, round and blue as cornflowers, met his. They were filled with mortification. Her cheeks were slightly flushed, her lips parted in an "o" of silent protest.

He did not immediately release her, but held her chin on the palm of his hand and regarded her in a reflective silence. No one could have been more unlike her sister. Diana had been as cool and stately as a swan. Never a hair out of place, her dress always impeccable. She had had a regal bearing, the arrogance of one who knew her own worth. And she had turned heads with her beauty whenever she entered a room.

Her little sister's hands were rough and chapped; her dress frequently in disorder. But as he examined her, Cato saw that Phoebe's complexion had all the glowing freshness of one who spent more time outdoors than in. He noticed how warm and expressive were her eyes, how soft and responsive her mouth.

Diana had been a wife to display. A wife to make other

men envious. She had been dutiful and submissive in his bed. Obedient to his dictates, although she had never left him in any doubt of her grievances when those dictates didn't suit her. But she had not been a warm and loving companion. Cato hadn't thought he wanted such a wife. He had thought Diana everything a man could desire. Now, the faintest inkling of something she had lacked niggled at him.

It was, of course, ridiculous to imagine that Phoebe, scatter-brained, untidy, tactless to the point of rudeness, could supply that lack. But she was younger than Diana had been. Less sure of herself. Less self-determined. She could be influenced.

Cato hadn't liked Lord Carlton's analogy with horse-breaking. It struck him as crude and unnecessary, but he still took the point. Such a very young and inexperienced girl could be molded to her husband's tastes. She could be taught to please him. And there was something most appealingly warm and open about the upturned face in his palm. A naive, inexperienced child with no preconceived notions. She wouldn't give him any trouble. *She could be taught to please him.*

He was surprised into a sudden smile. He released Phoebe's chin and with a word of farewell left the room.

"Well," said Phoebe with a touch of indignation. "I don't mean to speak ill of your father, Olivia, but did you see the way he was looking at me? Just as if I was a prize pig in the market place."

"Oh, no, he wasn't," Olivia protested. "It was just the milk on your lip."

"That was embarrassing," Phoebe conceded. "But I have to say that I really object to being examined like that. What could he possibly have been thinking?"

"I don't know." Olivia shrugged and returned to her curled position on the windowsill.

"Well, whatever it was, I'm sure I wouldn't care for it," Phoebe declared, sprawling once more upon the floor and taking up her quill.